Also by Willow Tickell

A Gift from Artemis
Merlinslade

Cooling Off

WILLOW TICKELL

SCEPTRE

First published in 1997 by Hodder and Stoughton
A division of Hodder Headline PLC
A Sceptre book

10 9 8 7 6 5 4 3 2

British Library Cataloguing in Publication Data

Tickell, Willow
    Cooling off
    1. English fiction – 20th century
    I. Title
    823.9'14 [F]

    ISBN 0 340 65795 2

Typeset by Palimpsest Book Production Limited,
Polmont, Stirlingshire
Printed and bound in Great Britain by
Mackays of Chatham PLC, Chatham, Kent

Hodder and Stoughton
A division of Hodder Headline PLC
338 Euston Road
London NW1 3BH

To Joss

Acknowledgements ∫

Many thanks to my agent Sarah Molloy for continuing to provide the best of encouragement and support, and to Sue Fletcher for her always excellent editorial advice. I should also like to thank Lance and Alex Tickell, Joss Kingsnorth, Geraldine Kaye and all the members of her writers' workshop, Eira and John Eastell, Judy Hodgkin, Enid Levin, Maggie Skinner, and Stella Weatherall.

Mick Day nobly unravelled the mysteries of postmodernism for me, and in Oxford Dr Schuyler Jones of the Pitt Rivers Museum and Jane Pickering of the University Museum were especially generous with their time and professional information.

Especial thanks are due to Dr Debra Hershkowitz who gave Gabriel Hall its name and helped in many other ways, and to Sarah Henry, who suggested Jericho and gave me a student's-eye view of Oxford. Ian Wilson and Asmara provided a delightful glimpse into life with an African Grey parrot.

Gabriel Hall, the Tucker Institute, and the Gabriel's Grounds Estate do not exist, and neither does the room I have described in the Balfour Library of the Pitt Rivers Museum. All the characters and events in this book are also entirely imaginary.

The worst wasn't over yet. With the sixth sense every war correspondent needs in order to survive, Christa knew that ahead lay the toughest encounter of her career. In a bitter role reversal she was about to have the media's scrutiny turned on her.

Outside the windows of the endless corridor to the immigration area at Heathrow, the world streamed with damp in a grey September dawn. On the tarmac planes sat like bloated silver cocoons. After three months in Bosnia it was hard to realise they were disgorging holidaymakers instead of soldiers and aid workers and refugees.

Briefly her view was obscured by an external wall. The glass darkened, and she saw herself plodding on alone, when Matt should have been by her side. Matt Brady, with his bald head and lanky frame, cracking terrible jokes and dragging on one of the smuggled Italian cigarettes he couldn't function without. Her laconic and imperturbable cameraman, who'd survived Vietnam and Beirut, only to be needlessly killed because she'd trusted another man too much.

All round her were brightly clad tourists returning from the Seychelles on the plane she'd picked up at a Rome refuelling stop. She felt incongruous in her scuffed boots, the anonymous blue jeans designed to make her look as unmilitary as possible, and the navy parka she'd slept in for too many nights. There were no souvenirs in her rucsac, apart from a flak jacket and helmet crammed in with her contacts book and a pile of dirty clothes. She'd been recalled to London so suddenly that there'd been no time for laundry, not that there was much water for such luxuries in Sarajevo anyway.

Apollo Television, her employers, had warned her the press would be waiting. At least her distinctive on-screen trademark, the thick French plait falling over one shoulder, looked reasonably tidy. She wondered whether to bundle it into a cap in a last-minute effort to sneak past, then decided she didn't have a hope of remaining anonymous.

She knew it was going to be even worse than she'd expected when she got to the immigration desk. An official who'd chatted her up many times before as he inspected her passport, now pushed it back without a smile. She remembered Matt had been a favourite of his too.

'Shame about Mr Brady,' he said. 'He was a nice chap. Looks like it's getting dangerous to work with you.'

Burning anger at the unfairness of it all, the only thing to carry her through the last week, rescued her once more.

'No more dangerous than with anyone else in Bosnia,' she said coldly.

'That's not what Gareth Hyde said on the telly the other night. He said you hadn't checked your facts.'

In the non-EU queue a family of Asians was patiently waiting while another official scrutinised their passports as though they were letter bombs.

'Why don't you go and help people who need you instead of hassling me?' she snapped.

She snatched up her passport and marched away, only to be delayed again by a surge of passengers making for the luggage carousels. As she waited, seething with impatience to get through and out of customs, she thought about Gareth with the sickly feeling of betrayal his name now induced in her. Until a few days ago she'd felt about him like the girl with purple love bites on her neck just ahead in the throng, who was gazing at her companion as though he was Bruce Willis, instead of a pasty twenty year old with a struggling moustache.

She pushed the thought aside as she saw one of Apollo's staff tripping purposefully towards her with a trolley between the carousels. Her spirits plunged again. Things must be bad if they'd sent a minder.

Christa tried to recall the woman's name. She could always remember names. It was one of her assets. But she was so tired that it eluded her completely, until the woman, exuding self-importance, came near enough for Christa to read the ID card pinned to her precisely tailored jacket.

Toria Green, that was it. She remembered her now. Three years ago, when Apollo had promoted Christa to foreign correspondent, Toria was Vicky Green in a white cotton blouse and creased miniskirt, hammering out assignment schedules in the typing pool. She must have worked hard to get into PR.

She grabbed Christa's arm.

'Christa, wonderful to see you! And you're looking great, you really are,' she gushed, as though assuring someone terminally ill that she was the picture of health.

Normally Christa, remembering her own early struggles to establish herself, would have shrugged off the flattery and tried to cooperate. But she was too wound up, and her minder was a little too clearly determined to get the upper hand over a potentially difficult charge.

'For God's sake, you don't have to give me that sort of rubbish. I know exactly how I look.'

'We all know you're bound to be stressed. That's why I'm here to help,' said Toria soothingly. She lowered her voice. 'Of course I don't have to tell you how desperately sorry everyone is about what happened to Matt.'

'So am I. But I can cope. I don't need a nanny.'

Firmly Christa disengaged her arm. She took the trolley, dumped her rucsac, and began to trundle it briskly past the luggage carousels. Long ago she'd learned to travel light. You could miss a scoop waiting for baggage from the hold. Anything that wasn't vital could come on later by air freight.

'You don't understand. Randall wants to brief you before you meet the press. He says it's essential.' Toria was starting to sound flustered.

'Don't worry, Vicky, I can handle anything they like to throw at me. There was really no need for this.'

'Toria – I'm called Toria now.' She was struggling to keep up on her high heels. 'You obviously don't realise just how tricky the situation is.'

'I can handle it,' repeated Christa, wrestling irritably with the trolley as its wheels kept trying to go in different directions.

'Christa, do stop, please.' Toria's voice was verging on the desperate. 'Randall's really, really worried about the media coverage you've been getting since Matt's death. The tabloids have been crucifying you, and there was even a hostile piece in the *Clarion* today.'

This did halt Christa momentarily. It was hard to imagine Randall, the chief news editor at Apollo and her boss, being anxious about anything. He was as unshakeable as a Chieftain tank. Even at the height of the Gulf War, when, according to old hands in the Apollo newsroom, fresh reports were coming in like Scuds, he'd sat in his office coordinating a network of contacts more labyrinthine than the CIA's, and producing coverage that won the company a run of awards.

She wondered if Toria was exaggerating to get her to cooperate. She was certainly beginning to lose her veneer of self-assurance. A slicked back strand had escaped from her dark cropped hair. She could only be about twenty-three, the same age as Christa when she'd first joined Apollo Television as a trainee home affairs correspondent. Christa decided to bluff.

'Randall, worried? I don't believe it. He knows the tabloids will have forgotten all about me by next week. And the *Clarion*'s too soft-focus liberal to have much punch,' she said airily.

'Gareth bad-mouthed you again in a long interview on Metro TV's "Probe" two nights ago. Yesterday's tabloids gave it huge coverage. You know how they love to rough up anyone with a high public profile who makes a slip. And after you talked your way out of Zepa with that lorry load of refugees, your profile couldn't have been higher.'

'What the hell do you mean, I slipped? I was *pushed*. Gareth pushed me, and the sooner everyone gets that straight, the better.' Christa tried to sound unimpressed, but again she was shaken. She'd heard nothing about the interview, and 'Probe' was almost top of the ratings.

'Obviously I don't know all the ins and outs.' Toria was beginning to sound slightly hysterical. 'But I do know Randall wants you to keep quiet until he's been able to talk to you and decide what line to take. I've fixed for you to leave here by a side exit. There's a company car waiting to take you straight to Apollo.'

Christa ignored her, grimly pushing the trolley on towards customs. In the heady early days of her affair with Gareth, when Sarajevo seemed like the heavenly city, she'd never dreamed that he would become jealous of her professional success, or so comprehensively betray her. But though she'd made a huge mistake, she wasn't going to run away, whatever Randall said.

In desperation Toria grabbed the side of the trolley, making it slew round.

'Christa, don't you see? You can't afford to upset Randall or the media any more. You've been so isolated in Bosnia that you don't appreciate the strength of public reaction here. Matt was everyone's favourite for a lot longer than you.'

'Do you think I don't know that? Matt was my closest friend. So how can you expect me to keep quiet when he's just been killed, because a colleague I trusted set me up with false information? I'm not going to dodge this interview. It'd be disastrous – more or less an admission that I was in the wrong. I've got to put my point of view before Gareth does any more harm.'

'Whatever you say at the moment, the press won't believe you. Randall's simply trying to work out the best form of damage limitation. I know you think you were set up, but at the moment that's not the way it seems. At least look at the latest cuttings file,' persisted Toria, trying to thrust a folder at her.

'Stuff the cuttings! Whose side are you on? I don't think I was set up, I know it! I'm doing this interview, and that's final!'

'For God's sake, Christa, this is my first big PR assignment. Please go along with me!' Toria looked as if she'd been round once too often on a roller-coaster ride. 'Randall will be wild if you don't, and it'll be ages before I'm given another chance.'

'I'll deal with Randall. I'll tell him it was my decision entirely. You don't really expect me to run, do you?'

'But he only wants to brief you, so that we can plan the best way to handle this. It's in your own interest to do it our way.'

'Tough!' rapped out Christa. 'I'm going to see the press now, and then I'm going home to have a bath and change. After that, when I'm ready, I'll come along to the studios.'

She wrenched the trolley from Toria, and shoved it at top-speed through the green customs channel, glaring at the officials, daring them to think she'd smuggle anything out of sad, exhausted

Bosnia. As she rounded a corner, Toria's high heels clicking frantically by her side, and emerged into the roped-off gangway which filtered passengers into the arrivals hall, her tiredness disappeared temporarily in an adrenalin rush.

A battery of flash bulbs exploded like shells in a night sky. Christa could hardly see as she pushed the trolley down the gangway. Now she was out of the gangway, and reporters were converging on her from all sides. Toria's voice squeaking 'No comment' was drowned in a hostile barrage of questions.

Keeping the trolley in front of her as a shield, Christa began to sort out the faces of people who'd been friends up to now. A reporter from Channel Six she'd known from her early days, the media columnist from the *Siren*, with whom she'd had several convivial lunches at the Groucho Club, even the women's editor of the *Clarion*, who had understood like no one else the pressures of being a young successful woman in a male-dominated profession. But their faces weren't admiring, as they'd been at the Newscaster of the Year award ceremony last year. Instead they ranged from openly vindictive to avidly salacious, and worst of all, in the case of the *Clarion* editor, pitying.

Christa halted the trolley, and grabbed her rucsac.

'All right,' she shouted, 'you'll get your story. Just let me have some space. I can't talk like this.'

She thrust her way out of the scrum, and made for a low box-like table between some sofas at one side of the concourse. The press rocketed after her. She stepped up on to the table, dumping her rucsac by her side, and again confronted them. Her heart felt as if it had gone into overdrive.

It was much too like the time she'd had to face the Serbs when she and Matt had been caught up in their surprise attack just before his death. The long, black threatening lenses of the cameras didn't look all that different from guns. Only the background rumble of heavy artillery was missing, though the sound of planes stacking overhead was nearly as loud. She was almost paralysed by a hideous presentiment that she wouldn't be able to handle the confrontation after all.

Pretend it's an assignment, pretend it's Matt behind the camera, pretend nothing's wrong, she said fiercely to herself.

A soundman suddenly dumped a metal container on the floor.

It sounded like a rifle shot. Christa stuffed her hands in her jeans pockets, and steadied her voice as she shouted above the renewed barrage of questions.

'OK, OK, I'll answer you all in a moment. But I want to make a statement first.'

She tried to summon up the words she'd put together on the plane but again, terrifyingly, her memory deserted her. It was something which hadn't happened since her trainee days.

The cameras were whirring like tiny buzz saws poised to cut her down. She pulled from her jeans pocket the crumpled piece of paper on which she'd mapped out the statement, and glanced rapidly through it.

Unnervingly she remembered Gareth's face, the last time she'd seen him, at Sarajevo airport. It was after he'd given her the information she'd trusted implicitly because it came from him. Olive-skinned, dark-eyed, with black hair she now suspected had been too black for a man in his late-forties, looking at her with the expression that made her turn to water as he said goodbye.

She took a deep breath of the dry, reconditioned air in the arrivals hall, and launched into her statement.

'Matt Brady and I went to a small village on the Serb front line on information given to me by Metro TV's correspondent, Gareth Hyde. According to him, a high-level secret conciliation process was taking place there, one which might well bring the war to an end. Gareth had just been posted unexpectedly to Rwanda, but he wanted me to have the chance of this scoop. He gave me the names of contacts at the front line, people he said he'd used before and trusted implicitly. Naturally I trusted him. But when Matt and I arrived it was clear that we'd been set up. There were no contacts, no conciliation process. Instead we found ourselves in the midst of a new offensive. We tried to salvage something from the incident by filming it, but instead Matt lost his life.'

As she'd learned to do over her years as a war correspondent, she tried to distance the sights and sounds of Matt's injury. Once again she forced from her mind the sudden stutter of the Kalashnikov and his gasp as the bullets hit him, her own despair as she realised he couldn't be moved, and the terrible drive in their armoured Land Rover to fetch help.

The Channel Six reporter waved a stick microphone in her face.

'That's not what Gareth said about it, Miss Keith.'

Christa knew now that she was going to have to fight for her professional life. They were calling her Miss Keith, the colleagues who'd shouted her first name across the smoke of a hundred bars to come and join them at the end of another exciting or frustrating, but always fascinating, day spent on the work they knew she could do better than most.

'Gareth says the whole venture was your idea – that he warned you against it, urged you to check your facts.'

'It's a lie,' said Christa. 'All the information originated from him.' She swallowed hard. 'It's well known that we were in a relationship. I saw no reason not to trust him.'

It was impossible not to mention her affair with Gareth. She'd never concealed it. Indeed, she'd been so much in love that her happiness would have been hard to hide. The gossip columns had devoured it like another Hemingway/Gellhorn romance.

Metro TV's reporter pounced on her reply. He'd had a grudge against her ever since she'd beaten him to a scoop in her early days.

'Gareth said on "Probe" that he had to end the affair because you were becoming too dependent on him. His own work began to suffer because you needed so much propping up.'

Christa stared, remembering Gareth's passionate assurances that he couldn't live without her, and the news leads she'd delighted in sharing with him because it brought them closer still. He'd used her to cover his professional laziness, and when her reputation looked like exceeding his, he'd cold-bloodedly betrayed her.

A reporter from the *Gorgon* produced his notebook and quoted from it with a vindictive smile.

'His actual words were that you used sex with him as a security blanket.'

Gareth's lie took her breath away. Even in her most dis-illusioned moments she'd never dreamed he would publicly misrepresent the most intimate part of their relationship. And he knew very well that she'd scorn to use the same weapon herself. What a fool she'd been not to look at Toria's cuttings file. If she had, she would have been prepared for this ultimate indignity.

'I've already told you,' she said angrily, 'Gareth set me up. I can't prove it, because Matt was the only witness when Gareth gave us the details of the so-called peace conference. But Gareth can't prove anything either. At least try to be impartial.'

'It's difficult to be impartial when someone like Matt dies. Poor old Matt. He wouldn't have harmed a fly.' The *Gorgon* reporter's voice dripped sentimentality. 'And Gareth's had almost thirty years' experience. How long have you been a correspondent, Miss Keith? Eight years, and not all in a senior post.'

'Eight years in which I've never betrayed a colleague,' she said angrily.

The questions were beginning to get to her. But she was so tired, and the adrenalin rush had almost faded, leaving her as useless as a burst tyre.

'Matt died. Wasn't that a betrayal?'

'A betrayal by Gareth, not by me.'

Nothing she said seemed to have any effect. Matt was everyone's friend, and Gareth would have had plenty of time to do the rounds, oiling the media with drinks and charm.

'How did you feel at Matt's funeral?' asked the Channel Six reporter.

'How do you think I felt? What a bloody stupid question. He was my friend, and he didn't need to die.'

At the back of the crowd Toria was signalling frantically at her not to say any more. Christa knew she wasn't placating her accusers, she wasn't doing any of the sensible things that might help to get the public on her side, but all she could think of now was Matt's burial: in the small town near the field hospital, as he'd requested. It had been at night, for the graveyard was constantly menaced by sniper fire. The only people present were a couple of acquaintances from the Red Cross who were not in the business of apportioning blame, some staff from the medical unit, and the local UN commander, who had been a friend of Matt's too.

She couldn't bear any more remembering. She had to get to her flat, to gather her strength before the encounter with

Randall. She'd lost Matt, but if she lost her job as well she'd lose everything.

To her left were the automatic doors which led to the taxi rank. And between the doors and her persecutors was what seemed like a whole Jumbo load of Arab businessmen, accompanied by black-veiled wives and a galaxy of children, progressing in a relaxed way across the concourse, halting everything in their path.

Christa snatched up her rucsac and made a dive through the ranks of the photographers. A tripod crashed to the ground. She shook off a dozen clutching hands, and sprinted across the highly polished floor.

She wove through the Arabs like a dodgem car, but the reporters were already moving up fast. A snake of interlocked trolleys stood by the exit. She thrust it careering across their path, and hurtled through the automatic doors to freedom.

A thin cold drizzle blew in her face, bracing her for one last effort. Shouting her address at the driver of the first taxi in the queue, and promising him double the fare if he lost the pursuit, she fell back in her seat with her arm over her eyes, as flashlights went off all around.

The driver, black and burly with razor-patterned hair, rose to her challenge with relish. He turned up the hip-hop on his radio, roared away ahead of a coachload of American matrons on a cultural tour, and by the time they reached the motorway had completely shaken off the pursuit.

It was raining hard when her taxi drove up to the red-brick Edwardian block where she'd rented a small furnished flat for the past few years. The block had no architectural merit, but the security was excellent, with a porter guarding the front door, and an entry-phone. It also had a fire exit into a back street, which had been useful more than once in the past.

She cut short the porter's greeting, told him not to admit anyone asking for her, and got into the ancient lift, listening to its creaks as it laboured up to the fifth floor. There was a stack of mail on the mat inside her door. She pushed it aside with her foot, and opened the inner door to the sitting room.

A stale dusty smell enveloped her. She let her rucsac drop

to the floor, and stood looking around. The owner of the flat, another foreign correspondent just coming to the end of three years in Mexico City, had let it to her while he was abroad. He'd bought and furnished it in the early-seventies, and done nothing to it since. The carpet was a dried mustard colour, the curtains faded avocado, and the matching sofa and chairs of black vinyl leather were beginning to split at the seams. It had never seemed like home, and she'd never been there long enough to make it one.

But suddenly, for the first time ever, because she was so tired, she longed for the place to welcome her, to see vivid colours, smell furniture polish and flowers, and feel the warmth of an open fire. She sat down on the hard slippery sofa, thinking that she must be really losing her grip if something so trivial seemed so important. Nothing, *nothing* mattered, she told herself fiercely, except her career, and getting it back on course.

The reminder had no effect. Christa had the even stranger thought that it would be good to see her mother. She imagined the shining sitting room in suburban Oxford where everything was arranged as precisely as a dental surgery. She imagined her mother fussing over her and bringing her tea in a flowered porcelain cup. She didn't even mind the thought of being nagged to put it down on a mat.

Except that being at home wouldn't work. It never did. After an hour or two she'd begin to feel as if she were trapped in a canary's cage. And anyway, independent thirty-one year olds didn't go round wanting their mothers, particularly a mother with as many problems as hers.

Coffee was what she needed, she told herself firmly, coffee to banish these insidious, destructive thoughts, and help her face the coming interview with Randall. She went into the tiny kitchen, which looked into a sunshineless well. As she automatically reached for the coffee percolator she saw on the draining board an empty takeaway box. It had contained the pizza she'd shared with Gareth at the end of a snatched weekend in London when they'd both had to make interim reports to their respective studios.

The sight affected her like a body-blow. Even worse, two

unwashed glasses and a half-empty bottle of Gareth's favourite whisky were still standing on the dresser.

She could feel tears gathering at the back of her eyes, but grimly she refused to let herself cry, because that would be letting Gareth triumph yet again. When the coffee was made she added a huge slug of whisky, and took it into the bathroom. The hot water which came from a central supply, and was one of the flat's major assets, shot steaming into the bath as though it had come straight from Rotorua.

She drank the coffee before getting into the water. As she washed she couldn't bear to look at herself, at the body in which Gareth had seemed to take so much delight, but which she now knew had meant nothing to him. Finally the whisky began to take the edge off her wretchedness. She wallowed there, dozing, for a long time, then washed her hair, and returned to the sitting room in her dressing gown.

It was nearing ten o'clock, almost time for Metro TV's mid-morning newscast. Christa made herself switch on. Metro would certainly have got the interview footage to the studio by now, and she must check it before the meeting with Randall.

The lead story was a cabinet reshuffle. After that came a report on a supermarket attack by an animal rights organisation called Howl of whom she'd never heard before. Shots of broken windows and wrecked meat counters flashed on to the screen. They seemed negligible compared to the havoc in Bosnia, and she watched impatiently until she realised the store was near her parents' home.

Christa began to pay a little more attention. Howl seemed to be a disturbingly effective set-up, for this was one of several incidents and so far no one had been arrested. There probably hadn't been so much excitement in her parents' Oxford suburb for years, she thought, then instantly forgot all about it as the report faded and her own interview came on.

She'd expected a biased presentation from Metro, but nothing as bad as this. The footage had been brutally edited to show her in the worst possible light. She was like a talking head, her face drained of expression, her voice dull with fatigue. Her replies had as little punch as a baby's fist, and a damning final shot showed her fleeing towards the exit.

Viewers were probably giving her the thumbs-down all over Britain, Christa decided, as she pressed the off button on the remote control. And Randall would be going through the roof. If she didn't get some sleep before she faced him, she'd never be able to cope. She took the whisky bottle into the bedroom, set the alarm for mid-afternoon, and pulled back the covers on the bed.

Instantly the smell hit her: the smell of Gareth's Aramis, of his cigarettes, even the faint smell of sex, trapped between the sheets she'd had no time to change. She was swamped by a terrible wave of longing and panic. I'm like one of Pavlov's dogs, still conditioned to wanting him, she thought. If I let him go on affecting me like this, I won't survive.

Frantically she ripped off the sheets and pillowcases, crammed them into a plastic bag, and padded outside to the garbage chute. As she heard the bag hurtle downwards and thud into the container below, it was as though she'd thrown her heart away.

Apollo's studios were situated on the South Bank, in a tower block with glass-sided lifts which rose and fell like surreal yoyos. As Christa was smoothly propelled towards the tenth floor she could see half of London spread out before her. The sun had emerged, and the city lay in an autumnal glow, basking in warmth before evening mist came stealing up the river. In Bosnia people would be thinking about how they'd survive the winter ahead, and Matt's grave would already be strewn with fallen leaves.

Christa always liked returning to the studios. It was far more of a home-coming than her return to the flat. But this time everything was wrong. As she got out of the lift, one of the newsroom staff who would normally have given her a rapturous greeting whisked past with only an embarrassed smile. The photo of her which hung with those of the other Apollo correspondents in the reception area had disappeared. Debbie, the receptionist, who usually had a stack of autograph requests waiting, greeted her in a strained voice, and there were no requests today.

Walking through the busy newsroom, which always before

when she returned from an assignment had been a slow trium-
phal progress, was quite different too. People seemed inordi-
nately interested in their monitor screens, or in suddenly making
intensely important phone calls which precluded anything but a
brief wave of the hand.

The charge was still there, the excitement of being at the cutting edge where the best news was made, an addictive charge she
knew she could live without even less than Gareth's presence,
but it was a very long walk all the same. When she got to the
door of Randall's office at the end of the room, she felt as if she'd
been down Sniper Alley on foot.

Randall was sitting at his desk, shelves laden with awards at
his back, some of which she and Matt had helped Apollo to win.
A bank of monitors flickered soundlessly by his side.

Immediately facing Randall were a couple of upright chairs
and a sofa covered in soft burgundy leather. Christa wondered
which he'd invite her to sit in. If he gestured her to a chair he'd
probably try to relegate her to reporting home news for a few
weeks, or else send her somewhere quiet, like New Zealand or
Alaska. It would all depend on how much he believed her story,
and on his estimate of her current market worth.

Randall was the only person she was slightly scared of at
Apollo. He was in his mid-fifties, the same age as her father,
but otherwise light years from her academic parent who was
the deputy librarian of an Oxford college. The only thing they
had in common was their insistence on accuracy.

Randall looked up at her entrance. His cropped grey hair sat on
top of his square head like a bathmat in shock. His steel-rimmed
half-glasses, red braces and bow tie made him look like the classic
news editor in an old Hollywood movie. She suspected it was an
image he liked to foster, though it was hard to believe he gave
much thought to his appearance. He lived for news, and now she
considered it, he was like her father in that as well. Her father
lived for Oxford and his college.

Randall didn't return her smile. Her confidence dropped
another few notches, then rose slightly when he waved her
to the sofa.

Randall watched Christa over the top of his glasses as she sat down, and wished he didn't have to do what he was about to do. She was his favourite among the news reporters. He'd given her the job which had made her name, luring Matt Brady to join her from Metro TV with a sum that reverberated round the Groucho Club for days, following a hunch that they'd make the best news team in the business.

She looked bushed, he thought. The tilt of her head and the direct challenging gaze were still there, but she'd lost at least a stone since he saw her last, and her skin was dull with fatigue. Even the barley gold hair which made her so easily distinguishable seemed subdued, not straying around her face as it usually did.

He'd already heard her version of the events leading up to Matt's death, over a satellite phone which magnified the tears suppressed behind the relating of an otherwise incisive, logical and absolutely believable report. He guessed Gareth Hyde had sold out on her because of professional jealousy. He was a devious bastard. He'd taken centre stage while she was out of touch, and manipulated the media so cleverly that overnight Christa had gone from being the darling of the public into a distinct liability.

He decided to be brisk. 'I know what's happened is tough for you, Christa, but it's dumped us in the shit here too.'

Her chin went up in one of the gestures which, when tempered by her smile, made her so attractive. Behind her toughness there had always been a hint of vulnerability, but he'd never seen that vulnerability surface until now.

'It was all Gareth's doing, and you know it,' she said.

'You wouldn't have been set up if you'd checked his sources first.'

'I told you on the phone, there wasn't time. He gave me the information late at night, just before he left for the airport. The meeting was supposed to take place early next morning. If I'd hung around we could have lost the scoop of the year.'

'As it was, Matt lost his life. Which was preferable?' Randall asked drily.

She coloured and swallowed hard. He felt like a sadist. She wasn't much older than his daughter, whom he still thought of as about fifteen.

'Matt was equally keen to follow up the lead,' she said stiffly. 'And I had every reason to trust Gareth. I'm sure you know the details of our relationship – he's given his twisted version of it to everyone by now.'

'OK, you were sleeping with him, though God knows how you found the time or energy in Sarajevo. But he was from a rival company, our major rival, and you must have known his reputation. His speciality is fucking up the opposition. In this case he did it by fucking you. Sorry to put it so crudely, but you've got to realise just how lethal he's been.'

She turned scarlet. He hated what he was doing even more, but he'd had Jimmy Judd, the media baron who owned the major shareholding in Apollo, breathing fire at him ever since Gareth's revelations. If he didn't dampen things down fast all their jobs would be on the line.

'I loved Gareth,' she said in a low voice. 'It sounds corny, but I did. Or I thought I did,' she added lamely.

'That makes it even worse. You aren't paid to fall in love, and especially not on assignment. You're paid, and generously at that, to deliver accurate reporting and look after your crew. You were responsible for Matt.'

'I know I was.' Her voice had almost disappeared. She felt in her pocket and pulled out a pack of cigarettes.

'And don't dare smoke in here,' he barked at her. 'I've just given up the bloody things.'

She glared back at him. He was glad for her sake. He'd rather see her angry than cowed. It made him feel marginally better about delivering the next blow.

'Matt knew as well as I did that it could be a set-up,' she said defiantly, 'but he was well in with the Serbs. We both felt we could handle things. It was a joint decision to go ahead. If he could, he'd tell you so himself.'

Her voice shook. He got up and poured her a cup of coffee from a percolator simmering under the window. It would be a disaster if she broke down before he'd sorted things out. That was one of the few remaining problems with women reporters. It was hard to put the boot in as he would with a male employee. Christa was strong enough to take it, but he didn't like doing it to her, all the same.

'Have some coffee,' he said more diplomatically. 'OK, I'll take your word for it, though I can think of many news editors who wouldn't.'

She couldn't quite conceal the relief in her smile. He braced himself to deliver the next blow.

'But the question is, where do we go from here?' he continued. 'You must be aware that your contract's due for renewal in a month's time. We have no obligation to employ you after that.'

She stared at him. He guessed she hadn't really believed that he might fire her. He didn't intend to, but she'd be more amenable if she thought there was a possibility.

'All right, I'll keep away from the front line for a while. Go somewhere quieter perhaps, where I can do human interest pieces instead. How about New Zealand, or Canada?'

He smiled. 'You must be joking, Christa. You mustn't go anywhere near a camera. It's going to take a long time to rehabilitate you in the public's eyes.'

Her cup clattered in its saucer as she put it down on the glass-topped coffee table before her.

'You mean, keep out of reporting altogether?' Her voice was incredulous.

'That's exactly what I mean.'

Christa clamped her hands together to stop them shaking. She felt as if her world was about to disintegrate. She'd never dreamed that Randall would go this far. He was looking supremely uncomfortable, and well he might, she thought savagely. Anger began to replace sheer terror at the prospect of life without work.

'Other people have survived worse, for heaven's sake,' she said. 'The media's loaded with people who've made mistakes, and bounced back.'

'Not strictly true,' he said. 'Loaded with men who've made mistakes, perhaps. But you're a young, attractive woman. The public already loved you, but they turned you into a sort of St Joan after you got those refugees out of Zepa. That was one of your strengths, but in this situation it's a weakness as well. A large section of the British public is still remarkably old-fashioned. It likes its heroines to be beyond reproach. If this were the States, with a huge feminist lobby to root for you, and where the public actually admires mistakes if they're spectacular enough, you might get by. But not here.'

He handed her a folder of press cuttings.

'Perhaps you'll deign to take a look through these now, and you'll understand what I mean. The PR girl said you didn't want to see them.'

'What happened at the airport wasn't her fault,' said Christa swiftly.

'Maybe. What's certain is that Gareth's done a magnificent hatchet job, and we can't even sue him because it'd be impossible to get evidence out of Bosnia. Presumably the only other witnesses were the Serb military.'

Christa leafed through the cuttings, wondering if she was going to throw up Randall's coffee. They were all hideous, but the last, and the worst, as she might have expected, was from the *Gorgon*.

'Matt Brady Killed by Christa's Foul-up', howled the headline, above a cruel montage photo of her apparently urging Matt on towards a wall of Serb tanks. 'Gareth Hyde told her not to risk the Serb front line,' said the copy underneath. 'She got too big for her boots, and now Brady's dead. We don't like the way Apollo gathers its news. We demand a more responsible approach.'

'That's good, coming from the *Gorgon*,' she said angrily.

A paragraph further on there was a quote from Gareth. '"Yes, I'd told her there were rumours of a conciliation process, but only rumours, which I advised her to ignore. You can imagine how I felt when I heard that she'd gone behind my back. Matt's death was totally unnecessary."'

'The last sentence is true, at least,' said Christa, slamming shut the folder.

If Randall believed only half this rubbish, he wouldn't want to go on employing her, she thought. She might as well get out of it with some dignity, and offer to resign before he fired her. He was clearly manoeuvring her in that direction anyway.

'All right, Randall, you've made your point. I'm willing to resign. But I'd expected a bit more support. I've done good work for you, and you know it.'

As soon as she'd spoken, all she could think of was that if

she couldn't work she'd fall apart. There was nothing else. No Gareth, no Matt, no flat even, for the owner was returning from Mexico at the end of the month. But to her astonishment Randall came round to her side of the desk, and sat next to her.

'Calm down, Christa. Those things had to be said, but I certainly don't want you to resign. You have to keep a very low profile, though, while we try to pick up the pieces. Whether you stay with us is up to you, of course, but I've a plan to patch up your career which may just work.'

He put the cup back in her hands. 'Finish your coffee, and let's look at this sensibly.'

He returned to his seat at the desk and produced her personnel file, which she normally saw once a year at the time of her annual assessment. In the past that had always been a formality, a flow of compliments and a gratifyingly large bonus paid into her bank a few days later.

'I think it would be best to put you on a retainer over the next year while you keep in the background. Then we can review the situation.'

'A year? You mean a whole year away from television? And how much money does a retainer mean?'

He named a sum which was a twentieth of her present annual salary.

'I couldn't survive on that. It'd hardly pay the council tax.'

'You must have savings. We've paid you more than generously.'

'I repaid you more than generously with good stories and even better ratings,' said Christa. 'I have to live while you put me on hold. I've got savings, yes, but I was hoping to put them towards a London base of my own.'

'Since the bad publicity over Matt's death our ratings have slumped. They'll come up again, but not with you on the screen.'

'If that's all you think of me, you can stuff your retainer. I've been humiliated enough. I'll get work somewhere else, even if I have to go abroad. CNN were putting out feelers in my direction a few months ago, but I turned them down. Obviously loyalty doesn't pay.'

In spite of the fighting words, she knew she didn't have a leg to stand on, and that Randall knew it too.

'Come off it, Christa. No news editor in his right mind would employ you just now. Won't you let me finish what I was saying?'

The flickering monitor screens kept breaking her concentration. Tiredness was creeping up on her again.

'I'll listen,' she said wearily, 'but don't think I'm necessarily going to go along with you.'

'Naturally the choice is yours. But you must acknowledge that a period of withdrawal from the public eye is in both our interests. A *managed* period of withdrawal, I must emphasise.'

'And exactly what form would this withdrawal take?' Christa enquired cautiously. Randall was quite capable of asking her to take the veil for a year.

'Spending more time with your family, getting in touch with the basics again, that's how we'll slant it.'

'My family!' Christa could hear her voice coming out in a screech of protest. 'You make me sound as if I've got a husband and six children. And even if I had, I refuse to act like some disgruntled politician.'

'But you do have a family.' He flicked through the folder. 'In Oxford, I understand?'

'Yes, I was brought up there. My father's a deputy librarian at one of the colleges, and my sister's married to a don.'

'And presumably you haven't been able to see much of them over the past few years?'

'I escaped a long time ago. I don't ever want to live there again.'

'Gabriel Hall, that's the ideal place for you at the moment,' Randall said. He didn't appear to have heard her at all.

'You mean the Oxford college? You can't be serious.' Christa began to wonder if Randall was suffering from overstrain as well. 'You can't expect me to have anything to do with that . . . that museum for male chauvinist dinosaurs! And I'm no scholar, for heaven's sake.'

Her father's college, a comparatively young foundation only a hundred years old, was reactionary enough. But Gabriel Hall, founded by Henry VIII, cushioned by huge endowments, clinging tenaciously to its ancient traditions and still blatantly favouring applicants from boys' public schools, was hardly changed since the days of *Brideshead Revisited*.

An old school friend, Piers Gurney, who used to teach at London University, had become a fellow of Gabriel a year ago. Though she'd not seen him recently, his Christmas letter had contained several acid comments on the prevailing state of affairs. And to make things worse, her brother-in-law, one of her least favourite people, was a fellow there too, though he spent most of his time at a research institute on the edge of town.

Randall looked at her file again. 'You've a very respectable first-class degree, and Gabriel Hall has a visiting media fellowship it hasn't yet filled – a fellowship endowed by Apollo.'

'It's ten years since I left college. You're not seriously suggesting that I could teach at that level? And I can hardly believe Gabriel would have courses in anything as modern as media studies anyway.'

He pulled a photocopied advertisement from his desk drawer. 'Take a look at this, and you'll believe me.'

The advertisement was dated three months earlier. Warily she skimmed the opening words. It was couched in incredibly antiquated English.

'"The Master and Governing Body of Gabriel Hall intend to proceed to the election of a Visiting Fellow in Media Studies with all the usual emoluments appertaining thereto",' she quoted. 'How retro can they get?'

She thrust the advertisement scornfully back at him.

'You're out of date yourself, Christa. Don't forget you've hardly been in this country over the last few years. Gabriel Hall has been trying to change its image. It's a stroke of luck for you that they haven't yet filled this post, and that Jimmy Judd's money is funding this fellowship, among several others.'

'No wonder they haven't filled the post. Who are they trying to communicate with? Erasmus?'

Randall ignored her outburst. 'Try to consider this rationally. It's not a bad salary, and it combines thoughtfulness for your family with concern for the education of the young. It'll make excellent PR.'

'But I've never even taught Sunday school! For heaven's sake, be reasonable.'

'If you'd read the job description which goes with the advertisement, you'd see it's perfect for you. The college is looking for someone who can present a measured, authoritative survey of women's role in newsgathering. You'd only have to give eight seminars a term, which at Oxford means one a week. You could even write a book on the history of women war-correspondents, and put in a chapter about your own experiences. It's ideal.'

'If it's so ideal, why haven't they filled the post already?'

'The college is trying to foster a less male-oriented image. It wanted a woman, and someone well-known in her profession. Unfortunately none of the other high-flyers has been interested so far.'

'I'm not surprised. What news reporter in her right mind would waste a year of her life in a place like that?' demanded Christa.

She stared gloomily at a tank of tropical fish next to the sofa. If she went to Oxford her existence would be just as pointless and just as confined.

'Come on, Christa, snap out of it! You know I'm talking sense, and you were due for a stretch of R and R anyway. A burnt-out reporter's no good to anyone.'

'I am *not* burnt-out,' Christa automatically rapped back.

'Not quite, perhaps, but you've been through a lot recently, and I'd hate to see you go under when it can be prevented.'

She remembered her performance on Metro TV this morning. Infuriatingly there was something in what he said. And Randall was starting to sound irritated. He'd probably been at his desk since 7 a.m., and he wasn't renowned for his patience. If she tried him too far she might lose out altogether.

'If I did go along with this plan of yours, you'd undertake to reinstate me as a news reporter at the end of the academic year?'

'I'd do my level best.'

'And at a reasonable salary, not this miserable retainer you've come up with now?'

'Again, I'll do my best.'

She probably wouldn't get a better offer, she thought. And assuming anyone wanted to buy it, a book might at least enable her to present the real facts of Matt's death.

'Then I suppose I shall have to accept,' she said despondently.

'Good,' said Randall in a brisk voice. 'I thought you'd see it my way in the end. Personally I think you're extremely lucky that JJ is willing to pull strings for you.'

Christa had never felt less lucky. She sat in a state of numb acceptance while he went through the rest of the advertisement with her. By the time he'd finished it seemed as if she'd agreed to consign herself to prison.

'That's settled, then,' he said. 'If you make a formal application by letter right away, I'll ask Jimmy Judd to speak to the Master of Gabriel. We'll have you fixed up in no time. You'll be too late to get residential accommodation in college, but I don't suppose you'd want it anyway.'

So she didn't have to live in the place, she thought, feeling slightly better. The obligations of the post seemed minimal, too. And remembering the Metro newscast had made her think of something which might just stop her going completely crazy with frustration in Oxford, if she could only get Randall to agree.

'I don't suppose you'd mind if I took a quick look at what's going on with this Howl organisation while I'm there? You never know, I might be able to sort out a lead or two.'

'Definitely, absolutely not!' exploded Randall, thumping his desk so violently that the images on the monitor screens juddered. 'You have to promise me here and now that you'll have nothing to do with that bunch of maniacs! Otherwise you'll be in the thick of it the minute you arrive, and that's not the object of this exercise. Promise me, Christa, or the whole thing's off, including the retainer with Apollo!'

'All right,' she said hastily. 'I promise. There's no need to go ballistic. It was only an idea.'

The next year seemed even more of a wasteland now. She listened unenthusiastically as Randall told her how the retainer would be paid, then let him see her to the lift. People looked up in the main office as they passed, no doubt wondering if she'd been fired. Soon they'd be pouring into their favourite watering-holes, going over all the latest gossip, but this time she wouldn't be with them.

'For God's sake, cheer up,' said Randall, as he said goodbye to her. 'It's not as bad as all that. Just look on it as a short period of cooling off.'

Staring gloomily at the view from the lift on her way out, she wished she could take his advice. The Thames stretched away like a gilded path to everywhere she'd rather be, while inexorably her perspective was being altered floor by floor, forcing her to face the mundane world.

Moments later she walked into the reality of her new life, into the choking air and the traffic's roar, to merge with the anonymous crowd of commuters hurrying towards Waterloo. Standing on the grey pavement, she felt almost as if she'd returned to the past, and was a struggling trainee reporter once more.

Christa straightened up, defiantly kicking an empty Coke can under the wheels of a passing taxi. She couldn't bear to sink to the bottom of the heap again. She'd fight her way back, whatever it took, and she'd have to start by trying to make something of the Oxford year after all.

2

Driven by duty, Christa phoned her parents on the evening of her return from Bosnia. They both seemed unsure whether to believe Gareth's revelations. She spent a quarter of an hour trying to explain, became exasperated with her mother, and then had to spend another fifteen minutes soothing her wounded feelings.

When Christa revealed that she was coming to Oxford for a while to work on a book, her mother instantly invited her to stay. She escaped by saying she needed to be near the centre of town, though she knew it would mean staying with Emma, her sister, instead. Nevertheless, though Emma would have been mortally offended if Christa hadn't asked for a bed, she wasn't particularly welcoming when phoned.

'I suppose so, but you couldn't have asked at a much worse time. Philip's been in a foul mood recently, Jamie's teething, Noelene's in love with a Rhodes scholar and seems incapable of concentration, and I'm trying to cope with the new term.'

Christa searched in her mind. Who was Noelene? She'd thought the au pair was called Chantal. But au pairs came and went like summer swallows in Emma's household, never able to stand more than a few months of her sister's relentlessly high standards.

'And it's not only that,' Emma went on. 'All this publicity you've been getting lately has been – well, a bit embarrassing.'

'I've already explained to you that Gareth double-crossed me. I thought you understood?'

'Of course I understand,' said Emma, with a little too much emphasis. 'But I was even asked about it by the headmistress at my school today. Imagine the mortification! And it may make things very difficult for Philip just when he's trying for promotion.'

Christa could imagine Philip's reaction to her fellowship, but she'd cross that hurdle later. Randall had agreed to ask the Master of Gabriel not to publicise her appointment before she arrived. Phil spent most of his time at his research institute rather than in college, and with luck he wouldn't hear about the fellowship until she'd moved into a flat.

'Can't you stay with Mummy and Daddy just this once? You know they'd love to have you,' Emma continued.

'And you know how I feel about that. It doesn't matter. I can find a hotel somewhere.' Christa's spirits immediately began to rise at the prospect of not having to conform to Emma's high domestic standards.

'There's no need to be so prickly. Of course you must stay. That's what families are for. I wouldn't dream your not coming here. But I'm just warning you that it may not be easy.'

It rained for the next two weeks. The weather suited Christa's mood as she hammered out an application for the fellowship. Any hope she had of Gabriel Hall refusing to take her because of the Bosnian affair vanished when she was given the post without an interview. The fact that she'd been appointed in such an underhand way made her still more annoyed.

Her closest friends were mainly foreign correspondents, and scattered across the globe. The others she tried to avoid. Their interest in the details of her downfall did her pride no good at all. Apart from a harrowing visit to Matt's sister, his only relative, in Ireland, she spent much of her time cleaning the flat, a job she detested, ready for the return of its owner, and packing her belongings. She'd lost all interest in getting a flat of her own, but before she left London she bought an irresistible silver Mini in a Fulham car saleroom in an effort to cheer herself up.

Now, cruising along the Oxford ring road, the squat little car clung to the wet surface like a waterbug, aquaplaning on the outside lane at seventy without the hint of a skid. Emma was bound to consider it flashy, which gave it even more appeal.

Her family seemed to bring out all her most childish reactions, Christa thought resignedly, wishing she didn't have to drop in on her parents before going to Emma's.

A BMW cruised past her on the inside. The driver threw her a smile that was half admiration, half challenge, a smile so like Gareth's that for a moment the Mini began to drift. She controlled the car at once, but it wasn't so easy to control her mind. Memories began to crowd in of racing across Sarajevo to press parties with Gareth in his armoured Citroën, and afterwards making love in his hotel room, their passion as always given an extra edge by the ever-looming background of war.

When she came to the turn-off for Botley, where her parents lived, she felt so wretched that she couldn't face dealing with their questions. Luckily she'd made them no specific promise about when she'd visit, and she decided to head straight for Emma's through the city instead.

Paul Simon was singing 'Slip Slidin' Away' on the car radio. It was like her life, she thought gloomily. Everything good kept sliding away from her. Yet in spite of her depression, as the car swooped onwards her first sight of Oxford made her catch her breath.

The fields surrounding it were flooded after heavy rain. The sun was setting, and the city seemed to rise from the water like a latter-day Avalon, its spires outlined against a sky suffused with apricot light across which drifted layers of deep grey cloud. Mist drifted from the meadows, lending even the pylons in the middle distance an air of unreality.

The city looked so serenely welcoming that it was hard to imagine not being happy there. Though she knew the serenity was an illusion, she drove into a lay-by and sat for a long time gazing at the view until the sun had gone and her hands were icy on the wheel. Unwillingly she switched on the headlights and swung into a stream of slow-moving traffic, which eventually ground into the Botley Road.

On either side rows of prim thirties houses closed in, changing to long Victorian terraces nearer the inner city. The congestion increased. To Christa it seemed to echo the way her life was slowing down. Better get used to it, she told herself.

A couple of students on unlit bicycles wobbled gaily in front of the Mini from a turning across the road, and into the bus lane on her left, pedalling unimpeded towards the city. The temptation was too much for Christa. She swung the Mini into the bus lane too, roared along it for a few hundred liberated yards, and was brought up at the lights of a pelican crossing. Ahead on the same side was a gap in the houses, filled by a red-brick warehouse pretending to be a pagoda, and topped by a neon sign proclaiming Pets' Palace.

As Christa wondered how anything so hideous could have got past the planners, she was almost startled out of her seat by an imperious hooting behind. A single-decker bus had pulled up within an inch of her rear bumper. In the wing mirror she could see the driver mouthing insults and shaking his fist.

The lights turned from red to pulsating amber. The lane on her right was still jammed with cars whose drivers showed no inclination to let her in. A little way ahead was another bus. She wound down the window and stuck out her hand in a V sign as she clamped her foot on the accelerator and screeched away. Her sudden turn into the car park in front of Pets' Palace almost made the bus behind her stall.

The store was closed, and the car park empty. The habits of Bosnia were ingrained in Christa, and she automatically pulled up at the side under the deep shadow of some trees. She switched off the Mini's lights, and decided to wait for a few minutes until the bus was well on its way.

Though the store was closed the windows were still lit, display-ing animal cages bounded on one side by plate glass. Christa was about twenty yards away, but she could see half-grown kittens scrabbling at the glass, a couple of disconsolate-looking cockatiels huddled on a plastic branch, some lethargic white rabbits, and a whippet pacing up and down in a frenzy of captive frustration. Every now and then it stopped and stared out into the darkness with huge mournful eyes.

Christa shivered, and thought that the store must be very sure of its security to have animals so openly on view. She put out her hand to restart the engine. As she did so a Cherokee four-wheel drive with crash bars lumbered into the car park. She watched it idly, thinking it was probably a security patrol, and wondered why it was reversing towards the store.

She soon found out. With a huge roar it accelerated and

ploughed straight through the entrance doors. The noise of shattering glass, much too reminiscent of a bomb's after-shock, made Christa's stomach contract violently.

The Cherokee's doors flew open, and four figures leaped out, all in dark hooded jackets and jeans except for one who almost fell as she tried to deal with the folds of a flowing skirt. Christa just had time to register that scarves swathed the lower part of their faces, and that the girl's headgear didn't quite contain a tumble of blonde curls, before they dashed inside.

A few seconds later she saw them in the window, scooping the kittens into a basket, enveloping the cockatiels in a sack, and throwing a blanket over the hysterically barking whippet. The girl was trying to catch one of the rabbits. Eventually she managed to grab it and stuff it under her jacket.

Behind the shrilling of a security alarm Christa could hear the splintering crash of display stands being overturned. She decided to make a quick exit. She didn't intend to confront a bunch of determined animal liberationists single-handed, and she had enough problems without being questioned by the police when they eventually arrived.

She was again about to switch on the engine when the girl appeared in the shattered doorway, the rabbit a pregnant-looking bump under her jacket. Christa sank down in her seat, peering over the top of the steering wheel. The girl hesitated, looked round frantically, then made a dash for the trees, plainly thinking that the Mini was unoccupied. She was only a few feet away from the car as she cowered in the shadows.

The others piled out of the store, moved the Cherokee forward and deposited the animals inside. They started looking around impatiently for the girl. One of them gestured towards the Mini. The girl was still lurking in the darkness, clearly terrified.

Christa opened the passenger door, and whispered fiercely, 'Get in. Get in here, and you'll make it.'

The girl started violently. Christa caught the gleam of her eyes as she registered that there was someone in the Mini. One of the others started to walk towards them.

'For Christ's sake, get moving,' hissed Christa. 'I won't wait.'

The girl scuttled to the open door, threw herself inside, and shut the door with a bang as the engine kicked into life. Christa rocketed out of the car park and into the bus lane, empty once more to her huge relief. She switched on the lights, and after she'd gone fifty yards saw the Cherokee shoot out of the car park in hot pursuit.

Christa pushed the engine to sixty, just caught the next set of lights before they turned to red, prayed they wouldn't meet any more wobbling, unlit cyclists, and hammered the Mini past the railway station. In the back the girl was giving gasps of alarm.

Christa scorched round Worcester Green, and as she came into the straight in Beaumont Street saw that they'd lost the Cherokee at last. She cornered down a side road into a quiet, tree-lined square, and switched off the engine.

Light from a street lamp filtered into the car. She turned and looked at the girl who was struggling to pull off her hood and scarf while trying to subdue the rabbit, busy practising Kung Fu under her jacket.

The girl's head appeared at the same time as the rabbit's. Their eyes had a similar startled, innocent gaze. Her ash-blonde curls were a triumph of the hairdresser's art, and her skin, pale and smooth as ceramic, was perfectly made up. She looked more like a cover girl than a die-hard activist. The rabbit, twitching its whiskers and ears while it surveyed its surroundings, seemed surprisingly unruffled.

'Well,' said Christa, wanting to laugh for the first time in weeks, 'that wasn't exactly a miracle of organisation, was it?'

'Thanks,' said the girl in a breathless Marilyn Monroe gasp. 'Thanks a lot. You were great.'

'And you were lucky. How on earth did you get mixed up in something like that?'

'I'm really grateful, honest I am. But I've got to be going now. I must get home. They're sure to come looking for me again.'

She started to fumble with the door handle.

'Hold on a minute,' said Christa. 'How about telling me who "they" are first? I suppose you mean Howl?'

The girl looked nervously out of the back window.

'We've lost them,' said Christa, 'and they're not going to waste time looking for you when they're dealing with half a zoo.'

The girl subsided into her seat.

'You must be crazy,' said Christa. 'You could be charged with breaking and entering, and God knows what else. You could be put inside, just for a rabbit!'

The girl hugged it protectively. It started to nibble the edge of her sleeve.

'The rabbit was in prison too,' she replied. 'Imagine being stuck in that horrible place, with no green grass, no fresh air, and lights blazing down on you non-stop. Anything's worth it to free animals from that sort of life.'

'Then why did you run out on the others if it meant so much?'

'I can't start telling you now,' said the girl nervously. 'It all took longer than I thought. I've got to get home before Glenn starts worrying about me.'

'Who's Glenn?'

'My bloke. He didn't want me to do this. We had a bit of a row over it.' Her voice had become wobbly as well as breathless. 'I think – I think he was right, probably. They never told me they were going to ram the store.' She stroked the rabbit's head. Her hands were trembling. 'Poor little thing. It's in shock, and no wonder.'

'I think you're the one in shock,' said Christa more gently. After the horrors of Bosnia it was still difficult to adjust to ordinary levels of distress. 'Sorry, I didn't realise you were quite so shaken up. I'll give you a lift home. Where do you live?'

'It's all right. I can make it alone. You don't have to bother.'

Christa guessed the girl was still too scared to reveal where she lived. But even though Christa had promised Randall she wouldn't get involved with Howl, and she intended to keep that promise, the lead was too good to miss, if only to satisfy her own curiosity.

'Then at least meet me tomorrow and tell me how you got into all this.'

'How do I know you won't grass on me to the police?'

The girl had managed to open the car door, and was settling the rabbit back into her jacket. She was in a frenzy of anxiety to get away.

'I could have stayed behind in the car park and waited for them to arrive if I'd wanted to do that. I'm just interested, that's all.'

The girl gazed at her suspiciously.

'And you do owe me,' said Christa with a smile.

She knew she was using coercion, albeit of a very gentle kind, but she was beginning to feel a reaction herself, the sort that still overtook her after any confrontation. All she wanted now was to be on her way too.

Embarrassed, the girl wrapped a curl of hair round her finger. Her hands were impeccably manicured.

'OK, how about Hockley's café in the covered market, around ten tomorrow? Glenn'll be there too. He usually has a second breakfast round that time.'

'Fine,' said Christa, thinking the arrangement would fit in nicely with her plans. She was going to see Piers at eleven, before an official meeting with the Master. 'You'd better tell me your name first, though. Mine's Christa.'

'I'm Stacey,' said the girl, extricating herself from the car. By the light of a street lamp Christa saw she was wearing flimsy black espadrilles tied with ankle bows. The square was empty and cold, with dead leaves blowing about in a crisp night wind which carried with it the sonorous tones of Boanerges, Gabriel's clock, beginning to strike the hour.

'Seven o'clock. I'm late, I'm late,' said Stacey distractedly, sounding just like the White Rabbit in *Alice in Wonderland*. The real white rabbit gave another kick. She clutched it more closely. 'Glenn'll have had tea ready half an hour ago. He'll be going spare. See you tomorrow, then.'

Christa watched her scuttle away. As she started the Mini and turned it towards North Oxford, she thought with wry amusement that if Stacey was like the White Rabbit, she herself was Alice about to enter the world of the looking glass.

Emma and Philip lived just off the Woodstock Road. They'd recently traded up from a modern house in Headington, and it was the first time Christa had visited their new home. She turned into a short drive whose gravel crunched beneath the Mini's tyres, parked behind an elderly Volvo with a ragged window sticker exhorting her to save the British Museum reading room, and looked up at the house.

It was a gaunt Victorian brick semi, with an ecclesiastical-looking tiled porch topped with a plaster griffin's head. The windows were framed in crenellated stone, and had top lights of Art Nouveau stained glass. Christa could almost feel the waves of high-mindedness proceeding from it.

She wished she were standing outside some cheerful hotel. It was a bad time of day, the time she and Matt had often had a drink together in whatever Sarajevo dive had some slivovitz for sale, while they set up their next shooting schedule. She made herself push the doorbell, which was set in a surround of gleaming brass, and heard it sound deep within the house.

After a long wait a hall light flicked on and the door was heaved open by a slender, leggy child of about five. She was wearing a tutu, wrinkled tights, and pink satin ballet shoes. Her dark, straight hair, tied back with a piece of velvet ribbon, and her eyes of spinach green, were unmistakably Emma's.

This was Pansy, whom Christa had last seen as a podgy three year old in the midst of a spectacular tantrum because Emma wouldn't let her go to the station to see Christa off on a late-night train.

Christa had only visited Oxford twice since then, the first time on a flying visit to her parents, when Pansy stayed at home with tonsillitis. On the next trip, Pansy was visiting Philip's mother, and she'd now evidently forgotten Christa completely.

'Do come in,' she said in a high regal voice. 'You must be Aunt Christa. Mummy's expecting you.'

Christa walked into the hall, which was panelled in dark oak, and dumped her rucsac next to a chair with an embroidered seat. One of Emma's hobbies was tambour work.

Pansy held out her hand. 'I don't s'pose you remember me. I'm Pansy – Pansy Laetitia Holdgate. How do you do?'

'Hi,' said Christa with a grin, taking the hand, which felt slightly sticky. 'I remember you very well. Why don't you drop the aunt, and just call me Christa?'

'That would be rude,' said Pansy, her gaze still fixed consideringly on Christa.

'So I must call you Niece Pansy, then?'

Pansy performed a series of wobbly pirouettes, and came round to face Christa once more. She gave a deep reluctant giggle, like water bubbling up in a well.

'That won't be necessary,' she said, sounding just like Emma in her most school-marmy mode.

'I didn't know your second name was Laetitia,' said Christa.

Pansy's eyes widened.

'But you're my godmother. Godmothers are supposed to know things like that. It's Latin. It means joy.' Her voice was outraged.

'Sorry,' said Christa, trying to look suitably chastened.

Pansy's christening had taken place when she'd a weekend to spare between assignments. She could just remember having to wear a hat, and trusting to luck that she'd never need to carry out the promises blithely made on Pansy's behalf in the arctic atmosphere of Philip's college chapel. The luncheon afterwards, with Philip toadying to the more senior academic guests, she'd tried to forget as fast as she could.

'It's all right,' said Pansy. 'Will you let me see your gun?'

'My gun? Sorry, but I don't have one.'

Pansy looked disappointed. 'Daddy said he wouldn't be surprised if you turned up with a Kal – Kal—'

'A Kalashnikov,' supplied Christa tersely.

'Mummy says she's never ever going to let Jamie play war games.'

'Quite right,' said Christa, though she was inwardly seething. She'd always suspected that her brother-in-law, whose IQ and intellectual arrogance were equally off the chart, made snide remarks about her behind her back.

'Would you like to see me do an entrechat?' Pansy asked.

'I'd love to.' Christa tried to assume an aunt-like expression of interest.

Pansy performed a not very polished jump and twiddle of her feet, landing with a heavy thud.

'I can go on my points, but I'm not allowed. Daddy says it's bad for my bones.'

At the end of the hall a door opened, and Emma appeared. Christa saw that she was still wearing her hair drawn into a Bloomsbury knot at the nape of her neck. A floury butcher's apron covered her white blouse and navy skirt. Her long face with its level brows and slightly beaky nose looked best when she was happy. Then she resembled one of the more commanding

Greek goddesses, but at the moment she was clearly tired and harassed.

'Hallo, Christa. Sorry I couldn't answer the door. I'm cooking for a dinner party tomorrow.'

She wiped her hands on her apron, and embraced her sister. Her hair, slippery with cleanliness and smelling of camomile, was pressed briefly against Christa's cheek. They never really hugged each other these days, Christa thought. Yet when she was Pansy's age she'd loved to crush her elder sister in enormous embraces like a teddy bear, to arrange her hair in outrageous styles, to squeeze close to her and distract her with butterfly kisses while she tried to read.

Emma released Christa, taking in her appearance with one wary glance, like a housewife door-stepped by a gypsy fortune-teller who might bring havoc to her well-ordered life.

'You've lost weight, but I suppose it's not surprising,' she said, in a tone which made it very clear that she considered the affair with Gareth the cause.

'So has everyone in Bosnia.' Christa kept her voice light, determined not to clash with Emma so soon.

'Mummy's going to wear her black velvet dress at dinner tomorrow,' said Pansy. 'What are you going to wear, Christa?'

'Aunt Christa,' corrected Emma, her eyes going to the well-worn rucsac on the floor. A worried expression crept across her face. 'You did bring a dress, didn't you, Christa? Phil's invited the Master of Gabriel and his wife, and they're rather old-fashioned about evening wear.'

'Yes, I've got a dress. It's not very new, but I won't let you down.'

She couldn't resist adding the last remark. Emma looked uncomfortable.

'How about some coffee?' she asked brightly. 'It's a little early for alcohol. Come and talk to me while I finish the pastry for tomorrow. We're going to have lamb *en croûte*.'

Christa, following her towards the kitchen, looked at her watch. Half-past six definitely wasn't too early. She urgently needed a very stiff vodka to prepare herself for the encounter with Phil.

'The kitchen's just been re-done,' said Emma, pushing open

the door. 'You should have seen it when we arrived – acres of white melamine.'

Christa cast her mind back to Emma's kitchen in the last house, which was crammed with lovingly rehabilitated pine and had the relentless cosiness of a Tyrolean chalet. Looking around, she saw that they were now in immigrant America. Tall Shaker cupboards were painted a faded grey so tastefully restrained that they seemed to merge into the walls. Ladder-back chairs surrounded the plain oak table in the centre of the room. On it stood a marble slab bearing a neatly rolled square of pastry.

Christa sat down cautiously on one of the chairs. Pansy joined her at the table and began to play with a handful of magnetic marbles. Christa continued her survey of the room. A snow white teatowel hung from the rail of an Aga whose hob covers shone like a vintage Chrysler's hub caps. Emma looked up from making coffee, and caught Christa's glance.

'I know Agas are loaded with all sorts of suspect social associ-ations,' she said defensively, 'but they're so wonderful for things like meringues and casseroles – and for drying Barbours, of course.'

'Barbours!' said Christa, pulling round her seat, which was as comfortable as an old-fashioned deportment chair, and propping her feet on the rungs of the one next to her. 'Since when did you wear a Barbour, Em? Have you and Philip started going to point-to-points?'

Emma didn't reply. Christa could sense her trying not to nag about the chair, and decided she'd better not push her luck by smoking. In theory she was trying to wean herself off the habit she'd started in Bosnia, but the way things were going she wouldn't be able to get through to bedtime without a cigarette.

'You'll have to tidy those away now, Pansy,' said Emma, bringing Christa a cafetière of coffee and some milk. 'I'm just going to get your supper. You'd better skip violin practice tonight, I haven't time to listen. But you can put out the empty milk bottles while you're waiting, and lay a place at the table.'

She gave Christa a mug, then parcelled the pastry in foil, and whisked it into the fridge.

The interior, in which already reposed a leg of lamb marinading in wine, was like an illustration from *Good Housekeeping*. Christa thought of her fridge at the flat. When she'd cleaned it before leaving the only contents were a whiskery piece of cheese and a forgotten carton of curdled milk.

With a long-suffering expression Pansy rolled the marbles into a table drawer. Emma winced at the noise. Pansy went over to a pinboard, and consulted a large chart headed 'Family Tasks'.

'It's Daddy's turn to do the milk bottles this week, not mine.'

'Daddy's been too busy.'

Emma cut two neat slices from a brown loaf with the texture of compacted compost. She glanced at her watch as she tipped some beaten eggs into a saucepan on the Aga.

'Where *is* Phil?' she said irritably. 'Jamie'll be going to sleep soon, and Phil's supposed to give him at least half an hour's quality time every night. It was part of our contract.'

'How can a baby be fitted into a contract?' Christa couldn't resist the tease.

'It's just a question of good organisation and people keeping their word,' Emma replied shortly. 'I wouldn't have dreamed of trying to handle a full-time job teaching, and a second child without Phil's complete cooperation.'

Pansy was still studying the chart. 'Noelene ought to have taken the newspapers to the paper bank when she went to Baby Aerobics with Jamie.'

'Isn't Jamie a bit young for working out?' Christa asked, thinking that though her nephew had no doubt inherited a stunning array of genes, he couldn't possibly be walking yet.

'Of course he's too young,' snapped Emma, 'though knowing you, Christa, I'm sure you've forgotten his age. He's only eight months old. At the moment Noelene simply rocks him to classical music, but as soon as he can walk he'll do some easy exercises. It's excellent for aural and motor development.'

The eggs were now ready. Emma piled them on to the toast. Pansy had taken a French edition of *Tintin in Tibet* from the table drawer, and was reading it with enormous concentration, mouthing the more difficult words.

'Tintin in French at five! That's pretty good going, Pansy,' said Christa. 'What are you going to learn next? Japanese?'

She gave Christa a withering look. 'I'm really too busy at the moment. But some of my friends are learning it. I've got a reading age of seven, they said at school.'

'Pansy's been going to French classes since she began to talk,' said Emma, approaching the table with the eggs. 'Put your book away now, Pansy. You know the rule about reading at meals.'

Pansy sulkily stashed the book behind her back, and glared at the eggs confronting her.

'Yuk! Chelsea has Pop Tarts for tea every day, *and* lovely white bread, *and* turkeyburgers and chips.'

'And God knows how many additives as well,' said Emma crossly, dumping the empty bowl in the sink.

'Who's Chelsea?' Christa asked.

'My best friend at school,' Pansy replied. '*Her* aunt works in a hairdresser's. She does Chel's hair with a hot brush and mousse. It looks brilliant.'

'It looks highly unsuitable,' said Emma. 'There's no question of state education later on for Pansy, of course. But we chose a local state school to start with, just to get her socially integrated. We fill the gaps with private tuition.'

Christa heroically refrained from comment. She herself had followed Emma to a private secondary school, but after a couple of years there, conforming to rules which seemed designed to make her miserable, she'd played truant so determinedly that her parents were forced to enrol her at the local comprehensive instead.

'Do get on with your food,' Emma snapped at Pansy, who was pushing the eggs round the plate.

She brought her a glass of milk. Pansy, clearly sensing an imminent explosion, started to eat.

'Sorry, my lovely, lovely, Mummy,' she said with an eggy smile.

Emma thought exasperatedly that her daughter and her sister were remarkably alike, and that it was hard enough to cope with one of them, let alone both. They were a disturbing mixture of stubbornness, independence, and occasional disarming tenderness, though it was years since she'd seen Christa display the last quality.

Since she left college she'd been dedicated to her career. When she became a foreign correspondent for Apollo it really took off. Her professionalism left Emma admiring and breathless, but Christa had in her sister's opinion become correspondingly hard.

Yet when they were at school together, Christa, who scamped her homework and broke the record for detentions, was always a teachers' favourite. Even now, thin and drawn, in frayed white jeans and an old blue cardigan under which she appeared to be wearing nothing at all, and whose buttons weren't done up quite far enough, she was attractive. She looked like a very cross, rumpled fledgling which had just fallen from its nest – a fledgling which, Emma knew from long experience, would peck vigorously if she tried to help.

Emma hadn't dared broach the subject of the Bosnian incident yet, but she'd have to warn Christa to be discreet about it at the dinner party tomorrow. Philip was gaining a reputation as a sound man in University circles, the sort who might one day become a Head of House himself. And a Head's wife automatically became mistress of a mouth-wateringly beautiful college residence.

Pansy crammed the last of the eggs into her mouth.

'I've finished. Can I have some ice-cream?'

'No, you may not. You know the rule – ice-cream only at weekends. Have an apple instead.'

She dumped a bowl of fruit in front of Pansy. An apple rolled out in Christa's direction. She flipped it back towards Pansy, thinking that there seemed to be a great many regulations in her young life.

'What's wrong with ice-cream?' Christa asked.

'Too much sugar. I don't want Pansy to end up with a mouthful of mercury,' said Emma.

She took a roasting chicken from the Aga oven, and carefully basted it. Christa, catching a waft of tarragon and garlic, suddenly felt hungry for the first time in a long while. If the sherry wasn't too slow in appearing she might just manage to survive the evening after all.

Pansy picked up the apple, a hard green Granny Smith, and returned it to the bowl with a look of contempt. Christa could sense Emma, en route to the sink to do the washing up, getting ready to nag her again. She felt an unexpected surge of solidarity with her niece. She'd been preached the gospel of deferred gratification all through her childhood as well.

'I'm surprised you don't have a dishwasher, or doesn't that go with the Shaker image?' The teasing would annoy Emma, but also divert her attention from Pansy.

'Philip says it wastes water.'

'Does Philip do the washing-up? He never used to.'

'He's working flat out on his research. And he's got other problems too.'

The Tucker Institute, where Philip worked, was a centre for biological research on the edge of the city near Wolvercote. It had been endowed by a patent medicine magnate, a graduate of Gabriel Hall, which owned the lease of the land on which it was built. Philip's fellowship at Gabriel was, like most of the posts at the Institute, part of the endowment.

'What sort of problems?' Christa asked.

'There's an underground animal rights group in this area called Howl. It's made several failed attempts at breaking into the Institute's labs. The security's excellent, but the fuss disrupts Phil's work. There's another local rights group too, called the Peaceable Kingdom, though luckily it's much more low-key.'

'And your problems take second place, as usual?' said Christa, thinking she'd better keep quiet about her own encounter with Howl.

Emma ignored her, glancing impatiently at Pansy, who was deep in *Tintin* again while she ate a banana.

'Go upstairs, Pansy, and ask Noelene to run you a bath. She must have put James to bed by now. I'll come and see you when I've finished here.'

Pansy wandered off, her nose still in the book, leaving the banana skin upside down like a yellow flower on the table.

'This dinner tomorrow is quite important,' Emma said. 'The post of Informator Agnorum comes up soon at Gabriel. It'd bring Phil a big increase in salary.'

'And what exactly is the post?' Christa asked, with renewed irritation at the way communications at Gabriel Hall seemed designed to exclude and confuse the uninitiated.

'Adviser to the first years, in effect. It used to be important, before the days of the student counselling service. But now it would simply entail having little get-togethers for them once a term here. If the Master takes away a good impression tomorrow, it'll help Phil's chances a lot.'

Christa was on the point of making a caustic remark about the disposition of funds at Gabriel Hall, when she suddenly realised that Emma was about to warn her to be tactful.

'So?' she said warily. 'Fine by me. It sounds a soft number. Naturally Phil would want it.'

'You don't quite understand,' said Emma, a slight note of desperation creeping into her voice. 'Luckily the Master doesn't have television, so he probably won't know who you are, and Phil's never mentioned that he's related to you . . .'

I bet he hasn't, thought Christa.

'Just tell him you're here to research a travel book if he asks. And if by any ghastly chance he does know about your recent . . .' she hesitated. '. . . your recent problem, you'll have to make something up. Tell him it's been totally distorted by the media.'

Christa, who'd been on the point of breaking the news to Emma about her fellowship, now decided not to just yet.

'What do you mean, make something up? It *was* distorted. Are you ashamed of me, Em?' Christa knew she was twisting the knife, but a wave of depression had begun to drag her down again. 'I can find somewhere else to stay if it bothers you as much as all that.'

'Of course I'm not ashamed of you,' said Emma, becoming very pink. 'And of course you must stay with us. You're family, for heaven's sake. It's just that we've taken out a massive mortgage on this place, and if Phil got this extra post we wouldn't have to worry about money so much.'

'Then why did you move in the first place? What was so bad about the other house?'

'What was bad? Everything! Almost on top of the ring road, tacky seventies architecture, and most of the neighbours were sales reps! Serious entertaining was impossible there.'

Christa thought that the first house had been a lot more cheerful than the present one. But Emma was starting to look suspiciously shiny-eyed, and Christa knew it had been unfair to take her own misery out on her.

She forced a smile. 'All right, Em. I'm sorry. I'll be a model of discretion. Come and have a cup of coffee with me, and mellow out for a bit.'

The mixture of apology and affection in Christa's voice startled Emma so much that she took another mug from the dresser and joined Christa at the table. As she poured herself some coffee an almost sympathetic silence fell between them. Emma wondered if she dared broach the subject of Gareth Hyde. She was longing to know what had really happened. Christa had always been so in control of her boyfriends in the past.

'You must be feeling pretty upset about Gareth still,' she said tentatively.

'I'm more upset about my career, and having to waste a year of it here.' Christa's voice was wary, and she didn't look at Emma.

'Were you really in love with him?'

Christa looked up, pushing away her coffee mug.

'Yes, I was in love.' Her voice was dispassionate but her face was wretched. 'Head over heels, fathoms deep . . . all the stupid things people say. I was so crazy about him that I didn't notice he was only in love with himself.'

'You'll meet someone else. You think you won't, but you will. And Oxford's full of unattached men.'

'I'm not interested. I just want to forget Gareth and get on with my life.'

She sounded so miserable that Emma didn't dare say anything else. She gave Christa's hand a squeeze. To Emma's astonishment Christa returned an almost grateful smile. For a few moments another companionable silence reigned, until the kitchen door opened to admit Noelene with a very wide-awake Jamie.

'Sorry, Mrs Holdgate, but he's in a really crook mood tonight,' said Noelene in a strong Australian accent. 'He doesn't want to settle.'

Jamie gave a crow of delight, and held out his arms to Emma. Once more Christa wrenched her mind from Gareth, and made herself focus on the new arrivals. It would have been hard to ignore Noelene anyway in her white leather jacket and minute red skirt which displayed legs tanned a peanut butter brown by the Antipodean sun.

'It's way past my finishing time and I've gotta run or I'll miss my bus,' she said.

She smiled vaguely at Christa, and dumped the baby in Emma's lap, making a swift exit through the back door in a wave of body spray.

'She might have waited another half hour,' said Emma crossly, looking at her watch. 'I know she's technically due to go off duty now, but she could try to be a little more thoughtful when I'm so busy. What do you think of your nephew, Christa?'

She looked warily at Jamie, who was wearing a rainbow-striped stretch suit and gnawing a bunch of plastic keys. He had a dandelion fuzz of hair and placid blue eyes. Dribble trickled down his chin, but at least he seemed more amenable than Pansy as an infant, who had howled all the way through her baptism looking like a tomato in a doily.

'He's sweet,' she said dutifully.

'Why don't you hold him?' said Emma, transferring him swiftly to her lap.

Christa waited for him to cry, but he continued to chew the keys, looking gravely around him. His warm, plump little body felt like an oversized hot-water bottle.

Emma was gazing at them both with a sentimental expression. 'I knew you'd love him. Babies are the best thing in the world, even though they're loads of hard work. Don't let this business with Gareth put you off. Don't leave it too long, will you?'

Christa was biting back a crushing reply when there was the sound of someone placing a key in the front door lock.

'Philip, at last!' said Emma.

Christa braced herself for the meeting with her brother-in-law. If she could get through that successfully the rest of the evening might not be too bad. His neat, precise figure came into the room, rimless spectacles planted firmly on his nose, dark hair combed carefully across a striking expanse of brow.

'Hallo, Christa,' he said, keeping well away from her, and bending over to give Emma a perfunctory kiss. Normally he was several inches shorter than his wife.

'Hallo, Philip. How are you?'

'Busy,' he said, picking up Pansy's banana skin with a look of distaste and putting in the rubbish bin.

'I was getting worried,' said Emma. 'I thought you wouldn't have time for Jamie.'

'Trouble with animal rights again,' he said gloomily, twitching the edges of the towel into perfect alignment on the Aga rail before sitting down. 'A demo by the Peaceable Kingdom this time, and they were egged on by a gang of estate lager louts with nothing better to do.'

The Gabriel's Grounds housing Estate lay next door to the Institute. Christa seemed to remember it had been built on land granted on a lease by Gabriel Hall, and funded by the same philanthropist who had endowed the Institute. He'd intended it to be a model estate, but it sounded as if something had gone seriously wrong.

'I had to wait for the police to clear them,' Philip continued. 'They seem incapable of understanding that the lab animals live the life of Riley on the whole.'

'But they aren't free,' Christa said.

He gave her a repressive look. 'The primates are doing a lot better at the Institute than in the hands of some unlicensed dealer in the Far East. And how are you? I gather you've been busy too. The media have kept us well informed.'

Christa couldn't stop herself from going on the offensive. 'But not accurately informed, I hope you realise,' she snapped back.

'Phil, why don't you take Jamie upstairs now?' said Emma desperately. 'You've still got time for half an hour with him before dinner.'

Philip glanced unenthusiastically at Jamie, who'd cast aside the keys and was vigorously chewing the sugar spoon instead.

'For Christ's sake, give me a chance to get my breath back. I haven't been sitting here having coffee like you two.' He turned his attention to Christa again. 'Shame about that cameraman you worked with. I gather he was a decent sort of chap. Lost your grip on the situation, did you?'

'I did not,' said Christa through gritted teeth. 'I told you, I was given false information.'

'By Gareth Hyde, you mean? But I thought he'd got a pretty sound reputation, if such a thing's possible in the media world.'

Christa couldn't decide if Philip was winding her up, or if he'd simply decided not to believe her version of the story. There'd never been much love lost between them since he'd criticised her for neglecting the family. He visited his doting and dictatorial mother without fail once a month.

The glances Emma was sending him at last began to register, but only had the effect of making him jump to another equally fraught subject.

'You're here to research a book, Emma says. I didn't know you had literary aspirations.'

'Apollo want me to take a break,' Christa replied shortly.

'I'm not surprised. Going to be an apologia, is it?'

'Not at all. There's nothing to apologise for.'

Philip lifted an eyebrow at Christa. 'Really? And how do you propose to do this research? You won't be able to use the university libraries, you know. You're not a member of any college.'

There was a marked sneer in his voice. Christa came to the end of her self-control.

'That's where you're wrong. I've got a visiting fellowship.'

'You, a fellow?' said Philip in disbelief. 'You don't have a higher degree.'

Emma looked equally stunned. 'You didn't tell me, Christa. However did you manage it?'

'It's a media fellowship,' she said nonchalantly, adding with more confidence than she felt, 'and the college jumped at the chance.'

'Which college?' Philip demanded. 'I suppose one of the newer places. They've had a few rather off-beat endowments recently.'

'Gabriel,' said Christa.

It was the best moment of the day. She'd never seen Philip speechless before. He turned a dull red before he was able to regain his voice.

'I don't believe it! Gabriel only has one female fellow, and she's among the finest minds in the country. Why would the college elect you?'

'Presumably to correct an imbalance the other colleges started to put right years ago,' Christa shot back.

Emma abandoned all attempt at peacemaking.

'But you're bound to stir things up, Christa. You always do. It'll make things so dreadfully difficult for Phil. How could you be so thoughtless?'

Jamie turned down his mouth at the distress in Emma's voice. She snatched him from Christa.

'You've upset him now,' she said.

Another wave of depression washed over Christa. As the newly established rapport between herself and Emma vanished, she was surprised to discover that she'd been expecting her sister's support.

'Gabriel's the last place I would have chosen. But I didn't have any option, and I've got to make the best of it. I'll try not to embarrass either of you in the process,' she said, battling not very successfully with tiredness and self-pity.

Emma looked even more horror-struck.

'Don't talk like that. You know it's not what we meant.'

'Maybe you didn't, but Philip certainly did.'

'Quite frankly, it seems like a recipe for total disaster to me,' he said in a tone of the iciest displeasure. 'And I've had enough trouble in college recently over that unfortunate business with your father.'

Christa stared at him. Her father, whom she loved dearly in spite of his ineffectual approach to life, was the most self-effacing of men.

'What are you talking about?' she demanded. 'Dad never makes trouble, and he has nothing to do with Gabriel.'

'Maybe he didn't tell you because he thought you'd be upset,' said Emma hurriedly.

'Tell me what, for heaven's sake? Do get to the point, Em,' said Christa, guessing from Phil's expression that it was something which would disturb her a lot.

'He applied for the post of head librarian at Gabriel last term. Everyone thought his appointment was a certainty, but he didn't get the job. It was a big disappointment for him.'

'Poor old Dad,' said Christa slowly. Her father would have revelled in having such a kingdom under his command. 'He never has much luck. What went wrong?'

Emma glanced at Phil. 'Apparently most of the appointments committee thought he was the best candidate, but I gather some of his ideas didn't quite coincide with the Master's,' she said evasively.

'Such as?' demanded Christa.

Emma looked nervously at Phil again. 'Well, Daddy was keen on making the books more widely accessible. At the moment the library's restricted to post-graduates, and it's not computerised.'

Christa's father was surprisingly enthusiastic about modern technology, and at home spent hours on the Internet pursuing family research.

'So why did the Master object?' Christa asked. 'I thought the whole idea of a university was to make knowledge available to everyone.'

'You would over-simplify, Christa,' said Phil. 'It's typical of you and the media. As it happens, I agree with the Master. Gabriel has a very special standard of excellence to maintain. It won't do so by opening its facilities to all and sundry. Luckily in the case of this particular appointment the Master had an overriding vote.'

'But Emma's just said that most of the committee thought Dad was the best candidate,' Christa burst out indignantly. 'Overriding a majority vote certainly doesn't demonstrate moral superiority.'

Philip was cross-eyed with fury. He leaped up from the table.

'You've got a bloody nerve to criticise when you're a guest! I knew this would happen.' He turned on Emma, who was clutching a teatowel distractedly to her breast. 'I've only been home ten minutes, but Christa's already wrecked the evening. I was particularly looking forward to a peaceful time with this tricky finance committee meeting coming up tomorrow. I'm going to Gabriel. I'll dine in hall.'

Jamie screwed up his face and began to howl as his father marched out of the kitchen. The front door slammed shut while Emma was frantically trying to soothe the screaming child.

'Oh, God,' said Christa, feeling another unusual pang of guilt, and finding herself apologising again. 'I'm sorry, Em, but you must see I really couldn't let Phil get away with it.'

Emma had retrieved the plastic keys for Jamie. He crammed them into his mouth. She smoothed his hair, and gradually his sobs began to subside. She gave Christa half a smile.

'I suppose not. It'd make life a lot easier, though, if you didn't pursue the truth quite so hard.'

'But it's so rotten for Dad,' pursued Christa. 'Surely you agree about that?'

'Yes, I do, as it happens, but I feel so tired these days, I try not to argue with Phil too much.' Emma looked down at Jamie, who was quiet at last, and then craned over his shoulder at her watch. 'Heavens, look at the time, and I haven't even done the vegetables yet.'

'Why don't you think about making your own life a bit easier?' said Christa, with a relieved grin. 'Leave the chicken for another day, and I'll fetch us a bottle of wine and a Chinese carry-out.'

'Well, it would be bliss not to cook any more tonight.' Emma's face was already brightening. She glanced at Jamie, whose eyes had started to droop. 'And I think he's ready for bed at last. But I meant what I was saying just now, Christa. It'd be a big help if you'd keep your home truths to yourself while you're here.'

'All right, I'll try to spare Phil's tender feelings, but only for your sake. And the day you find me not pursuing the truth professionally, you'll know I really am finished,' Christa replied, as she went to find the keys to the car.

3 ∫

'No, I can't drop Noelene and Jamie off at their class. My committee meeting starts in twenty minutes' time.'

Philip's voice carried clearly up the stairs to the landing. Rain was pelting against the window. Christa had just emerged the following morning from her bedroom above the porch, where a tepid radiator scarcely took the chill from the air. Yet she'd slept surprisingly well, once she'd wrapped her frozen feet in a pullover.

'Is there any good reason why Noelene shouldn't take Jamie in the buggy?' he went on. 'We pay her enough, after all. Or should I say subsidise her? She seems to spend most of her time enlarging her sexual experience.'

Intrigued, Christa peered down the stairwell. Philip was meticulously brushing his already immaculate grey suit as he studied himself in the hall mirror. Behind him Emma, in a voluminous caped macintosh, was hurriedly cramming exercise books into a plastic bag.

'It's too far in this weather. Do you have to be so bloody unreasonable? I'm teaching at nine, as well as walking Pansy to school. You go right past the aerobics place. And you were the one who wanted another child, if you remember.'

Christa couldn't have been more astonished to hear Victoria swearing at Albert. She craned further over the banisters.

'If we'd stayed in the other house, as I also wanted, if *you* remember, we could have bought a second car,' Philip retorted.

Pansy, a plastic lunch box clutched to her chest, was gazing at her parents as they argued, her eyes round beneath a red PVC sou'wester.

'Didn't you want Jamie, Mummy?' she asked.

'Of course I did,' said Emma sharply, frowning at Philip.

'And did you want me?'

'Do stop asking such ridiculous questions. Of course we wanted both of you.'

'Chel was a mistake,' Pansy remarked. 'I heard her mummy say so. How can a baby be a mistake?'

'Very easily.' Philip's voice was dry. He turned his attention to Emma again. 'Can't you ask your sister to take Noelene and Jamie? She's not slow to use you when it suits her, though it's obvious she doesn't give a toss about our welfare. This business over the fellowship is the last straw.'

'I told you, Phil, she was forced to take it. She explained it all to me at supper last night.'

'Doesn't sound very likely to me. I've never known Christa do anything she didn't want.'

All Christa's good resolutions of the previous night vanished. She took the Mini keys from her pocket, leaned over the banisters, and deliberately dropped them down the stairwell. They clinked to the ground at Emma's feet. She stared up at Christa, dismay dawning on her face as she realised she'd over-heard the conversation.

'Why don't you take my car for the day, Em, if it'll help?' Christa said. 'I won't need it in town.'

'Come on, Mummy, do.' Pansy tugged at Emma's arm. 'I shan't get my silver star this week if I'm late.'

Philip looked as if he'd swallowed a whole pickled egg. His Adam's apple bobbed above the pristine white shirt which Christa had seen Emma, almost dropping with fatigue, iron before she went to bed.

'Right, that's settled, then,' he said, snatching up a perfectly furled umbrella from the hall stand. 'Better make the most of your sister's offer, Em. I'll be amazed if it happens again.'

He wrenched open the front door, let it crash back against the wall, and stamped down the steps. As he got into the Volvo, Emma, scarlet-faced, picked up the keys at her feet. Christa slowly descended the stairs, not daring to laugh.

'Thanks,' Emma said awkwardly. 'It's a bit difficult at times when we all need to go in different directions.'

'Phil made that very clear.'

Emma blushed again. 'I'm sorry about what he said. He didn't really mean it. He's just a bit wound up generally at the moment.'

'He meant every word. I don't mind about myself, but I hate to hear him bawling you out. What's going on? You never used to have rows.'

Pansy, who'd followed Philip through the open door, had decided that the puddles were more interesting than her silver star, and was splashing from one to another in her wellington boots. Emma picked up the bulging carrier bag, bracing herself against the weight.

'Phil worries about the mortgage,' she said. 'But this house was a tremendous bargain, and living here really makes us part of the North Oxford scene.'

Christa sat down on the bottom stair. She clasped her arms round her knees.

'Which makes it all worthwhile?' she asked.

'I'm trying to give my children the best possible start in life. But what would you know about that? You've never had to look after anyone except yourself. In a way Phil's right.'

'I do know that marriage shouldn't be a one-sided sacrifice.'

'That just shows how little you understand. Marriage involves give and take, you know.'

'Philip seems to do most of the taking at the moment.'

'Oh, do – do be quiet for once, Christa. Why do we always end up arguing? And I'm going to be late for assembly at this rate.'

Emma lugged the carrier bag exasperatedly towards the front door, and hooked her foot round it to pull it shut. Her final remark as she manoeuvred herself outside was so breathtakingly unfair that it left Christa speechless.

'And for heaven's sake, if you run into Philip at Gabriel, try not to upset him again. I want the party to go well tonight.'

Christa was still trying to subdue her resentment as she made her own escape from the house an hour later. She hated the way Emma and Philip managed to make her feel like a child. And the atmosphere of marital discord which filled the house like razor wire was just as bad. It made her even more eager to find a place of her own.

The rain had finally stopped, and a flotilla of billowing clouds sailed in a pale blue sky above the thundering traffic of the Woodstock Road. Christa was wearing dark glasses and her hair was covered with an old striped Rasta beret. Though the media's interest had died down, people still occasionally recognised her in the street.

She'd managed to train herself to stop looking for snipers everywhere, but when she reached the wide expanse of St Giles' it was still difficult not to keep close to the wall and cross the side streets in a frantic dash. Yet apart from the traffic, nothing could have looked more peaceful than the ancient plane trees casting ragged golden leaves on the flagstoned pavement, and the dignified façades of St John's and Balliol.

She looked up at the Martyrs' Memorial as she passed. It was hard to believe that people had burned to death there for their beliefs. Yet Sarajevo and Dubrovnik were once just as serenely beautiful as Oxford, their ancient streets just as calm.

The covered market at least was reassuringly full of normal everyday life, almost souk-like in its labyrinthine corridors and richness of colour. The scent of cut flowers mingled with the reek of fish, the raw smell of butcher's meat, and the aroma of roasting coffee beans. Most of the cafés had gone upmarket since her youth, but Hockley's, one of the original market traders' haunts, seemed unchanged, though it now had Italian staff.

It had often been her refuge when she played truant from school, lingering as long as she dared over a cup of coffee before whiling away the afternoon in the anonymous darkness of a cinema. She'd got her first subconscious training as a reporter there: discovering how to listen, to draw out the heart of a story as she chatted to the other customers. And later, in the cinema, learning the art of the confident approach to brazen her way into adult movies, and then how to choke off the sad, furtive, approaches of lonely men so that she could concentrate on the story unfolding on the screen before her.

When she entered the café the neat rows of tables were still covered with green-and-white-checked plastic, and a half-curtain of net ran discreetly along the length of the window, so that customers could see into the shopping corridor, yet not be seen.

The clientele was the usual interesting mix. An elderly clergyman had folded himself away in a corner, and was reading poetry while he worked his way through a stack of buttered toast. A teenage couple shared a milk shake, and near the counter four workmen who seemed to overflow their chairs were demolishing huge fry-ups.

Christa asked for coffee at the counter, and then, suddenly tempted by the sight and smell of crisp fried bread, bacon and egg, and perfectly browned sausages, ordered the same for herself.

She took her coffee to one of the window tables. On the other side of the shopping corridor was a greengrocer's stall piled with ribbed globes of tawny pumpkin and all the harvest of late summer, including rarely seen quinces and medlars. Further on, outside a butcher's shop, hung Dickensian turkeys waiting for the American community's Thanksgiving, and a whole carcase of venison probably destined for a college feast.

As Christa drank her coffee, a man passed the window pushing a battered sit-up-and-beg bike. Over one handlebar hung an umbrella and a holdall bursting with books. He unstrapped a box of damsons from the carrier, their blue skins shining through the dusty bloom, and dumped them on the floor of the greengrocer's stall as he spoke to the proprietor.

The man had his back to her. He was tall, dressed in faded jeans and a sagging linen jacket. She amused herself by trying to guess what he'd look like when he turned round. Only the most venerable dons used such ancient bikes these days, but he was too upright to come into the golden oldie category. Though his jacket would have been perfect for a tea planter in the heyday of the empire, the jeans covered a pair of distinctly athletic legs.

Even when he turned she couldn't work him out. His eyes were concealed by wrap-around sunglasses and the turned-down brim of a brown trilby which a charity shop would have scorned. A loosely wound cotton scarf obscured his mouth and chin. He either had severe toothache, or wanted recognition as little as herself.

Her curiosity increased when he came into the café. He ordered an espresso and a toasted sandwich at the counter, chatting in

Italian to the attendant while he waited for the coffee. She decided he was probably a poverty-stricken expatriate drop-out from Tuscany on a duty visit to an academic parent.

Yet after he'd taken his espresso to a table on the other side of the room, he upset all her deductions by burying himself in an Arabic newspaper. A brown hand appeared from behind the screen of pages, and placed the hat and scarf on the chair by his side. Christa decided instead that he must be a dilettante Middle Easterner with a misguided liking for the English way of life.

She was still idly studying him when the rest of his order arrived. In the brief moment that the newspaper was put aside she was startled to glimpse a face very different from the one of her expectations. Though his tanned skin was almost as dark as an Arab's, his straight brushed-back hair was the colour of bleached grass. He'd taken off the glasses to reveal blue eyes set in a face which wouldn't have been out of place on an effigy of one of the more intransigent northern warrior-saints.

Her own order arrived as he disappeared behind the paper once more, and she forgot him once she started to eat. She'd just mopped up the last drop of egg yolk with the last piece of fried bread when Stacey pushed open the café door. Today she was immaculately dressed in a white lambswool tunic over a flowing grey skirt.

Though she saw Christa and waved, she made straight for the group of workmen, disappearing into the embrace of the largest and most muscular, who had a stubborn, amiable face and curling red hair. After a very long interval she emerged like Goldilocks from the arms of Father Bear, and dragged him over to Christa's table.

'Hi, this is Glenn,' said Stacey proudly, presenting him as if he were the biggest, shiniest prize in a TV game show. 'Glenn, meet Christa.'

Christa's hand was enveloped in a huge grasp. His skin was as dry and cracked as his dusty leather boots, the fuzz of russet hair on his arms spattered with emulsion paint.

'Cheers,' he said. 'Stace told me you did her a good turn yesterday. I warned her not to get mixed up with that crowd of nutters. Can I get you another cuppa? And the usual for you, Stace?'

Christa declined another drink for herself, and watched as he clumped across to the counter and planted his elbows on it to place his order. His shoulders were sensational. Stacey, gazing dreamily at his back view, clearly thought so too. She was even more perfectly made up this morning, and gave off wafts of tea-rose scent.

'So,' said Christa in a firm voice, determined to get something out of her before Glenn returned to destroy her concentration entirely, 'why don't you tell me a bit about those toughs you were with last night? Were they from Howl?'

Stacey looked round nervously, and began to rearrange the packets in the sugar bowl.

'It was my first time with them, I swear,' she said. 'Up to now I've been with another group, the Peaceable Kingdom. It's a really kosher sort of set-up, but I got pissed off by the way it never gets much in the way of results. The trouble is, it's full of middle-class types who can't do anything without a committee. People take notice of Howl.'

'I bet they do. How did you contact them in the first place? I thought the organisation was hush-hush.'

Stacey's gaze wandered anywhere but in the direction of Christa's eyes. 'I can't tell you, honest. And anyway I'm not going with them again. I promised Glenn. As it is, he says I'm lucky they aren't going to do me over for chickening out on them last night.'

'So you've been in touch with them since then?'

Stacey was almost squirming with embarrassment. She began to nibble a pearl-lacquered thumb-nail.

'I haven't, but Glenn made me give him the contact number when he saw the state I was in. He told them if they laid a finger on me, he'd put his mates on to them. Everyone knows there's no messing with Glenn.'

Christa wasn't sure she approved of Stacey letting Glenn solve her problems, but she looked at him with renewed interest as he reappeared with a laden tray. He gave Stacey a reassuring smile. Christa was surprised by a pang of envy at their closeness.

'And lucky for you they do, Stace,' he said, picking up the end of the conversation. 'You're the last person to get mixed up with Howl. It's nothing but trouble.'

He unloaded the tray, setting down herbal tea for Stacey, and a couple of cream doughnuts for himself. Something seemed to be bothering him as he sank his teeth into the first one. He gazed at Christa across the top of it with a puzzled frown. Suddenly he banged a massive fist on the table, making the teaspoons dance.

'A right jughead I am! I knew I'd seen you somewhere before. Stace and me don't watch the box much – we usually get videos – but we saw something about you on my mum's telly a few Sundays ago. Your beret put me off the track at first.'

He plonked down the doughnut and turned eagerly to Stacey.

'Don't you remember, Stace? She's the news reporter there was all that carry-on about, the one whose cameraman was shot. No wonder she's interested in Howl. Next thing you know, you'll be on the telly too.'

His voice had increased at least twenty decibels in his indignation. People were turning to look at them. Christa hastily put up her hand to shield her face. In despair she wondered how she could ever hope to restore her professional credibility when she was still getting this sort of reaction.

Stacey, who'd been staring at Christa open-mouthed, realised the extent of her distress. She shook Glenn's arm like a Yorkshire terrier worrying a Highland bull.

'Keep your voice down, Glenn, do. Can't you see you're embarrassing her?' She turned to Christa, her face glowing with interest. 'Of course, you're Christa Keith! The first name seemed familiar somehow, but I didn't recognise you in that beret. I said to Glenn at the time, that Gareth Hyde came across as a slimy sort of guy. Talk about kicking someone when she's down!'

'There's never smoke without fire,' said Glenn stubbornly, still regarding Christa with a frown. 'And the cameraman died. It's not a small thing, Stace.'

Christa clenched her hands together on the table. Her stomach had made its usual sick dive at the prospect of having to justify herself yet again.

'Look,' she said, 'it's up to you to believe what you want, but don't you think you should listen to my side of it before you make up your mind?'

'Yes, give her a chance, Glenn,' said Stacey. 'She gave me one, after all.'

He hesitated. 'I suppose that's fair. Go ahead, then. I'm listening.'

He started to munch at the doughnut again, eyes fixed on Christa as if she might make a sudden dash from the café.

She took a deep breath. 'Gareth set me up with false information. I believed it because he was – he was my friend.'

She hadn't quite been able to control the tremor in her voice, and to make everything worse Stacey was now looking at her in exactly the same soft, pitying way that she'd looked at the rescued rabbit.

'But you left your cameraman when he'd been hit. That's what Gareth Hyde said in the *Gorgon* just the other day. You dumped your mate. You don't do that, not ever,' Glenn pursued.

'Leave it, Glenn, just leave it! That's enough now,' said Stacey breathlessly. 'I believe her, even if you don't.'

'I didn't dump Matt,' said Christa, forgetting to keep her voice down in her eagerness to convince Glenn. 'I didn't dare move him. He was bleeding too much. All I could do was make for the nearest UN field hospital for help. I had no alternative. It was the worst journey of my life.'

She was back in the armoured Land Rover, driving with the terrified interpreter across nightmare terrain, her arms almost wrenched from their sockets as she tried to control the steering wheel, praying wildly to a God she didn't believe in that the Serbs wouldn't find Matt before she returned. And all the time she could see the blood relentlessly soaking through the field dressing over the hole in his chest.

She closed her eyes, lifted her fists from the table and thumped them against her forehead, as if she could beat the memory from her brain. The teaspoons danced in the saucers again as she let her hands fall back on the table, and felt one of them taken in Glenn's rough grasp.

'It's OK. You don't have to say any more,' he said awkwardly. 'I believe you now. Right on, I do.'

'Of course you believe her, Glenn,' said Stacey indignantly. 'She didn't dump me, did she? So she wouldn't have dumped her friend.'

Christa was too shaken to do more than give Stacey a weak smile of thanks. As it was, she'd already attracted attention to herself. The man with the newspaper had sent a repressive stare in her direction during her argument with Glenn. She was relieved when Stacey tactfully tried to change the subject.

'What are you doing in Oxford, then, if you usually work abroad?'

With an effort Christa pulled herself together. 'My TV company wants me to keep a low profile for a while, so I'm going to teach for a year at Gabriel Hall.'

Stacey made a scornful face. 'Sooner you than me,' she said. 'I'm a hair-stylist at a beauty salon in Jericho. We get loads of students from Gabriel – our salon's quite popular with them. You wouldn't believe the way some of the richer ones go on! They expect you to re-do a style if they don't like it, then have the nerve to tell you they're working too hard to have time to visit their usual London salon. Yet you see them bunking straight into the wine bar over the road afterwards. Too much dosh, that's their problem. They ought to try living on a grant like my kid brother. He has to work most evenings to pay his way.'

'I do a lot of North Oxford jobs,' said Glenn, attacking the second doughnut. 'They're a funny crowd, college people.'

'Glenn's got his own business,' said Stacey proudly.

'They usually pay on time,' he went on, 'but you have to take a load of rubbish from them, especially the wives. They'd rather die than call me Glenn, or sit down to have their coffee with me. I hear them on the phone telling their mates they've found a wonderful little man to help them, as though I'm some bloody magic gnome, and the next minute they're bullshitting about how tiring it is to have a workman in the house.'

'Go on,' said Stacey, nudging him in the ribs. 'You know most of them fancy you rotten. That's why you've got so much work.'

'Do you live in Jericho?' Christa asked, as Glenn gave a sheepish grin.

'Wish we did,' said Stacey. 'We're on the Gabriel's Grounds Estate, but we're saving every penny to get out. It's a bad place to live.'

'I thought it was supposed to be a model estate,' said Christa. 'Wasn't it set up by Sir Charles Tucker?'

'It was OK in the beginning. But when old Tucker died, it was handed over to a tenants' management cooperative who let things go for a while. The cooperative's improved a lot recently, but there are too many youngsters there with nothing to do but make trouble.'

'Yeah, getting stoned and vandalising everything in sight during the day, and joy-riding all night,' said Glenn. 'And when the Peaceable Kingdom put on a demo outside the Tucker Institute, the lads stirred things up there too.'

'Some of it isn't their fault,' said Stacey. 'Everything was all right while there was work at Gabriel's Mill close to the estate, but it closed down ten years ago. Gabriel Hall owns the Mill site, and promised then to lease it for small businesses and a sports and community centre to benefit the estate, but nothing's ever been done.'

'If Gabriel had kept its promise those lads wouldn't be going down the tubes,' said Glenn. 'To my mind something like that's a lot more important than all this animal rights stuff. Anyway, I don't understand why you're so interested in Howl, if you're not working for the telly now.'

'I heard something about it before I left London,' said Christa, 'and my brother-in-law works at the Institute. He said they've been getting a lot of trouble from Howl recently. I thought I might look into it in my spare time.'

'Fine,' said Glenn, 'but not using Stacey.'

'Of course not, if she really doesn't want me to. I can find other ways to investigate. But couldn't you just tell me what their meetings are like, what sort of people they are, Stacey? At least it'd give me something to work on.'

She hesitated. 'They don't have big meetings. They're organised in small groups – cells, they call them – and they meet in all sorts of odd places, never in people's homes. They use false names, too. Only the phone number's real.'

'And the intimidation, and the violence,' said Christa.

'It's no good trying to get at Stacey that way, either,' said Glenn, though this time with a smile tempering the warning in his voice. 'She's not giving you the phone number.'

'I wasn't trying to get at Stacey,' said Christa. 'I just don't like this sort of organisation.'

'We get enough aggro on the estate without looking for it.' Glenn yawned and stretched, revealing another magnificent expanse of muscles in the gap between his trousers and his T-shirt. 'I'd better go. I'm retiling a bathroom for an old lady in Southmoor Road. I've just got the original lot off, and it always looks bad at this stage. She'll be freaking out by now. I'll give you a lift to the salon on the way, Stace, when I've bought some rolls for my break.'

He ambled over to the counter, where the fair-haired man, now muffled up again, was paying his bill.

Stacey had been casting a severely professional look over Christa's appearance while she talked to Glenn.

'Why don't you come along to the salon some time?' she said. 'You wouldn't know yourself after a new hairstyle. We could do you a whole aromatherapy makeover if you liked – on the house of course.'

'Thanks,' said Christa, thinking she must look even more frayed than she'd thought. 'Maybe I will, when I'm settled here.'

She didn't have the slightest intention of wasting time in a beauty salon, but she made herself listen as Stacey enthusiastically ran through a long list of treatments. She'd just got to mud wrapping when a strange roar began to reverberate through the market.

It sounded so like a plane on a strafing run that Christa had to prevent herself from diving under the table. Stacey's recital stopped in mid-flow. A moment later a motorbike with two riders clad in leathers and half-face helmets stormed past the café windows, forcing passing shoppers to flatten themselves against the glass. The pile of pumpkins, caught by a wing mirror, cascaded like a shower of golden lottery balls to the ground.

As the bike screeched to a halt in front of the butcher's shop, the pillion rider leaped off, pulling a kitchen fire-extinguisher from inside his jacket. He blasted the turkeys and venison with foam, and hurled the empty canister like a grenade through the open shop door, narrowly missing a petrified shopper cowering by the counter. Then he produced an aerosol of spray paint with which he scrawled 'Meat is Murder' on the pavement in front of the shop.

The driver had kept the engine running throughout the attack, which was so sudden and so violent that everyone, even the butcher and his two assistants, was momentarily stunned. But when the pillion rider finally produced a baseball bat from beneath his jacket and began to smash the window, showering the trays of meat inside with splintered glass, the youngest and heftiest of the assistants rushed out of the shop and confronted him, brandishing a cleaver he'd snatched up from the block.

The onlookers in the corridor suddenly came to terrified life, and scrambled for cover wherever they could. The butcher made a wild lunge with his cleaver, which, if it had connected, would have severed the activist's arm. But the man stepped smartly to one side, swung the baseball bat at the blade in the butcher's fist, and sent it spinning to the ground.

The butcher slipped in a pool of extinguisher foam, and crashed into the venison carcase, half stunning himself. The activist hauled him up by the collar, and while he was still dazed began to goad him backwards with violent stabs of the baseball bat in his chest, propelling him towards the jagged edges of window glass. Christa watched in horror, rooted to the spot like everyone else in the café, not daring to risk a rescue attempt.

Everyone else except the fair-haired man. He'd just finished paying his bill at the counter as the attack began, and now unexpectedly shot through the café door towards the activist with a Samurai-like shout. The activist suddenly realised there was a new threat from the rear, released the butcher, and turned to face his new assailant, brandishing the baseball bat like a club.

The other man, silently confronting him in the glass-strewn arena before the wrecked shop, seemed to Christa completely defenceless. As she waited for the inevitable result, she thought grimly that it was a perfect example of useless self-sacrifice.

But she was totally mistaken. To her astonishment the fair-haired man spun round in a swift, near-balletic turn, and transferred all his weight into a single karate kick which struck at the activist's throat. The move was almost invisible in its rapidity, and yet it conveyed an impression of immensely controlled power.

The Howl activist folded into himself like a flattened box, clutching at his neck and gasping for breath. Desperately the driver of the motorbike revved his machine towards his accomplice, and hauled him on to the pillion. With the man clinging to his waist, the driver accelerated towards the exit, this time dislodging a pile of tomatoes which spattered his leather-clad legs with scarlet pulp.

By now the butcher had collected his wits. Though he hadn't a hope of catching up, he valiantly rushed after the bike, hotly followed by his colleague.

'My God, Howl doesn't stop at much, does it?' said Christa shakily, as the stunned silence in the café turned into a roar of comment. 'There could have been dozens of injuries in a place like this.'

'I told you, they're nutters,' said Glenn, his brow crinkled like a corrugated roof. 'And that other bloke was a right chancer too. It was lucky he didn't kill the Howl guy.' He shoved back his chair. 'Come on, Stace. I've got to get you out of here, before the police arrive.'

'You don't think Howl saw me, do you?' she asked in a wobbly voice.

'Of course not. They weren't interested in anything except smashing up the butcher's shop,' said Christa.

'Just come on, will you, Stace?' urged Glenn. 'The bike's bound to have been nicked. The police'll want to question everyone in sight.'

Stacey called breathless instructions on how to get to her salon as Glenn hustled her away. Christa decided to make an equally speedy departure. But when she went to pay her bill, the fair-haired man, who'd escaped the congratulations of the shoppers with difficulty, came back to the counter to retrieve his bag of books. Christa was unable to subdue her newsgathering instincts altogether, or a reluctant admiration. She knew Glenn was wrong. Luck had no part in what she'd just seen. The man knew exactly what he was doing. If he hadn't, he could have killed the activist.

'That was pretty impressive,' she said. 'Do you live in Oxford?'

He turned his dark glasses on her as he picked up the books.

'None of your business,' he said crisply, and was out of the door before she could say another word.

She'd received far worse brush-offs in her time, and was more interested than annoyed by his response. She watched him wheel his bike rapidly towards the exit, turning his head away to avoid any further attention from the crowd. He clearly had something to hide, but what exactly she'd lost her chance of finding out.

Ten minutes later Christa was walking down Holywell Street in the direction of Gabriel Hall, still thinking about the events in the covered market. Though she was accustomed to violence, it had disconcerted her in such an unexpected setting.

Gabriel Hall lay close to Holywell Church. It was almost as old and dignified as Magdalen, its nearest college neighbour. As Christa stood on the opposite side of the road, waiting for a knot of cyclists to pass, she gazed up at the façade of Cotswold stone.

Along the coping beneath the roof a succession of fantastic faces – green men, coiffed queens, grinning apes – stared back. Over the stone entrance archway was carved the Angel Gabriel, wings outstretched, face stern and serene, handing a lily to the kneeling and deeply subservient Virgin Mary.

The huge doors of iron-studded oak were firmly closed, but a wicket gate had been cut in one of them. Though the road was clear now Christa still hesitated on the edge of the pavement, reluctant to enter such an alien place.

A flash of red distracted her eye, and she saw that someone had lobbed a Coke can on to a ledge above Gabriel's head. The thought of Philip's disapproving expression cheered her up. Squashing her beret more firmly over her hair, she dodged across the road, and stepped over the threshold of the wicket gate into a vaulted inner porch.

A bowler-hatted porter who looked like an overgrown Stan Laurel sidled towards her between the trunks stacked on the cobblestoned floor. Beyond him, through an inner archway, she could see a large quadrangle.

'I'll have to ask you to leave, Miss. The public aren't admitted until the afternoon.'

The porter's expression combined pleasure in his official status with lugubrious delight in thwarting her.

'I'm a new member of college, a visiting fellow,' she said.

She started to walk on, but he dodged round a trunk and again barred her way.

'Oh, indeed, Miss, a visiting fellow are you? Then perhaps you'd care to show me your letter of appointment?'

Irritably she remembered she didn't have it with her.

'Presumably you keep a list of new members,' she snapped. 'You'll find my name there. Christa Keith. Apollo Fellow in Media Studies.'

The title sounded much too pretentious to have anything to do with her and he obviously thought so as well.

'Before taking up residence, all new fellows must present their letter of appointment at the porters' lodge,' he intoned.

'I'm not taking up residence today,' she snapped. 'I'm simply visiting an old friend, Dr Gurney, and then I have an appointment with the Master. If that bothers you, you can ring the Master and check.'

He cast a backward look through a glass screen into the porters' office.

'Phone's busy, Miss. Why don't you just run along and fetch your letter? Then we'll all be satisfied.'

'Perhaps you could just run along to another phone, and speak to the Master.'

'The Master's at a meeting.' His voice oozed satisfaction.

She should have realised that college security would be tight following Howl's recent activities, but that still didn't warrant the condescension in his tone. She longed to slap him down, but she suspected he had the power to make life difficult for her in many small ways if she did.

'Christa, what a delight to see you!'

Another, this time familiar, voice saved her from having to make an ignominious retreat. Walking towards her with a broad smile on his face was Piers.

'I thought I'd better come and meet you. Security's tight here.'

'Do you know this person, Dr Gurney?' demanded the porter, as though he'd encountered Prince Charles consorting with a bag lady.

'Of course I do. She's one of our visiting media fellows. I hope you haven't been giving her a hard time, Fred. Don't forget our new image.'

He hooked his arm through Christa's, and whisked her away towards the quad.

'What new image?' she demanded. 'I don't see anything new round here.'

'You may not see much at the moment, but the winds of change are actually starting to tremble a few leaves at Gabriel Hall,' said Piers with a grin.

Christa glanced up at him affectionately. They'd met in the sixth form at school, after his father had retired from a job managing a small chain of outer London newsagents. Then Piers had had a strong Essex accent, which, when he'd won a scholarship to Cambridge, underwent a rapid transformation into Brideshead English, with occasional renegade vowel slides and glottal stops at times of excitement.

'And about time too, judging by my welcome,' she said.

'Still the iconoclast, I see. Good. It's exactly what's needed here,' he said, turning an amused gaze on her through his spectacles.

As arts programme producers began to find they could rely on Piers for consistently witty and acerbic comment on the current literary scene, his appearance had changed as well, and he'd started sporting the subtly coloured jackets, Gap denims and round-framed Armani glasses of the media don.

They were walking round the edge of the quad, which was turfed with grass like living plush, devoid of even the smallest daisy. In the centre was a fountain rising from a circle of bronze dolphins. Tudor architecture at its most florid surrounded them, and over its rooftops presided a tower containing the famous Boanerges clock. The dial was enamelled blue with gilded hands, and beneath it two male figures brandishing hammers stood poised to strike a massive brass bell.

'King's Quad,' said Piers. 'It may seem quiet now, but it'll be like the Tokyo subway when the students return.'

On the opposite side of the quad, over an archway, was a statue of Henry VIII, feet planted firmly apart, hands hooked into his belt, looking more like a dyspeptic porker than ever.

'Our beloved benefactor,' said Piers. 'The statue was done just before Ann Boleyn's death.'

Christa averted her eyes from the baleful stone gaze.

'What are the students like?' she asked.

'Only a quarter from comprehensives. Recruitment's definitely dodgy here. The younger fellows have tried to change things, but it's hard going. Gabriel students are mostly well-heeled, fairly bright on the whole, but doing their utmost to conceal it. If any of the better-off ones feel guilty about their lifestyle, they'd rather die than say so. Their aim is to appear as laidback as possible while combining a hectic social life with a starred first.'

'And is that their only aim?'

Piers glanced at her. 'I'm sure they've got a few others tucked away. Just as you have too behind that die-hard façade. Or have your recent interesting experiences changed you?'

His voice was teasing, but his eyes were concerned. Christa had told him briefly about Gareth when she'd phoned him.

'I'm just the same,' she said stiffly.

'Really?'

'So presumably they're not particularly rewarding to teach?' she pursued, refusing to let him change the subject.

'Lectures aren't compulsory, and a lot of the students don't bother to turn up to them anyway, especially if they're before midday. Tutorials are one to one, and not so bad, as long as they've done their groundwork. Otherwise you end up giving a resumé of the source books they should already have read.'

'Sounds inspirational.'

'It can be, but only occasionally. The best thing about Gabriel is that teaching loads are light. There's plenty of time for research.'

'And for you to appear on the box. I thought Gabriel was supposed to be the best minds teaching the best minds?'

'In theory, yes. Unfortunately some of the best minds here don't know how to teach, and they haven't been encouraged to mend their ways as in the rest of the University.'

They entered a pool of shadow in a hallway beneath the statue, and began to climb a staircase with worn stone treads.

Piers pushed open a heavy oak outer door, then an inner one, and ushered her into his room. The partly open window overlooked the quad. Occupying almost the whole of one wall was a large mahogany desk. Not only was the surface stacked with books and papers, but they were piled all around it. They formed a rickety rampart, in which the various layers slipped and flowed like shale from a disintegrating rock face, gently coming to rest in outlying spoil heaps on the faded but still splendid carpet.

The only warmth came from a gas fire hiding in the back of a magnificent carved wood fireplace surround. In the hearth was a shiny brass toasting fork, and a tray containing a tea caddy, two mugs, and a gleaming silver teapot with the college crest on its side.

'How come all this polishing?' Christa teased him. 'Since when were you into housework?'

'Have you forgotten? Scouts do all that sort of thing at Oxford. And in the Gabriel Senior Common Room the fellows have butlers to look after them as well.'

Christa thought back to her own college days, where life was lived at a furious pace which left no time for domestic chores. She and her friends existed in a state of creative chaos where an Indian spread could quickly cover a tumbled bed, and unwashed dishes were stashed away in a cupboard if a parent appeared.

'I don't recall that you were particularly up in the housewifely arts yourself,' said Piers, 'so don't start knocking the system here. You'll be glad of your scout when you've your own set of rooms.'

'I'm not going to be in residence. Apparently there's a shortage of accommodation. But they say they'll find me a study, and it suits me to live out, anyway.'

Piers began to make a comment, then for some reason abruptly stopped and instead began to wander round the room, looking vaguely on shelves and behind chairs.

Christa went to inspect the line of invitations on the mantelpiece.

'You're moving in exalted circles these days,' she remarked, picking up a summons to a cabinet minister's drinks party.

'One has to circulate. You know what it's like,' replied Piers in a bored voice which didn't entirely conceal his gratification. 'Now where did I put that bloody kettle?'

He pushed open an inner door, and Christa had a glimpse of a smaller room with a narrow brass bedstead and a chipped white washbasin in which reposed the kettle and a carton of milk. Piers pounced on them, filled the kettle, and came back into the sitting room, firmly closing the inner door.

'The bedrooms here aren't conducive to much except monastic contemplation,' he said. 'But I rather like mine. Gives me a vicarious boarding-school experience.'

'What do the women dons think of them?'

'There aren't any except Leda Lennox, our new Vice-Master.' Piers gave a sardonic smile. 'An incredibly bizarre title for a woman, isn't it? But of course, it can't be changed. Leda's been here for several years and she's head of the Tucker Institute as well. Her fellowship goes with the Institute post. We have a few female graduate students, but none of them lives in.'

'Is that by design?'

'Not sure,' Piers replied unconvincingly. 'But now Leda's in office we'll have more. You'll like her, Christa. The younger dons ganged up to get her elected as Vice-Master. Luckily several of the old die-hards were laid up with 'flu last winter, and couldn't attend the meetings of Governing Body. For once we got our own way. It's no good trying to bludgeon things through at Gabriel. Everything's done sideways.'

He filled the kettle and took it into the outer room.

'Right,' he said, when he'd plugged it in. 'Now all I have to do is find the biscuits.'

While he continued his search Christa inspected the book-shelves which occupied most of the wall space. Contemporary French philosphers jostled the latest publications from the X Press, counterbalanced by an impressive display of classi-cal authors and long runs of literary periodicals. In a space between the books, a weathered stone hand of Buddha, broken off at the wrist as though casually garnered on a research trip to some ancient temple, lay next to a plaster statuette of Elvis.

Above a grainy photo of the stained concrete ramparts of her former school, the Lewis Carroll Comprehensive, hung a limited edition of an impenetrable Dada lithograph. Piers saw her looking at the photo.

'Hopeless to try to conceal one's educational roots at a place like Gabriel, of course. But I'm hoping that this photo may subtly suggest some overlooked strengths in a neo-brutalist education. Nothing worries my colleagues more than to think they may be missing the avant-garde bus.'

His tone was flippant, but Christa guessed that the room, which appeared at first to be such a haphazard jumble, was specifically designed to impress the onlooker with its occupier's eclectic tastes.

Piers would relish such a deception, but it wasn't for her. She hadn't thought particularly about the content of her classes up to now, but in this room, which, as a casual visitor, she would have enjoyed for its witty artificiality, she began to dread even more the year ahead, and to feel that she hadn't a hope of interesting her students.

She sat down in one of the leather library chairs which flanked the hearth while he made the tea, and forced herself to concentrate on the pictures on the shelves. There were no single portraits, but several holiday groups of friends, the women all the same type: short-haired, wide-shouldered, slim-hipped, the kind who looked wonderful in any clothes, but were far less pretty than the men who accompanied them.

When they were back in Oxford during their first college vacations Piers had suggested they sleep together, but had seemed more relieved than offended by her refusal. She was glad now they hadn't done so. It would probably have spoiled their friendship. Sex always did, she thought ruefully.

Watching his long fingers carefully measure pinches of tea into the pot, she considered the way their lives had diverged since leaving school. In many ways they'd both taken up abnormal existences, yet both of them had a profound need for their own particular worlds. Piers, who delighted in observing life from the sidelines, was perfectly at home here, but she was beginning to feel more and more that she'd die of stagnation in her new setting.

'What do you think of the Master? You'd better give me a rundown before I meet him,' she said, thinking that if this had been part of an assignment she'd have checked on him in *Who's Who* ages ago. As it was, she already disliked him intensely for his vetoing of her father's appointment.

Piers made a face. 'The smoothest operator in town. He lives on his reputation from the Waylandsbury dig.'

'So he's an archaeologist? I didn't realise he was in charge of that particular excavation.'

Christa had last seen the Waylandsbury Hoard, a stunning Romano-British find, on a school visit to the Ashmolean Museum in her teens.

'He hasn't published anything since he became Master ten years ago,' said Piers. 'He's absolutely besotted with the college, but it's a sort of smother love. He refuses to let anything change.'

'I've already gathered that.'

'The older dons don't object,' Piers went on. 'It preserves their privileges, but they can't see that the college is slowly rotting from the top. There's been a lot of unrest among the worse-off students lately. Accommodation fees have been upped enormously – I suspect to discourage the wrong kind of student from applying. Because there's a shortage of rooms, the second years have to live out, though Gabriel could easily afford to buy up more accommodation. Rents are very high in town, and those whose parents can't buy them a small house to share with their friends do badly again. Luckily this is the Master's last year before retirement as Head of House. Ten years is the maximum in the post.'

Christa frowned. Piers, watching her as he poured boiling water on to the tea, remembered how at school she'd been distinguished by an infectious interest in social issues. She'd had a chameleon-like ability to absorb all aspects of a question, and had argued her case in debates with a fierce integrity.

Though she'd learned to temper her enthusiasms in the interests of her television career, the integrity still remained, and would have been welcomed in any other Oxford college. Yet the woman by his fireplace wasn't at the moment much like the woman on the screen: thin, unusually shabby, as though she didn't care what she wore, and half the time looking as if she were miles away.

The change was all no doubt connected with Gareth Hyde, he thought. He was reputed to have a Don Giovanni-like effect on women, but even so it was hard to imagine Christa being attracted to him.

His gaze roved over her as he poured the milk into the mugs. He'd once tried to get her into bed with him in the days when he was anxiously trying to sort out his sexual identity. There had always been a Matisse-like impression of vividness about her. Now she seemed colourless and subdued, especially with her hair concealed beneath that beret.

He handed her a mug of tea, wondered whether to tell her it was his favourite Red Oolong, then decided against it. Christa, though she liked good food and drink, had a depressing lack of interest in its finer details, and none at all in preparing it herself.

She put the mug down by her side to cool, and shook her head at the biscuits. She looked uncomfortable in the chair. It was too big, too unyielding, made like all the college furniture to suit a man's frame. She clasped her hands behind her head.

'Christ, Piers, how am I going to stick it?' she burst out suddenly. 'It feels like a prison to me. Beautiful, but a prison all the same. It's not my sort of place, and never can be. And how the hell am I going to teach? I've nothing in common with the students here.'

He looked at her in alarm. Never in all the years he'd known her had Christa appealed to him directly for advice. Always she'd been the strong, optimistic one, he the pessimist who surveyed a hurdle three or four times while she was already over it and halfway to the finish.

'They must have thought you could cope, or they wouldn't have offered you the post.'

She laughed derisively. 'I've no illusions about that. I'm only here because Jimmy Judd endowed the fellowship, and my boss asked him to twist the Master's arm.'

'I very much doubt that's it entirely. The Master never makes concessions unless there's something in it for him or the college. The media fellowships are top dressing, something to make the college seem more up to date than it really is. There's been so much adverse comment recently about Gabriel's being a last bastion of gender privilege that I imagine even he realises it would be wise to appoint a few more female fellows. He's lucky to get you in the circumstances, and I'm sure he knows it.'

'That makes it even worse. As though I'm here to cover up a lie.'

'You won't be covering up anything if you make your course successful.'

'Easier said than done. You know very well that my work isn't academic. It's more rapid reaction to changing events – knowing how not to be manipulated, and how to file a balanced report. It'd be all right if I could show the students the nuts and bolts of reporting.'

'The Master wouldn't be too keen on hands-on stuff. That's taught at Oxford Brookes – what used to be the Poly. You'll just have to stick to your historical overview of the role of the female war-reporter. If no one comes to the seminars, at least you'll have more time for your book.'

Piers' brisk advice was slightly too practical for Christa's liking. As she stared gloomily out of the open window, wishing she could fly away like the pigeons on the roof, a thin brown cat crossed her line of vision and stepped delicately over the ledge. It inspected her with narrowed eyes before jumping on to the arm of Piers' chair, where it settled itself like a guardian deity in an Egyptian tomb.

'Meet Mehitabel,' said Piers, stroking the cat expertly under the chin, and producing an ecstasy of purrs.

'I didn't know you were an animal lover,' said Christa in amusement. Piers' face had taken on the same expression of concentrated enjoyment as the cat's.

'Nor did I. She simply walked in off the roof one night last year, and decided she was going to live with me. I find I've become rather fond of her. Unlike a human being she can be put outside when she becomes a trial.'

He'd stopped stroking Mehitabel for a moment to reply to Christa, and the cat waved her tail in furious protest.

'Looks to me as if she'd put you outside if you didn't toe the line,' said Christa. Mehitabel reminded her of something else she'd meant to ask Piers. 'Have you come across any of Howl's activities yet?'

He grimaced. 'Those fascists. Not here, but before the new security precautions were in place they made life a nightmare for the people at the Institute. Leda had to bear the brunt of it all. She coped brilliantly. You'll like her, Christa. She voted for the media fellowships, and took a lot of the middle-of-the-road dons with her. They might have tried to block them otherwise. Unfortunately the mood of Governing Body's very finely balanced. You'll soon find out – you should attend its meetings while you're here.'

Christa's emotional barometer was plummeting again. She'd heard plenty from Emma about the endless wrangles of academic committees.

'At least you're not alone in your sufferings,' said Piers. 'You can commiserate with our other visiting media fellow, though he's been holed up in his rooms in Bohemia Quad since the beginning of last month, and has only dined once in hall. He's almost as notorious as you.'

'Who's that?' said Christa listlessly, wondering how long it would take her to find a flat in which she could hole up as well.

'Mallory Farrar.'

Christa tore herself away from deciding which estate agent to go to first, and forced herself to concentrate on what Piers had just said.

'The traveller guy? The writer who's supposed to be tougher than Thesiger and more charismatic than Bruce Chatwin? The one who's been in the bestseller lists almost as often as Jeffrey Archer? I thought he was the media's darling.'

'Weren't you, as well?'

Christa winced at the sting in his remark.

'You're out of touch, Christa dear,' he went on. 'About two months ago he returned from some incredibly macho journey across Africa on foot. It took over a year, but even in this day and age there was a brave little woman waiting to marry our hero when he came home. Real Richard and Isabel Burton stuff – except that when Mallory Farrar got back he decided he didn't want to marry his beloved after all.'

'He sounds like a first-class rat to me.'

'Haven't people been saying that about you?' Piers' voice

was even drier. 'You haven't heard his side of the story, after all.'

'Christ, what do you expect my reaction to be, after everything Gareth's done? Who was the woman? Anyone well-known?'

'Yes, and definitely not a Victorian miss. She was Caitlin Trevor.'

This time Christa could instantly fit a face to the name. Caitlin Trevor was a young British film producer who'd recently made a hugely successful movie based on the story of Katherine Mansfield's life.

'I can't imagine she'd need to wait for any man. I interviewed her once. She seemed very much her own person to me. Why did he ditch her?'

'He'd just arrived home when she was offered funds to make a movie in Hollywood. It would have meant living there, but he refused to go.'

'Why did he duck out?'

'If you'd read his books you'd know that Hollywood is the last place he'd want to be. In the end they split, but it wasn't an ordinary split. She went berserk, and gave details of their affair to the press, making out that he used her.'

'That sounds even less like the Caitlin Trevor I met,' said Christa. 'What was his side of the story?'

'There wasn't one. Instead he preserved a gentlemanly silence which drove the press wild. They've been after his version ever since, but as you know it's not easy to get into Gabriel. Though King's Quad is open to the public in the afternoons, the porters go like Rottweilers for strangers who don't keep within bounds. Anyway, he still seems to have a large section of the public on his side.'

'Presumably because he's male,' said Christa, remembering Randall's observations.

She got up impatiently and went to the window. The room was beginning to make her feel claustrophobic. As she looked down into the quad, she saw a man enter it from the porters' lodge with his jacket slung over his shoulder. He cut straight across the grass with a long, loping stride, but the porters made no protest at all.

Piers joined her. 'Talk of the devil. There's Farrar himself, right on cue. If I walked on the grass like that, the porters would lynch me.'

As he passed under Piers' window he looked up briefly, and though his gaze was still shuttered by sunglasses, Christa instantly recognised the man who'd flung himself into the market brawl.

4

'Gloomy-looking guy, isn't he?' said Piers. 'But there's a lot of advance interest in his seminars. I strongly suspect my own attendances will fall as a result.'

'I strongly suspect my attendances will be nil,' said Christa, who had decided not to mention the incident in the market. They'd already talked quite enough about Mallory Farrar, in her opinion.

'The more feminist women students may feel a certain sisterhood with you. The men will turn up to see whether you look as good off screen as on. But whether they'll attend more than once is up to you.'

'You're so confidence-boosting,' she said acidly.

'As long as your historical groundwork's sound, you can jazz it up with postmodernist theory.'

'Postmodernist theory? Spare me. I told you, I'm a working journalist, not a philosopher.'

'Nevertheless, you're pretty good at getting to the heart of things, I seem to remember – ruthless, some might say.'

Piers was teasing her again. He'd gone back to his chair and was stretched out with his elbows on its arms and his long fingers tented together at the tips.

'Anyway,' he went on, 'I should have thought the Masters of Suspicion would be right up a journalist's street.'

Christa thought irritably that even he couldn't resist the ploy so many academics loved, throwing allusions into the conversation, and then with not-so-gentle pleasure watching the listener flounder.

'I suppose you mean Marx, Freud, and Nietzsche,' she shot

back, 'and the way they questioned all the old liberal ideas. But the postmods don't seem to believe in anything.'

'Everything's problematic these days,' said Piers, eyes shining as he got on to what was clearly a favourite hobby horse. 'That's what's so stimulating. The denial of certainty, the *jouissance* of deconstruction, the discovery of new *aporia*.'

'I've no idea what *jouissance* or *aporia* mean, and I guess most of the population doesn't either. If I tried to use those words on air, I'd be fired.'

'I'm afraid you're going to have to get to grips with post-modernism while you're here. In most arts subjects it's academic flavour of the month, if not of the whole late-capitalist age.'

To Christa's dismay Piers now looked utterly serious. Her spirits had descended so far that they were almost in the Gabriel wine cellars.

She looked at her watch, and saw with relief that there were only fifteen minutes until her appointment with the Master. Luckily it wasn't difficult to steer the conversation on to Piers' television programme, with which he seemed to have a love-hate relationship, and when Boanerges rang out the hour she was able to leave without offending him.

Piers walked with her as far as the Master's rooms, which led off a staircase beneath the Boanerges clock. She was wearing, very reluctantly, a gown borrowed from him, which he'd told her was obligatory at official meetings. The heavy wool dragged down her shoulders, shrouding her like a crow's wings.

'Good luck. And you really do look splendid in that gown,' he said, kissing her with an amused expression which belied his words before hurrying away.

Christa knocked cautiously on the door, above which '*Magister Collegii*' was painted in Roman script.

The face of the man who opened it reminded her of a painted egg. It was long and pale, with hair artfully arranged in grey strands across a balding pate. His eyes were egg-like as well, with slightly protruding whites, and irises the dull grey of over-boiled yolks. As if to make up for the tonsorial challenge, he had a small clipped moustache.

'Miss Keith? I'm delighted to meet you. Come in, do. I am

Vernon Slade,' he said, holding out his hand. When she took it the skin was cold and smooth. He too wore a gown, over a Donegal tweed suit.

He ushered her into his room, which was much larger than Piers'. What looked remarkably like a Turner of the University's spires from Christ Church meadow hung over a fireplace carved from Carrara marble. A log fire crackled sedately in a lyre-fronted basket grate, and under the window stood a wine jar of blue Chinese porcelain crammed with huge white chrysanthemums.

Christa took the fireside chair he offered her. She'd been in many grand rooms in her time, but this had an understated elegance which made it particularly impressive.

'We're delighted to have you with us,' he said. 'It was most fortuitous that you were in a position to offer us a year of your valuable time.'

Christa wondered if he could possibly be serious, but his face was completely grave as he went over to a tantalus on a rosewood side table. He appeared to glide rather than walk, an impression emphasised by the flowing folds of his gown.

'I hope you'll join me in a glass of our excellent Jubilee sherry?' he said, removing the stopper from a cut-glass decanter. His hands seemed disproportionately small, like those of an obstetrician Christa had once interviewed. It wasn't hard to imagine them delicately burrowing after some centuries-old artefact.

While he was busy with the drinks she made a further inspection of the room. One wall was covered with discreetly framed photos of what could only be the Waylandsbury dig, with the Master standing in not so discreet poses on the top of spoil heaps, triumphantly displaying his finds to an audience of venerating students. In the background dispirited-looking labourers trundled laden wheelbarrows away from the scene.

Propped upright on the chimneypiece was a magnificent silver dish bearing the figure of a sea god in bas-relief. It appeared to be Roman, and Christa wondered if it was real. Anything was possible in these surroundings. The Master saw her looking at it.

'Only a copy, of course. It's the Neptune dish, the crowning piece from the Waylandsbury Hoard. The original's in the Ashmolean, but I had this made to remind me of an extraordinarily happy period of my life. It isn't often granted to a young archaeologist to make such a discovery.'

He put a glass by her side, centring it fastidiously on a crested coaster.

'Now,' he said, sitting opposite her and raising his glass, 'your very good health, Miss Keith. I'm sure your stay with us will be a happy one. You'll find that Gabriel's atmosphere is unique.'

Christa took a sip of the sherry. It was as dry and flavourful as a ripe hazelnut. The Master had a dried look as well, as if he'd spent too long in the summer suns of his digs.

'I'm already realising that,' she said.

'We've managed to find you a study overlooking Bohemia Quad. Lord Judd intimated that a secluded part of college would be preferable. I fully understand the difficulties of your present situation. We're only too glad to be able to offer you a haven. In the past Gabriel has given a home to many refugees.'

Christa thought it highly unlikely that Gabriel was housing any real refugees these days. She also wondered what the wily Jimmy Judd had told him. He'd probably played heavily on the Master's sympathies, representing her as a helpless victim both of Gareth and the tabloid press. Though it was true, perversely she hated the thought of being presented in that way. It made her feel even more diminished.

'It's kind of you,' she said, 'but all this special treatment does rather make me feel as if I have a scarlet letter on my breast.'

'Like Hester Prynne?' He looked surprised. 'I see you know your American literature.'

'Is there any reason why I shouldn't?'

'You misunderstand me, Miss Keith.' His face was guileless. 'But while we're on the subject I would like to assure you that you need do no more than fulfil the most basic requirements of your fellowship. In view of the stressful nature of your recent experiences, I'm sure you won't want to give more than the minimum number of seminars. The Dean agrees with me that one a fortnight will be quite acceptable.'

'Again, it's kind of you, but I intend to give my full quota of seminars. One a week, I believe my contract said,' she replied, suspecting he didn't want to let her loose among the students for a moment longer than necessary.

'Splendid, splendid, if you're certain you feel up to it. We have a very high calibre of student here, but I'm sure they'll make allowances for your not being an academic.'

'And I shall try to make allowances for their unfamiliarity with the world beyond Oxford. I presume you expect things to be difficult for Mallory Farrar too,' she couldn't help adding, infuriated by his attitude.

'Ah, I see you know about our other visiting fellow. With respect, Miss Keith, his case is slightly different. He has an impressive corpus of literary achievement. The University recently gave him an honorary D. Litt., and his first book was based partly on research he did for a Cambridge doctorate. Your strengths obviously aren't the same, but the young today do have a strong interest in television and you may find that a help.'

Two doctorates sounded like academic overkill to Christa, and the Master was more evasive than a Balkan diplomat, she thought. The urge to argue with him was enormous, and she was almost relieved when he switched smoothly to a potted account of Gabriel's history which was clearly one of his standard entertainments.

Eventually, after a fulsome description of a recent royal visit, he put down his empty sherry glass.

'So you'll understand now, Miss Keith, why I regard Gabriel Hall as a sacred trust. All the fellows, whether visiting or tenured, have a duty to maintain our traditions. Naturally I like to obtain the assurance of new members of college that they will honour them too.'

Christa, who'd been trying not to yawn, snapped back into full alertness as she realised she was encountering a direct challenge at last.

She couldn't possibly give him the assurance he wanted, any more than her father had been able to at his interview. Thinking again of what it must have cost her gentle, scrupulous father to give the reply which had lost him the librarianship made her counter with a challenge of her own.

'I was already aware of your dislike of change,' she said. 'My father, Conrad Keith, recently made an application for the librarianship at Gabriel. I understand he didn't succeed because he wanted to make the library more accessible.'

The Master didn't turn a hair. 'I wasn't aware you were related,' he said. 'But in that case I'm sure your fellowship will go a long way towards making up for your father's disappointment.'

Christa's dislike of the Master was now so intense that she could hardly contain her anger. But open hostility could harm her father, who might try for another librarianship, and whose cause wouldn't be helped by the Master dripping poison into the ears of other college heads.

Above them Boanerges struck the half hour. The Master looked at his watch.

'I'm afraid I must leave you shortly. I have a luncheon appointment at Balliol. But there's just time to show you your room, for which the domestic bursar has very kindly given me the keys. Then I must be on my way. I'm so glad we could have this little chat before you settled in.'

They passed through the archway which housed Piers' staircase and into a smaller, less austere quad. A magnificent rambler rose with a late flush of blooms, petals shading from milk white to the colour of clotted cream, looped round perfectly proportioned seventeenth-century windows, a living contrast with the swags of stone flowers carved beneath them. Incongruously some of the windows displayed posters demanding better accommodation for second years and women post-graduates, but the Master appeared not to see them.

Christa caught a glimpse of a deer park through another entrance on the far side. Over it was a second statue, this time of a woman in Jacobean court dress, wearing an expression which even in stone had a quality of mingled wistfulness and charm.

'Bohemia Quad,' said the Master. 'Quite delightful, don't you think? Though personally I prefer the architecture of the Enlightenment. It's named after the daughter of James I, who became Queen of Bohemia, and endowed this part of Gabriel. The English called her the Winter Queen. The flowers here are always white in her memory.'

As they crossed the quad, a young woman emerged from a

passageway on the far side, clutching a bulging black plastic sack. When she saw them she hesitated, and then struck out in their direction.

The Master immediately increased his pace, forging ahead like a presidential limousine, and completely disregarding the oncomer. She was equally determined to be recognised, and halted directly in their path.

'I need to speak to you about my vacation grant, Professor Slade,' she said. 'It's still not come through.'

She had a strong northern accent, and was small and thin, with dark eyes peering intensely through a straggly fringe. Beneath it was an expanse of forehead almost as impressive as Phil's.

The Master's gaze lingered on a pair of tights trailing from the bag, and then with even greater distaste on the gold stud in her nostril.

'Ah, Miss Caldwell, isn't it?' he said vaguely.

'Yes, Donna Caldwell. I've sent you three letters in the past month about my grant, but I never get a reply.'

'I do seem to recall something of the sort,' said the Master blandly. 'Haven't you approached the Bursar?'

'Of course I have. He says you've still not signed the form for the release of funds.'

'It is a discretionary grant, from the Isaiah Granby bequest for the relief of indigent scholars in the vacations, as I recall,' said the Master. 'Refresh my mind as to why you need it.'

Donna looked acutely embarrassed, but ploughed on. 'Me mother died last year, and me stepfather sold up our home. I'd nowhere to go in the vacation, so I stayed on here. I've got a job waitressing, but it's not enough for accommodation and keep.'

'I expect the committee is still investigating your case. You'll just have to be patient a little longer, my dear. You seem to have managed up to now.'

Donna reddened. 'Only by scrounging off me mates.'

The Master's gaze passed again over the plastic bag.

'I very much hope that hasn't entailed taking advantage of some post-graduate's hospitality. Students can be sent down for the unauthorised sharing of college accommodation.'

'So where else do you expect me to stay?' Donna burst out angrily. 'On the streets? It's not fair that the college lets rooms to conference visitors when someone like me has nowhere to go.'

'You are lucky that I have chosen not to hear that remark,' said the Master icily. 'If you have any problems I suggest you address them to the student counselling service. Good morning, Miss Caldwell.'

As he swept past her, Christa could see that she was on the verge of tears. Seething with indignation, Christa could only give her a sympathetic smile and hurry on.

'Some of these scholarship students have a most unfortunate social manner,' the Master said. 'A person of that sort will never feel at home at Gabriel.'

'It's hard to feel at home anywhere if you're worrying about money,' said Christa.

'We simply don't have the resources to look after the students' welfare in the vacation,' said the Master.

'But isn't the Isaiah Granby fund specifically for that purpose?'

'The fund is already considerably depleted. We had to send a couple of our rugby blues to the States during the last vacation on a recruitment tour.'

'And were they indigent?' demanded Christa, incensed at his lack of concern.

'It was in the interests of the college. I think you must allow me, Miss Keith, to know more about these matters than you.'

They had now crossed the quad and begun to wind up a spiral stair. Christa saw that her name had already been painted in black lettering over the topmost door.

The Master unlocked the outer door, pushed open the inner one with a flourish and stood aside to let her go in. It was hardly more than a box room, with sloping ceilings, and a mullioned dormer window whose ancient glass oddly distorted the clouds outside.

The desk was most definitely not an antique and had a splay leg, the two sagging armchairs wouldn't have fetched ten pounds in a street market, and the rusty electric fire looked hardly capable of warming a cupboard.

'A trifle small, perhaps, but delightfully secluded, and I'm sure you'll work wonders with a few feminine touches.'

The Master's voice was as persuasive as a used car salesman's, but Christa's patience had run out. It was a room which the humblest of college employees would have scorned, and he knew it.

'I'm afraid I can't share your opinion,' she said coldly, 'especially as I've already seen the standard of accommodation normally enjoyed by fellows of Gabriel.'

The Master sighed. 'Really, Miss Keith, I do assure you that as a latecomer you're lucky to have a room at all.'

'All the same, I must insist on better furniture – some carpeting, an efficient heater, and a desk lamp at the very least,' said Christa firmly, thinking that the college store was probably stuffed with Chippendale chairs and Persian rugs. 'I expect to entertain visitors from Apollo in college during the coming year,' she added, praying her words wouldn't come true. 'I'm sure you wouldn't want anyone connected with the media to get the wrong impression of Gabriel.'

'Well, well, I'll see what I can do,' said the Master, hastily shunting her from the room and locking up before she could ask for anything else. He gave her the bunch of keys. 'One of these unlocks a side entrance through the fellows' garden. It means you can come and go as you please.'

So at least she could avoid the porters' lodge, Christa thought. As she began to negotiate the downward spiral, and paused on the next landing, her eye was automatically drawn to the view through open doors into two interconnecting rooms. She just had time to get an impression of space and light, and a dazzling view over the deer park to the river beyond, when Mallory Farrar appeared, obviously about to leave. He closed the inner door firmly behind him.

'How opportune,' said the Master. 'One of your neighbours, and our other visiting fellow.'

His voice lingered a fraction of a second too long on Farrar's academic title as he introduced him. Christa's irritation had already returned now she'd registered that his accommodation was sumptuous compared to hers.

'Hallo,' she said, with a curt nod.

'Dr Farrar will tell you that it's possible to live very comfortably here,' said the Master.

Mallory Farrar's expression was the sort which Christa would normally have treated with extreme caution, but she'd decided she had taken enough.

'No doubt, Professor Slade, given adequate space, one could.' She absolutely refused to address him as Master to his face. 'I don't understand why there should be such a difference between Dr Farrar's accommodation and mine. As far as I know the terms of Apollo's media fellowships are the same.'

'That is so,' said the Master imperturbably. 'But Dr Farrar took up residence a month ago, when there was no suitable candidate for your post. Normally the allocation of rooms is done in the most democratic way.'

'Good,' said Christa. 'Then in that case I'm sure, Dr Farrar, that you won't mind exchanging accommodation with me halfway through the academic year.'

'I should mind very much,' he said, turning a gaze on her which made her feel as if her foot had gone through ice.

'I'm afraid there's nothing we can do, Miss Keith,' the Master put in hastily. 'College regulations state that fellows shall not ordinarily be required to give up their accommodation once the year has begun. You were simply unfortunate to be appointed so late. "*Nescia mens hominum fatis sortisque futurae*", as Virgil has it.'

'Exactly,' said Farrar, unhurriedly locking his outer door.

Being ganged up on by a couple of men in a dead language was too much for Christa.

'And didn't Webster say, "Fortune's a right whore"?' she countered sweetly.

Farrar turned a long look on her, but to her satisfaction said nothing more. He merely nodded to them both again, and slipped away down the stairs, negotiating the steep spiral unexpectedly fast for someone so tall.

'Shall we follow?' said the Master, who hadn't turned a hair. 'You must excuse Dr Farrar's abruptness. He too has had a difficult time lately, and he was naturally a little disturbed when he learned that he was to share a staircase with someone connected with television news. He's an immense asset to

Gabriel,' the Master added, as they began to walk back across the quad, letting the unspoken words 'unlike you' hang heavily in the air.

He looked at his watch again.

'I'm so sorry that I haven't the time to show you around any more. But I've asked the Dean to introduce you to the Senior Common Room tomorrow. You could pick up your timetable from his office beforehand, if that's convenient. And please remember, Miss Keith, I'm always available, whatever the problem.'

The moment the Master left her, Christa dived into the nearest pub and fortified herself with a sandwich lunch and a stiff drink.

She knew Emma wanted her to see her parents that afternoon, but the need to find a place of her own was now urgent. She rang her mother on the pub phone, promising to visit the next day, and then set off to do the rounds of estate agents.

Her first impulse had been to find a flat in East Oxford, which was less self-consciously academic than the northern part of the city and possessed an ethnic mix she'd always liked. But to her dismay East Oxford had gone upmarket since her schooldays, and none of the local estate agents could offer her anything reasonable to rent for less than £600 a month.

'There were students in here, so the decor's a little tired,' said the last agent, after he'd shown her round a flat off the Iffley Road with reeking drains, damp-stained wallpaper and a kitchen thick with grease. He plainly thought her mad not to take it right away. 'But it's a snip at the price, and it's got loads of potential. The landlord would have no objections if you wanted to redecorate. You could strip the floorboards and give the walls a dragged finish in no time at all.'

'How can students possibly pay rents like this?' asked Christa.

He shrugged. 'Most of the parents are well-heeled. If the kids get into trouble we just slap on a court order and sue for arrears. So are you going to take it or not?'

'I'll let you know,' she said with deliberate indecision.

The estate agent dropped her in the city centre hardly bothering to conceal his annoyance. It was four o'clock, and the streets were suffocatingly full of tourists and carbon-monoxide. Christa trudged along feeling tireder than she would have openly admitted. She decided she'd like to sit by the river for a while, remembered it would be just as crowded, and headed west towards Jericho and the canal instead.

Though she didn't know the area well, as she turned into its narrow side streets she began to feel less gloomy. Emma always dismissed Jericho as a raffish kind of place, the resort of those who weren't interested in making the grade. But the terrace houses, though small, had a certain light-hearted exuberance. With their cheerful façades of parti-coloured brick, and their miniature Gothic windows and doorway arches, they looked as if Mr Pooter had redesigned the lofty residences of North Oxford while in the throes of speed.

Everything here was on a cosy human scale. Jaunty snap-dragons, untidy drifts of Michaelmas daisies and straggling nasturtiums blazed in small front gardens. Bicycles cluttered doorsteps. Cats sunned themselves on tiled front paths, mothers trundled babies along the pavement.

The declining sun was warm on Christa's face. She wandered on past pubs, a small enclave of council houses and a delicatessen, skirted the florid bulk of St Barnabas' church which looked like a Hollywood version of an Italian basilica, and finally arrived by the canal.

On the other side, just visible through a screen of trees, lay the railway line and some overgrown allotments. The willows overhanging the canal bank had shed a cargo of umber leaves into the slowly flowing stream. A couple of narrow boats moored alongside were clearly inhabited despite their peeling paint and general air of decrepitude. In one of them a girl sat on deck, smoking and reading. Christa could see a young man in the galley, and a smell of frying onions issued from the companionway.

Christa sat on a bench by the towpath. A family of mallards came paddling by, the ducklings almost full grown. She could hear a distant train shunting along the railway line, and the occasional sound of activity in the ironworks further down the canal, but otherwise an undemanding peace prevailed.

Eventually the church clock struck the half-hour – silvery,

frivolous chimes compared to the solemn knell of Boanerges. Reluctantly Christa got up, thinking she'd better try the Jericho estate agents before they closed. But as she walked along a street which ran parallel to the canal, an end-of-terrace house caught her eye. She paused briefly on the opposite side of the road for a longer look.

The walls were a patchwork of silver, russet and yellow, with impertinent pointed window arches of herringbone brick like a clown's eyebrows. The front garden extended along the side of the house, where a Virginia creeper ran riot up the wall, smothering part of the roof and threatening the chimney pots.

A row of sunflowers paraded inside the front garden fence like golden grenadiers. The front lawn had been roughly mown, and was bordered by springy cushions of catmint and camomile.

By the front door sat a very old woman on a wooden kitchen chair. Her feet were thrust into camel-hair slippers with bobbles on the toes, and her dress was covered with a jaunty royal blue cardigan.

She too wore her hair in a plait, but it was coiled into a complicated bun on top of her head. Her back was so bent that Christa was surprised she could stay upright, yet the rheumaticky hands were wielding a set of steel knitting needles so fast that the movement appeared as a silvery blur. By her side, in a cage hanging from a stand, a grey parrot basked in the sun. She only needed a long skirt and a bonnet to become part of a Victorian cottage watercolour.

Christa began to walk on. If she stared any longer the old lady might become alarmed, in spite of her air of doughty independence. But as Christa turned for one last look, she saw that the street was no longer empty. A youth in sunglasses was weaving along the pavement in the direction of the cottage, playing football with an empty beer can. He wore black jeans and a black T shirt, the uniform of the aspiring hard man everywhere.

Briefly Christa was reminded of Howl, then just as quickly dismissed the idea. This youth was obviously half drunk and simply had nothing to do.

But as he came level with the old lady's front gate the parrot caught his eye. Suddenly he booted the can into the road, kicked open the gate, and shambled up the garden path towards her. Christa, watching in horror, was certain she was going to be mugged. But instead the youth grabbed the parrot's cage from its stand and lumbered back with it towards the street.

The bird let out a series of piercing screeches. They were joined by the shrieks of the old lady, who tottered down the path after him brandishing her knitting, the ball of wool unwinding in her wake.

Nonchalantly the youth stood on the pavement laughing at her, with the cage dangling from his hand.

'Keep your hair on, Grandma,' he shouted. 'No need to get your bloomers in a twist.'

Christa couldn't bear to see the mindless cruelty of Bosnia repeated here. She tore across the road. In her soft-soled canvas boots she was silent, and the youth didn't see her till she was on him.

She grabbed at the cage. He almost overbalanced, but swiftly regained his footing, and wrenched it back again. In the tussle the door flew open. The parrot hopped out on to the fence, and began to climb one of the sunflowers, still squawking furiously.

'Piss off, you stupid, fucking bitch!' the lad yelled at Christa, shoving her aside and trying to grab the sunflower as the parrot swayed around on it like a drunken trapeze artist.

The old lady, who'd got as far as a pear tree halfway down the garden, with surprising nimbleness began hurling windfalls at the thug.

'Leave my bird be, you young villain, you!' she screeched. 'I'll teach you not to thieve!'

'Cut it out, Grandma, or I'll teach you a lesson as well!' he shouted angrily, as one of the windfalls hit him on the arm.

His words seemed to have no effect on the old lady, who redoubled her barrage and seemed to be almost enjoying herself. He swore, and started to clamber over the fence.

Christa, still half-winded from his elbow in her ribs, hurled herself into the attack once more, locking her arm round his neck from the back and pressing against his windpipe. He was tall, and her feet swung off the ground, but somehow she managed to punch her other fist into the base of his spine

He swung round howling with pain, dislodging her so violently that she fell. As she began to pick herself up from the pavement, and saw him make again for the parrot, a bicycle scorched to a stop by her side.

Its rider, a girl in a tennis dress, leaped off and hurtled towards him with her racquet. She gave him a hefty forearm swipe across the shin which momentarily doubled him over. As he unbent, he saw her arm swing back again. He gave a howl of terror and ran for his life. By the time Christa got to her feet, he had disappeared ignominiously round the end of the street.

Unsteadily she readjusted her jacket, which he'd almost pulled off.

'You don't hang about, do you?' she said to the girl with a shaky smile. 'Thanks for helping. He was stronger than I thought.'

'Always make sure you're one step ahead of the opposition, that's what my dad says. Are you all right?'

The girl was tall, with skin the colour of mocha coffee, and glossy black hair braided back into a bunch of narrow plaits. She wore brilliant green Lycra shorts under her tennis dress.

'I'm afraid these have had it,' she said, picking up the sunglasses from the pavement.

Christa's legs felt decidedly rubbery, and she leaned against the fence. Her beret was slipping off. She removed it, shaking out her own plait. The girl's eyes widened. Christa guessed she'd been recognised.

'He was one of those kids from Gabriel's Grounds, I bet,' said the girl. 'They've nothing to do but look for trouble. Most of them are all bark and no bite. Are you sure you're OK?'

'I'm fine, but how about the old lady?'

'Looks all right to me. Better than you, in fact.'

Christa turned, and saw that she had hobbled over to the sunflower and persuaded the parrot on to her wrist. It waddled up her arm to her shoulder, where it sat nibbling her ear.

'Hooligans, the lot of them!' said the old lady. 'They ought to bring back conscription, and give them something to do.'

She seemed oblivious of the fact that she'd been in considerable danger as well. The girl raised her eyebrows at Christa in amusement.

'I think you'd better let us ring the police for you,' said Christa gently to the old lady, resigning herself to not escaping their attention as easily as last time.

'Police! What do I want them for? They'll get the welfare down on me like a ton of bricks, trying to push me into a home. But I know my rights. I'm not doolally yet, and that's the only way they'll get me out of here.'

She looked sharply at Christa. 'A nice cup of tea, that's what you need. You'd better come inside, and sit down for a bit. The darkie can come too – you've both been good girls to me.'

She stumped away up the path, the parrot swaying on her shoulder. Intensely embarrassed, Christa glanced at the girl.

'Sorry,' she said. 'Remarks like that make me want to apologise for the whole white race.'

'Forget it,' said the girl easily. 'You can't expect too much from someone who was probably brought up on golliwogs and Little Black Sambo. And at least she's straightforward, unlike some of the people I have to deal with in college.'

'You're a student?'

'A grad student. I'm doing a D.Phil. at Gabriel.' She gave a mischievous grin. 'A token female and a token black all in one. I was an offer they couldn't refuse.'

'What's your name?' asked Christa, warming to her still more. 'I've just taken up a year's fellowship there.'

'Rebekah. And I know you, of course. You're Christa Keith. I didn't like to say anything at first, but I recognised you as soon as you took your beret off. I heard you'd come to Gabriel.'

The old lady paused halfway up the path. 'Stop that chatting and hurry along, do. I can't leave the front door open for you. There's a nasty wind getting up.'

Rebekah looked at her watch.

'I'd love to stay, but I can't. I was supposed to see my supervisor ten minutes ago. Can you manage here all right on your own?'

'I should think so,' said Christa drily.

'Yeah, sorry, I guess you could cope with most things.'

Rebekah got back on her bike, pushing the racquet into a sports bag hooked over a handlebar. She balanced herself with one foot on the pavement. 'It's a huge bit of luck for me that you're here. My dissertation's about postmodernist attitudes to the Gulf War. I wonder if we could discuss it sometime when you're settled in college?'

'Yes, of course,' said Christa, astonished to find that she actually had a fan at Gabriel. 'But I'd better warn you now that I haven't got much of a grip on the postmods.'

'No one has! That's what so fascinating about them,' said Rebekah, pushing herself off from the kerb. 'See you in college, then.'

She shot away down the street, and scorched round the corner with a farewell ring on the bicycle bell. If only the rest of the students could be like Rebekah, Christa thought as she watched her go, she might even look forward to the coming year.

The old lady was beckoning impatiently from the front door.

'Bring the cage with you,' she called.

Christa collected it from the lawn, and stepped after her into a long hallway. It smelled of baking and coal tar soap. The old lady pushed open an inner door into a small parlour. Near a fireplace with porridge-coloured tiles stood a much larger cage. The parrot allowed itself to be inserted deftly inside. It hopped on to a swing and began to preen itself, fluffing out a feathery ruff round its neck.

A clock in a figured maple case ticked away quietly over the fireplace. Above the clock hung a watercolour of an orange and purple sunset glimmering through the trees of a bluebell wood. Goss ware and commemoration mugs marched along the mantelpiece, and between them was tucked an impressive array of birthday cards.

'Sit down,' the old lady commanded, taking the other cage from her, and dumping it in a corner. 'Enough to turn anyone's stomach, a nasty young lad like that.'

She appeared to be in perfect health herself. Christa, who'd been worrying in case she started to show signs of delayed shock, began to relax. The parrot too seemed unaffected, muttering quietly and incomprehensibly as it delved among its feathers.

'What's the parrot called?' Christa asked.

'Poppaea,' said the old lady. 'Silly name. She's Poppy to me. I used to work as a cleaner at Gabriel, and Dr Jephson, one of the dons, gave her to me when he left. Speaks a lot of foreign languages she does, when she's in a good mood, but I can't understand a word.'

The old woman threw a serge cover over the cage, and trotted off into the back of the house. Avoiding a sofa almost extinguished beneath antimacassars and cushions of ruched burgundy satin, Christa settled down to wait in one of the fireside chairs, which was adorned with a rainbow-coloured crocheted blanket.

A coal fire burned in the grate, its flames reflected in a highly polished brass scuttle. Beneath Christa's feet was a hooked hearthrug depicting a galleon breasting mountainous seas. Emma would have cringed at the decor, but Christa liked it. The little room radiated a warmth which didn't just come from the fire.

The old lady reappeared with a tray, and proceeded to ply a teapot encased in a cosy. There was a third cup and saucer on the tray. She saw Christa looking at it.

'My son Derek always pops in on his way home from work,' she said.

Christa took a cautious sip from the cup she'd just been handed. The tea was so strong that it furred the roof of her mouth, but the accompanying slice of madeira cake on a fragile china plate was homebaked, and liberally sprinkled with chopped angelica and caraway seeds.

'That's better,' said the old lady, after sitting down in the chair opposite Christa and taking several noisy sips of her own tea. 'What's your name, dear?'

Christa told her, and was relieved to see that it meant nothing. There was no television in the little parlour, though an old-fashioned radio with a fretwork pattern over the loudspeaker stood on a fireside table.

'Mine's Jessie, Jessie Hutt,' said the old woman. 'Mrs Hutt, *if* you please. There's no respect these days. "Jessie," say these chits from the welfare, "Jessie, you'd be so much better off in a nice rest home." Huh! What do they know about it? Rest homes is for the weakly ones, not for the likes of me. I don't need rest. There's enough rest when you're dead. How old do you think I am?'

'Sixty?' said Christa with a grin.

Mrs Hutt gave an answering cackle of laughter. 'Trying it on, you saucy young wench, aren't you? But you don't get round me so easy. I've told you, I'm not daft yet. I was eighty-nine last Sunday. What do you think of that?'

'Terrific,' said Christa, feeling like someone on "This is Your Life."

'What do you mean, terrific? Old age isn't terrific. It's misery all the way.' This was said with tremendous relish. 'But I can manage as long as people don't interfere.'

'Have you always lived in Jericho?'

'St Barnabas, we old ones call it, not Jericho. I came here on my wedding day. My pride and joy this house was then, and it still is.'

Mrs Hutt gestured to a photo of a thirties bride standing by a heavily brilliantined young man in a dashing double-breasted suit and spats.

'That's my ex-hubby. He was a carpet salesman, a real charmer. He had a lovely little Austin Seven, but it gave him too many chances to put himself about. When I was eight months gone he ran off with a woman over Bicester way.'

She took another draught of tea, and disconcertingly veered on to a completely different subject.

'Plaits is for schoolgirls and old women, not a lovely young thing like you. You ought to make more of yourself, get yourself a perm. You won't catch any boys like that.'

'But I don't want to catch a boy,' said Christa, highly amused.

'Had a bad time with one of them, have you?' Mrs Hutt gave a hoot of laughter. 'Think your heart's broken? I could tell you a few things. But I had to make the best of it or I'd have lost my house, and that *would* have broken my heart.'

'How did you manage?'

'I found myself a job as a college cleaner and did some charring on the side. My mum looked after the baby for me, bless her.'

Christa wondered what her own mother's reaction would be

in such circumstances. Instant retreat, probably, as it always was in the face of anything unforeseen.

'What do you do for a living, then, dear?' Mrs Hutt asked.

'I'm a television reporter.'

'Waste of time, the telly. I wouldn't give it house room. I've too much to do. The welfare'd love to see me let my chores go.'

Christa was increasingly torn between amusement and admiration. The running battle with the social services was clearly one of Jessie Hutt's main interests in life. Nevertheless it must have taken a lot of courage not to be intimidated by the events of the afternoon.

'Of course, the students was nearly all men before the war, and I was quite a looker in them days, so I had plenty of fun. But I never really let myself go, of course. I wasn't going to get in the family way again. That's the secret with men – enjoy yourself, but never let them have the upper hand.'

She was obviously longing to tell Christa the exploits of her youth, and it wasn't difficult, with a few tactful prompts, to unleash a pack of racy reminiscences. They'd finished their second cups of tea when Mrs Hutt finally came to an end, yawning hugely and settling back in her chair.

'I've talked too much, but you're a good girl to listen. I must have a little shut-eye before Derek arrives. You make yourself at home, dear. Go upstairs and tidy up if you want.'

She took a very large, very clean white handkerchief from her pocket, spread it over her face, and appeared to fall into a deep and instant sleep.

The room was absolutely silent, apart from the old lady's regular breathing and the minute sounds of the fire. Christa wondered whether to slip away, then decided she should really wait for Mrs Hutt's son and try to tell him discreetly about the afternoon's events. In any case she was longing to see the rest of the house

Upstairs the larger of the two bedrooms looked through dazzlingly white lace curtains on to the street. It was dominated by a double bed with semi-circular head and foot boards with a walnut sunburst veneer. There were a matching wardrobe and dressing table, on which were another wedding photo and a silver-backed dressing set whose chasing had been almost polished away. The bed was made up with a double set of pillows, and on its faded pink satin eiderdown lay a nightdress case embroidered with a crinoline lady among a riot of hollyhocks.

Something about the determined preservation of the decor of the old lady's short married life gave Christa an unexpected catch in her throat. She closed the door gently, and peered into the bathroom.

Over a large claw-footed bath the pilot light in an old-fashioned geyser flickered and hissed. The pedestal of the washbasin was patterned with blue ivy trails. In the lavatory next door more blue ivy rampaged round the bowl, and a brass-handled chain hung from the gently gurgling cistern.

Christa was about to look into the back bedroom when she heard the front door open, and a male voice. She waited tactfully on the landing for a minute before retreating downstairs. In the sitting room a man with greying hair, wearing a neat dark suit, was standing on a chair, struggling to replace a bulb in the ceiling light under a barrage of instructions from Mrs Hutt. He eventually got it into position, and clambered down.

'This is my boy Derek,' said Mrs Hutt. 'I've been telling him how you saved poor Poppy this afternoon.'

Derek took a handkerchief from his pocket, and wiped the dust off his fingers before solemnly shaking Christa's hand.

'Pleased to meet you. It was really good of you to give Mum a hand. Something like this was bound to happen, but she will live alone. Me and Jen – that's the wife – have been asking her to move in with us for years.'

'Who's she? The cat's mother?' demanded Mrs Hutt. 'And now you've messed up your hanky. Give it to me and I'll put it in the next wash.'

Meekly her son handed it over.

'You can show Christa the garden and cut some of my dahlias for her before she goes. I'm going to wash up the crocks. And bring me in another pail of coal while you're about it. Don't touch my chrysanths, whatever you do. I'm keeping them for your grandma's grave.'

Derek winked at Christa as he ushered her through a small

breakfast room, and into a kitchen with a mottled grey enamel gas cooker. Next door was a scullery with a copper and a Belfast sink, in which was propped a much-worn washboard. In a corner stood a heavy iron mangle.

Derek caught Christa's look of amazement.

'We've offered to get her a washing machine time and time again, but she just won't change. She worries me to death. I come in here every day to check she's all right, but she hates me to interfere.'

'Perhaps it'd be a good idea to tell the police what happened today, all the same.'

'She was bothered by lads scrumping pears last year, but she said if I got the police round, she wouldn't open the door to them. There's nothing anyone can do if she refuses to make a charge. I'll just have to try to persuade her not to sit in the front garden in future.' He sighed, his forehead crinkled with concern.

The back garden, which ran down to the canal, was a warm, damp tangle of flowers and creepers, with a small vegetable plot at the end, and a couple of gnarled plum trees. Derek produced an efficient-looking pocket knife, and began to cut an armful of dahlias.

'The lad you saw this afternoon probably came from Gabriel's Grounds,' he said. 'The unemployed kids walk across Port Meadow looking for a bit of excitement. Things might improve when they get a community centre, and the chance of work.'

'Do you live in Jericho?'

'Just over the way, in Walton Manor. I've worked with a local firm for the last thirty years. Steady, that's what Mum wanted me to be, and that's how I've turned out.' He laughed. 'I expect she's told you about my dad – she was always terrified I'd take after him. But she was good with me, let me have my head within reason when I was a boy.'

As he went into a ramshackle shed to find a piece of string for the flowers, Christa wondered what it would have been like to have a mother like Jessie Hutt, and not one who spent her life expecting the worst. She was touched and flattered when, back in the house, the old lady made her promise to come to tea again in a week's time.

'Mum's taken a real fancy to you,' said Derek, as he saw Christa off at the gate with an enormous bunch of dahlias.

Christa thought wrily that so far Jessie Hutt and Rebekah were the only people in Oxford who had. It was too late to see more estate agents now, but she decided to spend half an hour in the public library, researching Howl in the archives of the local papers. She didn't intend to arrive back at Ethelred Road a moment earlier than necessary. Emma's dinner party, now uncomfortably close, had less potential for meeting soul-mates than a dental check-up.

5

Emma pulled a face when she saw the dahlias. 'Not particularly subtle, are they?'

'I like them,' said Christa, bringing the flowers to the table in a jug she'd just filled with water at the kitchen sink. Their clashing colours and pungent autumnal scent gave a distinct lift to the sombre room.

'So do I,' said Pansy, who was drawing a complicated spiral in a school exercise book with one hand, and wiggling a loose tooth with the other. 'They're lovely and shaggy, like Chel's sitting-room carpet. Her mummy fluffs it up with a plastic rake. Why can't we get one like it, too?'

'Why don't you concentrate on finishing your homework, instead of wanting things you can't have?' said Emma.

Pansy gave a resigned shrug, unerringly copying one of Emma's favourite gestures, and began to colour the spiral a violent purple.

'What's that, Pansy?' Christa asked, trying to conceal her amusement. 'A double helix?'

Pansy waved the exercise book at Christa. 'Don't be silly. It's a sweet little ammonite going for a walk at the bottom of the prehistoric sea,' she said, ignoring her mother's frown. 'I should have thought anyone could see that. Our class went to the Science Museum today.'

Christa decided her niece had put her down quite enough.

'I should have thought someone as clever as you would know ammonites didn't walk. They swam.'

Pansy looked up, frowning. Christa returned an identical challenging look. Emma held her breath. Pansy was already in a bad mood at having to go to bed early because of the impending dinner party.

'How?' demanded Pansy. 'They haven't got fins, so they must be like snails.'

'A squid lived in that shell. It put out its tentacles when it wanted to swim. I'll show you how.'

Christa took up a black felt pen, and drew a Disneyesque squid with goggle eyes peering from the mouth of the shell.

Pansy gave an unwilling giggle, and began to gather up her work. Emma breathed a sigh of relief.

'That's right, run upstairs to Noelene now, darling. The guests'll be here in half an hour. I'm afraid I shan't have time to read to you tonight.'

'Chel's mummy lets her watch a video at bedtime when she's busy,' remarked Pansy as she mooched towards the door.

'I'm surprised Chel can read at all,' said Emma, who was frequently made to feel inadequate by the way Chel's mother, a single parent running her own small business, managed with such little fuss to bring up a remarkably well-adjusted child.

'She's got more stars for reading than me!' said Pansy, delivering a triumphant exit line.

Christa transferred the dahlias to the dresser. Emma flinched at the effect against her restrained grey paintwork. The vivid colours were as impossible to ignore as Christa herself. But her sister was looking almost happy for the first time since her arrival, and with a crucial dinner party coming up Emma knew it was in her own interests to keep her that way. She decided to play safe and not ask Christa to read Pansy a bedtime story.

'So, how many people will there be at this banquet tonight?' Christa asked.

Judging by the table laden with silver and cut glass she'd glimpsed through the dining-room door, it was destined to be a meal worthy of *Barchester Towers*.

'Seven altogether. The Master and Mrs Slade. Tom Carver – he's the new librarian at Gabriel – and his wife. Phil and me. And you, of course.'

Three cosy couples, thought Christa, and presumably Tom Carver was the man who'd taken the job her father wanted.

'What are you making?' she asked Emma, who'd been

arranging sliced nectarines in a dish, and was now beating a bowl of cinnamon-flavoured cream.

'Crème brûlée,' said Emma. 'A bit old-fashioned, but everyone likes it and it's easy to prepare.'

Christa remembered her last meal with Gareth in Sarajevo, a severely limited meal which had seemed ambrosial at the time, and pushed the thought from her mind. She put out her hand to filch a slice of nectarine, saw Emma's tense expression, and stopped.

'Why don't you let me do that?' said Christa. 'Or why don't you use an electric whisk?'

'It's easier to get the consistency just right by hand. And it's quicker in the long run if I do it. Remember that Hollandaise sauce for Pansy's christening lunch?'

Christa did remember. She'd tried to help Emma, who hadn't fully recovered from a difficult delivery. Instead she'd overbeaten the sauce, reducing it to a curdled mess. Philip curdled things still further with a sour observation on Christa's lack of helpfulness, she couldn't resist pointing out that he'd never changed a nappy in his life, and Emma had burst into floods of tears.

'I really don't see why you have to work yourself into the ground like this,' Christa said. 'Couldn't you have bought a pudding?'

'You don't understand,' said Emma, pushing back her hair from her forehead. 'It isn't just any dinner. If Phil gets promotion I shall have to do a lot more entertaining. It's important how I perform tonight. The Master's wife is a fabulous cook.'

'So in other words you're being vetted. But you're already overstretched. You know you are.'

'You've always gone for things you've wanted. Why shouldn't I?' said Emma, a dangerous tightness creeping into her voice.

'Because we're different,' said Christa. 'Because you're not really like that.'

'How do you know what I'm like now? We've hardly seen each other since I married. You've not the slightest idea what it's like to have to think of someone else.'

'I thought of Gareth, for Christ's sake.'

'I'm not talking about obsession. I'm talking about steady everyday loving, the sort that brings long-term rewards.'

'You make it sound like an emotional building society. Marriage certainly has changed you. What about all those plans you had to do a post-grad course in art history? You know you never meant to teach.'

'Phil and I agreed that it was the most sensible thing,' said Emma, carefully spreading the thickened cream over the fruit. 'We needed to save for the deposit on a house.'

'How strange that he still managed to do exactly what he wanted. You're brainwashing yourself into thinking you want it too.'

Christa's face had been getting progressively cloudier ever since the mention of Gareth's name. By now Emma was so exasperated she could have tipped the dish over her head. She almost ran into the hall when the phone started to ring.

Christa knew from the tense set of Emma's shoulders just how infuriated she was, and suddenly felt ashamed of her pleasure at such a petty triumph. Though Emma's assumption that Oxford's prizes were worth any sacrifice maddened her, she had just decided to make a placatory remark when her sister reappeared, her face radiant.

'That was the Master's wife. She asked if they could bring another guest. I was worried about the uneven numbers but now it's going to be absolutely perfect. We couldn't have got anyone better.'

'Who is it?' said Christa, trying not to laugh at Emma's reverent expression. 'John Major?'

'Don't be silly, Christa, a Tory prime minister wouldn't do at all, not after Oxford refused Mrs Thatcher an honorary degree.' Emma's face became abstracted. 'The food should just stretch, and I'll lay another place when I've done this.'

'But who is it?' Christa persisted.

'Mallory Farrar! I can't believe our luck!'

On her way back from the library Christa had been trying to hype herself into a more positive frame of mind about the dinner, but now her good resolutions instantly departed. Mallory Farrar three times in one day was too much.

'I've met him already, at Gabriel this morning. He didn't look much of a party-goer to me.'

'He isn't. That's why it's such a scoop to have him here

tonight. Apparently the Master persuaded him that he ought to mix a little more.'

'I don't see what's so wonderful about him.' It wasn't hard for Christa to make her voice dismissive. 'All that macho solo travelling just seems like a form of showing off. What good does it do anyone except himself?'

'How can you say that? His books are extraordinary,' said Emma, sprinkling a layer of Muscovado sugar over the cream. 'Surely even you must have read them?'

'I haven't had time to read anything much in the last few years.'

It wasn't strictly true, she thought, for she had plenty of time on the innumerable air flights that were part of her job. But then she was usually so tired or so scared that the only way to relax was with the lightest of fiction.

Emma looked shocked. 'You really ought to try his last book. He has some seminal ideas on the developing world,' she said reprovingly.

'There are too many male-engendered ideas around this place already,' said Christa. 'I think it'd be much better if I had a curry in town, and left you all to it,' she added hopefully.

'Christa!' Emma's voice was shrill with exasperation again. 'Just go upstairs and get ready, will you? And don't forget to put on a dress, please. It doesn't matter how old it is, as long as it's got a skirt.'

They'd reached the dessert stage of the dinner party, but an inhibiting decorum still prevailed. Emma was clearly nervous after a near disaster with the main course. The lamb had been tough in spite of her ministrations, provoking a shower of sarcastic remarks from Phil.

She was wearing a severely plain black velvet dress, relieved by a gold locket on a ribbon round her neck. The Victorian jewellery suited her, but the colour of the dress drained her skin.

The dining room wasn't quite warm enough in spite of the emotion being generated between Emma and Phil, and the table, covered with yards of white damask, was slightly too large for conversation across its width. In the background, from Phil's state-of-the-art sound system which he alone was allowed to operate, the atonal notes of a Schoenberg quartet scissored into the chilly air. The greenery-yallery Morris wallpaper was in such muted good taste that in the subdued lighting the room looked as if it had been decorated with watered pea soup.

Over the empty fireplace hung a plush-framed and deeply sentimental steel engraving by Marcus Stone which had once belonged to their grandparents. It was entitled 'The Broken Vow'. As teenagers Christa and Emma had made delicious, secret fun of it. But earlier in the evening she'd been astounded to hear Emma gravely discuss its delightful naivety with the Master's wife.

It was a measure of how much she and Emma had grown apart in the last few years. Depression began to join Christa's already severe boredom. Phil, assiduously taking round an excellent college Sauternes to accompany the dessert, had ignored her empty glass, presumably in an effort to keep her as quiet as possible.

Not that he needed to, she thought bitterly. The Master, on her left, had chatted mainly to Emma at the head of the table, and to Farrar who sat opposite him. Christa guessed he felt he'd bestowed enough of his valuable attention on her earlier in the day.

On her right Tom Carver, Gabriel's librarian, was maundering on, as he had been most of the evening, about the dangers of computerisation. He spoke as if technology were a subversive force.

Christa was thinking how much better her father would have been in the job when she noticed that Phil, who'd been unexpectedly summoned away to the phone by Noelene in the midst of replenishing glasses, had left the bottle on the table. She filled her empty glass, and began to drink steadily, hoping to get in another refill before he returned.

The Sauternes was excellent, and she relaxed enough to look across the table towards Farrar, whom so far she'd ignored as comprehensively as he had her. He was refusing a second helping of Emma's dessert. He didn't look as though he much enjoyed the pleasures of the flesh, Christa thought. Perhaps that was why the relationship with Caitlin Trevor had gone wrong.

Yet his clothes were surprisingly fashionable for an ascetic. He was wearing a suit which had almost certainly originated in Milan. The loose unstructured jacket would have made a shorter man look like a mafioso, but it suited his spare good looks, and he probably knew it.

The Master's wife certainly did. She was listening to him as though Lawrence of Arabia were by her side. She had given Christa exactly two minutes of her attention when they were introduced before dinner. During that time she'd managed to tell her that not only did she run the twelve-roomed Master's Lodge single-handed, but she was also a JP, a Relate counsellor, and an expert on Cyrillic script.

Christa thought dispiritedly that when she came home on leave before, people used to queue up to talk to her at parties. But now exactly the opposite seemed to be happening.

Philip reappeared, removed the Sauternes from her reach with a beady glare, and sat down again at the end of the table. Christa, who'd just poured herself another glass, smiled sweetly back at him.

'Problems at the Institute, Dr Holdgate?' the Master asked.

'I'm afraid so. There was another raid this evening. That was the police, asking me if I'd seen anything suspicious before I left. Some Howl activists got over the ring fence, and tried to force a window. Our security patrol caught up with them, but unfortunately they managed to escape.'

'How very distressing,' said the Master.

'It was indeed, particularly as a guard was injured in the scuffle.'

'These thugs need to be put down for several years. They would if they came before me,' said the Master's wife, passing her plate to Emma for more crème brûlée. 'We've never had this sort of trouble from the Peaceable Kingdom.'

At least Mrs Slade seemed to approve of the pudding, Emma thought, but the dinner party hadn't taken off as she'd wanted. Phil was anxious, which made him over-ingratiating, and Christa hadn't helped by sitting stony-faced as the guests' conversation skated round her but never quite drew her in.

She stole a glance at her sister, and saw that she was looking less tense at last. The old dress at the bottom of her rucsac had emerged as a bias-cut shift of mulberry coloured silk, which made Emma feel instantly dissatisfied with her own frock.

'The sooner the government sets up boot camps the better,' Mrs Slade went on. 'It's a great pity we don't have an empire any more where these people could find something useful to do, instead of disrupting the Institute's valuable work.'

'The issue's not quite so simple, is it?' said Christa. 'The Institute never lets the public in on its activities, and I gather its patrols had already used unnecessary force on some of the Peaceable Kingdom's protestors. Any kind of closed institution is bound to raise certain doubts in the public's mind.'

She lounged back in her chair, staring at Philip in a way that Emma knew would provoke him like nothing else.

'You've been in Oxford for forty-eight hours, Christa. That hardly makes you an expert,' he snapped.

'Oh, I don't know,' said Christa. 'I've seen a couple of Howl incidents since I arrived, and I was reading up on the situation in the city library this afternoon.'

Emma groaned inwardly. It would have been too much to hope that Christa would spend her leisure safely among the antiques of the Ashmolean Museum, but how had she managed to encounter Howl already?

'It scarcely constitutes an in-depth appraisal of the situation,' said Philip, giving Mrs Slade an unctuous smile as he refilled her glass.

Christa thought how Gareth would have laughed at Phil's pomposity. His cynical wit was one of the things which had helped to make life in Sarajevo bearable. She remembered how much he'd always liked the dress she was wearing, remembered him slowly taking it off, and again had to subdue an irrational pang of longing.

'I expect Miss Keith's presentation of information on television has of necessity to be superficial,' said the Master's wife in a gritty voice.

The party wasn't going to start flying now, however quiet she kept, so she might as well defend herself, thought Christa recklessly.

'We don't have much time, but I try to put over the core facts as truthfully as possible.'

'Some people say the media's turned war into an entertainment, almost a video game,' said Farrar unexpectedly.

His face was half in shadow as he leaned back in his chair, but Christa was sure she could see a combative gleam in his eyes.

'Possibly in the hands of the political analysts, but not in the hands of the reporters themselves – not the correspondents I know, anyway. Unfortunately we can't control how others use our copy once it's been filed.'

Even Gareth, with all his cynicism, wouldn't have subverted the accurate reporting of events, Christa thought, and then suddenly wondered if perhaps he'd stooped to that as well.

'So at second hand the news becomes still further divorced from reality. A simulacrum, an artificial reproduction of what's gone before,' Farrar went on.

'I doubt if Miss Keith is fully conversant with the jargon of contemporary philosophical thought,' interposed the Master.

There had been an amused edge to Farrar's voice which instantly spurred Christa on.

'I suppose you're implying that the representation of reality becomes more meaningful than reality itself, *Dr* Farrar.' Christa loaded her voice with sarcasm as she accented his title. 'You're trying to say that television news can't ever adequately report events.'

'What you think of as truth has first been filtered through your mind, then through your editor's, then through the minds of the viewers themselves. One could ask if the end product has any validity at all?'

'Doesn't exactly the same argument apply to your books? I haven't read them, but I gather they explore the problems of the developing world. However hard you try, you can never totally enter the feelings of a peasant woman who has to watch her children starve.'

Philip moved restlessly in his chair. 'Perhaps not an entirely appropriate topic for a First World dinner party,' he said with a quelling glance at Christa. 'Let's have some port, and a change of subject.'

'I'll ask Noelene to start the coffee,' said Emma in a bright voice.

'It's an interesting subject, nevertheless,' said Farrar lightly.

'All right, I take your point, *Ms* Keith.' He too accented the title, in a way which made Christa feel irrevocably consigned to the looniest feminist left. 'But I've as much right to comment as you, and at least my comments aren't shaped to suit the media's demands.'

'So are you saying your work isn't a construct?' demanded Christa.

'Of course not. I'm merely trying to point out that the sort of cultural comment I make in my books isn't subject to an exterior selective process.'

Christa wasn't sure which infuriated her most – his teasing, the general assumption that it wasn't possible for her to enter the rarified realms of the academic mind, or Philip's bland dismissal of poverty as an inappropriate subject for discussion.

'A news reporter doesn't have that luxury,' she rapped back. 'And in any case, I wouldn't work with an editor I didn't trust. Without the press the facts either wouldn't be reported at all, or else the public would get them via some propaganda machine. Try telling a victim of ethnic cleansing that what she's suffered has no validity. But if I report what's happened as accurately as I can, at least I enable some rational judgements to be made.'

'I really don't think we should get on to a subject like that,' said Emma desperately.

'I agree,' said the Master's wife.

She got up as though rising from the magisterial bench, and fixed Christa with a look which made no secret of her verdict. 'I think this is most definitely an opportune time to adjourn and leave the gentlemen to their port.'

Christa stared in utter disbelief as the Master's wife, with Mrs Carver following her like a pet lamb, progressed from the room. She hadn't even bothered to ask her hostess's permission, yet Emma meekly got up too, made a frantic face at Christa, and gestured with her head towards the door.

Christa's first impulse was to stay as a matter of principle. If the men tried to ignore her, she'd make sure they didn't do so for long. But Emma looked exhausted as well as distraught. Christa remembered she'd been up half the night with a teething Jamie, through whose wails Philip had slumbered as peacefully as an old lady hooked on Mogadon.

Reluctantly Christa got to her feet, and let Emma shepherd her into the hall.

'I do not believe this,' she hissed as Emma hurriedly closed the dining-room door behind them. 'We're nearly in the twenty-first century, and women are still leaving men to their port? How could you let that old battleaxe get away with it, Em?'

'Shhh,' said Emma, nervously glancing towards the drawing-room door which was slightly ajar. 'The Master thinks it's a fine old custom which should be maintained. I know it's awful but I promised Phil I wouldn't object, just for tonight. Please, Christa, go and chat to the women while I bring the coffee. They'll think it so odd if you don't.'

Christa braced herself, and went into the drawing room, where a sullen coal fire burned in the grate. The Master's wife and Mrs Carver had taken the only comfortable chairs, and were engaged in a discussion on soft furnishings. They didn't even look up at her entry.

Christa decided that self-sacrifice only went so far. She had no intention of sitting in a corner waiting for them to acknowledge her, and in any case she was desperate for a cigarette. So far she hadn't dared to smoke in Emma's house, but she wouldn't be able to get through the rest of the evening without one.

Upstairs she found a squashed pack of Camels in her rucsac, and took them on to the dimly lit landing, where she could keep an eye on the dining-room door. She threw up the sash window as a precaution before sitting on the chest beneath it to light her cigarette.

The smoke drifted into the cold night air. A new moon, the harbinger of luck, was rising serenely above the housetops. The last time she'd seen it was just before Matt died, and nothing good had happened since then. She took another drag on the cigarette, desperately trying not to let her unhappiness push her into a morass of self-pity.

'Mummy doesn't allow smoking in the house,' Pansy's voice piped from across the landing.

Christa peered through the half-light. Her niece was squeezed into a space between a chest of drawers and the banisters at the head of the stairs.

'Tough,' said Christa. 'This is an emergency.'

'My teacher smokes. She says she's stressed out.'

'She's not the only one. Why aren't you asleep?'

Pansy padded across the landing, and plonked herself down by Christa's side. She wore a dressing gown and Mickey Mouse slippers. Under her arm was a dog-eared catalogue from a discount store, and a doll with an insipid porcelain face and balding scalp which had belonged to Emma as a child.

'There's too much noise,' she said. 'Why were you looking so sad? Have you got a tummy-ache?'

'I was thinking of a friend of mine who died.'

'Was he your best friend?'

'More or less.'

'Chel and Mummy are my best friends. Mummy promised she'd bring me some pudding if I was still awake after dinner, but she hasn't. I suppose it's because she's got too many things to remember since Jamie was born.'

Pansy began to wiggle her loose tooth while surreptitiously sucking her thumb at the same time. The attempt at grown-up rationalisation mingled with a forlorn note in her voice made Christa remember how hard she'd found it to cope with her mother's preference for quiet, compliant Emma when she was a child.

'I'll get you some pudding,' she said.

The kitchen was empty, apart from Noelene, who was languidly washing up with frequent rests to peruse the latest edition of *Hello*. Christa heaped a plate with the last of the crème brûlée, found a spoon, and returned to the landing.

'Yummy scrummy,' said Pansy, falling on the food like a famished puppy.

'What's the catalogue for?' asked Christa, retrieving her cigarette from its resting place in a cache-pot on the window sill.

'So I can look at the Princess Perfect dolls. Mummy won't let me have one. All I've got is boring Belinda.' She waved the doll in front of Christa by its thinning locks.

'And what's so good about Princess Perfect?'

'She's brilliant. I can't think why Mummy doesn't like her. Look, I'll show you.'

She leafed through the catalogue, breathing heavily as she found the right page. Christa tried not to laugh. Princess Perfect had waist-length blonde hair, Bambi eyes, the bosom of an operatic diva, and hips which were an obstetric emergency in waiting. Her wardrobe appeared to be made entirely of technicolour satin. She was the thinking woman's nightmare and an absolute knock-out.

'She's got a Wonderbra, and real French knickers too,' said Pansy, who'd propped the catalogue on her knees and was poring over the picture as she finished her pudding.

'What do you know about things like that?' asked Christa, even more amused.

'Chel showed me them in her mummy's drawer.' Pansy put down the empty dish, and shut the catalogue with a sigh. 'Anyway, it's no good. Now Jamie's here, I never ever get what I want.'

She drooped disconsolately, rubbing her eyes. Christa threw her cigarette end out of the window, and put her arm round Pansy. She smelt of soap and cinnamon.

'You and me both, Pansy. But you'll get it one day. You'll grow up faster than you think, and so will Jamie,' she said, thinking she was a fine one to dispense advice in her present state. Unfortunately growing up never seemed to stop.

The dining-room door opened, releasing the sound of male voices into the hall. Pansy ran to peer over the banisters.

'They're all going into the drawing room now. I'd better go back to bed before Daddy sees me. He'll only get mad and that makes Mummy forget things even more,' she said with a theatrical sigh.

She trailed towards her room, the luckless Belinda dangling from her hand. Christa almost offered to read her a story, but if she didn't put in an immediate appearance downstairs Emma would go over the top. With a sigh nearly as big as Pansy's she went to join the others.

Mallory Farrar followed his host into the drawing room thinking that dinner with a group of fundamentalist mujaheddin would have been more relaxed than the one he'd just endured. He'd been a fool to allow the Master to persuade him into it.

The only person he felt in tune with was Emma Holdgate. She showed a sensitivity to other people's reactions which must make life difficult for her, particularly with a husband so hungry for success. Philip Holdgate needed a wife like the Master's, a woman more thickly armoured and with less peripheral vision than a giant tortoise.

The Master himself, in the few weeks he'd had to observe him, Mallory considered one of the most devious men he'd ever met. Vernon Slade had taken up his post as Head of House several years after Mallory graduated from Gabriel. Under the previous Master, a brilliant, genial liberal of the old school, it had been the most stimulating college in Oxford. The statutes of its Governing Body had never been used as a straitjacket, as they were now. Though the college was wealthier today than ever before, it was heading towards intellectual bankruptcy, paralysed by Slade's refusal to consider any new ideas which might jeopardise its privileges.

The fellowship he'd accepted with such alacrity had already become a burden, but though Mallory found the present situation in college intensely oppressive, he had no intention of fighting it. There had been too much turmoil in his life recently.

Instead he was beginning to think of throwing in the fellowship and lying low abroad, in Zanzibar perhaps, or Mozambique, while he finished his present book. At least he wasn't likely to meet any rampant animal rights activists there, he thought, remembering the morning's events.

His gaze fell consideringly on Christa Keith, whom he'd recognised immediately in the market café. He'd seen her on television reporting from Bosnia, delivering a coherent, incisive summing-up of current events with almost inhuman self-possession while tracer bullets seamed the night sky behind her and the camera was rocked by shell-blast. She was clearly as hard-boiled as most of the war-reporters he'd met, inured like a surgeon to blood and pain.

She'd latched on to him this morning with the media's usual alacrity. Yet she was brave, he admitted grudgingly to himself. She'd talked herself and a truckful of refugees out of Zepa. But stupid as well, to get involved with a notorious womaniser like Gareth Hyde, for the media didn't spare even its own. Almost as stupid as himself, he thought, crushing the memory of Caitlin for the hundredth time.

Tom Carver had just started a long diatribe about the Internet. Jesus, he's at it again, Mallory said to himself. He took the cup of coffee Emma was handing him, and wondered how soon he could reasonably leave.

At least he had one thing in common with Christa Keith. She was clearly just as fed up with the conversation. He felt almost sorry for Tom Carver as she homed in on him.

'I still don't understand what valid objection there could be to making the Gabriel library more widely available,' she said.

'Because many of our books and manuscripts are irreplaceable. It's hard enough protecting them from the depredations of our own students,' Tom Carver answered testily. 'In fact Governing Body has been giving serious consideration to restricting the more valuable part of the collection to post-graduates only. If the library were linked to a global information network, we should have every Tom, Dick and Harry wanting to come here to look more closely at our books.'

'Surely the whole point of the Internet is that they wouldn't need to come here? And the British Library and the Bodleian seem to manage, anyway.'

'They have far greater financial resources for ensuring the safety of their stock.'

'Gabriel doesn't seem to me to lack financial resources. But if it's a problem I believe the Senior Common Room has the services of several butlers. If you dispensed with some of them, perhaps the money saved could be put towards a library security system.'

'You are evidently not conversant with the exigencies of college bequests, Miss Keith.' The Master's voice was like a dollop of melting butter. 'The salary of our invaluable butlers is provided from a fund set up specifically for that purpose in the last century by a royal duke who was a student at Gabriel.'

'And, of course, the high standard of domestic service still prevailing at Gabriel makes it possible for our dons to concentrate exclusively on their research, and produce the outstanding results they do,' said the Master's wife, using her voice on Christa like a bludgeon.

'Did Einstein need a butler to help him work out the law of relativity?' she asked with an innocent expression.

Mallory, against all his inclinations, wanted to applaud. But Emma, watching a flush like raspberry juice over summer pudding suffuse the face of the Master's wife, knew that her dinner party was almost beyond repair. In a last attempt to smooth things over, she dredged up something Phil had told her after a committee meeting the previous term.

'The new library store proposed for the Gabriel's Mill site is a splendid idea,' she said brightly, 'especially as it's going to free more space in college for student accommodation.'

Every expression except Christa's and Mallory Farrar's registered instant dismay.

'Emma, for heaven's sake, I told you that in complete confidence! I warned you not to mention it to anyone,' said Phil through clenched teeth. 'Nothing's settled yet.'

Oh, God, thought Emma wearily, how could I forget? But I'm so damned tired all the time these days. She glanced over at Christa, knowing that she wouldn't be able to resist pursuing the remark. As she feared, her sister was now looking like Boadicea about to mow down her enemies with the knives on her chariot wheels. She obviously knew far too much about that subject as well.

'But I understood that the Mill site would be redeveloped for the benefit of the Gabriel's Grounds Estate?' Christa said. 'Is something going on that the public doesn't know about?'

No one answered her. An eloquent glance passed between the Master and his wife. Mrs Slade stood up and tucked her handbag firmly under her arm.

'It's been a most pleasant evening, but I'm afraid we really have to go. Vernon has a meeting with the Minister for the Environment early tomorrow, and I'm on the bench.'

The Carvers hurriedly began to take their leave as well. Even Mallory Farrar, whom Emma was desperately hoping would stay and perhaps defuse a little of Philip's anger, was unfolding himself with alacrity from the sofa. It was as though Christa's question had never been asked, yet because of it the party was finally in ruins.

Afterwards, in the kitchen, Philip made it clear that his hopes for academic advancement were in ruins too.

'Well, that's it,' he said, sitting down and irritably pushing away the empty brûlée dish, which Noelene had abandoned in favour of bed and the Radio One Rap Show. 'Thanks to you, Christa, I've very little chance of promotion now. I hope you realise this means Emma will have to continue working full-time to pay off the mortgage. And we've got the fees at Pansy's next school coming up soon.'

Christa, who'd just brought in the empty coffee cups from the drawing room, contained her temper with difficulty.

'It's hardly fair to make me responsible for your choice of lifestyle,' she said coldly.

'That's rich coming from you. When were you ever responsible for anything except your own interests?'

'Phil, please.' Emma spoke from the sink, where she was putting saucepans to soak overnight. Her voice was high with fatigue and controlled tension. 'I shouldn't have made the remark about the library in the first place. It really wasn't Christa's fault.'

'Rubbish,' said Phil. 'She could have asked me about it quietly, in private, afterwards. But when does Christa ever do anything quietly? My God, no wonder Gareth Hyde got shot of her so fast. I bet he's thinking he had a lucky escape.'

Christa felt sick. She hadn't realised quite how much Philip resented her, or how shaky her self-esteem still was. His words again raised all the doubts about her effectiveness as a woman which she'd been trying so hard to dismiss. As she straightened up she struggled to make her face impassive and to quell the sudden lump in her throat.

'If you feel so threatened by a simple question, one which I had every right to ask, perhaps you shouldn't be applying for this particular post anyway,' she said. 'Understanding others never was your strong point.'

Her throw-away tone brought Phil to his feet.

'You've gone too far this time, Christa! I know Emma said you could stay as long as you liked, but quite frankly I've already had enough. The whole bloody household's been upset ever since you arrived. I'd like you out of here by the end of the week!'

'No problem at all,' said Christa airily. 'I'll leave tomorrow.'

Emma had been scrubbing a saucepan like an automaton. It fell into the sink with a crash.

'You promised Christa could stay till she'd found a flat, Phil! I haven't seen her for over a year. I won't have her turned out. Your mother was here for a month in the spring, don't forget.'

Christa, who'd been thinking joyfully that now she'd be able to make a legitimate escape from Ethelred Road, was touched and dismayed by this unexpected support. Things must be worse than she'd realised between Emma and Phil for her to oppose him so directly.

'My mother's an angel compared to Christa,' said Phil.

'I want her to stay, Phil. I mean it. This is half my house, don't forget.' Emma's voice was ominously wobbly.

'For God's sake, don't start one of your crying jags,' said Phil exasperatedly.

Now he was being even more unfair, Christa thought. Emma hardly ever cried. Her rare outbursts were always the accumulation of months of stress.

Emma shot Philip a furious look, and he had the grace to look slightly ashamed.

'All right, all right then,' he said tetchily, 'if it really means so much to you. But just till the end of the month, and not a moment more.'

Christa was surprised by the rapid capitulation, until she remembered how much he'd hated coping with Emma's tears at Pansy's christening. With difficulty she refrained from saying that she'd make sure she was gone long before the end of the month.

Philip got up and took his jacket from the back of the chair, folding it fussily over his arm.

'I'm going to bed,' he said. 'I'll leave you two to get on with it, since you're so fond of each other's company. But perhaps it wouldn't be too much to ask, Emma, if you'd bring me a cup of tea when you come up.'

As they heard Phil's footsteps fade away upstairs, Emma filled the kettle and plugged it in with a taut expression on her face. She ran herself a glass of water at the sink, and came back to the table, pressing the glass against her forehead.

'You needn't have done that, Em, but thanks all the same,' said Christa. 'You look ready to drop. And why on earth can't Phil make his own tea?'

'He would have if you hadn't been here.'

'So he won't help if there's another woman around? How chauvinist can you get?'

'He feels threatened by you,' said Emma tiredly. 'He always has. You're everything he's not: dynamic, successful, probably two or three times as well-paid.'

'And now I'm on the ropes he's making the most of it. You let him get away with too much.'

As soon as she'd spoken she remembered uncomfortably just how much she'd let Gareth get away with. Perhaps he'd felt threatened. Perhaps in the unlikely event of her ever having a new lover, *he* would feel threatened too.

'Sorry,' she said, attempting a smile. 'I'm not exactly an expert in male management, am I?'

'You just don't realise how tough you can seem,' said Emma. She got up and pulled Pansy's lunch box from a shelf.

'I'll do Pansy's lunch,' said Christa firmly, taking it from her.

'But you don't know what she likes,' protested Emma.

'I know exactly what *you* like her to have,' said Christa with a grin. 'I saw you make up her box last night. I think you should go to bed, and I'll finish the washing up too. It won't take long.'

'You?' Emma looked stunned. 'But there's still an awful lot to do, and you know how you hate housework.'

'At least I'll be an improvement on Noelene.'

'Well, it would be heavenly to get some sleep before Jamie starts up again,' said Emma doubtfully. 'But you will make sure you turn everything off when you've finished? And lock the back door too.'

'Stop fussing, and go on, do.'

Emma had made the tea and was halfway to the door when she hesitated again.

'Christa, promise me you won't pursue this business of the library extension any further? I should never have mentioned it. You'll stir up trouble for all of us, and waste your time into the bargain. The Master always gets what he wants in the end.'

'So the Gabriel's Mill site definitely won't be developed in the interests of the Gabriel's Grounds Estate? Is that what you mean?'

'I don't mean anything definite,' said Emma, starting to look anxious all over again. 'You do jump on people's statements so. The Master's worried because the students have begun to stir up a fuss about the lack of accommodation. Lots of them have to live out at the moment, and rents are so high in town.' She rested the laden tea tray on the dresser briefly as she tried to convince Christa. 'He just happened to remark at the committee meeting that if the present library store were moved from the college to the Mill, the old building could be converted into student quarters. I'm sure Phil's right, and nothing's fixed.'

She picked up the tray as an imperious wail floated down the stairs.

'God, there's Jamie. He's early tonight. I'll have to go before he really works himself up.'

Christa, who'd been torn between wanting to banish Emma's anxiety over her indiscretion, and an increasing desire to investigate, realised with relief that she wasn't going to have to commit herself.

When she'd finished all the chores she stood for a few minutes in the back porch, smoking another illicit cigarette before locking up. It was darker at the back of the house, and the stars shone brilliantly through a rustling tracery of withered leaves. In the distance she could hear the rumble of late-night traffic on the Woodstock Road.

She'd been in Oxford two days, and her gloomiest expectations had not only been confirmed, but exceeded in the case of Gabriel Hall. The place was rotten with mismanagement. If she started to look into it, she'd be entirely on her own. If she attracted the slightest adverse attention, she was sure Randall wouldn't hesitate to cancel her retainer.

Yet to go along with what seemed to be happening would be to give it her tacit agreement, and leave her with no self-respect at all. If she were careful, investigating the workings of the college would be infinitely easier than investigating Howl. And if she didn't have something constructive to do she'd be out of her mind by the end of the year. As Christa crushed the cigarette against the wall, she'd already decided to turn the Master's latest piece of empire building very discreetly inside out.

6

The office of Miss Harker, the Dean's secretary, appeared to have been last modernised in the 1950s. She was typing up a storm on an Underwood manual with a double-length carriage, from which projected an immensely complicated timetable. The tab release shot the carriage sideways every few spaces with a grinding crash. Here as well, the electronic revolution might never have taken place. Christa wasn't surprised to see a packet of aspirins next to the biscuit tin and empty mug on her desk.

Power dressing had also passed Miss Harker by. Her considerable bulk was covered by a white blouse with a Peter Pan collar, and a knife-pleated navy skirt. She trained the lenses of a pair of NHS spectacles on Christa.

'Copies of college regulations have already been sent to new graduate students in the internal mail. Dr Anstruther can't see anyone until the official beginning of term,' she snapped, returning the typewriter carriage so violently that it hurtled the tin of biscuits to the floor. The lid flew off, scattering the contents beneath her desk.

'Drat the things!' she exclaimed, as she dived after them.

Christa joined her beneath the desk, helping to gather up the pieces. Miss Harker smelt of Apple Blossom dusting powder, and was breathing heavily as they came up for air together. She was in her late fifties, but had the unlined skin of the chronically overweight. Christa carefully put her handful of fragments on the edge of the desk.

'My name's Christa Keith. I'm a new visiting fellow, and I've an appointment with the Dean at eleven.'

'Why didn't you say so then, for goodness' sake?' Miss Harker demanded, hastily sweeping the biscuits into a waste-paper basket, and consulting an imposing leather-bound diary. 'You're quite right. Dr Anstruther must have written it in without my knowledge. I'll let him know you're here,' she added, casting a jaundiced look at the shabby jeans Christa had donned in a mood of continuing protest.

When the Dean appeared through an inner door his physique cast Miss Harker's into the shade. He was a mountainous man, with a broad, bald head. Pipe smoke billowed from the room behind him.

'Miss Keith, isn't it? How delightful. The Master told me to expect you,' he said in an asthmatic wheeze.

He too distrustfully eyed her jeans. It had become depressingly clear to Christa that to establish any credibility in Gabriel's sartorial time-warp, she'd have to acquire some new clothes.

He glanced at his watch. 'Shall we cut along to the Senior Common Room, then? I'm afraid time is of the essence today.'

As he rolled beside her through a labyrinth of draughty corridors, Christa endured more emollient chat which included a long eulogy on the warm-heartedness of Jimmy Judd, a financial assassin who rarely let his finer feelings get in the way of enhancing his reputation. She replied with sugared remarks of a sort she hadn't employed since breaking the ground in an interview with a particularly slippery Far Eastern dictator.

'You'll be pleased to hear that your seminars are scheduled for first thing on Monday mornings,' said the Dean, as they crossed a cloistered quad dominated by an ancient cedar tree. 'There's nothing like an early start.'

The worst possible time, when her students would still be recovering from the previous weekend, Christa thought, and of course the Dean knew it.

'I gather you're short of space, and had some trouble finding me a room,' she said, determined to find a way to introduce the subject of Gabriel's Mill.

'We always do our best for Lord Judd.'

'But I understand your accommodation problems will soon be solved by the removal of the library store to the Gabriel's Mill site?'

Dr Anstruther burst into a volcanic fit of coughing.

'I can assure you that it's only the most tentative of ideas,' he said, stopping under the cedar to wipe his eyes with a paisley handkerchief, 'and one which most certainly should not be in the public domain.'

'How odd, then, that I heard it mentioned last night during a dinner party at which the Master himself was present,' Christa said with her most guileless expression.

'Then I can only think it was a dinner attended solely by members of Gabriel Hall. Perhaps I should take this opportunity to remind you that fellows are expected to maintain absolute discretion on the college's internal affairs.'

She managed to avoid a direct answer, trying another dose of flattery instead.

'It's such a neat solution, and one in which I suspect you played no small part.'

It was a lucky guess. He put away his handkerchief, and puffed out his chest like a self-advertising toad.

'Well, yes, I believe I was in fact the first to moot the idea.'

'I understood the previous Master promised that the land would be redeveloped to benefit the Gabriel's Grounds Estate. I wonder if you've considered the adverse publicity?'

'I doubt if there'd be any once the full facts were known. The land on which Gabriel's Mill is built was given to the college by Elizabeth of Bohemia in perpetuity. The Deed of Gift in our archives states that it cannot be sold.'

'I thought the previous Master promised to lease rather than sell it.'

'The late Professor Saltash may have made some sort of rather rash verbal undertaking,' said the Dean, avoiding her eye, 'but there is nothing to that effect in writing.'

'I gather plans have already been drawn up for the library store. How exciting. I'd love to see them.'

She'd pushed her luck a little too far.

'I'm afraid you have been been informed incorrectly on that count. I must emphasise that the plan is still only a suggestion. Nothing has been settled yet,' he said, turning on her a gaze as innocently genial as Friar Tuck's. 'Shall we walk on? I can take the opportunity to tell you the history of the Senior Common Room as we go.'

As he started to drone away about Queen Anne, Christa thought gleefully that she was getting somewhere at last. The Dean was well aware of the former Master's promise, and from his reaction she strongly suspected that plans for redevelopment already existed. If she could only discover the architect's name, the rest should be comparatively easy.

A bright log fire crackled in the Senior Common Room hearth, which was surrounded with antique Isnik tiles in a formalised design of turquoise flowers. Through the windows a stiff breeze was chasing leaves across the fellows' garden, but no draughts penetrated the heavy curtains of dark blue brocade, and the deep Wilton carpet instantly absorbed any footfall.

The walls were lined with pale green watered silk, and adorned with portraits of the great and good, all former students at Gabriel. As Christa studied them, she noted sardonically that though the atmosphere was now one of insulated privilege, the college in its hey-day had specialised in social reformers.

She'd hoped to see Piers, but he wasn't there. Instead the Dean introduced her to several ancient dons sunk in the depths of enormous sofas. Like hedgehogs roused from winter homes of dried leaves, they peered dimly at Christa round their newspapers, gave her limp hands to shake, and returned without ceremony to crosswords and obituaries.

A gathering of middle-aged fellows with grey hair and grey expressions seemed equally unwilling to abandon their discussion of European politics. And another group gave her the most perfunctory of greetings before returning to a savage dissection of an article in *Granta*. In a far corner, in a library chair with his back to the room, was Mallory Farrar reading a magazine, whom the Dean carefully did not disturb.

'So now you know everyone, I'm sure you'll make yourself at home,' he said breezily. 'Unfortunately I have another appointment, but please help yourself to coffee, and do ask the butler if there's anything you especially require. I shall look forward to seeing you again at the Master's drinks party at the beginning of term.'

He whisked away towards the door. The butler raced to open it for him. Though he almost genuflected as the Dean passed,

Christa was amused to catch the hint of a sardonic smile once the door had closed behind him.

On a side table was an impressive array of silver coffee pots, Coalport china ornamented with the college crest, and a bonbonnière of biscuits. She poured herself some coffee, and decided to tackle the middle-aged men first. As she approached the group, she realised they were now discussing the Balkans. It was the perfect lead. Smiling, she picked up one of their comments and added an observation of her own.

The man who'd been speaking raised an eyebrow.

'Really?' he said in a bored voice, and plunged straight back into his original conversation.

She waited a few moments, and tried a further comment when another of them referred to the fall of Zepa. Again she was ignored.

She decided to tackle the other group instead. She knew the journalist who'd written the article they were still tearing apart. But when she offered a remark, they simply smiled vaguely at her and wandered off to the other side of the room, leaving her stranded in the middle of the carpet.

By now she was too furious to finish her coffee. She marched over to the fire and abandoned her cup and saucer on the mantelpiece in front of a simpering Meissen shepherdess, before fishing out her cigarettes and lighter. The most ancient don was sucking away at a cigar, so at least no one could tell her not to smoke.

As she lit up, reminding herself that this cigarette really must be the last, she saw that the high-backed chair before the fire had an occupant whom both she and the Dean had overlooked.

A woman with thick gun-metal grey hair in a perfectly disciplined bob was watching Christa as if she knew exactly what she was thinking. Ironic eyes gazed at her from a strong, shield-shaped face confidently made up with a slash of water melon-red lipstick. She wore what could only be a Jean Muir suit, several years old but still perfect, and had a copy of the *Lancet* in her lap.

'Hallo,' she said. 'You look as if you need that. I'm Leda Lennox, the Vice-Master, though I don't much care for the term, and you must be Christa Keith. It's good to have some reinforcements at last. Why don't you join me?'

She smiled as Christa took the chair next to her.

'I'm always lecturing people on the evils of cigarettes, but I still succumb every now and then myself. I imagine you've just experienced the full force of the Gabriel welcome. Unfortunately some of my colleagues aren't known for their ready charm. But I'm absolutely delighted to have you here. I've been longing for reinforcements.'

Christa warmed to the unexpected friendliness. Whatever her colleagues lacked, Leda Lennox made up for in full.

'So far they've treated me like a new boy at prep school,' said Christa, with a rueful laugh.

'Exactly. You have to demonstrate that you know the unwritten rules before they'll accept you. And it doesn't help that for centuries the Senior Common Room has been an exclusively male retreat.'

'How did you get them to accept you?'

'I was given a DBE just before I came here. I don't much like the honours system, but I took it for the sake of my team. It helps funding, and in the case of the older fellows there's absolutely nothing like a Dame. It virtually makes me an honorary man.'

'I doubt if any honours are going to come my way,' said Christa.

'You mean after that sad business with Matt Brady? It must have been extremely tough for you. But the college is lucky to have you, all the same, and you shouldn't forget it.'

'Thanks for saying so,' said Christa. It was good to have another ally besides Piers. 'What am I supposed to do, though? Wait indefinitely until they discover my true worth?'

'I think you'll find some kindred spirits among the younger fellows. Unfortunately they aren't here today, but they're as keen for change as I am. And the others will have to talk to you when you dine with them in hall. It's college etiquette.'

Christa didn't say she'd already decided to dine in college as little as possible. The thought of having to sit next to Philip or Mallory Farrar held no appeal.

'You must know my brother-in-law, Philip Holdgate,' she said, longing to find out what Leda thought of him. 'He works at the Institute.'

'Yes, I know him well, of course.' Leda's voice was carefully noncommittal. 'He was appointed by my predecessor.'

'Phil tells me you've been having trouble with Howl activists. I've seen enough of them already to know what that must mean. What sort of animals do you use in your labs?'

'Most of our work's done with small rodents. But my own research on meningitis involves primates. Howl has the idea that the Institute is some sort of animal Colditz. Unfortunately it's too risky to invite them to see how untrue that is.' She smiled. 'I've no family of my own. You could say the Institute and the animals are my family instead.'

Though the remark might have sounded slightly odd from anyone else, Christa immediately believed her. She'd rarely encountered anyone who appeared so sincere and well-balanced.

'Being Vice-Master must seem rather unimportant compared to your scientific work.'

'It's important in a different way. Gabriel still doles out research funds for graduates almost exclusively to men. As Vice-Master I automatically chair the Bursaries Committee. With the help of the younger dons I managed to push through a bursary for a very able black female student last year. I'm hoping to do even better in future.'

So Rebekah too owed her place at Gabriel to Leda, thought Christa.

Leda glanced at the knot of fellows who'd been discussing Bosnia as they drifted from the room, still immersed in conversation.

'The older dons haven't yet recovered from the shock, but they'll get the message eventually. They've simply not been exposed to enough change.'

'And I can guess exactly whose fault that is,' said Christa.

Leda gave her a swift, conspiratorial smile. 'You can guess, but you'd better not say.'

Mallory Farrar had just replaced the magazine he'd been reading on a table laden with newspapers and periodicals, and was making for the door with his usual remote expression.

'You should find a sympathiser in our other visiting fellow,' said Leda, following Christa's gaze. 'He dislikes the current state of affairs at Gabriel as much as you.'

Christa was astonished. 'That's not my impression. He's gone along with the Master every time we've met.'

'I think he's still feeling bruised after the Caitlin Trevor affair, and simply wants a quiet life.'

Christa thought acidly that this was carrying sympathy too far. Caitlin Trevor must have more bruises than a defeated world heavyweight. Leda put the copy of the *Lancet* on a table by her side.

'Strictly off the record,' she said, 'because I don't want to alarm the older fellows too much at this stage, I've every intention of trying to get the college back to how it was under Professor Saltash – caring properly for the students, whatever their background. The poorer ones get a rotten deal over accommodation at the moment. They live in a state of permanent financial anxiety. It affects their work and their health.'

It was the perfect moment to bring up the development of Gabriel's Mill, Christa decided.

'I gather the kids on the Gabriel's Grounds Estate have a poor deal too. I don't think much of the Master's plan to put things right for the students by doing the estate out of the Mill site.'

Leda gave her a curious look, then said cautiously, 'Let's go into the quad. There may be hearing aids turned up a little too high in here, and I've got to get back to the Institute, anyway.'

She walked with Christa as far as the cedar tree before saying, 'I'd heard you were quite a newshound, but I didn't realise how good. Who told you?'

'I heard it mentioned inadvertently at a dinner party. I've been trying to find out more. I can't believe you're involved, but anything you can tell me would help.'

Leda seemed to be inspecting the cracks in the flag-stoned path. 'Help what?' she asked quietly.

'Why, to stop the scheme, of course. After what you've just said, you surely wouldn't want the college to exploit the people on the estate?'

Leda sat on the circular wooden seat surrounding the tree, and gazed directly at Christa.

'Look,' she said gently, 'I know you've had a rough time

recently, and I can guess how hard it's been for you to give up reporting. But don't let yourself be tempted to investigate. You'd be wasting your time, as well as endangering your future. No one's seen any plans: there's nothing concrete. At the moment I'm certain it's just an idea skating about between the Dean and the Master, the sort of idea that's often mentioned in committee simply to test the water, and just as often dropped.'

It wasn't Christa's impression. She brushed some fallen needles from the seat and sat down next to Leda, preparing to argue her case.

'But supposing it isn't? Supposing the plans are already prepared and he's thought of some way of hustling them through?'

'Though the Master's compulsively devious, even he would have to put a plan like that to Governing Body first.'

'What if his plans for the site were so potentially lucrative that Governing Body couldn't refuse?'

Leda shook her head. 'Aren't you getting into the realms of fantasy? The Master's destroyed too many good people already. He has a huge talent for manipulation – probably the only talent he has left, as he hasn't produced anything new academically for years. Better to concentrate on motivating your students. They need someone like you. The better-off majority are too little concerned with the state of the world.'

She got up, her expression so genuinely concerned that Christa was temporarily silenced.

'And after that little homily I really must go,' said Leda, smiling at her. 'We've a group of researchers from the States visiting the Institute this afternoon. But I hope I'll see you at the Master's drinks party on Tuesday night.'

Christa sat for a little longer when Leda had left. Above her in the tree a magpie was searching for insects, dislodging showers of pollen from the cedar's cone-shaped flowers.

Leda hadn't convinced her about Gabriel's Mill, but on all other counts Christa had been totally won over by her concern. If only her own mother were as tactful, she thought, and remembered gloomily that she'd agreed to make her long-postponed visit to her parents that afternoon.

Emma had taken the Mini again, so this time Christa braved

the Botley Road by bus. Juniper Grove was still the same well-ordered suburban enclave of her childhood. The trees after which the road was named paraded the grass verges like guardians of respectability. Its Betjemanesque semis had been designed for a vanished age when housewife mothers hung out snowy lines of handwashed sheets and fathers raised vegetables in the long back gardens, with their children playing round them.

When Christa's parents moved there in the early sixties, soon after their marriage, it was still an ideal area for young couples wanting to start a family, but the sort of place any aspiring professional would leave the moment a good promotion came along.

Her parents had never moved. Because of her mother they were imprisoned in their surroundings like the wooden couple forever fixed to a weather house's floor. Only it wasn't the weather which motivated her parents, but her mother's neurosis. Not that it was ever referred to in that way. It was always, from her father, 'Your mother's nervous attacks', and from her mother, 'My little problem'.

Walking towards the house from the bus-stop, Christa remembered how, as a twelve-year-old, infuriated beyond endurance by some petty errand inflicted on her by her mother's inability to leave the house, she'd gone down to the public library and wrestled with the long words in a medical dictionary until she'd worked out exactly what was wrong with her.

Back at home, when fifteen-year-old Emma had pleaded with her to be more sympathetic, she'd yelled furiously, 'It's not a little problem! It's a great big neurosis. It's called agoraphobia, and she has no right to let it mess up our lives as well as hers! Why didn't you tell me? I'm old enough to know, instead of always having to pretend it doesn't exist.'

Christa recalled with painful clarity her jumbled feelings at the time. Pity for her mother, whom she'd loved unreservedly before she stopped seeing her with a child's eyes, anger at her refusal to accept psychiatric help, and more anger towards her father for not making her do so. And above all, a determination not to let her own life be circumscribed, as she saw Emma already sacrificing large chunks of her freedom to the role of their mother's escort.

Taking a deep breath, she opened the front gate and walked

up the path bisecting the front lawn. It was bordered with the usual autumn display of African marigolds.

She wondered if her mother was watching from behind the net curtains as she pressed the bell. Evidently not, for a couple of minutes elapsed before her father answered the door, wearing his unvarying off-duty uniform of cavalry twill trousers and a college blazer.

She used to cringe when he turned up at school open days, standing out like a crow in his dark suit among the bright colours of the other fathers' casual clothes, and commenting in his penetrating Oxbridge accent on the rows of popular fiction in the sixth-form library. Yet at least he did appear, unlike her mother, who'd never dared face such unfamiliar territory.

'Christa, my dear, it's so good to see you,' he said, holding out his arms, and beaming at her through his spectacles.

Hugging him back, with his neatly clipped beard grazing her cheek, she thought how much she loved him, and yet how ineffectual he was away from his work. When she'd been bullied as a new girl at comprehensive school by a gang of older boys, his only solution had been to read Kipling's 'If' to her, and counsel endurance. Consulting her mother was out of the question, and so she did endure until she'd hit on the idea of attending evening classes in self-defence. After that her tormentors left her alone.

He looked at his watch. 'You'd better come and have tea right away. Your mother's made some scones, and she's been worrying about them for the last twenty minutes in case they get cold.'

Sometimes, to distract herself during bad situations in Bosnia, Christa had played a sort of Kim's game with the contents of the Juniper Grove sitting room, remembering the exact position of everything in it. Like her mother's life, nothing ever altered.

There were the mushroom-coloured slub silk three-piece suite, the spindly walnut occasional tables, and the glass-fronted cabinet holding her mother's collection of china thimbles, which no one else was allowed to touch. On top of the piano, where Emma had dutifully practised Mozart, and Christa picked out pop tunes, were their graduation photos, the ultimate trophies of the middle class. Her mother disliked fresh flowers for the mess they made, but on the sideboard stood a bowl of silk roses, forever scentless and unchanged.

Christa braced herself as she heard the sound of rattling wheels outside which heralded the full afternoon tea scenario. A moment later her mother appeared, pushing a laden trolley which she kept carefully away from her mail-order dress with its usual inoffensive print and safe mid-calf hem.

'Christabel, sweetheart, it's lovely to see you at last!' she cooed.

Christa just in time refrained from snapping at her not to use the full version of the name chosen by her father in a moment of poetic excess. She'd shortened it in her first hour at comprehensive school.

'Hallo, Ma,' she said with deliberate casualness, as she was enfolded in a *L'Aimant*-scented embrace.

'You haven't been looking after yourself,' said her mother accusingly, standing back and inspecting her. 'You must put on some weight while you're here. Mustn't she, Conrad?'

Christa's father was trotting to and fro like a well-trained labrador, trying not to trip over anything as he dispersed the occasional tables in a sequence learned over many years.

'Yes, of course, Alice, my dear,' he said.

Christa sat down on the sofa, remembering to keep the heels of her boots well away from the pale silk. Her mother, rattling out family news while handing round plates, knives, cake forks and lace napkins, kept shooting covert glances at her. When they all had scones and jam, and she'd made sure the cups of tea were on their mats, she dispatched Conrad into the kitchen for more hot water.

The moment he'd gone she said, with the little intake of breath that always preceded difficult questions, 'Sweetheart, we really were worried to death about this business with Gareth Hyde. I can't understand how he could be allowed to say such terrible things about you if they weren't true. I thought your father should consult a solicitor, but he said you wouldn't like us to interfere.'

Christa abandoned her scone. It suddenly tasted like foam rubber. She picked up a cushion, hugging it defensively to her chest.

Alice's spirits sank at the gesture. As usual, she'd said the wrong thing to her youngest daughter, though oddly enough she always felt better with Christa. Her optimism and energy were infectious. Sometimes they even made Alice feel it might be possible to find a way out of her cage.

'Dad's right,' said Christa. 'More than anything I simply want the fuss to calm down. Gareth's in the past. I'm fine now.'

Then she should look happier, thought Alice anxiously. If only they could go out together, have a cosy lunch at some quiet little pub, as other mothers did with their daughters, she was sure she could get Christa to confide in her. But it was no good. She hadn't managed a trip like that for years, not even with Emma.

At the thought of her elder daughter more worries came sneaking up.

'Emma rang us about your fellowship at Gabriel. We're delighted for you, of course, but I'm afraid it's upset her a lot. She's so concerned about not spoiling Phil's chances of promotion. You must try to be extra tactful with them both.'

'I'm sorry. I didn't mean any of it to happen this way.'

Christa's voice was curt. She looked as though her jaw was aching from controlling her expression, but Alice, thinking how tired and overworked Emma had been lately, felt it her duty to plough on.

'Perhaps you don't realise, darling, quite what a responsibility Emma has, with two young children and the mortgage dependent on her earnings as well. One day you'll have a family yourself, and know what it's like.'

'For God's sake, stop trying to change me!' Christa burst out. 'You ought to be working on your own life, not mine!'

Alice felt as if Christa had hit her. The accusation was so cruelly unfair, she thought. Christa didn't seem to realise that she never stopped thinking about her problem. It was always hideously there. Only Conrad and Emma understood, but even Emma had been less sympathetic lately, after the unfortunate incident with Pansy in the shop.

She couldn't bear the way Christa was ruining her longed-for visit. Alice's eyes switched agitatedly from her daughter's face to a loose piece of braid on the cushion, which she was systematically unravelling. If the house, the only part of her life over which she had any control, started falling apart, what would happen to her then?

'Darling, stop it, do! You're ruining the trim!'

She darted forward and twitched the cushion away. Conrad, returning with the hot water, sent Christa a sympathetic look as Alice hurried over to her sewing box, threaded a needle, and began to attack the braid.

He put the hot water jug on the trolley, and said diplomatically to Christa, 'I've discovered some Tasmanian members of your mother's family who emigrated early last century. It's opened up a most interesting branch of the family tree. You must come and see the chart after tea.'

Sometimes, thought Christa, her father seemed more interested in the dead than the living, but any diversion was better than none. It had the effect of making her mother plunge into family anecdotes, all of which Christa had heard many times before. She was only just fifty-five, but her interests were getting narrower all the time. When tea at last came to an end she decided to risk speaking to her father about it as soon as they were alone.

As Alice started to push the trolley out of the room, refusing all offers of help, for only she was allowed to wash up the best china, Christa thankfully followed Conrad upstairs.

His retreat was a small box room, crammed with county histories, a photocopier and fax machine, and a computer on which, when released from garden chores, he surfed the Internet. The remaining shelf space was occupied by books of poetry, his other passion. He wrote it himself, spare bleak little offerings which he could never be persuaded to submit to a publisher, just as he would never reveal any of his deepest emotions.

Conrad was rooting about in a bulging box file. On his desk were a photo of Emma, dressed for a Greek play at school, intensely serious beneath a crooked laurel crown, and one of the few of Christa herself which she liked, clipped from the *TV Times*, taken by Matt in Haiti as she joked with a gang of street urchins.

'How is Mother at the moment?' she asked. 'Truthfully, Dad?'

'About the same,' he said distantly, extracting a black and white photo of a tombstone. 'Look at this! "Sacred to the memory of Lionel Glenridding, died in Hobart, Tasmania, 1833". He must have been one of the first settlers. Perhaps that's where you got your love of travel.'

'He certainly didn't pass it on to Mother,' said Christa. 'She really should see a specialist. She seems worse to me.'

Her father sighed and put down the photo, clearly loath to leave Tasmania. 'Her doctor keeps on suggesting it, but she won't agree.'

'Couldn't you try to be a bit firmer? She's wasted half her life already.'

'The idea distresses her so much that I can't bear to mention it any more. And she keeps assuring me she's perfectly happy.'

'But doesn't it depress you to think of spending the rest of your lives this way?'

'I promised to look after her when we married, and I will,' said Conrad doggedly, with a weary expression which made Christa long to rush downstairs and shake her mother.

'I'm sorry, Dad, but I think there's a better way of looking after her, and it ought to be done now, before it's too late.'

'Well, perhaps I might try talking to her again while you're here,' said her father doubtfully. 'I must say your stay in Oxford is most providential in many ways.'

'How do you mean?' Christa asked, studying a faded Victorian view of Southwold, where her great-grandfather had owned a grocery store.

'I've been wanting to do some more family research along the Suffolk coast. I'd like to spend a week there in December and another in April, during the vacations.'

'So?' said Christa cautiously. 'How does that affect me?'

'I thought you could stay with your mother while I was away. It would set my mind at rest, and give her so much pleasure. You don't realise, Christabel, how fond she is of you.'

'Why can't Emma stay? She never minds.'

'Things have been a little difficult with Emma and the children lately. I don't like to ask her.'

Christa looked at him in astonishment. Emma usually went to enormous lengths to please their parents, turning up religiously for Sunday lunch and birthdays, a fact she never allowed Christa to forget.

'Emma visits you regularly still, doesn't she?'

'Yes, but she doesn't often bring the children these days. Your mother adores them, and she feels it very much.'

'So what's stopping Emma? Was it something Mother did?'

Conrad was shuffling around the contents of the top drawer of his desk. He didn't look at her as he answered.

'A few months ago your mother needed something from the corner shop. It was one of her better days, and she felt she might just get there without help. Pansy was here on her own for the afternoon, and Alice took her along. She had one of her attacks in the shop. Unfortunately Pansy was extremely scared. Emma lost her temper when she found out, and wasn't as – as forgiving as she might have been.'

Christa remembered her own childhood again. Her mother had been more adventurous then, and would set out with herself and Emma on shopping expeditions which were occasionally successful, but more often ended in a panic attack.

The first time it happened Christa had been about Pansy's age, and thought her mother, ghost pale, shaking uncontrollably, and scarcely able to breathe, was going to die. In those days Alice always managed somehow to get them all home, but as the children grew older the attacks increased in severity. Christa and Emma became skilled in their management, one of them calming their mother and shielding her from curious eyes, while the other rushed to find a taxi. Christa's refusal, at twelve, to cooperate any more, had caused consternation in the family.

'For heaven's sake, Dad, how did you expect Emma to react?' she demanded. 'Can't you remember how it was when we were young? We should never have had that sort of responsibility.'

'But what could I do?' said Conrad helplessly. 'You know what your mother's like.'

'Yes, and that's why I won't live with her again.'

Christa felt like a traitor as her father's shoulders sagged. The urge to agree just to cheer him up was almost irresistible. But instead she forced herself to say, 'I think you should make a stand for once, and insist she sorts herself out. If you do, I'll help you all I can.'

'I don't know,' he said, spreading his hands helplessly before him on the desk. 'You're so determined, Christabel, so strong –

so unlike your mother. You've always handled your life with such confidence. You must give her a little sympathy.'

'But I'm the same as anyone else,' Christa broke out. 'I've simply had to learn to be strong in order to survive. Can't you see Mother's had too much sympathy? Don't you understand she needs to learn how to cope as well?'

'So I'm not a very satisfactory father or husband, it seems,' said Conrad with a faint smile.

'That's not fair! You know how much we all love you. I just hate seeing you worried like this.'

He frowned at Christa warningly. Alice's tread was coming up the stairs. A moment later her head appeared round the door with its usual concerned expression, as if they might have disappeared in her absence.

'You'll stay for dinner, won't you, Christa?' she said. 'There's a Pavlova for dessert, your favourite.'

'She was making it all morning,' said Conrad to Christa in a meaningful voice.

Christa had never liked Pavlova. It was one of her mother's pet stratagems to slave over some special unasked-for delicacy, then to be deeply hurt if one didn't stay and eat it. She'd already made it clear on the phone that she wouldn't be staying for dinner.

'Sorry, I'm meeting someone,' she lied.

Alice advanced into the room with the wounded look that was too familiar to be effective any more.

'But you've stayed such a short time, and I see so little of you as it is. I try so hard to make you welcome. I don't know what I do wrong.'

'You haven't done anything wrong to me,' said Christa, beginning to lose her patience as Conrad slipped from the room in his usual disappearing trick whenever arguments between his wife and daughters arose. 'You're doing it to yourself. You know exactly what I mean.'

Her mother's face crumpled. 'How can you be so insensitive? I can't help how I feel. You don't understand what I suffer – you never have – and now even Emma's turning against me.'

Tears were already rolling down her cheeks. Christa remembered a Bosnian refugee she'd seen on the road from Zepa, a woman of about her mother's age whose only son had just been killed, distraught with grief, yet still trying to hide her tears behind her shawl.

'I've seen enough lately to know that some women would be glad to have your problems instead of theirs.'

Alice gulped, and looked at her uncertainly.

'Poor, poor souls. I know I must seem so hopeless to you compared with them. But I can't help it. I can't!'

'You could, if you agreed to see a specialist.'

'A psychiatrist!' said her mother, as if Christa had suggested consulting Frankenstein. 'But I saw one years ago, when this all started, and he wanted to treat me in a mental hospital. I'd rather die than go to one of those places.'

'Phobias like yours aren't treated by staying in hospitals these days. It's done through group therapy. Your doctor must have explained it to you.'

'Group therapy!' said her mother even more dismissively. 'Sitting around all day with a lot of misfits!'

'And what are you doing now? Sitting around here, being a misfit on your own!'

'That's not fair, Christa! I'm never off my feet. I made forty pounds of jam this summer. You seemed to like it enough at tea.'

'And you really think forty pounds of jam makes up for what you're putting Dad through? You might at least give therapy a try, for his sake, if no one else's.'

'I can't, I can't,' Alice wailed, the tears starting to flow in earnest.

Christa, not entirely able to subdue a maddeningly irrational impulse to comfort her mother, who sometimes seemed more of a child than Pansy, put an arm round her.

'Think how wonderful it would be to get yourself sorted out. You could visit Emma, and go out with Jamie and Pansy whenever you liked. You've just got to be brave enough to take the first step. I know you can.'

Alice gulped again, and sniffed, wiping her eyes with a lace-edged handkerchief produced from her sleeve.

'Do you really think so, darling?'

'Of course. So why don't we go downstairs now, and ring the doctor for an appointment?' coaxed Christa, determined to make her mother commit herself. 'The sooner you do it, the sooner you'll be better.'

Alice smiled mistily. 'I always feel better anyway when you're here.' She hesitated, sniffed again, and said after a cliff-hanging pause, 'I suppose I could have one more try, if it means so much to everyone.'

'Terrific,' said Christa. 'You know we'll all help,' she added rashly, thinking that with a breakthrough like this, she'd even volunteer to take her mother to the therapy sessions.

'I'm such a coward, though,' said Alice. 'I know I'd never manage it without you. But if you were living here it'd give me such confidence. Please, darling. You've just been telling us that you haven't found a place of your own yet, and it would be so lovely to have you at home again.'

In her intense disappointment and frustration, Christa didn't bother to soften her reply.

'It'd make everything worse, and you know it. You wouldn't be able to resist trying to run my life, then I'd become angry, and you'd be even more upset.'

'I don't know what you mean,' quavered Alice. 'All I want is for you to be happy.'

'Then ring the doctor. Nothing would make me happier. The whole point of seeing a therapist is for you to learn to manage alone. You won't if you have me around as a crutch all the time. And after what happened in Bosnia I'm the last person to take on that role, anyway.'

'There! I knew you hadn't got over that man yet!' said Alice.

'For God's sake, stop changing the subject. Just go and make the phone call.'

'I'm much too upset now after the way you've spoken to me. I shan't discuss it with you again if this is going to be your attitude,' Alice added, with a pathetic attempt at dignity.

By now Christa was so torn apart by the resentment and pity she'd experienced so often as a teenager, and whose intensity she'd half forgotten, that she delivered an ultimatum of her own.

'Fine by me,' she said. 'Because I won't be visiting you again until you've tried to sort things out. I can't bear to watch what you're doing to Dad and yourself any longer.'

Her mother's mouth dropped slackly open. Even her curls seemed to wilt.

Christa whirled out of the box room before her mother could work on her a moment more, and rushed down the stairs. Her father was pacing uncertainly about the hall like an elderly, moulting heron. She gave him a quick hug, near to tears.

'Sorry, Dad, to leave you to pick up the pieces. But it's the last time. I've told Mother I'm not coming here again. She understands exactly why.'

Unable to stand his hurt, disappointed look any more than her mother's, she added, 'I'll phone you as soon as I've got my own place. You know I'd love to see you there any time,' and fled out of the front door.

Christa was desperate for a cigarette after her visit to Botley, but so far she'd managed not to smoke that day. She made for the Eagle and Child in St Giles', and ordered herself a whisky instead, thinking that at this rate, if smoking didn't get her, alcohol probably would.

It was one of the few pubs in Oxford retaining some original character, with small, intimate oak-panelled rooms. She headed for one of them with her glass, and found a seat in an inglenook. As the events of the afternoon slowly receded she began to take more notice of the people around her. That led to different but equally unwanted thoughts, for everyone there except herself seemed to be with someone.

She watched a man chatting up a girl who was equally clearly on the make, and was inevitably reminded of her first meeting with Gareth at the Sarajevo Hilton.

She'd been sitting on one of the purple-upholstered chairs in the foyer, thinking that if it weren't for the thudding of mortars in the surrounding hills, she could almost pretend she was in any international hotel. Already she'd decided to spend part of her stay in lodgings with someone local, so that she could properly get the feel of the place.

Gareth changed all that. He'd been having a drink with his woman interpreter before she went off duty. She appeared to be in an advanced state of melt-down as he gave her a farewell embrace.

Christa looked more closely at the man who was producing this effect, and caught his gaze over the interpreter's shoulder, a lazy, amused gaze which seemed to say to her, You and I are people of the world, and it's our lot to put up with this sort of thing.

He was about her height, with broad shoulders crammed into a bomber jacket. His tight-fitting denim jeans, she discovered later when she couldn't have cared less, restrained a sizeable roll of middle-aged spread. He had the most alive brown eyes she'd seen, and hair cut short at the front but falling in waves to his collar at the back, a style which would have looked ridiculous on anyone else of his age. But she never noticed his years at that first meeting. All she saw was his air of immense vitality.

When the interpreter finally left, Gareth was, most unusually for him, alone. Christa was also alone. Matt had a hangover brought on by too much drink on the plane. Though unshakeable in every other respect, he was terrified of flying.

Within ten seconds of the interpreter's departure Gareth had introduced himself. Though she'd heard all about his reputation, after a couple of hours she was falling in love with a rapidity that terrified and delighted her. Matt, joining them later for a hair of the dog, had taken in the situation at once, and read her a lecture while Gareth was buying another round.

'What the hell's got into you, Christa? If this weren't our first day here, I'd think you needed some R and R. Gareth's a good reporter, one of the best in his line, I'll give him that, but he's a first-class creep, and much too old for you. We were on assignment together at Woodstock in the seventies, for God's sake, and he was pulling girls all over the place then.'

Matt had been even more disgusted when Christa accepted an invitation from Gareth to share a night-cap in his room.

'Now I've seen it all,' Matt hissed at her, while Gareth was again at the bar buying a bottle of brandy. 'You make bloody sure he's got some Durex. He's had more lays than a carpet fitter!'

And next morning, when she'd wandered downstairs, hazy after Gareth's love-making, Matt was still grumpy.

'Would you get your act together and concentrate?' he'd grated at her. 'I don't want to go out there and get shot just because Gareth's fucked you out of your mind.'

*   *   *

They had been prophetic words, and as Christa remembered them, they seemed to fill the smoky air of her present surroundings. She delved in her pocket for her cigarettes and lighter, and nearly burned her fingers in shock when a voice once as well-known to her as Matt's sounded above the chatter.

'Christa! It's really you! I don't believe it!'

Hastily jettisoning the cigarette, she looked up and also couldn't believe her eyes. A man was advancing towards her through the smoke, arms outstretched, hair in a short Afro of grey peppercorn curls, his lively brown face splitting like a conker case into a huge smile.

'Wesley! Wes!'

She rushed at him, almost overturning her drink, felt him embrace her, and found herself trying not to sniffle like a baby into his jacket.

'Hey, hey, what's all this about, Christa? Take it easy, now. I know I'm good-looking, but don't forget I'm a married man.'

A moment later she was sitting with him in the inglenook, one of his arms still round her as she furiously rubbed away her tears. Though he was several years older than when she'd seen him last, and slightly more wrinkled, he was definitely real.

'So, *jambo, mama. Habari?*' he asked, using the Swahili he'd tried to teach her in their few quiet moments on assignment.

'*Mzuri* – good, the news is very good now I've met you.' She smiled at him damply. 'God, it's been too long, but you went freelance, and then I went abroad. And somehow I thought you might have retired.'

Wes was in his mid-fifties, the age at which heaving a cameraman's gear about the globe began to lose its appeal.

'Never. I've got four kids to support in First World luxury, don't forget. I shan't retire till they can support me.'

Wes Mukasa came from Kampala. He'd trained as a cameraman in Kenya, married a Swahili from the coast, then moved home to Uganda TV in the late-sixties. When General Amin appeared on the scene, one of Wes's many foreign friends had managed to get him a job in the UK with Apollo.

He'd become one of the company's top cameramen by the time Christa joined Apollo as a home correspondent. They'd frequently worked together until she went abroad, and he'd taught her almost as much as Matt.

'Are you here on assignment?' she asked.

'I live in Oxford now, just off the Iffley Road. I do a lot of work for Dreaming Spires TV these days. It's one of the local stations.'

'So you're a fully paid-up Oxonian,' she teased him.

'Miriam as well. She teaches Multicultural Studies here.'

'And the children? How are they?' She couldn't remember their names.

'The twins have just started secondary school. As for the two eldest, Ronnie's taking a year out in Africa after "A" levels, and Rebekah's doing a doctorate here at Gabriel.'

'Rebekah? Then I know her! How astounding! We met, quite by chance, only yesterday in Jericho.'

Wesley was equally astonished. 'She never said a word at supper last night! That girl certainly likes to pull the wool over her old dad's eyes.'

Christa was puzzled. 'So she didn't tell you I was here at Gabriel on a visiting fellowship? She must have known I used to work with you.'

Wesley shook his head, smiling. 'At one time Rebekah hankered after camera work, like me, but her mother wasn't keen. Luckily she got interested in other aspects of the media instead, but Miriam still thinks she might change her mind. I guess Rebekah didn't want to worry her mother. Miriam knows she admires you.'

'Nothing much to admire these days,' said Christa. 'I suppose you've heard the full horror story about Gareth and me?'

'Yes – sorry. You must have flipped completely when you found out he'd double-crossed you.'

'At least you believe my story. Not many people do. It was even an effort for Randall, and he's shunted me out of the way pretty damn quick.'

'So this fellowship at Gabriel was his idea?'

'Damage limitation, he calls it. But I'll probably cause just as much damage here. I've never taught in my life, and you know how I feel about Oxford and my family.'

'Yes, I remember you going on about them,' said Wes with

a grin. 'Sorry I can't buy you another drink, but I was on my way out. Miriam's teaching night school, and if the twins are left to themselves they won't touch their homework. How about walking a little way with me, and filling me in on your news?'

They threaded their way to the door, Wes greeting acquaintances as he passed. He had an enviable knack of adapting himself to any company, and an equally enviable domestic life. His Ugandan relatives celebrated for days whenever he went back, and his family in England adored him.

The moment they were outside, Wes began to ask her about Bosnia. It was such a relief to talk freely that she hardly noticed time rushing by until they'd walked the length of the High and were almost at Magdalen bridge. Then she suddenly thought that if Wesley was working for a local TV station he must be well up on all the Oxford gossip. She couldn't let him leave until she'd pumped him about Gabriel.

'It'll be good to have Rebekah around in college. How's she coping?' Christa asked. 'Gabriel's such a hotbed of prejudice.'

Wesley grimaced. 'It's not the place I would have chosen for her, but it offered the best deal even without accommodation, and it takes a lot to faze Rebekah.'

'I didn't get accommodation either.'

'So where are you staying? I haven't even had time to ask you that.'

'In the bosom of my family, with my sister, but not for long, I hope. My brother-in-law's a fellow at Gabriel too, and sees my presence there as one huge threat.'

'Heavy,' said Wes, shaking his head. 'Still, you've got Mallory Farrar in college this year. He should help.'

'Not you as well!' said Christa. 'He seems to be everyone's good old boy. Does this mean you approve of First-World authors at last?' Wes was renowned for his partisan attitude to African writers.

'Not those clapped-out white males like Proust and James. But Farrar's OK. He gets Africa right most of the time. Miriam thinks he's the cat's pyjamas.'

'He seems like a typical reactionary to me.' Christa paused on the bridge, looking over the parapet at the lights reflected in the water below. 'Tell me, Wes, have you heard about any specific scams at Gabriel on the grapevine? To do with the Master, in particular? He seems to be at the heart of everything that's wrong with the college.'

Wes shrugged. 'The Dreaming Spires newsroom hears all sorts of rumours, but it's never got anything definite on Gabriel. The Master's a slippery fellow – like a djinn, nothing to get hold of, ever. The Swahili still believe in djinns, you know, Christa. You should hear the stories Miriam's mother tells.'

Christa laughed. 'How about the business of the Gabriel's Mill site being developed to benefit the Gabriel's Grounds Estate? Have you heard anything new?'

'Only that the college is still dragging its feet. Gabriel's always chronically slow. It's a shame. The estate urgently needs more facilities. I was filming unemployed kids there a few weeks ago. They aren't basically bad, but they've nothing to do. Why do you ask, anyway?'

'This is strictly off the record, but I think the college is going to renege on its promise.'

Wesley whistled in amazement. 'That'd be some let-down! It'd cause a huge outcry. How do you know?'

As the traffic thundered by at their back, Christa described the dinner party, and her subsequent conversation with the Dean.

'I talked to Leda Lennox about it this morning. She thinks I'm jumping to conclusions. But if I'm not, it's an incredibly clever scheme. However much the tenants' management association objects, the Master can always win by saying the college's resources must be used to put the welfare of his students first.'

'Well? To be fair, what's wrong with that?' said Wes. 'No one likes the man, but it could be true. The students do need more accommodation.'

'Yes, but it could be a very different story when the old library store's been converted into student accommodation, and the new store's in place, and the fuss is all forgotten. Then it'd be so easy for Governing Body to up the students' residence fees yet again on the pretext of improved facilities, and sneak in some lucrative commercial development on the rest of the Gabriel's Mill land. I gather it's a very large site.'

Wesley slowly shook his head.

'It's exactly the sort of thing the Master would do, but you don't have any proof, and he really doesn't have much time. He's retiring next summer.'

As a swirl of fallen leaves eddied along the pavement in a lorry's back draught, Christa doggedly ignored cold feet in every sense, and didn't reply.

'Come on, Christa. You know I'm right. In any case, I don't think you'd ever pin him down through official channels. The only way would be through some spectacular public exposé which caught him completely on the hop, and you simply haven't the resources for that.'

She sighed. Boanerges struck seven, reminding her that she was delaying Wes. She put her arm through his and they started to walk on.

'Best to forget it,' he said. 'Your seminars are going to be more than enough to cope with, if what Rebekah says about the students is true. Your first priority is to keep your head down, and make sure Randall doesn't fire you.' He squeezed her arm sympathetically. 'Look, we're almost in St Clement's. You can get a bus from here. But you must come for a meal and meet all the family soon. I'll send a message by Rebekah.'

Though Christa kept telling herself that she really must be sensible and follow Wes's advice, by the time her bus arrived she knew she wouldn't. The Gabriel's Mill lead was too important to ignore. But he was right at least about getting her teaching under control. She felt panicky every time she thought of her seminars, and they were now only a week away. She'd have to wait a while before taking on Goliath.

7

On the afternoon of her second visit to Jericho, Christa walked through the bright, windy streets thinking how good it would be to see Jessie again after the frustrations of the weekend, spent struggling to prepare her seminars between fruitless searches for accommodation. As the marital skirmishing at Ethelred Road increased she had become desperate to move, but Emma seemed equally desperate for her to stay, and so she'd again dropped the idea of taking temporary refuge in a hotel.

Though the leaves on the Virginia creeper had turned scarlet, and the sunflower petals were gone at last, yellow fruit still hung like lamps among the pear tree's branches in Jessie's front garden in Kitchener Road. Yet as Christa walked up the front path something seemed wrong. The front curtains were partly drawn, and there was no smoke spiralling from the chimney. She knocked on the door, expecting to hear Jessie's light tread, and instead picked up the thud of male feet.

Derek opened the door. Dismay spread over his face. He clapped his hand to his forehead.

'Miss Keith! I'd forgotten you were visiting today!' He stood aside to let her enter. 'Come in,' he said awkwardly. 'Come in and sit down. Mum isn't here, I'm afraid.'

She went into the sitting room, and took a seat, still puzzled. The fire was out. Jessie must be ill, in hospital perhaps.

'Is your mother not well? I'm so sorry. I wouldn't have bothered you if I'd known.'

He sat uncomfortably on the edge of the chair opposite her. 'I'm afraid it's worse than ill.'

The large-knuckled clumsy hands which had so carefully

gathered flowers for her at their last meeting were clenched. He was wearing a black tie, and she suddenly knew with horrible certainty what he was about to say.

'Mum's dead!' he burst out.

His face was twisted into the expression she'd seen too often in Bosnia on the faces of men trying not to cry. She'd never expected to witness it in Jericho, and for a moment it winded her.

'It was the day after your visit,' he went on. 'I came in on my way to work, and there she was, sitting so peacefully just where I am now. I thought she was asleep, but she'd passed away! It gave me a terrible shock. I can still hardly believe it.'

Christa couldn't take it in, either. It was as if the heart of the house had gone.

'I'm so sorry,' she said again, her voice catching in her throat. 'She was such a splendid old lady. She – she was one of the few people who felt like my friend here.'

'I'm really sorry I had to tell you this way,' said Derek. 'But what with the funeral and everything, I completely forgot about your visit until I saw you at the door.'

'She's been buried already?' Christa could still scarcely grasp that the larger-than-life Jessie was dead.

'It was a straightforward heart attack, and there was no reason to delay. We had the funeral yesterday. Jen did a slap-up tea afterwards.' Derek gave a rueful smile. 'Mum would have enjoyed it.'

He pulled his handkerchief from his pocket, and blew his nose like a trumpet blast. 'I've taken a few days off work to sort out her things. Jen took the clothes to Oxfam, and we're going to keep some of the ornaments, and one or two other bits. The rest'll go to auction. Mum'd turn in her grave if she knew, but her furniture's too old-fashioned for us.'

'What about the house?' Christa asked, forcing herself to make conversation. Talking about practicalities seemed to make him feel better.

'Mum was a fly old bird. She made it over to me some years ago, so the Social couldn't force her to sell it if she went into a home. She was a bit of a handful sometimes, but her heart was in the right place.'

He gave another trumpet blast, and put away the handkerchief. 'Still, life goes on, as she would have said. You look as if you could do with a cuppa. I was just about to make one anyway. Stay there, I'll be back in a mo.'

Christa sat quietly while he clattered about in the kitchen. She guessed he wanted to have something to do while he regained his equilibrium. She felt unexpectedly rocky herself. She wasn't ready for another death, even that of an old woman whom she scarcely knew.

Except that Jessie wasn't any old woman, Christa thought. In her own small way she was as much an affirmation of the human spirit as the Bosnian grandmothers she'd seen keeping the remnants of their families together on the road. She smiled to herself at the high-flown image, which Randall would have edited instantly out of any report, but it was a good thought that even in Oxford she'd found a victory for determination over the odds.

She went over to the parrot's cage and lifted the cover. It gave her an infinitely knowing look, sidestepped neatly along its perch, winked a yellow eye, and let out an ear-splitting screech.

'No use crying over spilt milk,' it cackled, sounding so like Jessie that for one heart-stopping moment Christa thought she must be in the room.

She let the cover fall as if she'd been stung, and shot back to her chair. As she collapsed into it, she had to suppress a strong inclination to burst into hysterical laughter. The cushions seemed to fit her back perfectly, and though Jessie had gone and the fire was out, the little room still had a welcoming effect. She rested her head against the crocheted throw, and thought how tired she was of never having a real home.

The realisation of what had just passed through her mind startled her almost more than the parrot's screech. She sat bolt upright, nearly knocking over a pot of maidenhair fern on the table at her elbow, as a yet more extraordinary thought occurred to her. She could offer to buy the house from Derek.

Immediately she tried to dismiss the idea. She wasn't even sure if he wanted to sell, the price would probably be far too high for her to buy outright, and her job situation was too shaky to get a mortgage. But the idea wouldn't go away. It became more enticing by the minute, until, veering sharply in the opposite direction, she told herself she was being a hopeless defeatist, and that it was worth a try.

Derek reappeared bearing two mugs of tea with a strange yellowish tinge.

'I'm afraid it's evaporated milk,' he said. 'Mum kept a great store of the stuff. I wish you could have come to the funeral tea. Jen made a plum cake, and we had sherry as well. Mum always said she wanted a good send-off.'

Christa let him talk about it a little longer, then said with unusual diffidence, surprised by how scared she was at the thought of losing her chance, 'Are you going to keep the house? Perhaps you've children of your own who'd like to live here?'

'Our daughters are already settled. No, it's a big break with the past, but I'm going to put it on the market. The longer it's empty, the more likely we are to have trouble with vandals, especially with lads from Gabriel's Grounds roaming about.'

'I'm looking for somewhere myself,' said Christa tentatively. 'I'd love to buy it, but it depends how much you're asking.'

He stared at her for a moment. 'I thought you were staying in one of the colleges.'

'I've a fellowship, but no accommodation.'

'Wouldn't it be too old-fashioned for someone like you? I don't intend to refurbish, you know.'

'I like it exactly as it is,' said Christa, with hasty mental reservations about the scullery, and the terrifying bathroom geyser.

'How much could you afford, then?'

Cheerfully saying goodbye to a vacation holiday in the Maldives, Christa named a sum which would almost wipe out her deposit account, but which she knew was probably at least ten thousand pounds below the house's true worth.

He sighed. 'That's a good bit less than I was expecting.'

'Cash,' said Christa. 'And I'm not in a chain.'

'The Oxford yuppies fight over cottages like this.'

'There aren't many yuppies left these days. And as long as a surveyor said the house was basically sound, I wouldn't quibble over minor repairs. Some buyers can haggle for ages over details, you know.'

'I'd never have let Mum live in a house that wasn't sound,' said Derek indignantly, but she could see he was beginning to waver already.

'I suppose it would save on estate agent's fees,' he went on, 'and a lot of bother into the bargain.'

He produced a small notebook, and proceeded to jot down some sums with a stub of pencil.

'How about if you bought the contents outright for another two thousand?' he said, looking up when he'd finished his calculations. 'It's still way off the price I'd thought of, but Mum did take a great fancy to you. It'd be good to have someone she liked in the old place.'

'Done, subject to a survey and so on, of course,' said Christa recklessly, thinking she'd be almost cleared out financially, but it was still worth it.

'Hang on a minute. There's something else. We've been wondering what to do about the parrot. Jen's never taken to it – she hates mess – but Mum would have wanted it to have a good home. Would you keep Poppy here with you?'

Christa swallowed. She'd never had a pet in her life, let alone one with attitude, but it wasn't much to do for Jessie, after all.

'Fine by me, 'she said.

Derek scribbled a few more calculations. 'Right then. One last point, and if you agree, we can call it a deal.'

'Yes?' she said, wondering if he was going to ask her to take over a troop of Scouts as well.

'The sale'll probably take two or three months to go through, and I'd prefer the house not to stay empty so long. Could you rent it at the going rate, say six hundred a month, until the sale's complete? I'd get a proper tenancy agreement drawn up, of course.'

The business Derek worked for must run like clockwork, Christa thought. He was no softie financially. He'd effectively added several thousand more to the price she'd offered, but she was keener than ever to close the sale. The more she committed herself, the more right it felt.

'No problem. I can move in right away,' she said.

Christa arranged with Derek to take over the house the following

Friday, though she could hardly spare the time. Her first seminar at Gabriel now loomed like a major operation. She'd pinned a course reading list on the senior tutor's noticeboard, but Piers was in a discouraging mood when she pumped him for more advice.

He scanned the list of students she'd given him.

'You'll need to keep an eye on the trouble makers here. Justin Seddon, for instance. He's easy to spot. Looks like Lord Fauntleroy grown up, has media ambitions, a daddy with mega-bucks, and wastes a bloody good mind on anything but learning.'

'I suppose that means he wants to be a television presenter without any of the spade work?'

'Afraid so. And Steve Drew could be a problem. He fought his way up through an inner London comprehensive. He's extremely bright too. Gabriel gave him a bursary, mainly as a PR move, I suspect. But Steve's a bit rough round the edges, and some of the older dons let him know it. As a result he wastes most of his time trying to hammer the system. He's been making a lot of waves about student accommodation.'

'Poor kid. I know how he feels.'

'Wait a bit before sympathising. He has media ambitions as well, though he's not as pretty as Justin.' Piers handed her back the list. 'And the Dean's sure to give you some hole-in-the-wall lecture room, so make sure you check it out first.'

Christa's confidence level had sunk alarmingly by the time she arrived at the Dean's office to borrow the keys to her seminar room for a preliminary survey. But Miss Harker at least seemed less fraught than before. She became pink with pleasure when Christa presented her with a replacement box of biscuits.

'How kind of you, my dear,' she said, as she gazed delightedly at the ranks of Bourbons and custard creams nestling within their paper frills. 'Perhaps you'd like to join me for elevenses when you return.'

Christa needed something stronger than coffee after inspecting her room. Narrow poorly fitting windows looked on to a feature-less wall, and a rusty heating pipe snaking round the ceiling failed to dispel a strong smell of damp. There was a lecturer's desk of Dickensian proportions, and the metal chairs were welded together in rigid rows which made any less formal arrangement impossible.

She felt so dispirited as she headed back towards Miss Harker's office that she took the wrong turning, and found herself walking down a long oak-panelled passage in a part of college she didn't know. One of the doors was slightly open. She was startled to hear Mallory Farrar's voice, and couldn't resist peering inside.

He was giving an impromptu talk, obviously by popular request, to those students who had already arrived. The room was crowded with them, their attention riveted on him as he sat sideways on a table, his gown half off his shoulders. Even the bunch of rugby scrum halves in one corner was enthralled. In spite of herself, Christa began to listen too, then wished she hadn't, for his reputation was clearly deserved.

Imagery laced with wit and magical powers of description were underpinned by comment as trenchant as any war-correspondent's. It wasn't an ego-trip, either, Christa thought irritably. He encouraged participation, treating dull and percep-tive questions alike with the same attentive courtesy.

Most infuriating still, the room he'd been allocated was perfect for seminars: intimate, yet large enough not to feel crowded. Autumn sunshine flooded through the windows, waking the mahogany hue of chairs arranged in a casual semi-circle, throw-ing into relief the acanthus-moulded ceiling, and falling as if prearranged on Farrar's smooth blond hair.

Frustrated and despondent, wondering how she could hope to match such a performance, Christa marched straight back to Miss Harker's office, clashed the keys down on her desk, and demanded to see the Dean.

Miss Harker was checking through carbon copies with one hand clamped to her temple, and reacted as if she'd asked to speak to Gabriel himself.

'Really, Miss Keith, I'm telling you the truth. He's here, yes, but he never sees anyone without an appointment.'

'Why not? I can't hear any voices through the door, so he's obviously alone.'

'He's trying to work out a schedule for the royal visit. It needs all his concentration. I think you should sit down and have a quiet cup of coffee with me.'

'My seminars need all my concentration, and I've been given an impossible room. I have to see him now.'

'I truly wouldn't advise it, Miss Keith. You've already . . .'

She broke off, looking deeply embarrassed. Christa instantly guessed what she'd been about to say.

'I've already rocked the boat. Good, and I'm about to rock it a whole lot more!'

She wrenched open the inner door. The Dean reposed in a magnificent high-backed Sheraton chair, some typewritten papers held loosely to his chest, trembling to his snores. His walnut roll-top desk, strewn with more papers, would have sent an 'Antiques Roadshow' expert into ecstasies. Behind him a log fire crackled beneath a wooden chimney piece carved with pineapples and palms. The room was warm enough to raise real pineapples, unlike Miss Harker's cubby hole which could have doubled as an eighteenth-century ice-house.

Christa kicked the door shut with her foot. The Dean sat up in the midst of a strangled gurgle like an airlock in a pipe.

'Miss Keith!' His eyes focused hazily on her. 'I'm not available now, I'm afraid. Didn't Miss Harker tell you?'

'Yes, she did. But you look very available to me. I want to know why I've been given a seminar room with all the facilities of a dungeon?'

His chins shook like ripples of pink blancmange as he pulled himself together. 'I thought the Master had explained to you – the lateness of your appointment and so on,' he bumbled.

'The timetable had only just been made up when we first met. I can't accept that excuse, especially when Mallory Farrar has again been given such ideal facilities. It's gross discrimination, and I intend to complain directly to Lord Judd.'

The Dean burst into a fit of coughing which left him almost speechless. She watched, forcing herself not to offer help. She had no intention of whining to Jimmy Judd, but she guessed the Dean wouldn't dare to call her bluff. As he began to regain his breath he realised there were papers in his hand, gave Christa a highly suspicious look, and shuffled them quickly into a desk drawer.

Instantly she began to wonder if they had something to do with Gabriel's Mill.

'I might be able to find some alternative, but I certainly can't arrange anything before next week,' he said, his chins going into overdrive in his eagerness to convince her.

'And I certainly can't wait longer than a week before faxing Lord Judd,' Christa replied, her mind still on the papers in the drawer. 'So I shall expect greatly improved surroundings for my second seminar.'

'Of course, of course. Just leave it in my hands,' he said smoothly, though when the telephone rang he snatched at the receiver like a life-belt.

He listened for a few moments, then turned to her with a smile of pure relief.

'The Duke's aide has just arrived to discuss his visit. Do forgive me, but I really must leave you now.'

He rose from the chair like a surfacing hippo, swept the folds of his gown about him, and ushered her into the outer office. Miss Harker bunkered down behind her typewriter as the Dean sailed past, totally ignoring her.

'I'm so sorry, Miss Keith. I can assure you the allocation was nothing to do with me,' she said, popping out like a rabbit once he'd disappeared, and looking as if she might burst into tears.

Christa, still grappling with frustration, only just refrained from tapping her foot impatiently on the floor, and suggesting that Miss Harker took classes in self-assertion as well as word-processing. She consoled herself with the thought that the Dean wouldn't last an hour at Apollo.

'Why do you put up with it, Miss Harker? It's obviously not good for you here,' she asked impulsively. 'Why don't you take early retirement?'

Miss Harker took a second aspirin with a sip of water.

'It's kind of you to be concerned. Not many people care at Gabriel these days. Though I'd love to take early retirement, I stay on because the office is preferable to home. I live with my elder sister. She's a dear soul, but she has the beginnings of Alzheimer's.'

Christa's anger began to evaporate as she took in Miss Harker's words. She had the disconcerting thought that in a different way her bravery was probably quite as great as anyone's in Sarajevo.

'Of course, doing one's duty is quite alien to the young today. It's all doing one's own thing instead,' Miss Harker went on.

'Aren't you being a bit hard on us? And I'm sure you could find a less stressful job if you tried.'

'I suppose I stay out of a sort of loyalty to Gabriel as it was,' Miss Harker replied, distractedly sorting carbon copies into numbered heaps. 'I loved my work when old Professor Saltash was Master. Now there was a most delightful and thoughtful person. Though I shouldn't say so, the Dean has changed completely since he left.'

She pursed her lips, and gathered up the papers. 'I just have to take these along to the general office. They're urgent. I'll be back in a moment to make some coffee.'

Christa could scarcely believe her luck. She had no idea how far away the general office was, but it was too good a chance to miss. The moment Miss Harker disappeared, she rushed back through the inner door, feeling like an industrial spy as she delved into the drawer.

Exactly as she'd suspected, she found a proposal from the Master for a library store, administrative offices, and staff housing at Gabriel's Mill, though with infuriating caution he didn't mention the architect's name. The document clipped to it made her head reel. She'd just skimmed through the proposal for a second-stage development incorporating an up-market shopping mall, when she heard Miss Harker clopping back like a busy donkey along the corridor.

Christa longed to take the report, but daren't. Suspicion would instantly fall on her, or, worse still, on Miss Harker if she did. She only had time to shuffle the papers back into the drawer and scurry into the outer office, just before Miss Harker reappeared.

'Now,' said the secretary happily, 'if you wait another moment I'll put the kettle on, and we can have our elevenses at last.'

By the time Christa left Gabriel, she was convinced that Miss Harker knew nothing about the plans. She hadn't reacted to the heaviest hints, and it was impossible to imagine her telling a lie, even in the interests of the Dean. Christa was so buoyed up at having her suspicions confirmed that it was hard to think of anything else, even though any futher investigations would be considerably hampered by not knowing the architect's name.

By now it was almost midday, and she had to drag her mind from her newly acquired information, and dash back to Ethelred Road to pack before the move to Jericho. Emma and Phil were at work, but the primary schools were closed for the day for a teachers' conference. Pansy sat on the front step watching Christa cram her possessions into the Mini.

Noelene, who was entertaining another au pair to coffee, had refused to take her to visit Chel, and in revenge Pansy was wearing Noelene's high-heeled snakeskin boots. Her hair, plaited too tightly because Noelene was in a hurry, stuck out beneath one of Emma's hats, a cylindrical black felt recently acquired for autumn gatherings of the college wives. She looked like a pixie peering from a stove pipe.

'My Mummy's got *hundreds* more things than you,' she observed.

'So I've noticed. Don't get too many things too soon, Pansy, or you'll miss out on a lot of fun.' Christa shoved the last box into the boot, and just managed to close the lid.

'Well, I'm off now,' she said with a smile, careful not to attempt the smallest embrace.

Pansy was sucking the end of a plait and still scowling horribly, but she suddenly hurtled off the step, throwing herself at Christa and hugging her tightly round the waist.

'I don't want you to go,' she mumbled into Christa's jacket.

'Hey, hey, Pansy. Calm down,' said Christa in amazement. 'I'm not going far, only to Jericho. You can visit me any time.'

'Any time Mummy's got time, and that's never. Daddy won't let me, anyway. I heard him tell Mummy you were a subversive influence. What does subversive mean?'

'Enjoying yourself,' said Christa under her breath. It was something Phil knew little about. Aloud, she said, 'I'm sure Mummy will bring you over soon.'

Pansy looked doubtful, hung her head, returned her plait to her mouth, and mooched back to the step. She dumped herself down and sat staring reproachfully at Christa, her eyes enormous under the brim of the hat.

Christa got in the car, switched on the engine, and opened the window. She leaned out to wave goodbye to Pansy and saw two fat tears trickling down her cheeks.

'Damn, damn, damn!' muttered Christa, trying to quell the lump in her own throat. She clashed the gears furiously as she accelerated out of the drive. 'I refuse to be dragged into the family again, even by Pansy, I absolutely refuse!'

Christa was still trying to forget Pansy's expression when she arrived outside her new home in Kitchener Road. Derek had brought her the keys on his way to work that morning. She unlocked the front door, lugged her suitcases and boxes up the leaf-strewn path, and dumped them by the hall stand.

The house was very quiet. It seemed to be waiting to see what she would do. All she could hear was the clock ticking like a busy mechanical heart. It was a strange feeling to be responsible for bricks and mortar of her own. She'd always thought it would make her feel trapped, but strangely enough it didn't.

She went into the sitting room. The sun was falling on pots of scented-leaved geraniums at a table by the bay window, filling the air with their gentle fragrance. The parrot clambered up the side of the cage and hung there, as if she too was sizing Christa up.

In the grate Derek had neatly laid a boy scout edifice of twigs and sticks topped with clinker and small pieces of coal. The scuttle was full, and on the mantelpiece reposed a note under a box of matches.

In neat handwriting was written: 'Services all on. Please use contents of Mum's kitchen store. Best of luck, D. Hutt'.

Christa set a match to the fire. The sticks caught at once. She shoved the guard in place and wandered into the kitchen. Derek had placed some onions, a cauliflower and a huge bunch of carrots in a basket on the table. She still held the matches, and lit the gas under the kettle, carefully adjusting the flames with a brass tap.

She peered into the pantry. The shelves were groaning with the strongly flavoured, nostalgic food beloved of the very old: tins of pineapple, pilchards and rice pudding, drums of cocoa, jars of Ovaltine, tea and instant coffee, and a mountain of canned evaporated milk. On the tiled floor were some bottles of homemade wine.

Christa walked through the scullery, averting her eyes from the copper as she resolved to get a washing machine next day, and went into the garden. Derek had even tidied it for the winter. She made her way along the path to the water's edge. A narrow boat came by, its wake rocking the drifting weeds by the bank.

When she'd picked a few late sprays of buddleia, she came back into the kitchen where the kettle was whistling like a hysterical referee. She found a vase, made herself some coffee and returned to the fire, where she put the flowers on the mantelpiece, which was now empty except for a couple of bulging-eyed china puppies.

It looked bare without the rest of Jessie's ornaments. Christa fetched her cassette player and a framed photo of Matt from one of the boxes in the hall. She put them next to the flowers, slotted in an Eddie Grant tape, and carried away as always by the music's lazy charm, took a few light-hearted steps. Poppaea clearly approved. She too began to perform a stately hopping dance, weaving back and forth along her perch and bobbing her head.

Christa laughed and sat in Jessie's chair to finish her coffee before unpacking the rest of her things. She looked at the photo of Matt, and for the first time was able to think of him without the usual sense of guilt and loss. Her newfound calm emboldened her to take the ever-present problem of her seminars from the back of her mind, and try to deal with it rationally.

She wondered what Matt would have said, and remembering his boundless optimism, was tempted to jettison Piers' advice and her carefully prepared plans entirely, and teach the students in a hands-on way after all.

But to do that, she mused, it would be necessary to have at least two video cameras, and an editing console, which she now couldn't possibly afford. Most difficult of all, she'd need a project which would grab both herself and the students, who, according to Piers, weren't interested in current affairs.

Christa looked at Matt's photo again. He'd always been a great one for impromptu decisions. She decided to trust in whatever luck she had left, and play the whole thing by ear.

*　　*　　*

Christa's weekend was spent settling into the house and trying to inject some life into her notes for the first seminar. On Monday morning she came into work early to set up an antiquated projector from the college store. Though it weighed at least a stone, and the lens adjustment and slide changing were manual, it had to do. Afterwards she took refuge in the deserted SCR, and when Boanerges sounded nine strokes, deliberately waited another five minutes before setting off for her class.

The students' rooms were still quiet after the weekend, though a morose porter was collecting up empty beer cans from the dew-soaked grass in King's Quad. Christa braced herself against the chill breeze rustling the withered rose heads on the college walls, and thought that she'd rather be going to the worst front-line assignment.

The seminar room had not been changed and was more dismal than ever, though as a concession she now had a table instead of a desk, and moveable chairs which she'd arranged less formally. The students looked cold and dismal too. The only cheerful face, in the front row, was Rebekah's. She was wisely wearing a fake fur jacket in lipstick red over a heavy sweater and leggings.

Christa's seminars were open to all the students, but her audience was only about twenty. Some harassed-looking third-years were feverishly reading books quite unconnected with her class, presumably for looming tutorials. Donna Caldwell, the student she'd met earlier with the Master, was there, and a knot of male rowers appeared in sweat shirts and jogging pants at the last moment. Piers had told Christa that Gabriel was head of the river, but only by slanting its scholarships heavily in favour of applicants with more brawn than brain.

'They're dead wood intellectually,' he'd said. 'Most of them'll be lucky to scrape by with thirds, but they have to turn up at a few lectures to keep their tutors happy. They'll see your seminars as a soft option.'

If Randall had wanted to punish her, he couldn't have found a more effective way of doing it, Christa thought. Apart from Rebekah, nothing was going to interest this lot. Grimly she took a roll call, determined to identify the trouble makers Piers had mentioned.

Justin Seddon sat at the back, tall and indolent with waving hair pushed back from a face like a deviant angel's. He wore a dark red jacket and narrow camel-coloured chinos. His brogue-clad feet were propped on the chair in front of him.

Steve Drew's hair was like harvest stubble. He had round black-rimmed spectacles and a truculent expression. His feet, in calf-high, battle-scarred boots, looked as if they were itching to trip someone up.

Feeling like a suicide pilot, Christa plunged into an account of the women reporters of the Boer War. It was a subject which fascinated her, but, it soon became apparent, not her students. Though she'd worked very hard on her presentation, they were determined to be bored. Halfway through, the projector stuck, and even her hard-won expertise at coping with mechanical failures couldn't fix it.

By this time the students seemed almost asleep. Three-quarters of the way through the seminar Justin sloped out of the room, and reappeared a few minutes later in a strong aura of ganja. Christa almost felt she could have done with a joint herself. All her attempts at initiating discussion were met with bored, or sleepy, or disengaged stares.

She ploughed on to the end, and then rashly asked for questions. After Rebekah had made her feel falsely confident with a good query on Reuters, no one else spoke up. The silence became embarrassing as the students began to look pointedly towards the door. Christa knew that if she didn't get a grip on them now, she'd end up next week without an audience. And though that would be a relief in a way, she couldn't bear the thought of the malicious glances in the SCR.

'Right,' she said, in a voice she normally only used when it was necessary to impress on obstructive officials that she intended to have her way, 'it's not been hard to get the message that you were deeply unimpressed by the last hour. So, before you go, perhaps you could tell me what would interest you? Or, indeed, if anything interests you? For instance, you may have noticed that I've been talking about human suffering on a huge scale. Do I take it that you feel insulated from that sort of thing here?'

It was a risk to try goading them. She could alienate them

all. As it was, several of the first-years were already looking embarrassed and sidling towards the door, and most of the rowing set were gathering up their books.

Justin Seddon flicked back a lock of hair in a curiously insolent manner.

'We've zapped out of the past. Don't you agree with Fukuyama, that we've arrived at the end of history?'

Christa remembered Piers had urged her to study the postmodernist philosphers in depth, but she'd only skimmed through their latest books in the most cursory way. The rowers were already hurtling like panicked buffalo towards the door, leaving just one stolid representative behind. She waited for the thud of their feet to subside before answering.

The remaining students had suddenly become amazingly alert at the prospect of some teacher-baiting. Christa frantically called up her small store of information on Fukuyama's work.

'Only the end of history in that most nations now accept democracy as the best kind of government,' she replied.

'Democracy is a construct of the bourgeoisie,' said Justin witheringly. 'In fact everything's a construct, as far as I can see, so why bother?'

The few freshers left were gazing at him wide-eyed. The remaining rower looked as if his brains were full of polystyrene granules. Christa glanced at her student list again. Justin was reading PPE – Politics, Philosophy and Economics.

'Democracy's to do with politics. Presumably you have some interest in that?'

'Politics sucks,' he said languidly. 'Everyone knows that running about in the cold with a placard is as much use as listening to a scratched John Lennon disc.'

Christa suddenly saw how she might still win the argument, if he wasn't already too stoned to take in her answer.

'What about college politics? I gather some of you have some fairly strong ideas about your accommodation, for instance.'

'Ever seen what the Master does with democracy?' Justin asked. 'That's why the students never get anywhere except up shit creek.'

He must be stoned, or infinitely sure of himself and his father's money, to risk criticising the Master so openly to a college fellow, thought Christa. But in an odd way she admired his frankness. With his assets there was no need for him to knock the system.

'Yeah, the Master turns democracy arse over tip,' said Steve, folding his arms over his chest, and jutting out a pugnacious chin. 'He blatantly favours middle-class kids. That's why fuckers like you, Seddon, won't fight back. You don't need to.'

'I don't fight because I'm not a naive peasant like you,' said Justin, grinning amiably at him.

'Why don't you just bog off to your dad's grouse moor, then, where you can exploit the peasants as much as you like?' retorted Steve, equally unperturbed.

Rebekah, buttoning her jacket in the front row, raised her eyebrows at Christa. 'They're always like this, poor little lads, full of hot air. They're both longing to work in telly, but ask them to repeat what they've just said about the Master to camera, and they'd both chicken out.'

'Typical post-grad talk,' said Steve. 'You slag off the way things are run here just as much as us, but you won't risk your bursary by doing anything about it. I would. I think smashing the present system at Gabriel is worth it.'

'I'd have a go if someone came up with a good enough plan,' said Rebekah calmly. 'But no one has.'

It was too much for Christa. She'd suddenly seen how she could teach them in a hands-on way after all, and manage to keep their interest at the same time. All she had to do was get the film equipment, and let them have their heads making a programme from a student viewpoint on what was wrong with Gabriel. She'd simply act as the facilitator, and they could decide themselves when it was finished whether to risk trying for actual transmission.

'OK, OK, I get the message,' she said, before she lost her last vestige of control. She longed to say she agreed with them, but that would make her own position even more precarious. 'If you feel so strongly, perhaps you'd like to put your money where your mouth is. None of this is official yet, so you haven't heard me say it, but if you're here next week we can discuss ways of getting you all in front of a camera, and you can try to put Gabriel right.'

Boanerges began to ring out ten o'clock, providentially signalling the end of the seminar, for she'd had no time to work out
a format for the programme. Her mind was rushing ahead like
a souped-up Nintendo game as she scanned the students' faces
for a reaction.

Justin and Steve were already moving towards the exit. For
an awful moment Christa thought she'd lost them, but at the
last minute Steve stopped in the doorway, lounging against the
frame with one booted foot crossed over the other so that no
one else could leave.

'Do you really mean that?' he demanded.

Suppressing a sergeant-major impulse to tell him to stand up
straight, she smiled and said, 'Yes, I do, if you feel you can
take it.'

'You mean, show us the proper inside TV stuff, so we'd all get
a chance at making a programme and it'd go out on air in real
time?' said Justin, actually beginning to look excited.

'Yes,' she said even more rashly, though she had no idea if
she'd be able to persuade any TV company to screen it. 'But
when the programme was in the can, you'd have to make
a decision between yourselves about whether you wanted it
shown. Don't forget you'd be laying yourselves on the line. It's
what all good programme-makers do to a certain extent, but it
has special dangers for you.'

'We can hack it, no sweat,' said Justin grandly. 'So what form
would this programme take? Would it be like "Newsnight"?'

Justin was hooked, thought Christa with growing amusement.
He clearly saw himself as a second Jeremy Paxman. It would be
fun educating him.

'Turn up next week, and you'll find out.'

'OK, then,' he said, 'we'll see what we can do. I expect we can
persuade some of the others to come in on it, can't we, Steve?'

'Maybe.' Steve stared belligerently at Christa. 'But you'd better
not be bull-shitting us, or you won't have a class any more.'

'It'll work out, I promise you. All I ask is that you don't talk
about this outside until next week. I need a little time to set it
up first.'

'Right,' said Justin. He turned on the other students. 'So you
lot had better not go shooting off your mouths in the bar tonight.

We don't want things fucked up before they've even got off the ground.'

Rebekah's eyes were even rounder as the last student filed out.

'It sounds great, but how are you going to carry it through?' she asked. 'You'll have to get the Master's permission before you can even begin.'

'Don't worry. It's no problem,' lied Christa.

'You're certainly chancing your arm,' said Rebekah admiringly. 'If it misfires, the Master'll be your enemy for life.'

'I've a fair number of enemies dotted around the world already. I'd be no good as a reporter if I hadn't. Now how about fixing a time to discuss that dissertation of yours?'

After Rebekah had arranged to visit her in Jericho, and left for another seminar, Christa sank on to one of the empty seats. Though there were enormous obstacles ahead, the surge of enthusiasm which always accompanied a new professional commitment was already kicking in. It had been absent so long that she felt almost drunk with the effect.

She'd spend the rest of the day sussing out the best deals on camera equipment, she told herself excitedly. And next morning, after she'd visited Stacey's salon to see if Glenn could give her a quote for some alterations to the house, she'd shop for a suit to wear at the Master's drinks party. If she wanted to beat him and the Gabriel system, she had to put on a very good show of joining them first.

8 ∫

When Christa arrived outside Stacey's salon in Walton Street next morning, she found that Howl had been been at work overnight. Glaziers were replacing the window of a butcher's shop a few doors away. The marble display slabs had been shattered by hammer blows, and jars of pickle and chutney lay smashed on the floor.

The proprietor, a man in his fifties with a grey, distraught face, who was painting out a 'Meat is Murder' slogan sprayed on the wall, stopped to speak to a neighbour as Christa passed.

'They even ruined the meat in my cold store,' she heard him say. 'And they left a note threatening to return if I didn't close down. My wife's been taken to hospital with the worry of it all.'

Again Christa felt sickened by Howl's bullying violence, and her reaction was intensified by a strangely proprietory rush of anger that they should target Jericho.

But at least Stacey's salon was unharmed. A menagerie of toy animals peered coyly from the tropical plants framing the window, and as Christa pushed open the door she was greeted by a warm, scented blast of air. A bird-like babble of voices, and the music of Deep Forest wafting from a cassette player, made her feel as if she'd been transported to the Amazon.

A junior bustled about collecting used towels. Stacey, in a pale blue angora crop top and stretch jodhpurs, hovered over the last stages of a blow-dry. She caught sight of the new arrival in the mirror, thrust an armful of magazines at her client, and hurried over.

'Christa! I'd given up hoping to see you here! Have you come for a re-style after all?'

'I just wanted Glenn's address. I've taken on a house in Jericho. I wondered if he'd come over and discuss some alterations.'

'No probs,' Stacey answered, proudly handing Christa one of his business cards from a pile at the front of the reception desk. 'He's doing some work in Plantation Road just now, so he can easily give you a quote.'

'Thanks. How are things? I see Howl's been at it again. I hope they kept away from you?' Christa had lowered her voice as she pushed the card into her pocket, but the other assistant was engrossed in painting highlights into a client's hair.

'I was lucky. Glenn must have really put them off, bless him.' Stacey bent to adjust a koala bear with candy pink fur peering from a fern by the desk. Though Christa couldn't see her face, she could hear the embarrassment in her voice. 'But they wrecked the shop down the road last night, and the butcher's not a bad old bloke in his way. I'd just persuaded him to stop selling factory-farmed chicken.' She kept her face turned from Christa as she added, 'It made me feel bad about not giving you that contact number.'

Christa just managed not to comment. She might still get her lead, if Stacey had already changed her thinking this much. But it would be only too easy to scare off someone so stubborn and so timid.

'Why don't you and Glenn come round for a drink on Sunday?' she suggested. 'He could give me a quote then, and you could see the house as well.'

Stacey straightened up, relief blossoming all over her face at the change of subject.

'Thanks. That'd be great. I'd love to.'

Christa took up another of Glenn's cards from the desk, and a pencil with a rubber Teddy bear's head on the end.

'I'll put down the address and phone number for you, then you can give me a ring.'

As she wrote she could sense Stacey's eyes on her. When she looked up to give her the card, Stacey leaned forward and burst out eagerly, 'Honest, Christa, I wish you'd let me fix your hair. It's brilliant – the colour, the texture, everything – but it's doing nothing for you, and French plaits went out ages ago.'

Christa glanced in the mirror behind the reception desk, and seeing herself under the bright salon light, thought that perhaps she did look a little too like the post-tornado Dorothy in *The Wizard of Oz*.

'If you've got an hour to spare I could do you a re-style now,' pressed Stacey. 'My present lady's almost finished, and lunch-time's usually quiet.'

Christa hesitated. After three months in the midst of the harshest of battles it was hard to adjust to the ambience of the salon.

'You won't be disappointed, honest,' said Stacey earnestly.

Christa began to give way. The Deep Forest music, the rushing of water as the junior cleaned a washbasin, and the light-hearted background chatter, were all having a surprisingly releasing effect.

'And if you haven't had lunch I can send for a carry-out from the Jericho Café along the road. They do terrific filled baguettes,' Stacey said triumphantly.

Christa finally succumbed. 'Sounds like an offer I can't refuse,' she said with a grin.

Fifteen minutes later her hair had been doused in coconut shampoo, and she sat cocooned in a pastel cape while Stacey scissored away with the concentration of a surgeon perfecting her amputation technique.

Christa tried not to look at the locks of hair falling noiselessly around her. Stacey, in a brief pause, misinterpreted her expression.

'You don't need to worry about the products we use. They're not animal-tested.'

'Are you back with the Peaceable Kingdom again?'

'Yeah, but it seems a bit like an old dears' tea-party after Howl.'

'Maybe you could try to shake them up a bit.'

'I'm no good at things like that. They need someone more like you.'

'I'm not much good at anything at the moment.'

Since her return from Bosnia, Christa hadn't admitted her feelings so openly to anyone, apart from Emma. In the mirror Stacey's eyes were wide with sympathy.

'This is just a bad patch. Your luck's bound to change. And you're really lucky to have a house of your own.'

Christa's gaze moved apprehensively to her own image in the mirror. Her hair, damp and bedraggled as seaweed at low tide, now hung limply on a level with her shoulders. She looked like an escapee from *Waterworld*.

'I think you're lucky to have found someone like Glenn,' Christa said, hoping that she wasn't going to have her appearance wrecked as well as her life. 'Gareth couldn't leave me fast enough once he'd put the boot in.'

'Did you really love him?' Stacey was lifting the damp hair with a comb and studying it intently, teeth clamped on her lower lip in deep concentration.

'Yes, I did,' Christa answered miserably.

As Stacey began to anchor clumps of hair to the top of her head with butterfly clips, Christa wondered what it was about hairdressing salons which made women act as if they were in a confessional. Before Gareth she never had any trouble attracting or keeping men, but neither had she wanted to live with any of them. The problem was always how to extricate herself without too much damage to their self-esteem. Yet Gareth, the one man she could have lived with, had ditched her without a shred of sensitivity or remorse.

She watched the scissors approaching her defenceless head again, and suddenly knew that she couldn't cope with another disaster. She began to struggle out of the cape.

'Sorry, Stacey, but I don't think I can take having more cut off at the moment. Just leave it as a long bob, and I'll dry it at home.'

Stacey looked horrified. 'You can't go out into the street like that! I swear to you, it's going to look terrific.'

Christa shook her head, fumbling still with the cape, and longing to be alone.

'And what about my professional reputation?' Stacey was beginning to sound as desperate as Christa. 'I know it can't seem any big deal compared to yours, but you are my responsibility, you know.'

'I'm sorry,' Christa said again, feeling a complete heel. 'Truly, it's nothing to do with you. It's just the way things hit me sometimes.'

She pulled herself free from the cape and threw it on to the ledge in front of the mirror. Stacey was almost as pale as she had been on the night of the Howl attack. Clutching the back of Christa's chair, she gulped and said in a breathless rush, 'If I let you have the contact number for Howl, will you stay?'

Christa subsided into the chair, gazing at her in astonishment.

'I thought it was so important for you not to take any more risks?'

'I think it's important for you to let me finish your hair.' Stacey's voice was shaking in her desperation to express herself. 'Otherwise it'll be just another defeat for you, if you see what I mean.'

God, how selfish can I get, thought Christa, when I drive Stacey into offering to do something for me that terrifies her and might endanger the salon? Reluctantly she picked up the cape.

'It's all right. I'll stay. And I don't want the number, either,' she said, resigning herself to a double sacrifice.

'But I want you to have it,' said Stacey. 'I've been thinking about Howl all morning. The butcher's wife along the road collapsed with shock, and the Institute security guard's still in hospital. It's just as bad to hurt a human being as an animal, in my opinion. Howl needs investigating. So how about it?'

Christa gazed first at Stacey's solemn face in the mirror, then at her own. Her hair was beginning to dry and didn't look quite so bad after all. She smiled.

'Glenn'll probably do me over, but OK, throw in an espresso with that baguette, and it's a deal.'

'I'll cope with Glenn, and your hair's going to be great, trust me,' said Stacey, picking up the scissors again with a huge smile of relief.

An hour later, leaving the salon with the Howl contact number safely in her pocket, Christa was amazed to discover that Stacey had been right. Casting surreptitious glances at her reflection in the shop windows of Walton Street, she took in her altered image at leisure: hair cut short at the nape of her neck, longer at the sides, swept in a provocative wave over one eye, with the gloss and movement of wind-rippled wheat, and nothing faintly Dorothy-ish about it any more.

She even felt she might just survive the Gabriel drinks party the following day. While she was still on a high she spent the rest of the afternoon in the boutiques of Little Clarendon Street shopping for clothes which were sexy but serious, clothes designed to generate the maximum of sober allure. Investigating Howl would have to take a back seat for a while. She would never have thought it possible, but she was suddenly far more interested in her seminars.

Still determined to out-Herod Herod next morning, Christa walked to the Public Library and spent a couple of hours catching up on old reports of the Waylandsbury dig. The only hope she had of lulling the Master into trusting her was with his own weapon: flattery. And for that she needed to know everything about his crowning professional glory.

She turned up treasure of her own in the shape of a yellowing edition of the *Illustrated London News* which was almost entirely devoted to an account of the dig. The story of the Waylandsbury Hoard had clearly enthralled the public of the early sixties, only just emerging from the austerity of the post-war years. Best of all, it had pages of remarkably clear photos.

She spent some time at the copier, and on the way out in search of coffee, passed a notice board with details of local events. One of the notices was headed by the Dreaming Spires logo, a silhouette of the Oxford skyline. She began to skim through it, idly at first, and then with rising excitement when she realised it was advertising a competition for media students.

The requirements were satisfactorily loose: a forty-minute television programme, including some reportage, on a subject of local interest, produced by any tertiary college within a fifty-mile radius of Oxford. Transmission was guaranteed for the short-listed entries, which would be shown the following summer. It was perfect for her class, and Randall couldn't possibly object to her part in something with such an educational slant.

The enquiry desk was even able to supply an application form, which she tucked away with the photocopy of the Waylandsbury article to study later. It had been a profitable day so far, she thought. She'd pay a quick visit to the Ashmolean to inspect the Hoard itself, and then she'd be fully equipped to tackle the Master.

Christa returned home with just enough time to prepare for the drinks party. The porter in charge of the sacrosanct fellows' car park had finally adjusted to the Mini's presence, and admitted her without demur. As she slipped it into a tiny space next to the Master's Daimler, she was amused to see that she was surrounded by a solid cohort of Volvos and Saabs. The fellows were out in force tonight.

She went first to King's Quad. Piers, whom she'd already phoned to relate the full horror of her introduction to the older fellows, had suggested that she meet him beforehand, so that they could walk over to the SCR together.

He took in her altered appearance the moment she entered his rooms.

'*Love* the hair,' he said, as she waited while he made sure the window was open enough for Mehitabel to come and go as she pleased. 'You'd been looking like Rapunzel for much too long. And didn't I see that suit in Hobbs' window just the other day?'

He turned from the window, and surveyed her again.

'What are you up to, Christa? I've never seen you dressed to kill before. Do fill me in.'

'I simply thought the Senior Common Room needed a little enlivening,' she said nonchalantly, while he bent to turn off the fire.

He gave her a quizzical look, and ushered her on to the landing.

'You could do that dressed in a sack,' he said, locking the door. 'But I wonder if it's entirely politic to put the Master's wife in the shade?'

'Stop needling, Piers, or I shall have to work out what kind of statement your clothes are making tonight.'

He was wearing a sumptuous grey brocade waistcoat beneath his black jacket. He looked down at it complacently.

'Just trying to brighten the scene in my own small way.' He

glanced at his watch. 'So, shall we throw ourselves to the lions now?'

They walked round to the south side of King's Quad. Christa could hear laughter and the steady beat of music from the Junior Common Room bar. People were spilling from it into the quad, talking eagerly to each other.

'First week get-togethers, first college romances,' said Piers. 'God, how exhausting to be that age again!'

They passed under another archway and crossed the quad with the cedar tree.

'Cloisters Quad,' Piers remarked. 'This used to be part of a monastery before good King Hal got to work. But there's not much self-denial around these days,' he added in an undertone as they approached the common-room door.

Two tail-coated butlers were ranged just inside, bearing salvers laden with flutes of champagne, fresh orange juice, and Malvern water. There was nothing so plebeian as crisps, but silver dishes on side tables held toasted almonds and plump Kalamata olives spiked with pimento. A third butler was circulating with a tray of canapés.

The room was lit by a hanging crystal candelabrum and discreet rose-shaded lamps. Most of the older fellows had congregated near the fireplace, but tonight there was a large leavening presence of younger men.

The Master's wife, wearing a stiff red moiré dress in which she looked like a badly packed Christmas gift, was busy dispensing gracious chit-chat, and keeping a sharp eye on Leda Lennox. In a sherry-coloured panne velvet suit she was cutting a swathe among the middle-aged dons.

Christa was the only other woman there, and after a round of lively introductions by Piers she'd soon attracted an entourage of her own. She wasn't sure whether the champagne had something to do with it, or her new image, but even though Phil had decided not to acknowledge her presence, she decided to enjoy herself. There was still plenty of time to tackle the Master, and it wouldn't hurt to let him see her in demand.

She'd already accepted two offers of dinner the following week, and was trying to persuade a sweet but mind-numbingly earnest young theologian that the Dead Sea Scrolls didn't really turn her on, when there was a lull in the conversation. People were looking towards the door, and automatically her eyes turned in the same direction.

Mallory Farrar had just appeared, and was standing on the edge of the room in another casually elegant suit, with his usual expression of having his eyes fixed on a horizon no one else could see. Though he did nothing to make it happen, people began to flow in his direction. Attractiveness like that would make it difficult for any woman, let alone Caitlin Trevor, to live with him, thought Christa irritably.

The charm was clearly working on Mrs Slade. She bustled towards him, gesturing the other party goers aside like Moses parting the Red Sea. He didn't conceal quite fast enough an expression of terminal boredom before letting polite interest blanket his face. Christa, watching from a seat in the window bay, thought amusedly that it served him right. It also suited her perfectly, for now Mrs Slade's attention was diverted she could approach the Master herself.

Making her way towards the fireplace, she was delighted to see that she was able to create as much of a stir with her progress as his wife. The Master had been buttonholed by an ancient don, and glanced hopefully towards the diversion. When he registered Christa's new image, a look she usually associated with bored businessmen in foreign hotels appeared on his face. As he glided towards her like a Dalek, she almost laughed at the thought of the Master having some basic instincts after all.

'Miss Keith. How delightful to see you here tonight. Do come and tell me how you've been getting on.'

He took her arm and guided her towards a corner sofa. As she sat down he patted her knee. It could have been interpreted as an avuncular gesture, if he hadn't then given it a decidedly unfamilial squeeze. So the Master was a bit of an old goat as well, she thought, with a mixture of amusement and distaste. She'd let him get away with it this time, but only to suit her own purposes.

All the same, she hoped Piers hadn't been watching. If he had, his comments were bound to be acid. She looked around for him, and to her surprise saw Mallory Farrar's gaze fixed on her instead. Her astonishment grew when he shot her a look of disapproval Calvin couldn't have bettered. It instantly spurred her on.

She dipped her head slightly so that a wing of hair drooped over one eye, and smiling at the Master, gave him the long upward glance which she'd last used to persuade a pig-headed Serb army captain to let her truckload of refugees through a road block. The Master's thin lips actually parted in a smile.

'You've been so welcoming that I already feel at home, Professor Slade,' she said, lying in her teeth. 'I'm delighted to have another chance to chat with you. I was in the Ashmolean this morning, looking at the Waylandsbury Hoard. I couldn't help thinking what an outstanding achievement it was on your part.'

He threw out his chest like one of the peacocks which strutted on the fellows' lawn.

'I think I may modestly say it did cause quite a stir at the time. Of course, there was very little media exposure in those days, but it might interest you to know that I appeared on one of the *Monitor* programmes.'

'I wish I could have seen it,' said Christa, privately thanking heaven she'd been spared. She couldn't imagine a bigger screen turn-off – pedantic, smug, not even possessing some eccentricity which might make the public take to him.

Yet for someone who so despised the media, there had been a surprising amount of regret in his voice, and she suddenly wondered if she could turn it to her advantage. He'd be much likelier to agree to the students' film if he could make a personal appearance.

'I'd be only too glad to help if you thought of branching out into television again. But I imagine you're so busy these days that a media appearance would have very low priority.'

To her delight he now looked like the peacock spying a particularly juicy grub.

'I wouldn't entirely say so, not if the opportunity were sufficiently rewarding. I did in fact ask Dr Gurney to mention to the producer of his programme that I might be available, but apparently all the slots were filled – I believe that's the correct term?'

'I can see you're as au fait with television as everything else,' said Christa, imagining Piers' face at the request. 'What a pity, when so many people thought you were a screen natural. But it's just occurred to me that there is a way in which you could appear on television again, and greatly enhance the college's reputation as well. I know how tirelessly you work for Gabriel.'

May heaven forgive me for such gross flattery, she thought. The Master certainly wouldn't, when he ultimately discovered her true intent, but by then it would be too late for him to stop her. She knew she was flirting with danger, but the addictive buzz was too strong to resist.

She leaned towards the Master confidentially. His eyes became more boiled egg-like than ever as they tried to peer down her camisole top.

'I've been thinking that rather than focus all my seminars on historical events, I'd like to involve the students actively in the television presentation of current college topics,' she said. 'It'd be particularly appropriate at Gabriel, which has such a reputation for new ideas,' she added, recklessly piling on the blandishments.

'Most appropriate,' said the Master, his gaze still hovering over her camisole. 'But perhaps a little unwise. Unfortunately we do have a few somewhat restless students in our ranks.'

'This would give them something to do – provide a focus, and force them to apply a little clear thinking to current issues.'

'That's all very well in theory, but I couldn't possibly give my agreement unless there were some extremely strong counter-balancing views.'

Smiling persuasively at him, she pulled the lapels of her jacket together. Self-sacrifice had its limits.

'I envisaged the programme containing a major contribution from yourself. It would more than adequately counterbalance any dissident voices. And the mere act of agreeing to take part would bring you enormous popularity among the students.'

She'd disliked adding the last remark, for if her plan worked he'd have no popularity left at all. But the Master wasn't easy to persuade, and she knew from Piers that some of the students had been complaining openly about his remoteness from their affairs.

The Master was no longer focusing on her neckline, but entirely on her face.

'Though I'm hardly likely to be motivated by a desire for popularity, Miss Keith, I have always hoped that every student would regard me as a friend. But I'm sure you'll appreciate that it's not always easy to come down to their level, especially these days. Would any television company be interested, I wonder?'

As Christa realised exultantly that she'd landed the Master at last, she also became aware that Farrar was progressing across the room in their direction, his expression more forbidding than ever. She'd have to move fast before he arrived to ruin everything.

'Dreaming Spires Television is holding a competition for a student video documentary on a subject of local interest,' she said. 'Don't you think it would be splendid to film a debate on some current college issue in the Great Hall at Gabriel? The participants could use video footage to support their case. You would be the key speaker, of course, and you have such presence that we're bound to reach the competition short-list at the very least.'

'Hmm.' The Master ran his finger reflectively along his moustache. 'Yes, the idea has distinct possibilities.'

'Imagine the drama of the setting,' said Christa craftily. 'The candlelit hall, you in your gown, the camera panning round the ancient portraits. Why, I shouldn't be at all surprised if a programme like "Probe" snapped you up afterwards. Press interest would be enormous.'

'Well, I suppose for the sake of the college I might be persuaded,' he said with poorly feigned reluctance. 'It would be an opportunity to employ our splendid official publicity film, which speaks for itself. And I'm sure one or two of our illustrious alumni would be willing to support me.'

To Christa's fury Farrar was almost upon them. The Master raised a hand to beckon him over. Damn the man, thought Christa, glaring at Farrar, willing him not to accept the invitation, yet knowing he would.

Mallory Farrar had just escaped being steam-rollered by Mrs Slade into attending a fund-raising dinner in aid of replacing the college's official cars. Money seemed to pour into Gabriel's coffers from all sides, but not to benefit the students, he thought. At least the younger fellows were present tonight, though, and he'd been having a reasonable conversation at last, when he caught sight of a woman in a short-skirted suit sitting next to the Master on the other side of the room.

He noticed her legs first, long and slender in glossy black tights which subtly defined the curve of knee and calf. And her suit, the colour of bitter chocolate, somehow managed to convey an intriguing mixture of seriousness and desirability.

He felt a tug of physical attraction that he'd not experienced since first seeing Caitlin. If he'd believed in astrology, the stars should have been going backwards in their courses at that meeting.

He was lunching in Soho with Warren, his agent, to celebrate the signing of a new contract. She was at another table with an actor whose autobiography Warren had recently sold, and introductions were made. Mallory had been hard pressed to conceal from the ever-watchful Warren his immediate interest in her. They were in bed within twelve hours, and the affair had raged all summer, made white-hot by the knowledge of his imminent departure.

The memory still had such power to hurt that when his gaze travelled to the woman's face, and he saw it was Christa Keith, the shock was correspondingly intense.

Instantly he crushed his initial reaction, though he'd been obliged to accord her some grudging admiration during the run-in with the Master over their respective rooms. She appeared to have done a complete about-turn since then, and was gazing at the Master as if she were a disciple at her guru's feet. Simply because she was so clearly up to something, he decided to investigate.

Farrar took a quick precautionary look at Mrs Slade, who so far was unaware of the developments on the other side of the room, and headed towards them. He was only waylaid once, and his journey was made easier by the Master's gesturing to him.

'Dr Farrar, do join us and hear Miss Keith's most interesting proposition,' said Professor Slade, when he arrived at their corner.

Farrar balanced himself on the arm of a chair facing the sofa. To sit down properly was far too dangerous a commitment.

'She's suggested we should make a television programme based on Gabriel. An excellent idea, don't you think? You might even appear on it as well,' said the Master.

Farrar looked at her suspiciously. What trouble was she stirring up, and what had she done to her hair? Before, it had been tightly braided into a head-girlish plait, not the stuff of fantasy at all. Now it was short, skimming the lobes of her ears, and sliding across her forehead in a pale amber fall like peaty water in the sun. At the back it was shorter still, cut to reveal her nape in a way which made her seem oddly vulnerable – not an adjective he would ever have associated with Christa Keith.

She was looking at him quizzically, waiting for his reply.

'I'd rather not,' he said. 'In my experience, there's always a slant.'

She tucked the fall of hair behind her ear, gazing at him in an amused way, as if a Flintstone had just wandered in.

'I do believe Dr Farrar's scared of the media. I suppose that's why he's so keen to escape on these enormous journeys of his. It's a good thing there are people like you about, Professor Slade, who understand how to handle media power.'

Christ, she's got a venomous tongue, Farrar thought. Not much vulnerability there. He had no compunction about hitting back.

'Gareth Hyde certainly knew how to, as well,' he said. 'Perhaps coming to Gabriel is your escape?'

Though she flinched perceptibly, she recovered at once.

'We're not talking about me, we're talking about the college, and ways of giving it a more positive public image. Professor Slade's forward-looking enough to recognise the need. I hoped you would be generous enough to cooperate.'

Bitch, he thought. Gareth Hyde, much as he disliked him, had been lucky to escape so easily. If only it had been as easy to get away from Caitlin. Christa Keith was clearly made in the same equally lethal mould, and he didn't hesitate to put her down again.

'Television isn't what Gabriel needs,' he said, then wished he hadn't, for it was impossible to tell the Master what was missing.

Personally all he wanted still was the peace he'd hoped to find at Gabriel, but which was continuing to elude him.

'I'm usually the one who's accused of being reactionary,' said Professor Slade. 'But I think in this instance you are. What reasonable objection could there be?'

'I dislike any invasion of privacy,' said Farrar.

'You'd be perfectly free not to cooperate,' Christa said.

'I'm sure Miss Keith would use the utmost tact,' added the Master.

'Tact is not a word I associate with television cameras, and in any case you still haven't told us how you intend to slant this documentary of yours, Ms Keith,' said Farrar, fixing Christa with a wintery gaze.

He was a total bastard, Christa decided. He'd guessed she hadn't worked out any details, and was determined to knock the stuffing out of her plan. Those eyes were as hard as glacier ice. She couldn't imagine them melting into any expression of tenderness.

'I haven't had time to get down to a discussion with my students yet,' she said. 'I want them to be fully involved. But of course I shall keep the Master informed all the way.'

Across the room she saw the Master's wife finally come out of a huddle with the Dean and check up on the party. Her gaze homed in on Farrar, then on her husband and Christa. Once more she began to power her way through the crowd.

'Oh, look!' said Christa wickedly. 'Mrs Slade's coming to chat with you again, Dr Farrar. You *are* being honoured tonight.'

The freezing stare switched away. An expression of pure horror crossed his face. She saw him fix a desperate glance on a French ormolu clock adorning the common-room writing table.

'I'm afraid I shan't have the pleasure of another talk with your wife, Master,' he said, getting to his feet as if he'd just heard a fire alarm. 'I'm expecting a phone call from New York. Please give her my apologies and thanks for a very pleasant evening.'

He nodded to Christa, and she watched in amusement as he rapidly skirted the room towards the exit. Luckily for him Mrs Slade had been briefly intercepted by the Senior Tutor. Farrar's head was outlined momentarily against the panelling as one of the butlers opened the door, and then he disappeared.

The Master too was keeping a wary eye on his wife's approach. Christa focused all her attention on him again. There wasn't much time left.

'The students will be thrilled that you've agreed to take part,' she said. 'We shall need a little financial help for our equipment, of course, but I'm sure the college funds could run to it.'

'Equipment?' he queried vaguely, as though TV programmes were produced with the wave of a magic wand.

'We'd need two video cameras,' she replied, trying to keep her voice patient, 'film stock, and an editing machine. They can be kept in my room for safety. The editing could be done there as well.'

'Two cameras?' The Master's voice was doubtful.

'We don't have much time. Oxford terms aren't very long, and if we're going to do justice to Gabriel and the Waylandsbury dig, we'll need a couple of camera teams. The more footage we have, the more leeway there'll be with cutting. And good cutting will be what gives the programme impact. That, and your participation, of course,' she added quickly.

'Won't it all be rather expensive?' he asked.

'Not necessarily. I can arrange a discount if we promise to mention our suppliers in the credits, and the equipment can be sold on afterwards.'

'I'd have to consult the Bursar. Most of our endowments are entailed in one way or another.'

'There must be some fund with a fairly loose interpretation. I'm sure it's been done before. Someone as versatile as you . . .'

She let her voice trail meaningfully away, and kept her face completely innocent while putting her hand persuasively on his arm.

'If the film is as successful as I expect, we shall have the major networks fighting for reproduction rights. And the Gabriel setting should have instant transatlantic appeal.'

'Well, I suppose I might make a few enquiries,' he said. She could see he was already imagining himself being interviewed by Dan Rather in the States. 'How much would you need, do you think?'

She quickly named an amount the paltriness of which would have made an Apollo producer threaten instant resignation. The Master's face made it clear that he considered the sum hugely over-optimistic, but luckily for Christa his wife was bearing down on them like a U-boat with all torpedoes primed.

'We'll discuss this again,' he said, disengaging his arm smartly from beneath her hand, and looking like a small boy caught stealing toffees. 'And I must ask you not to mention it to my wife. Unfortunately she's never been keen on my appearing on television.'

Mrs Slade plumped herself firmly down on the Master's other side.

'I can't allow you to monopolise my husband any more, Miss Keith,' she boomed. 'There are too many people here who haven't had a chance to talk to him yet. What have you been chatting about for so long?'

'Miss Keith is feeling a little at sea with her seminars, my dear,' he answered, giving Christa a distinctly beseeching look.

'Your husband is very generously going to help me,' she said to Mrs Slade. 'Isn't that so, Professor?' she added, shooting him a meaningful look in return.

'Yes, yes. I suppose I'll have to,' the Master answered tetchily.

'What sort of help?' demanded Mrs Slade.

'It's merely a small matter of presentation,' said the Master. He rose from the sofa and slipped his hand under his wife's arm. 'Now, who are these other people you wish me to meet, my dear?'

Christa hid her amusement behind her champagne glass as he steered Mrs Slade smartly into less troubled waters, but she felt surprisingly drained by the encounter. She hadn't expected to take on Farrar as well, and she didn't like the way he'd made her feel as if she was about to do something underhand. The room, heated by a mass of glowing logs and the chandelier, was by now extremely warm, and she decided to slip out into the quad for a few minutes before rejoining the fray.

The branches of the cedar tree were black against a dark blue sky, echoing the pattern of the ribbed vaulting in the cloister roof above Christa's head. The quad was very quiet, and an almost monastic sense of calm and order prevailed.

As she sat on the stone parapet, leaning her back against one of the pillars which supported the roof, she felt her confidence slowly return. In spite of her distrust of everything to do with the college, it was possible in a setting like this to understand how some of the greatest humanitarian movements had once been generated at Gabriel. She decided that if the students' documentary led to a renewal of that influence, her plans would be more than justified.

She was about to return to her networking among the dons, when she caught a movement beneath the tree. A solitary figure stood with his back to her, head tilted, gazing at the stars through the branches. The darkness of his clothes against the cedar's black bark had provided perfect camouflage until he moved.

It was Mallory Farrar again. As usual, his detachment irritated her profoundly, but she wondered if she should make one last effort to get on better terms. She was going to have to use her room in college more than she'd expected, and she didn't have the time or energy for a skirmish every time they met on the stairs.

There was a flagged path to the cedar across the grass. She set off along it, her heels tapping on the stone. She could sense waves of resentment at the approaching invasion of his privacy, but he didn't react when she arrived by his side. He was the stillest person she'd ever met.

'That was a quick phone call,' she said, hoping to tease a response out of him.

It was like trying to strike up a conversation with one of the stone busts in front of the Sheldonian. Though he looked at her, he didn't reply. She abandoned all attempts at finesse.

'We've got to co-exist until next summer. Wouldn't it be better if we tried to get along till then?'

There was a long silence. 'So what do you suggest?' he finally asked.

'It'd help for a start if you stopped trying to put me down, especially in front of the Master.'

'I'd call it presenting another point of view. I thought you were all for that.'

'What I do is absolutely no concern of yours. I don't interfere in your business.'

He jammed his hands in his pockets and began to walk impatiently up and down beneath the tree. She felt a moment of triumph that she'd broken through his self-possession.

'What you do to the college is my concern,' he said. 'I know you're out to make some sensational television programme which will restore your reputation and leave Gabriel worse off than ever. This place needs constructive rescue, not destruction.'

His words infuriated her after the decision she'd just made.

'I've never been involved in a sensational programme in my life.'

'Come off it. Your whole way of life lately has been sensational. It couldn't be anything else.'

'I could say the same of you,' she said angrily.

'It's not the same at all.'

'Because you're producing great literature, and the sort of thing I do is on a lower scale? How arrogant can you get?'

'I simply happen to care about the college. I don't think you have the slightest understanding of how it used to be. The Master's spoiled most of that, but if you begin to stir things up at this stage it'll make his successor's task impossible. You'll be more destructive than he is.'

'So you admit he's destructive?' She jumped on the statement.

'Yes, I do, but your way of fighting him hasn't the slightest chance of success.'

'I'd rather do something than nothing,' she said, not caring that she'd now openly admitted she intended to fight the Master. 'There's still a year until he retires. A lot can happen in a year, yet all you seem prepared to do is sit on the fence and watch Gabriel rot. And when it's all over, and you're thousands of miles away from here, I suppose you'll write some exquisitely elegiacal little piece for the *Spectator* about how sad it is, and think you've done your bit. You might as well go back to star-gazing if that's your attitude.'

Christa didn't bother to wait for his reaction. She turned on her heel and marched straight back to the common room. She'd spent too much of her life recently trying to make sense out of blindly partisan views.

'How are you getting on?' said a voice by Christa's side, as she sat with a second glass of champagne wondering which group of fellows to tackle next. 'I've been meaning to ask if you needed any help, but I've been at the Institute a lot lately.'

Leda had taken the Master's seat, and was looking at Christa with a face full of sympathetic interest. She put down her glass of orange juice on the table in front of them, and helped herself to an olive. Her hands were ringless and compact, the nails enamelled with colourless varnish.

'I'm never going to be the world's greatest teacher, but I'll survive,' Christa responded. 'How about your research? It sounds as if you're busy.'

Leda pulled a face. 'Too busy. The security procedures hold things up. But we're starting to get encouraging results.'

Christa looked again at Leda's hands. She could easily imagine them engaged in some experimental procedure to help sick children, but never inflicting unnecessary suffering on the animals in her charge.

'Meningitis is an awful disease. I saw some children in a Sarajevo hospital who'd been brain-damaged by it. The symptoms tended to get overlooked among all the other horrors of war until it was too late.'

She was silent, thinking about the uncoordinated movements and halting speech of children condemned to an institution for the rest of their days.

'It is bad, but there's a lot to be hopeful about as well.' Leda hesitated. 'From your expression I think you remember too much,' she went on. 'Forgive my lecturing you but I am a doctor as well as a researcher, and it's not good to rake over some memories too often.'

'Yes, you're probably right,' said Christa slowly. Surprisingly, she found she didn't resent Leda's talking to her in this way.

'It can become a habit that's hard to break.'

'I know,' said Christa, thinking of her mother, and for the first time in her life she had a disturbing inkling of how easy it might be to head in the same direction.

'I'm glad your work's going so well,' she said, trying to smile as she changed the subject. More out of politeness than because she had any hope of a visit, she continued, 'I asked Phil if I could look round the labs, but I gather outsiders aren't admitted.'

'I wish we could let in the public, and show them just how good our animal houses are, but it's too risky with Howl on the rampage. I could arrange it for you, though, if you're really keen. Normally we only admit professional colleagues these days.'

Leda looked towards the ormolu clock. 'Only five more minutes to go, thank God. Mrs Slade closes down these college functions on the dot. I'm going to the Institute afterwards for a quick check on an experiment. Would you like to come with me?'

Christa was staggered. She'd never expected the offer. The only problem was that Leda had made it purely out of the kindness of her heart, and if she did see anything wrong it would be horribly difficult to betray that kindness in an exposé afterwards.

'It won't be like Frankenstein's laboratory at all,' said Leda in a gently mocking voice. 'There's absolutely nothing going on there to trouble your reporter's mind, I promise you. Gabriel's in a mess just now, but not the Institute.'

'I'd love to see it,' said Christa, still scarcely believing her luck.

'Good, and I can drop you back here afterwards. I must have a quick word with the Senior Tutor before I leave, so let's meet in the car park in five minutes' time.'

9

'Where did you do your medical training?' Christa asked Leda, as her car moved smoothly along South Parks Road.

'In London, and for a couple of research years at Harvard. I worked as a paediatric registrar when I came home, then got on to a project where I could combine clinical work and research. It was the perfect job so far as I was concerned. We had some good breaks, and because of them I was offered the headship of the Institute.'

Christa glanced sideways at Leda's blunt, decisive profile. She was handling the car effortlessly in the heavy traffic. Christa couldn't imagine her wasting time regretting any decision she'd made, yet there was a certain wistfulness in her voice.

'Do you miss the clinical side?'

Leda spun the car towards the Woodstock Road, neatly skirting a group of students spilling off the pavement.

'That's perceptive of you. Yes, I do, very much, though I'm occasionally called in on difficult cases. But doctors needn't retire till their late-sixties. I hope there'll be time to crack the problem of meningitis, and still have some years left to spend entirely on clinical work. How about you? How did you get into war-reporting?'

She certainly had the good clinician's knack of drawing out information, Christa thought. By the time they were approaching the Gabriel's Grounds Estate she'd even told Leda all the background to her affair with Gareth.

'Bad luck for you,' commented Leda. 'The one colleague I had an affair with did all he could to boost my career. I realised afterwards how risky it had been, though.'

Christa waited, hoping for more revelations, but Leda didn't elaborate. Instead she said, 'The quickest route to the Institute is through the Gabriel's Grounds Estate, but it's full of young joy-riders at night, so we'll go by a back way.'

Five minutes later they were driving down a country lane, and then a concreted slip road. Brick walls topped with razor wire and blazing with lights loomed up before them. The Institute resembled the Maze prison more than a centre for scientific research.

Leda slowed the car at a massive pair of gates. A guard stepped towards them from a control point and minutely inspected the boot, the back seat, the bonnet, and even under the car with an angled mirror. Eventually he waved them through.

Again Christa was reminded of Northern Ireland. 'It's like the Falls Road area used to be,' she said.

'And just as necessary, I'm afraid,' answered Leda, parking the car outside the main door of a large bunker-like building. 'Howl's a dangerous organisation. I can understand their concern but not the psychology that could release potentially lethal organisms into the community if they set our experimental animals free, as they've threatened to do.'

'Howl would say that if you weren't doing these experiments in the first place, the problem wouldn't arise,' Christa replied as they walked towards the door of the Institute.

Leda shook her head as she searched in her shoulder bag. 'I'm afraid the views of Howl and the people who work here are irreconcilable. We believe carefully controlled experimentation is justified to save human life. They never will. Even if you showed them the brain-damaged children you saw in Sarajevo, they'd say animals came first.'

She found a plastic card, and inserted it into a slot in an electronic control panel, punching in a six-digit number. Christa tried to see what it was, but Leda was too fast. The door swung open, admitting them to an entrance lobby which could have been in any public building, except for another guard intently scanning an enormous console of monitor screens.

When they'd both signed a register, he briskly searched Christa's bag, asked her to pass through a metal detector, and waved them on through a labyrinth of anonymous office corridors.

'These are the labs. You can have a look round while I'm checking my experiment,' said Leda, as they finally approached a pair of massive double doors.

Next to them was another control panel with a small illuminated screen. She pressed her palm against it.

'Handprint recognition. A useful double check,' she said. 'It only admits researchers and technicians, not office staff.'

As the doors rolled smoothly shut behind Christa, the characteristic smell of a zoo greeted her, a combination of wood chippings, over-ripe fruit, and warm fur, the whole tinged with a waft of ammonia.

'We're in the holding rooms now,' said Leda. 'Most of these animals have been or will be experimented on. We run a breeding programme for small mammals too.'

Christa followed her on a tour of cages almost as well-kept as her parents' house. They contained a bright-eyed assortment of rats, rabbits and mice, who looked no less contented than Basil, Pansy's much-loved guinea pig. A grey-haired motherly-looking woman was crooning to the animals as she dished out an assortment of fresh food from an enamel bowl. She smiled and nodded at Christa.

'This is Betty, one of our technicians,' said Leda. 'She's giving the animals their evening feed. It'll be lights out soon.'

The atmosphere was so relaxed that Christa had to remind herself that this was not a nursery at bed-time with Nanny handing round cocoa to her charges, but for the animals a cross between a hospital and a prison. And these were only the small mammals, anyway. Things would probably be very different with the monkeys.

'I'm working with our primates at the moment,' said Leda. 'You won't be able to come into the isolation area, but you can observe the animals from an outer room. I've had the labs redesigned for maximum openness. That way any malpractice can be quickly picked up. Very occasionally a young researcher becomes impatient and tries to skip the rules, but so far we've always managed to catch that sort of thing in time.'

The primate holding area was much larger than the one they'd just left. A large high-ceilinged enclosure partly walled with plastic glass contained a troop of vervets. Their chattering echoed through the room as they scampered along branches and swung from ropes. They were provided with sleeping platforms and some heavy duty plastic toys. The quieter animals were busy grooming each other. There were some smaller enclosures containing family units of huge-eyed marmosets, each with its own nesting box and communal play area. The animals appeared not in the least deranged by captivity. There was none of the obsessive pacing and rocking Christa had seen in some zoos.

'Where do you get your primates?' she asked.

'They come from a licensed breeding centre. Importation from the wild is forbidden.'

Christa wondered if the animals had any sub-conscious longing for the freedom they'd never known. Researchers would probably say they didn't, but the near-human expression in the monkeys' eyes made her rejoice that the imprisonment of wild primates was banned.

'We try to keep our animals going as long as possible, not just because they're expensive to replace, but because we become so fond of them,' Leda continued.

The monkeys weren't even slightly afraid of her, but had rushed to the front of their enclosures and were trying to attract her attention. Leda produced a bunch of small bananas from her shoulder bag which she distributed through the bars. She knew each monkey by name and spent several minutes talking to them while they peeled the fruit with amazingly delicate movements, their dark eyes fixed on her as if they understood every word she said.

Christa marvelled at the way Leda was able to experiment on creatures with whom she was so closely bonded. She knew she'd never be able to exercise such immense self-control herself, even in the interests of saving human life.

'Here's Betty with some grain for the vervets,' said Leda.

Betty had appeared in a connecting corridor at the back of the enclosure, and was tossing handfuls of wheat into the vervets' litter. They'd already eaten the bananas, and immediately began to search for the grain with long, probing fingers.

'We like them to have plenty to do,' said Leda. 'It's so easy for them to become bored, and then turn on each other.'

'Do you have any chimpanzees?' Christa asked.

'No. There's too much public feeling against their use, and we don't have large enough holding facilities here, in any case.'

While Christa wandered round the cages, Leda moved to a side table to examine charts recording the animals' care.

'I've got to shower and robe up before entering the experimental zone, so I'll leave you now. But you can watch through the observation screen,' she said, when she'd initialled the data.

Again Christa followed her, this time into a smaller room, one wall of which was partially panelled in glass. Facing her through the screen was a row of smaller holding cages. The animals in them looked extremely lethargic, and at least half seemed to be asleep, but she couldn't detect any signs of obvious distress.

She continued to watch as Leda reappeared, dressed in hooded white overalls, rubber boots and gloves, and a mask. Carrying a kidney dish containing a stab needle and a slide, she gently extracted a marmoset from its cage.

Like the others it was very sleepy, but awake enough to cling to Leda like a child. She soothed the small creature for several minutes before cradling it in the crook of one arm, and deftly transferring a drop of its blood to the slide. It hardly appeared to notice the procedure.

'Wonderful, Dr Lennox is, with those animals,' said Betty, who had joined Christa in the observation room. 'And she's even better with kids. My neighbour's three year old got meningitis last year. It was touch and go whether she'd live, but Dr Lennox was called in and pulled her through. It's wicked the way Howl's trying to ruin her work.'

While Christa waited for Leda to reappear she mused that Howl's activities must make it harder still for her to compartmentalise her interests. Her ability to cope with so many demands on her emotions was remarkable.

Christa couldn't remember any other woman who'd impressed her more. Thinking about how much she owed Leda personally, she began to wonder whether to contact Howl sooner than she'd planned. She might be able to convince them that everything at the Institute was above board, and perhaps prevent another attack. By the time Leda returned from the isolation zone she'd made up her mind to get in touch with Howl the following day.

* * *

Christa was woken by the sun casting a patterned net through Jessie's lace curtains on to the faded silk eiderdown. In the mirror between the wardrobe doors the short-haired stranger she still wasn't quite used to stared sleepily back at her. Outside all was silent apart from the whirring of a milk float.

She lay drowsily for a while, her body fitting neatly into the shallow dip made in the mattress by Jessie's frame. The silence no longer disturbed her. She'd finally got used to the idea that guns weren't going to crack across the street, and since the recent truce she'd stopped worrying so intensely about the Bosnian friends she'd left behind. Neither was she waking in the small hours to think obsessively of Gareth's betrayal and Matt's death.

Her gaze moved to her contacts book on the dressing table. Odder still, the thought of the Howl number waiting to be rung didn't give her the usual frisson of excitement before a confrontation. She smiled to herself, thinking how Randall would approve of her new frame of mind, and drowsed again, only to be roused by the chimes of the St Barnabas clock striking seven.

As the last stroke died away Poppaea set up a series of hideous squawks. Christa groaned. She'd forgotten to put the cover on the cage when she went to bed, and the parrot still kept Jessie's early hours. She knew there'd be no peace now, and stumbled, still half-asleep, from the bed.

She was wearing one of the thermal vests she'd acquired for an assignment in Kabul the previous winter. They'd been washed so often that they'd become tunic-like, and were as soft and comfortable as old flannel. Apart from the things she'd bought in Little Clarendon Street, all her clothes over the last three years had been gathered on the wing from one assignment to another.

She dragged on the equally limp towelling wrap hanging on the back of the door, thinking that at least in her manless state she could wear whatever she liked in bed. On her first short leave from Bosnia she'd stuffed her rucsac with satin underwear to please Gareth. It had all been given away when she left, thrust into the arms of an overwhelmed chambermaid to exchange for black market food.

Downstairs Christa gave Poppaea a snack of sunflower seeds, made herself some very strong coffee and sat on the sofa with her newly acquired mobile phone and her contacts book, while she pondered how to approach Howl. She might as well try to get as much information as possible, though her first priority was to put them right about the Institute.

If she tried to infiltrate them by saying she wanted to join the organisation, it would be almost impossible to keep up the pretence. Safer to stay on known ground, pass herself off as a freelance reporter, and give an assumed name, she decided.

Quickly she organised some questions into a list, pulled up the aerial and punched in the number. Just in time she remembered to add the code which prevented her own number from appearing on any display screen at the other end of the line.

'Yeah?' said a distinctly unfriendly male voice, sounding only too ready to slam the receiver down.

Christa braced herself. Dealings over the phone were always difficult without the advantage of body language.

'Hi. My name's Lee Grant,' she said, giving a pen name she'd once used years ago to keep some newspaper articles distinct from her television work. 'I'm a freelance reporter doing an undercover investigation on Gabriel Hall. That includes the activities at the Institute. I've got a contact there who's just given me an inside tour. How about an information exchange?'

There was a long silence. Christa had no way of knowing if there was anyone else in the room with the disembodied voice, but she thought she could hear whispering in the background.

'Who gave you this number?' a new voice, a woman's, asked.

'A colleague.'

'Name?' barked the voice. It had a marked Midlands accent.

Christa mentioned a colleague from her early days, whom she'd got out of big trouble over a libel action. She had taken the precaution of priming him the night before.

'Where did he get the number?'

'He couldn't remember exactly, just that it was in connection with some other story.'

'You lot aren't usually forgetful.' The voice didn't sound any more receptive. 'But we might consider a limited information exchange if you could get us into the Institute as well.'

'Sorry,' Christa said. 'My visit was strictly a one-off.'

'What sort of animals were they using?'

'Meet me and I'll tell you,' she said.

Christa hadn't intended a meeting, but she was becoming curious to see the person attached to the voice.

'You'd have to offer us some really hot information for that. Were there chimpanzees?'

Christa deliberately ignored the question. 'I saw the experimental area as well as the holding rooms,' she said tantalisingly. 'But if you're not interested, let's forget it. I have other leads to follow.'

She heard a short muffled conversation at the other end of the line.

'OK, then,' said the voice. 'We've better things to do, but how about half-ten at the bowling green on the Gabriel's Grounds Estate?'

'Fine,' said Christa, though she couldn't imagine an odder or more unsuitable place for such a meeting, swarming with elderly people with ample time to check up on strangers. But at least with so many people about it should be relatively safe.

'Right, the door round the back of the pavilion. We'll be waiting for you.'

Christa had just given Poppaea and herself breakfast before leaving the house, when someone hammered furiously on the front door. The postman had already been with a large advance bill from the solicitors who were dealing with the sale of the house. She frowned, wondering if he'd forgotten to deliver some other demand.

Looking out of the window, she recognised an equally unwelcome caller. Emma's car was parked in the street. Christa had known she wouldn't be able to resist an inspection for long, but it was odd that she should choose a sacred school day for her visit.

When she opened the door, Emma was standing on the step wearing an expression which combined extreme embarrassment and fury. Her hair was slipping from its moorings, and her tailored navy jacket had been buttoned askew.

'You've got to help me, Kissie!' she said peremptorily, using the childhood nickname Christa loathed, her own first attempt at her name, which she'd hoped was safely buried in the family past. 'I'm absolutely desperate, and there's no one else to ask!'

'Mummee!' wailed a voice behind Emma. 'Why can't I come and see Christa's new house? And I'm going to be late for school *again*!'

Pansy was hanging out of the Volvo window with her arms draped pathetically over the side.

'Stay right where you are, Pansy, and look after Jamie, or I won't let you go to *Pocahontas* with Chelsea tomorrow. I mean it, too,' Emma bellowed back at her.

Pansy subsided on the car seat.

'Can I come inside for a minute?' said Emma. 'I don't want Pansy to hear me. She's got ears like radar.'

Without waiting for Christa's reply she charged past her into the hall, and through the open sitting-room door. Christa followed, wondering what new domestic calamity had occurred. It must be something serious, for Emma didn't even stop to inspect her surroundings before bursting into a storm of indignation.

'It's bloody, bloody Phil! He's let me down again!'

'So what's new? And what's it got to do with me? I moved here to get out of Phil's way, at his request, if you remember.'

Emma stomped over to the fireplace, and turned to Christa again. Her face was as pink as if she'd been toasting bread at the flames.

'School's closed because of a maintenance problem today. I'd arranged to have it all to myself in London, shopping and doing the museums. Lucinda said I could stay overnight with her. There's a private view and a party afterwards at her gallery – loads of people I knew at Cambridge'll be there.'

'Sounds a great idea,' said Christa encouragingly. Lucinda was the best of Emma's ex-college friends, laidback, fun, and the manager of a highly successful North London art gallery. 'It's about time you did something just for you.'

'Phil said he'd work at home and look after Jamie and collect Pansy from school. I'd got everything sewn up, then he had the nerve to announce at breakfast that it wasn't on after all! Some scientific big-wig's visiting Gabriel, and Phil thinks he ought to make himself known.'

'Does he ever not?' said Christa, wondering why there was all this drama when Emma had a perfectly able-bodied au pair. 'Can't Noelene look after the children?'

'Her ex-boyfriend's just turned up from Sydney, and asked her to meet him in London for a long weekend.'

'I thought she had a big thing going for a Rhodes scholar?' said Christa, thinking that Emma must be intending to leave James at Botley, and ask her to collect Pansy from school.

'Apparently Noelene was in love with this Sydney boyfriend all the time, but they'd had some sort of row before she left home. The poor girl's desperate to get back together with him. It would have been so cruel not to let her go.'

'Why not tell her to wait till tomorrow? Sounds to me as though she's the one who's done the sewing up,' Christa couldn't resist observing. 'Honestly, Em, you've got to stop letting everyone use you.'

'Well, it's done,' said Emma crossly. 'And anyway, I can still make the ten o'clock train if you take over Jamie now.'

'Me?' Christa stared at her in horror. 'I can't look after Jamie! You know I'm hopeless with babies.'

'You're only hopeless because you haven't had any practice. And you're not teaching today, are you? So you've nothing else to do.'

'As it happens I've got a lot to do,' said Christa indignantly. The appointment with Howl had suddenly taken on the appearance of a friendly harbour light in a force-ten gale.

'What exactly?' Emma demanded.

'An appointment.'

'If it's the dentist, you can take Jamie with you. Nobody minds these days.'

'It's not that sort of appointment,' said Christa, vividly imagining Howl's reaction if she turned up with a squalling child. The interview would be an instant write-off.

'Most people get to like babies, even if they think they don't at first,' said Emma.

'Not these people. And I don't know how long the meeting'll go on, anyway. Why don't you ask Mother? She'd jump at the chance.'

Emma frowned. 'I never leave the children alone with her

these days. I can't trust her not to take them out and then have a panic attack.'

'That's a bit hard on her, isn't it?' said Christa, remembering how her mother had adored looking after Pansy as a baby, and how carefully she'd tended her. It was the one time Christa had seen her completely happy and relaxed. 'Dad told me what happened with Pansy, but he said Mother had promised not to take either of the children out again on her own, and you know she always keeps her word.'

'You really are the end, lecturing me about Mother when you can scarcely be bothered with her yourself. Can't you change this appointment of yours? It's my first chance of a day out alone since Jamie was born. You can't imagine how I've been looking forward to it. I've tried everyone else, and Phil swears he'll collect Pansy from school and be home by tea. It's not for long. Please, Kissie.'

'No, I can't. This is a one-off chance.' Christa was beginning to feel so mean that she didn't even tell Emma off for using the hated name.

Fury finally replaced the frustration in Emma's voice.

'You're just bloody selfish! That's why you won't do it. And that's why you can't get yourself together, not because of Gareth!'

'Don't you dare lay that sort of guilt trip on me,' Christa flung back, struggling with the usual feelings of inadequacy at the mention of Gareth's name. 'I had enough of it at home. I'm perfectly happy, thank you, and I don't need your comments.'

Emma looked round distractedly as if to find some other ammunition, and for the first time became aware of her surroundings. Slowly she took in the furnishings, her gaze lingering with particular incredulity on the bluebell wood and the galleon-bedecked carpet.

'Perfectly happy?' she said. 'In a place like this? Haven't you any taste at all? How can you live with that ghastly sentimental thing over the mantelpiece? It's the ultimate in stereotyped art. And the rug's even worse. I feel seasick just looking at it.'

'I like them,' Christa retorted, though she'd been planning to replace them eventually. 'They're cheerful, and they're honest. Your decor's what you think you ought to like.'

Emma glowered at her.

'Don't be so ridiculous. There's no comparison. You must have been mad when you bought this tacky little dump. House values in Ethelred Road are going up all the time, but you'll be into negative equity by Christmas. And you're sure to have dreadful problems with damp so near the canal.'

She glanced out of the window.

'Oh, God, why won't that child ever do what she's told?'

Christa followed Emma's gaze. Pansy was opening the car door. Emma clapped her hands distractedly to her head, dislodging a shower of hairpins.

'I've got to go,' she said. 'I suppose I'll just have to put off the shopping and museums till another day. At least I'll still make the preview, though. Phil should be back by four.'

Christa followed her to the door, her resentment draining away at the sight of Emma's disconsolate expression.

'I would help if I could, truly,' she said.

Emma turned, and paused to look at her.

'Would you? I wonder how much you care for anything except your career. Because I bet that's what this mysterious appointment is about. Your bloody career.'

'Of course I care. You just asked me at a bad time.'

'We'll see,' said Emma, pleating her lips into a thin, disbelieving line. 'Next time I ask you, we'll see.'

'Next time you ask me, I'll help, I promise,' Christa said.

Christa took a bus to the edge of Gabriel's Grounds, and walked the rest of the way. She wanted to discover if the estate was really as bad as people made out.

The outskirts were a treeless maze of concrete block row houses built on a grid system which converged on an inner ring road. The front gardens were mostly choked with weeds, or else turned into parking lots on which stood ancient Cortinas and rusty vans in various stages of repair. Christa reflected that Sir Charles Tucker's philanthropy had clearly not extended to a good architect.

A few houses in a brave attempt at personalisation had been given stone cladding, or a coat of pastel paint further individualised by roving graffiti artists. But in general their occupiers seemed to have abandoned all hope of external improvement and retreated indoors behind impenetrable screens of net.

Within the circle of the ring road were a couple of high-rise blocks whose balconies burgeoned with washing like a Neapolitan alley, and a small shopping centre built round three sides of a paved square. The shops were made of the same stained concrete as the houses, and were notable only for the security guards lurking within every entrance door. It didn't take long for Christa to discover why they were there.

In front of the shops was a raised brick flowerbed in which the only blooms were greasy chip wrappers and empty cartons from a nearby take-away. Lounging around a ghetto-blaster perched on the parapet was a gang of young men. They were patently unemployed, but nothing like the patient hollow-cheeked, stooped-shouldered men of Depression dole queues. These were tough, beer-drinking youths, back pockets of their jeans bulging like holsters with extra cans.

A few older women scuttled in and out of the shops with laden carrier bags, keeping a wary eye on the lads in spite of the security guards. A bunch of girls in chunky-heeled boots and skirts like pelmets had no such misgivings. They were slowly cruising along the pavement, arms safely linked, sending the youths challenging stares. Confrontation was heavy in the air.

On the open side of the square an impromptu game of football kept spilling into the road, occasioning much flashy footwork and swearing as the players retrieved the ball from under the wheels of passing cars. The precinct was clearly a Tom Tiddler's ground where Christa guessed the main entertainment was pushing authority to the limit. Yet in spite of the violence of the game, the standard of play was remarkably high. The youths looked as if they practised for hours every day.

The ball spun again into the road, and was deflected by a passing motorcyclist, who almost fell from his machine as he gave it an angry kick. It hurtled back towards Christa. She trapped it neatly beneath her foot, a trick learned in the girls' football team at school, and punted it back into the game. The lads let loose a fusillade of wolf whistles and started to make good-humoured but deeply suggestive gestures in her direction.

Annoyed with herself for attracting so much attention, Christa slipped down an alleyway between two shops, and emerged into a car park showered with broken glass, and almost devoid of vehicles. After dodging behind an evil-smelling garbage bin to consult a street map, she headed off in the rough direction of the bowls pavilion.

It was enclosed behind high unclipped privet hedges, and she paused for a moment in their shelter to cram her beret over her hair, and don a pair of rarely used reading glasses. It was safest to look as unlike her usual self as possible.

She needn't have worried about encountering swarms of bowls devotees, for the deserted greens were thick with couch grass and scored by the tyres of mountain bikes. Most of the surrounding seats had splintered slats, the walls of the pavilion were decorated with more graffiti, and the windows boarded up. As the bowling green appeared to be the only games facility in the whole neighbourhood, apart from a similarly run-down children's play area she'd seen on her way in, Christa couldn't help feeling a sneaking sympathy with the football players.

Cautiously she brushed through the privet branches at the back of the pavilion, and found a door marked 'Greenkeeper's Office'. She took a deep breath, remembering that though she'd left a precautionary note on the table at home saying where she'd gone, if any of the Howl members had homicidal tendencies her absence probably wouldn't be remarked on for several days. Cautiously she pushed the door, which had a Yale lock, found it was open, and stepped into near darkness.

'Make sure it's properly closed,' commanded a disembodied voice as the door swung to behind her.

She managed to put down the latch, and turned towards the voice. The room was lit only by a tiny fanlight in the roof, and smelt of decay. When her eyes eventually became accustomed to the gloom she could just make out two figures sitting at a table on the far side, with an empty chair in the middle of the floor facing them. Warily she moved towards it.

The people opposite her were muffled in the same hooded jackets and scarves as the night of the Pets' Palace raid. Christa encouraged herself with the thought that in the prevailing gloom they'd be able to see as little of her as she could of them.

'Hallo. I'm Lee,' she said conversationally, sitting in the empty chair and trying to sound as unthreatening as possible. 'Thanks for meeting me.'

'Haven't written much lately, have you?' said one of the figures, in the Midlands accent she'd heard on the phone.

'I've been abroad for a few years,' Christa replied, thinking they hadn't been slow to check up.

'And you've not written on animal rights, either.'

'No, it isn't particularly my line of country. As I told you before, I'm gathering information for a general investigative piece on Gabriel Hall.'

'So who's your contact at the Institute?'

'You don't really expect me to tell you that, do you?' Christa tried to sound sweetly reasonable. 'If I didn't respect confidences I'd be finished as a journalist.'

'Even when it's a matter of life and death for defenceless animals?'

The other figure had spoken at last. It was a young male voice, high-pitched with fervour, but with no recognisable accent. Her eyes were becoming accustomed to the lack of light. He appeared to be tall and lanky behind his wrappings.

'You almost made it a matter of life and death for that security guard,' she said, thinking that she was on Tom Tiddler's ground as well. 'I can understand your wanting to see inside a closed institution,' she added quickly, 'but human beings are animals too. Why hurt them in the process?'

'Humans have had their chance to create a better world, and they've screwed it up.'

'Animals are genuine innocents, yet they don't have any chance,' added the woman.

'The experiments at the Institute are conducted under licence. Some of them involve meningitis research. What if a child of yours got the disease?' Christa asked her.

'I don't have a kid, but if I did it'd have to take its chances rather than use a drug tested on animals. And anyway, kids have a whole load of laws to protect them.'

The woman's voice was as unemotional as her companion's was vehement. She was either unbelievably naive or equally cold-blooded, thought Christa, remembering Bosnian women she'd met who'd submitted to rape to save their children's lives.

'Sounds to me as if you wouldn't put over our point of view even if we did give you information,' the man said to Christa, his voice breaking with indignation.

She guessed he could only be in his late teens. It was sunny outside, and the airless room was becoming very warm. He kept running his fingers impatiently inside the folds of the scarf at his neck as if to loosen them.

'You've read my writing, so you'll know I always put both sides of an issue,' said Christa. 'You want to suss out the real state of affairs at the Institute, and I'm interested in doing exactly the same at Gabriel. Since both places are connected, don't you think an information exchange makes sense for us all?'

Christa didn't like the sensation of supping with the devil, though she intended to be severely discouraging, and she was confident that Howl wouldn't be able to penetrate the Institute's security system in any case.

Her plea had been directed at the woman, but the man answered again.

'Join us first, then we'll know you're on the level,' he challenged. 'Or maybe you're too scared. It takes bottle to belong to Howl.'

'I'm sure it does,' said Christa drily. 'I've already explained, I can't go along with your methods. Of course I think animals shouldn't suffer unnecessarily, but I believe human beings are capable of suffering more.'

The young man shoved back his seat, scraping the legs along the floor, and began to walk restlessly up and down.

'The rich don't suffer, do they?' he said. 'And they're the ones who eat most meat and keep the butchers going. They pollute society. The scientists don't suffer either – they're torturers. We'll get them all in the end. You've seen nothing yet.'

In spite of his dramatic language Christa had to check a strong desire to laugh. He still came across as an adolescent Rambo, and was obviously using Howl as a focus for other deep-seated discontents.

'People like you who stand on the side-lines are the worst of all,' he flung wildly at her. 'People like you make the Holocaust happen. Can't you understand there's an animal Holocaust going on here in Oxford?'

Christa no longer wanted to laugh. If he'd ever seen genocide in action he'd know there was no comparison.

'Remarks like that don't fight fascism, they feed it,' she said, unable to keep the disgust from her voice.

'Are you calling me a fucking fascist?' he shouted at her across the table.

'Sit down, Paul,' the woman commanded. 'That's enough.'

Her curiously flat voice carried more menace than all his rantings. Christa, who'd been preparing to make a speedy exit, watched him subside on to his seat like a collapsing soufflé, and changed her mind.

The woman turned to her.

'He gets a bit carried away at times. All our young ones do.'

'Do you live round here?' Christa asked, as much to defuse the tension as learn more about them.

'Do you think we're daft?' said Paul. 'We wouldn't meet you on our own patch. No, I'm from Witney, and Eileen's a Brummie.'

Again the woman interrupted him.

'Before you get excited, those aren't our real names,' she said to Christa. 'And I'm still waiting to hear one good reason why we should talk to you.'

'Because I've got access to contacts in Gabriel, and I've seen inside the Institute. If something is wrong there, and you're really sincere, you shouldn't mind who takes it apart as long as it's done soon.'

'Of course we're bloody sincere, but how do we know you aren't working for the fuzz?' Paul demanded.

'You'll have to take a chance, just like me. I'm ready to trust you. And I'll acknowledge your help. You could do with some good publicity for a change.'

'Any publicity is good if it makes people aware of what animals suffer,' said Eileen.

She tilted back her chair, and gave Christa a thoughtful stare. Her eyes appeared to be a muddy brown. Christa wished with increasing frustration that she could pick up more clues to Eileen's appearance. Her task was made harder by the way her reading glasses blurred the only part of Eileen that she could see properly: her broad, stubby-fingered hands.

'OK, if your information's good enough, I'll give you something in return,' Eileen went on. 'You'd better start by describing the internal security at the Institute.'

It wasn't the deal of the century, but Christa decided she wasn't going to get any better.

'It's high tech stuff and lots of it,' she said briskly. 'An electronic barrier at the main door, and another before you can enter the research area. They work by code and handprint recognition, and there's video surveillance as well as security guards everywhere. You don't have a hope of getting through,' she added with immense satisfaction.

'Could you draw us a map of the internal layout?' asked Paul.

'Not a chance,' said Christa. 'We went through very fast, and it's like a maze inside.'

Paul gave a snort of disgust. 'Some reporter!' he said.

'What about the animals? What were their conditions? And how much evidence of surgery?' Eileen asked.

'No evidence of surgery at all. And you won't like this, but the holding rooms looked no worse than a good zoo.'

'Oh, yeah?' jeered Paul. 'Forgot to put on your specs, did you?'

At least Eileen seemed to be taking the information seriously.

'Did you take photos?' she asked.

'No. It wasn't that sort of visit.'

'What animals did you see?'

'Mice, rabbits, rats and some primates.'

'What kind of primates?'

'Vervets and marmosets. They had plenty of room to move around.'

'Any chimps?' demanded Eileen.

'None.'

'You're absolutely certain?'

'Positive,' said Christa, wondering why she was so insistent.

Whatever the reason, she guessed it wasn't at all the sort of information they were expecting. Paul had begun to walk impatiently up and down again, obviously longing for something more sensational. She could hear a plane droning high up in the sky, and the distant shouts of children, and longed to escape into the world outside, away from their paranoid questioning.

'It was all set up for your visit,' he said.

'It couldn't have been. The visit was made on the spur of the moment.'

'OK, things may have looked all right on the surface, but you didn't see any of the procedures, did you?'

'I watched a blood sample being taken. There was no obvious suffering, and the person who showed me around seemed to care a lot about the animals' welfare.'

Paul snorted in derision. 'Pull the other one!'

'Look,' said Christa, trying hard to restrain herself, 'as far as I'm concerned everything seemed completely above board at the Institute. In my opinion you're wasting your time there. I've told you all I know, so how about some information from you for a change?'

'You've told us nothing,' said Paul contemptuously. 'Nothing that'll help us liberate those animals. The meeting's been a dead loss as far as we're concerned.'

'There are other ways of changing things besides yours,' said Christa. She'd encountered his unlovely combination of brashness and aggression in young militants all over the world.

'Fat chance you'd get anywhere. You're just another middle-class liberal who's scared of rocking the boat.'

'I've a much better chance of putting things right than some half-baked Marxist,' said Christa, deciding she must have blown it by now, and determined to have her say before she made a very hasty exit.

'Who the fuck are you calling a Marxist? I'm English, not a bloody wog.'

'I told you, that's enough, Paul!' said Eileen. 'This isn't getting us anywhere.' She leaned towards Christa.

'Not everyone in Howl would agree, but I think we sometimes have to fight the bastards with their own weapons as well, so I'm going to give you your lead. And when you've heard it you'll know there's something wrong at the Institute.'

Eileen put her elbows on the table, and resting her chin on her clasped hands, spoke so softly that Christa had to strain to catch her voice.

'We've heard from a foreign animal rights group that someone at the Institute plans to smuggle in a baby chimp from the wild. It'll be done through a dealer on the continent. A deposit has already been made in a foreign bank account. Though the account is numbered and not named, we understand it's operated by someone at Gabriel Hall.'

For a moment Christa was stunned. She'd expected Howl to produce wild rumours of illegal methods of vivisection, but nothing like this.

'I was told categorically that the Institute doesn't use chimps,' she said. 'And the researchers are very closely supervised. Why would it need chimps from the wild anyway?'

'Not clued in on everything, are you, Miss Know-all?' Paul jeered.

'Some strains of disease originate among wild primate populations. Would you like me to tell you what happens to the baby chimps when they're taken?' said Eileen.

'Go on,' Christa said, steeling herself to listen.

'Their mothers are hacked to death, the infants dragged from their corpses and crammed into boxes like coffins. They're hidden in larger crates of fruit, and freighted in the freezing hold of an aircraft to some middleman in Europe. If they haven't died by then, they're doomed to a wretched existence in a laboratory cage at the mercy of the vivisectionist's knife.'

Christa shuddered. Eileen's emotive description was all the more horrific delivered in her flat unemphatic voice. But such an undertaking still seemed unthinkable in connection with the Institute. Her mind couldn't make sense of it, however hard she tried.

Leda would never collaborate in such a venture. Her senior researchers, whom Christa had met at the Master's party, and who as fellows of Gabriel were the only other people with a direct connection with the college, appeared honest to a degree. Phil had sufficient ambition, but was much too careful of his reputation to risk anything illegal.

'Don't you have more evidence?' she asked. 'Could you give me a contact number for your informant abroad?'

'Useless,' said Paul. 'He's just been put inside.'

'Have you tried talking to the lab technicians and the office staff after hours?'

'Yeah, we've tried, but they're all too fucking loyal to the murderer at the top.'

'It's not much to go on,' said Christa, keeping her temper with difficulty at hearing Leda described this way.

'Chickening out already?' sneered Paul.

'We believe our source. You'd better do so too,' Eileen interposed evenly, 'because we expect to see some concrete results from you soon.'

'I'll do my best, but I never promised results,' said Christa.

'Please yourself,' said Eileen. 'Just remember, Howl doesn't like to be let down.'

'Right. We're not a load of suckers like some other outfits round here,' said Paul.

Christa had had more than enough of him by now. Luckily Eileen appeared to feel the same way too.

'We're off, then. We've wasted enough time,' she said, getting up from the table. 'You'd better wait till we're out of the way. And don't bother to try that contact number again. It's been changed.'

Christa had no wish to follow them. Even she was daunted by the prospect of penetrating further into such a volatile organisation without back-up. She'd decided not to go any further with her enquiry. The threat she shrugged off. She'd heard worse a score of times before, and in any case she was sure they still didn't know her true identity.

Nevertheless, once Eileen and Paul had left, Christa was still interested enough to rush to the boarded-up window, snatch off her glasses, find a chink in the planks, and peer through.

They were already halfway down the path by the green, Paul hurrying in front, and Eileen stumping along behind. She was shorter than Christa had thought, but her shoulders strained against her jacket and she had the distinctive walk of someone who was either overweight or very heavily-built.

The couple disappeared round the end of the privet hedge, and as Christa heard a motor bike roar away she reflected that Eileen was clearly not someone to tangle with. The Gabriel's Mill investigation was a far safer bet.

10

Back at Gabriel Hall, Christa was astounded to find a note from the Master in her pigeon-hole promising her a cheque for most of the amount she needed by the end of the week. He was even vainer than she'd suspected. After hustling round the Oxford camera shops all afternoon, she got the promise of an excellent deal on equipment, heavily reduced in return for a mention in the credits, and arrived back in Jericho feeling unusually pleased with herself.

She poured herself a large vodka before collapsing in Jessie's chair while she decided which of the meals in the new freezer to defrost for supper in her equally new micro-wave.

The seat had been positioned to give Jessie the ultimate in surveillance on passers-by. Christa hadn't yet closed the curtains, and sat gazing idly out of the front window while the last light drained from the garden, leaving a bank of Michaelmas daisies by the path a pale blur in the dusk.

The street lamps were already lit, but she didn't register the arrival of a car outside until the garden gate was pushed open, and a woman came up the path struggling with some heavy rectangular object in one hand, and a bulging bag in the other. A moment later she gave the letter box flap a furious rattle.

Christa switched on the light, and went to open the front door. Emma confronted her again. This time her hair was under control. She was wearing her best suit and an expression like a government chief whip. Jamie was lying in a carry-cot on the step, sleeping sweetly beneath the hood. Christa guessed at once what Emma was going to ask.

'Phil's let you down again, hasn't he?' she demanded.

'I'd run myself into the ground getting Jamie ready for bed, so he'd only have Pansy to cope with.' Emma's voice vibrated with anger. 'I was all ready to go when he casually announced on the phone that the visiting scientist was dining in hall tonight, and he felt he had to stay on. Then he had the nerve to get stroppy when I objected!'

'You'd better come in,' Christa said. 'It's cold out here.'

She picked up the carry-cot and hefted it on to the sitting-room sofa. A large pack of disposable nappies was wedged into the foot, and the bag Emma dumped next to it was stuffed with baby gear.

'You promised you'd help me next time, remember? Well, this is it.' Emma's face was fierce with determination.

'All right, all right, I guess I'll just have to manage,' said Christa, who'd already resigned herself to the inevitable. 'There's no need to go over the top. You can bet Phil's probably putting away caviare at this very minute, so the sooner you get to London and start enjoying yourself, the better.'

'You're an angel!' said Emma, face now wreathed in smiles of relief. 'Honestly, you'll love looking after Jamie. He's so good most of the time. And at least you won't have Pansy. I've fixed for her to stay the night at Chelsea's house.'

Emma hesitated, twisting the Victorian silver cuff bangle she always wore.

'I suppose – I suppose you wouldn't keep Jamie till tomorrow afternoon, would you? That way I could do some shopping before I leave. Tomorrow Chelsea's coming back to our house with Pansy for the day. Phil was planning to work on a paper, but he'll just have to look after them instead. I'm afraid if I try to dump Jamie on him as well, he might refuse.'

Christa could scarcely imagine making it through the night with Jamie, let alone a whole twenty-four hours, but the thought of Phil's face when he discovered he was in charge of not just one, but two temperamental five-year-olds, urged her on.

'No problem,' she said nonchalantly. 'I'll expect you this time tomorrow – but this is strictly a one-off, don't forget.'

'I'll fetch the buggy from the car,' said Emma. 'Everything else is here. Don't let him have anything sweet, and don't let him watch the television. It could do all sorts of harm. The mind's extremely receptive at this stage. But he should sleep through like a lamb till the morning.'

Emma's forecast was disastrously inaccurate. The moment she drove away, Jamie woke up and decided to stay awake forever.

In vain Christa consulted the baby book. She tried nappy changing, but he squirmed under her ministrations like a trapped ferret, and simply became livelier still. The green and yellow globs of baby food from the jars provided by Emma, which Christa had laboriously heated to just the right temperature, he instantly spat out. Worst of all, he ingested a bottle of milk like a human vacuum cleaner, and when she held him afterwards to pat his back, regurgitated the feed in massive burps until her shoulder looked as if it was covered in guano.

By midnight Jamie was continuing to hang on to wakefulness like a party guest who wouldn't go home. Eventually, in guilty desperation, she propped him on the sofa in front of her newly acquired television, and switched on a late-night movie. It was *The Sound of Music*, Christa's least favourite musical, but to her amazed delight Jamie was mesmerised.

For the first time ever Christa felt friendly towards the family von Trapp. Though Jamie had an attention span as small as himself, with a bit of luck she might get ten minutes' peace. She sat next to him, gave him a rock hard ginger nut to chew, poured herself another vodka, and put her feet up on Jessie's shiny leather pouffe.

One moment she was watching Julie Andrews twirl through Alpine meadows, and 'The Jolly Goatherd' was pounding hypnotically into her ears. The next she woke to find a test card on the screen, and Jamie asleep at last with the biscuit reposing on his chest. She tiptoed upstairs to her bedroom with the carry-cot as if it were dynamite. Her final thought before falling into unconsciousness was that he must surely sleep until mid-morning at least.

At first light a human alarm call bored relentlessly into her dreams. Jamie, scarlet-faced, dribble pouring down his chin, was crying in the high-pitched miserable wail which meant real trouble. He was teething again.

Even Poppaea had had enough. When, after half an hour of trying to soothe Jamie, Christa carried him downstairs, the parrot took one look and went into a deep sulk, hiding her head in her feathers at the back of the cage. Christa put on another bottle to heat. When the phone rang, she dumped the still-howling Jamie on the sofa, and snatched it up eagerly, praying it was Emma.

Instead her mother's voice sounded down the line.

'Phil told me Emma had left Jamie with you. I can't think why she didn't let me have him. How are you getting on? I've been worrying all night about you both.'

Christa looked at her watch. Eight o'clock, so her mother was phoning as she made early-morning tea. Christa could imagine her anxious face under its crown of pink plastic rollers.

'We're both fine,' she said. 'I'm just fixing Jamie's morning feed,' she added nonchalantly, as if she'd been preparing bottles for years.

'But there must be something the matter with him. I can hear him crying. He doesn't sound at all happy to me.'

'He's simply got a little problem with his dentition,' said Christa, using one of the emollient phrases from the baby book, though Jamie's incisors had reached sabre-toothed tiger proportions in her mind.

'Teething!' screeched Alice. 'That's just when they pick up all sorts of infections! Have you taken his temperature?'

'No, I haven't, because it's not necessary.' The thought of trying to keep Jamie still while she held the thermometer in the place recommended by the baby book was too awful to contemplate. 'For heaven's sake, Mother, will you please stop interfering?'

'But the poor little mite sounds completely hysterical. Why aren't you cuddling him? Babies need lots of affection, you know.'

'I'm not cuddling him because I'm holding the phone to talk to you,' said Christa. 'And he doesn't like my sort of cuddling, anyway.'

She resisted an irrational urge to give in and confide in her mother, who would instantly take her back into favour and dole out the sympathy she so badly needed. The price was too high.

'I've got to go. The bottle's ready. Don't worry, everything's under control,' she said, slamming down the aerial on the phone, and pressing the No Call button to cut off any further advice.

Jamie drank most of the bottle, then promply burst into tears once more. Bracing herself, she held him to her shoulder, his hot, wet little face plastered against hers, and waited for the inevitable regurgitation. His entire body shuddered with misery. Cautiously she tried putting him back on the sofa. With tears streaming down his face he held out his arms piteously in his first ever real demonstration of affection towards her.

For a moment Christa was so taken aback that she simply stood and stared at him. To her astonishment she felt herself being swamped by a huge unnerving surge of protective love. She picked him up and as he burrowed into the space between her chin and her neck, found herself murmuring all sorts of ridiculous baby-talk into his ear. After several minutes his sobs began to subside, he gave a series of hiccups, and became unbelievably silent.

Cautiously Christa peered at him. His thumb was plugged into his mouth, and though his lashes were still spiky with tears, his blue eyes gazed serenely back at her. Feeling like a single-handed yachtsman trying to batten everything down between squalls, she rushed him upstairs, changed his nappy, and wiped his face and hands, all without a murmur of protest. While she held him in her lap to brush his hair, she even dredged up a couple of nursery rhymes and sang them to him, rocking to their beat. If Randall could see her now, she thought wrily, he really would think she'd lost her grip.

Emboldened by her success, Christa decided to postpone her own breakfast and take Jamie for a walk. She inserted him into his outdoor suit, discarded her sweater, which smelt like a cheese factory, and dragged on her old blue cardigan and Sarajevo jacket over her jeans.

Ten minutes later she was trundling Jamie along the canal tow path. After long pauses to look at some ducks and a woman shaking out rugs on a narrow boat, they crossed the railway bridge to Port Meadow. On the far side, where the Isis wound away to Wolvercote and Gabriel's Grounds, a trail of mist still lingered along the river bank. The sun hadn't yet broken through, and the air was damp and cold.

By now Christa was desperate for coffee, but Jamie remained determinedly ready for entertainment. She turned down a track into Cripley Meadow allotments, which lay to her left between the river and the railway. With fewer diversions he might take a nap and allow her to snatch a pit stop at the Jericho Café.

In the final luxuriant flush of autumn the allotments were as lush as an urban Garden of Eden. To the right of the track a tributary of the Isis threaded silently between banks of rustling sedge and overhanging willow boughs. Water weed, combed by the current into strands of long green hair, streamed over its gravelly bed.

Christa's feet were already wet, but though the buggy was lurching along the potholed path like a miniature tank, Jamie seemed happy still. The track stretched as far as she could see, and she pushed determinedly on, diverting herself by studying the characterful assortment of garden shacks which had sprouted among the allotments as naturally as mushrooms.

Some of the plots were completely overgrown. Others, especially those near the stream, burgeoned with vegetables which would have satisfied the greediest still-life artist. There were feathery rows of carrots, enormous grey and jagged artichoke heads, knee-high leeks with leaves like bunches of stiff green ribbon, and courgettes which had swollen into vegetable zeppelins.

In the distance an elderly couple tended a bonfire, and a little way ahead a man was digging, but otherwise the allotments were deserted. The smell of woodsmoke and freshly turned earth lingered in the chilly air. Christa stopped for a moment to rest her arms, remembering the gardens cultivated against all odds in Sarajevo, and now like Matt's grave under a mantle of snow.

As Jamie began to wriggle in his harness, she was glad to continue the walk. The man ahead was working one of the largest plots, which ran almost to the stream's edge and boasted a shed with marked delusions of grandeur. It had a steep corrugated-iron roof, a stove-pipe chimney, a proper window picked out in red paint, and even a rudimentary verandah with steps made from sections of railway sleepers. To one side were some gnarled fruit trees, and on the other the boiler of an old engine now in its second career as a rainwater tank.

The man had his back to her, and was shaking potatoes like huge pearls from the dark earth before throwing them into a pail. He wore wellingtons, threadbare cords, and a navy sweater with thinning elbows. He paused for a moment to stretch his back, and the light gleamed on straight blond hair.

Irritably thinking that Mallory Farrar turned up more often than a motorway contra-flow, Christa prepared to make a swift exit in the opposite direction. In her haste she tripped over a rut. Jamie, jolted once too often, let out a roar which made a marauding band of gulls soar into the air.

Farrar turned and saw her. He hesitated, then stuck the fork in the ground, picked up the bucket and came clumping towards them, his boots heavy with earth. The fellows of Gabriel generally considered that too much physical exertion produced a muscle-bound mind, and had commensurate physiques. But Farrar looked as if he'd enjoyed wrestling with the potatoes, and gave an annnoyingly attractive impression of restrained energy.

'Hallo there,' he said. 'Nice day, isn't it?'

'I suppose so.' Her voice was curt as she struggled to turn the buggy, which had suddenly developed rigor mortis.

'Those wheels are stuck. They're clogged with mud.'

'I don't need two doctorates to realise that,' she retorted through the noise of Jamie's howls. Her arms felt as if they were about to snap from their sockets.

Farrar put down the bucket, lifted the buggy by the foot-rest at the other end, and neatly swung it round. Jamie was startled into momentary silence. He gazed at the figure above him. Farrar stared gravely back, then turned to Christa, his eyebrows raised.

'Yours?' he asked. 'He's very like you.'

How dare he jump to such a conclusion? Christa thought angrily. And no doubt he'd added charges of immaturity and social irresponsibility on her part.

'Of course he isn't mine,' she snapped back. 'He's Emma's child.'

'So that explains it. Somehow I couldn't quite see you in a parental role.'

'I don't know why not. It's no big deal.'

Jamie's howls had begun to change into a whining grizzle. She bent to adjust a loose buckle on his harness, and worriedly noticed that his cheek was scarlet once more. She'd left her gloves at home, and her hands were so cold they were scarcely functioning. She accidentally gave his arm a slight bump, and the grizzle notched up several more decibels. Her manufactured nonchalance started to disappear fast.

'Now look what you've done,' she hurled at Farrar through the din, squashing the unwelcome thought that she was echoing Emma's words to her. 'We were having an OK walk till you came along. It'll take me forever to calm him down.'

'Aren't you exaggerating rather?' he asked coolly.

He picked up the potatoes again with the obvious intention of escape and glanced towards the shed, where, Christa instantly decided, he probably had waiting for him all sorts of delightful refreshments dear to the male gardener's heart: a thermos of steaming tea, slabs of fruit cake, perhaps even a warming slug of alcohol. Her last cup of coffee was twelve hours away, and she lost her patience completely.

'You've obviously never looked after a baby,' she said. 'But go on, run away to that . . .' she broke off, casting about for inspiration, and remembered another of Pansy's story books. '. . . that ridiculous gingerbread house of yours! Whenever you're losing an argument you never stick around.'

Angrily she unclipped the harness she'd so laboriously adjusted, hoisted Jamie against her shoulder, and with her free hand prepared to drag the buggy along behind her until she reached tarmac again.

Mallory felt as if a whirlwind had descended on him from a cabbage patch, and was now just as suddenly about to depart. Her discomfiture might have amused him, if he hadn't been having some productive thoughts about his new book for the first time in days. She was the one who'd ruined things, though he had to admit the baby was giving her an extremely hard time, flinging his rigid body backwards in paroxysms of rage. And she did look wretchedly cold, he conceded grudgingly.

He grabbed the buggy from her.

'You'd better come inside and do something about that child,' he said, setting off purposefully towards the shed.

'What do you mean, *do* something?' he heard her indignant voice exclaim behind him. 'I bet you know as much about babies as a Buddhist monk.'

'That'd have to be more than you, by the look of it,' he flung back.

Unexpectedly, the ridiculousness of the situation made him want to laugh. They were both bluffing like mad, he thought. He cast a quick glance over his shoulder as he climbed the steps to the hut. He'd half expected her to storm off without the buggy, but she was gingerly picking her way towards him, scowling at the inoffensive vegetables whose dew-laden leaves overhung the narrow path.

'Leave your shoes on the verandah,' he called to her. 'Harry Buller's fussy about his hut.'

Christa's trainers were so heavy with mud that they felt like a deep-sea diver's boots, and the ankles of her jeans were soaked. Kicking off the shoes outside the door, she vowed never to be cast in the role of long-term child-minder again. A few hours of this sort of endurance test were all she could take at the most.

The inside of the shed smelled of creosote. It contained an unlit stove, a frayed piece of carpet, and two rusty metal folding chairs slung with daisy-patterned nylon. Above rows of tools, sagging shelves were crammed with more gardening equipment and a stack of dog-eared seed catalogues.

Farrar, standing in his socks at a table with gashed legs and a ringed top, was about to light a camping gas burner. A tin kettle stood by its side.

'Who's Harry Buller?' Christa asked, warily taking one of the chairs and settling Jamie in her lap. In the new surroundings he'd become magically silent.

'My scout. He's in hospital. I'm looking after his allotment for him until he's well again.'

So it was Mallory Farrar, philanthropist, now. She'd never expected that particular manifestation, thought Christa, watching him adjust the flame. His hands, seamed with earth, were long-fingered with blunt tips. Catching her gaze, he unexpectedly smiled, and his mouth acquired a quirky and totally transforming tilt.

'Go on, now tell me you run a soup kitchen for down and outs,' he said. 'I wouldn't believe you, but I can see you're longing to go one better.'

Christa, again thoroughly wrong-footed, was still punch-drunk enough to slam back an automatic reply.

'I did once cook for a truckload of refugees in Bosnia,' she said, then was astonished to find herself adding, 'but I was hopeless at it. Someone else had to rescue me.'

She smiled to herself, remembering the very large, very Slavonic matron who'd forcefully shooed her away.

Farrar glanced at her. The flame was roaring steadily under the kettle.

'It'll soon be warm in here,' he said. 'I'm going outside to get the dirt off my hands. I'll fix those wheels at the same time.'

The chill was already fading from the air, and Christa quickly divested Jamie of his outdoor suit while he was still in a good mood. To her relief the nappy seemed to be holding out. She shrugged her arms from her coat, remembered she'd put some ginger nuts in her pocket, and gave him one. He began to gnaw at it, his eyes fixed on the flame.

She decided to try one of the nursery rhymes again before Farrar returned to catch her in such an undignified activity. It worked even better this time. By the third verse, Jamie fell asleep as suddenly as if the gas flame had been put out. She removed the biscuit, and rested her chin on his downy fuzz of hair, feeling unaccountably satisfied as the warm pulse beneath his skull beat against her skin.

Farrar, after returning from a tap by the main track, quietly pushed open the door. His gaze met Christa, ensconced like a fin-de-siècle Madonna in the rickety chair, legs tucked beneath it, not quite concealing a couple of impressive holes in her socks. The baby slept, his mouth corked with his thumb. The other small hand was stranded starfish-like on the skin of her breast, which swelled away into a warm, shadowed curve beneath her loosely buttoned cardigan.

She had already surprised him with her brief display of self-deprecating humour. Now her usual back-to-the-wall expression had gone, and was replaced by an unsettlingly tender, wistful look. Inconveniently for his own peace of mind, her story that

Gareth Hyde had exploited her became suddenly much more credible.

The kettle was sending a plume of steam into the roof. Taking his supply of coffee from the shelf, he made a brew in Harry's old aluminium percolator. He retrieved a second mug from behind a roll of twine, put it on the table with a carton of milk, and decided that the cinnamon Danish he'd bought himself would have to be sacrificed. Using the flattened bag as a plate, he placed it on an upended vegetable box by her side.

'Sorry it isn't gingerbread,' he said.

Her slightly ashamed smile almost made the sacrifice worthwhile. He saw her look round and establish that the pastry was the only one.

'Let's share it,' she said.

'I don't have a knife.'

'I thought explorers were always hung about with weapons.'

He poured out the coffee, and took a mug to her side.

'Not this one. But maybe there's something here which would do,' he replied, going to investigate the shelves.

'Of course, I'd forgotten. Karate's more your line. Where did you learn?'

'In Japan, a few years ago. The philosophy of it appeals to me.'

'I suppose you've got several black belts.' Her face was decidedly mischievous now.

He found a broken table knife which looked as if it had been used for digging out dandelion roots, and decided to join the tease.

'Nothing so showy. I'm a second dan.'

'What's that?'

'A second dan teaches black belts,' he replied, cutting the Danish pastry neatly in half, and taking a piece for himself.

She settled the baby more firmly, and gave him a swift smile of complicity, as if she'd enjoyed the riposte. He liked the easy way she'd adjusted to the situation, and thought with an odd sense of guilt that he'd been so uptight over his own problems that perhaps he hadn't given her much of a chance. If Hyde's defection really hadn't been her fault, she was bound to be self-protective.

She took a sip from her mug. 'That's good,' she said in a surprised tone. 'I suppose you were taught how to make coffee by some incredibly charismatic old Turkish sage?'

'Almost right. I was taught by his incredibly charismatic young Turkish wife. Strictly in the pursuit of research, of course.'

'Of course.'

Though he'd accompanied his reply with a derisive look, and though her reply was heavy with irony, Christa believed him. She suspected that once he started to concentrate on his work, all other interests would be forgotten. Rather like herself, except that she hadn't been able to forget Gareth.

Her thoughts were going in a dangerous direction. She hurriedly began to eat the pastry.

'So, where are you off to when this book's finished?' she asked. 'There can't be many unspoiled places left.'

He sat down in the other chair, and propped his feet on a reel of hosepipe. His socks at least looked as if they belonged to an explorer. They were made of thick grey wool, and the toes had been neatly darned, no doubt by an adoring little woman in some far-flung bazaar whom liberation hadn't touched.

He looked at her over his coffee as if he suspected what she was thinking.

'Ladakh, perhaps. It's a fairly closed society still.'

'Like Gabriel, don't you think?' she couldn't resist saying. 'Though you're obviously a great fan of the system.'

'When I was a student under Professor Saltash, the college was a marvellous place. Even you would have approved. You've got me wrong. I don't much like what's going on just now.'

'Then why don't you try to put it right?'

'You've asked me that already.' His voice was dry.

'I don't think you gave the real answer.'

'At the moment I'm more interested in a quiet life.'

'But the whole college is so obviously riddled with malpractice. I don't understand how you can let things slide.'

'You must know better than most that it isn't possible to join every crusade.'

'This is on your own doorstep, though.' She tried to keep her voice down as the baby stirred in his sleep. 'And if something like this isn't controlled, in the end it becomes unstoppable.'

He shrugged. 'How do you propose to stop it, then? I suppose through this film you're trying to persuade the Master to support?'

'Have persuaded,' she interrupted.

'If we're pursuing a mutual reckoning, it's only fair to tell me what's behind the film.'

'You don't really expect me to let you in on my plans?'

'No, but I promise I won't split on you if you do.'

Surprisingly, Christa discovered she believed him, but at this stage she didn't intend to take any risks.

'I think you'd turn all moral on me if I did.'

'If you'd read my books, you wouldn't say that.'

'If you'd seen my reporting, you wouldn't be so suspicious.'

'I have seen your reporting. It's almost too good. As I was trying to say the other night, it's one thing to expose a first-class shit like the Master, and quite another to do so much damage to the college that it doesn't have a hope of getting back to how it was.'

'I thought you weren't interested.'

'I'm not,' he said. 'It was simply an objective observation.'

'One of your specialities, Dr Farrar,' she said wrily.

'You aren't so bad at them yourself. And don't you think you've ribbed me enough over that honorary doctorate? My name's Mallory, or even Mal if you like. And I'd much rather call you Christa. How about it?'

Christa, still thinking about the college, absent-mindedly capitulated. 'All right,' she said.

Jamie stirred again, snuffled, and opened his eyes, staring at his surroundings as if he'd never seen them before. Christa produced another biscuit, but he flung it on the floor. Hastily she began to insert him into his outdoor suit.

'Thanks for the coffee, but I'll have to go,' she said, struggling back into her own coat. 'It's way past Jamie's next feed.'

She got up, and glanced through the window. The colour of the clouds had gone from pale grey to charcoal while she'd been inside. Mallory stood up as well, and took a jacket from a peg behind the door.

'I'll walk you home. It's starting to rain. Where do you live?'

'Jericho. Really, you don't need to. It's not far, and the buggy has a hood.'

'But you haven't, and I've an umbrella. I'm teaching after lunch, and Jericho's on my way.'

Neither of them spoke as they walked along the sodden allotment track. Christa was fully occupied with the buggy, and Jamie had been reduced to silence by the tall umbrella-wielding figure who strode beside him. But when they reached the canal path again, an old lady in a pleated plastic rainhood feeding the ducks gave them such an approving smile that Christa suddenly became aware of their familial appearance. She almost burst out laughing, knowing there couldn't have been in Oxford that day two people more determined to stay free.

'What's the joke?' Mallory enquired.

'I was thinking we must look exactly like a building society logo,' she said, stopping the buggy so that Jamie could take another look at the ducks.

'What a fate,' Mallory said, but a smile pulled up one corner of his mouth as he halted by her side.

He was being so unexpectedly good-tempered in a situation where Gareth would have run a mile, that Christa suddenly decided she must clear up the business of the student documentary after all.

'I swear to you I'm not gunning for the college itself,' she said, as the ducks squabbled in the murky water. 'But you must acknowledge that nothing'll improve until the Master goes. And I've actually seen written evidence that he intends to go back on Professor Saltash's promise to develop the Mill site for the benefit of Gabriel's Grounds Estate. I'm going to use the documentary to show him up.'

'You have been busy,' he said drily. 'So I was right. It's to be a night of the long knives. Have you thought about the consequences for your students if it goes wrong?'

'They know they can pull out whenever they like. And if it shows any signs of going wrong, I'll scrap it. But I'm pretty sure I can make it work.'

'What's the format going to be?'

'A debate in the Great Hall with the participants producing

video evidence, and the Master in a key role. He won't realise what's happening until it's too late.'

'Why not simply give Leda your information, and let her deal with it?'

Christa frowned, watching a marauding swan barge in among the ducks.

'She's too above board to take him on effectively at his own game. And she's got too much to lose if she doesn't win. It'd be a disaster if she didn't become the next Master.'

'At least we agree over that,' said Mallory.

He sounded fractionally more receptive. She wondered whether to tell him what she'd heard from Howl as well. It was still weighing on her mind, and it would be good to have an objective opinion to back up her own.

'Oddly enough, I've also been given information about a scam at the Institute, but it's so far-fetched I've decided to ignore it.'

'What kind of scam? And how would you know what goes on at the Institute?'

She hesitated, unsure of trusting Mallory any further. But if she didn't give him some firm evidence to back up such a radical statement, he'd discount everything she said in future.

'I fixed a meeting with Howl,' she said. 'They told me.'

He turned and looked at her.

'Wasn't that rather risky?' he asked quietly.

'Yes, but I'm sure you often take risks.'

'I draw the line at psychopaths.'

She ignored the barb. 'Howl's heard that someone at the Institute plans to smuggle in a baby chimpanzee from the wild.'

'Without Leda knowing? She's got an iron grip on the place, and her reputation's whiter than white. It sounds like some paranoid Howl fantasy to me.'

'That was my reaction, too,' said Christa, feeling surprisingly comforted by the scornful disbelief in his voice.

'To go back to the business of Gabriel's Mill. If you're so sure you can produce firm evidence, why not simply put it before the fellows at a meeting of Governing Body? Even the Master can't go against a majority.'

'Too risky. The Master has too strong a grip on the older dons, and there are just enough of them to sway the vote. As far as I can see, the only way to discredit him would be academically. It's the one thing they wouldn't forgive. But he's got such a stainless reputation in the archaeological world.'

Mallory began to laugh. 'You don't believe in doing things by halves, do you?'

His face became grave again as he kicked a stick into the water, and watched it being drawn to the centre of the stream.

'If you're really set on this crazy scheme, your last idea at least has some potential,' he said after a long silence. 'I probably shouldn't tell you this, given your bloodhound tendencies, but I heard something interesting from a retired fellow the other day. Years ago he was the Master's tutor, and he's disliked him ever since. He said that after the Waylandsbury Hoard was discovered there was a rumour that he'd hijacked someone else's data to locate the site.'

Christa's hands were frozen again after the stop, but she hardly noticed. She turned the buggy away from the water, and began to walk on excitedly.

'Did he say how he'd heard the rumour?' she asked.

'I didn't ask, but the Master's got plenty of enemies outside Gabriel. Apparently some of them have already tried to topple him that way, but so far no one's found a shred of evidence.'

He looked sideways at her. 'It'd be the academic kiss of death if it could be proved, but personally I'd lay off the whole business if I were you. Why risk your own career?'

'It wouldn't be the first time,' said Christa, as they reached a footbridge back into Jericho. 'I'll manage.'

He looked so unconvinced as he helped her lift the buggy up the steps, that by the time they reached the other side of the canal she'd decided to let the subject drop.

She started to push the buggy briskly along the pavement, longing for the encounter to end so that she could think about this new revelation. Mallory loped easily along at her side. Like a camel making for the next oasis, she thought, as she steered the conversation to the ever-useful climate.

'This weather must seem dismal to you after the desert.'

'Not at all. I like the rain. The British don't know how lucky they are.'

She wasn't sure if it was meant as a rebuke, but it felt like one, and made her decide to spike the small talk with something sharper.

'Do you have any family here, or were you raised in a Bedouin tent?' she asked.

'Nothing so exotic. I was brought up in Cheltenham.'

'Cheltenham!' It seemed an unlikely setting. 'I don't believe it!'

'No need to sound so dismissive. It's a good place.'

'What do your parents do?'

'My father died last year. He was a musician. And my mother's an anaesthetist. Nothing very out of the ordinary.'

'That's dashing compared to mine. Dad works as a college librarian, and my mother's the champion housewife of Botley.'

He smiled, lengthening his step to avoid a puddle swimming with leaves. 'Lucky you. When I was a child I never saw much of my mother. But I've three elder sisters who stood in for her. I had to leave home in self-defence.'

'I'm sorry about your father,' said Christa, thought it was still hard to imagine Mallory with any sort of family, except perhaps some romantic band of misguidedly devoted retainers.

'So am I. I was staying in a God-awful flop-house in Tamanrasset when I got the news. I didn't think I'd mind so much.'

Christa wondered if the jacket he was wearing now, a somewhat fogeyish blue and brown check tweed which nevertheless hung remarkably elegantly on his spare frame, had belonged to his father. But she didn't like to ask, and in any case they'd progressed at such a rate that they were already at the house.

She stopped, and leaned over the front gate to release the latch. When she turned back to Mallory he was scrutinising the façade. She braced herself for a comprehensive send-up.

'So this is *your* gingerbread house,' he said with a grin. 'What a splendid place. Is it as good inside?'

Christa was so disarmed by the genuine admiration in his voice that she came dangerously near inviting him in. But the sitting room and kitchen were disaster zones after Jamie's occupation, and she refused to give him more evidence of her incompetence.

'I don't have Gretel's domestic talents, but why don't you come and take a look one day?' she said, half hoping the invitation was vague enough for him not to take up.

'Maybe I will,' he said, sounding equally non-committal. 'The man I'm writing about, Quentin Stannage, is buried nearby, in St Sepulchre. I ought to look around there sometime as well.'

'Thanks for the rescue.'

'Any time. I'll see you round college, then.' He glanced at Jamie, who was chewing determinedly on a loose end of his harness. 'And don't let the infant Dracula get you down.'

Christa shoved the buggy through the gate. When she looked round Mallory was almost at the end of the street. She opened the front door, thinking in amusement that they'd spent the whole of their enforced time together emphasising their independence, when nothing could have been more obvious anyway.

As if programmed, Jamie began to wail the moment she stepped into the hall. Altogether, she thought more soberly, as she bore him towards the kitchen, the morning had been a steep learning curve. She'd made totally unexpected discoveries about herself as well as Mallory Farrar, and the information he'd given her about the Master's academic piracy was so fascinating that it more than made up for having to abandon Howl's lead.

Eight students had turned up for Christa's second seminar. Justin, in Levis and a striped shirt, stood at the table where she'd been demonstrating how the camcorders worked.

'What are we waiting for?' he demanded. 'Let's go and try them out.'

His hands lingered proprietorially on one of them. Steve was next to him, poised to grab the other.

They'd monopolised the action so far. Christa guessed that Rebekah, absorbing everything but making little comment, knew how to use a camcorder anyway. But Donna, wearing a droopy black sweater and skirt, was standing at the back, biting her nails in frustration and glowering at Justin's girlfriend Annabel, a sleek blonde who spent most of her time concentrating on him rather than the matter in hand.

'So you want to hurtle off into the blue and waste your stock filming everything in sight?' said Christa acidly. 'Sorry, but our budget won't run to it. You've got to have a project and a shooting script before you start.'

With satisfaction she saw Justin's hands fall to his sides.

'How can we, when you haven't told us your great idea?' he said petulantly. 'Or maybe there isn't one after all.'

'I've got an idea. Whether it's great will be up to you.'

Christa sat on the edge of her table, first removing a film of chalk, and pulled a sheaf of photocopies from her bag. She felt unusually nervous. She was about to steer them into a project which could be as hazardous for their careers as hers, and at some stage she'd have to make the risk very clear.

'Dreaming Spires TV is running a student competition,' she said. 'It could be perfect for you. See what you think.'

She handed out the details and waited while the class studied them, at first lethargically and then with increasing interest. Even Annabel stopped filing her nails as she read over Justin's shoulder.

'Terrific! It's made for us,' said Steve, raising his cropped head. 'But it says here we need official permission. The Master's always run a mile from any student involvement in the media. He's too scared of criticism. And if we entered the competition we'd certainly want to criticise.'

'You bet,' said Rebekah, who, in a tartan mini-skirt and canary yellow sweater, was decorating her photocopy with a cartoon of the Master.

'I thought that's how you'd feel, and so I've already spoken to him,' said Christa nonchalantly. 'He's agreed to let you set up and film a panel debate between the students and the establishment. It can be on any subject of current concern, and it'll probably take place in the Great Hall.'

There was a long silence, in which the sound of the choristers practising in the chapel floated faintly towards them. The whole class was staring incredulously at her.

'Wow!' said Rebekah. 'How did you fix it? We've never been allowed an in-college debate on anything to do with Gabriel.'

'It's a fucking miracle,' said Steve.

Christa thought so too, but remembering her role, produced a suitably sober response.

'It was hard work, and it's going to mean hard work for all of you too. The Master intends to bring in some heavyweight alumni to support the establishment's case, and he wants to use clips from the official documentary on Gabriel as well.'

'That'll load things in the college's favour from the start,' said Justin. 'There'll be squads of Nobel prize winners sounding off about the need to preserve Gabriel exactly as it is. And that bloody documentary shows Oxford just as the oldies would love it to be – clear-eyed, clean-limbed youth learning how to become leaders of men.'

'With never a mention of women, of course,' said Lallie, a quiet, intense girl who sat next to Donna.

'Then you'll be pleased to hear I've also persuaded the Master to let you back up your own views with video material which you can shoot yourselves,' said Christa. 'His side will find it very hard to argue with screen evidence, so long as you make it strong enough, and so long as you keep it under wraps until the debate.'

Justin was looking at her with dawning respect. 'You really get to it, don't you?' he said.

'Since you aren't going to be able to work on your programme full-time,' Christa went on, 'I think you should choose just one student grievance for the moment and focus on that.'

'Hard to know where to start!' said Donna happily, sinking her teeth into an apple. The students seemed to graze all day long on a succession of fast foods.

'How about college funds?' proposed Mike, a quiet post-graduate at the back of the class. 'Most of the surplus goes on perks for the senior fellows.'

'Yeah, that's true,' said Steve. 'A promotion trip to the Virgin Islands for the Bursar, new custom-made sofas for the SCR, celebration feasts at the drop of a hat – but strictly limited to high table of course. Whereas Rebekah here has to grovel for the fare to give a paper in Cambridge, the Junior Common Room looks like a penitentiary, and most of the poorer students can't afford to dine in hall at all.'

Donna abandoned her apple, pushed past Annabel and arrived breathlessly in front of Christa, her eyes shining with fervour.

'The big issue, the one where we'd grab everyone's sympathy, is college accommodation! Specifically the cost of it, and the way nothing decent's provided for second years or female post-grads.'

Justin grinned. He squared off his hands in an imaginary frame and squinted through them at Donna.

'We could get lots of great shots there,' he said. 'Students starving in garrets on one chip butty a day.'

'Sod all you know about starving! It's a bloody disgrace the way you were given second-year accommodation in college because of your dad's hand-outs,' Donna said angrily. 'But we've got it easy compared with kids outside. At least we have some chance of a job.'

Justin began to saw at an imaginary violin. 'Spare us your Tyneside socialism, Donna, please. If you don't look out for yourself these days, no one else will.'

'This kind of argument isn't getting us anywhere,' said Christa firmly. 'But Donna does have a point. Don't forget you'll have a wider TV audience besides the one in college, and the public at the moment isn't especially sympathetic towards privilege.'

Steve, sitting hunched forwards with his hands on his knees while the others talked, stopped drumming the heels of his boots impatiently on the floor.

'You mean link our issue to a larger one, preferably within the town?'

'Well done, Steve,' Christa said, trying to keep the irony from her voice. She was rewarded by an almost amiable look.

'Hey, that's a nice one!' said Rebekah. 'But the only real link Gabriel has with the locals is over the development of the Mill site, and the college has promised that it'll benefit the estate tenants' association anyway.'

'Yet the development seems to be taking a surprisingly long time to go through,' said Christa, trying to sound all innocence.

She scanned the line of faces in front of her, and waited hopefully. There was a moment's startled silence. Even Annabel stopped admiring her nails, and gazed at Christa with her mouth dropping open in a crimson O.

'You mean perhaps the college doesn't intend to benefit the tenants after all?' she said wonderingly.

'It's not for me to say what the college intends,' answered Christa, remembering scores of similarly dusty answers she'd had from politicians in her time. 'But it might be interesting for you to try to find out.'

'What's it to do with our accommodation, though?' Annabel asked, widening her eyes into a Betty Boop stare.

'For God's sake, dumbo, no wonder you've only two Ds at "A" level. I suppose Daddy's money got you in here too,' said Steve impatiently. 'It could mean Gabriel's planning to build new student accommodation out there. That'd be way out of order because it's miles from college. Or else Gabriel could want to move something big like the library store to the Mill site, to free up land in town for student flats. Either way it'd really fuck up the locals' plans.'

'Yes!' said Justin, punching his clenched fists into the air. 'That's it! So let's zip along to the Dean's office and see what we can find out. We'll try the Bursar if he's not around.'

He was already moving towards the camcorders again. Christa smartly side-stepped into his path.

'What do the rest of you think?' she demanded.

'It's a crap idea,' said Steve. 'The establishment's never going to admit anything.'

'Exactly,' she said, wondering just how long she'd be able to keep up this lengthy approach to a problem it would have taken her two seconds to solve. 'So where else could you look for information?'

'On the estate?' said Donna doubtfully.

'Yes, of course!' exclaimed Rebekah. 'Someone there's bound to know if the college has been up to anything at the Mill site lately.'

'The estate!' echoed Justin, his face falling. 'That dump? Do we have to?'

'You only want to interview nice sanitised people like yourself,' said Steve.

'What you do is voluntary and entirely up to you,' said Christa. 'It's only fair to point out that there could be certain risks attached to upsetting the Master. You're all dependent on the college for your degrees. So if at any time you want to pull out of the project, I shall understand completely.'

'I think it's a great idea. We should go for it. I bet everyone else thinks so too,' said Rebekah.

To Christa's gratification there were nods, and from Ted the remaining rower, who appeared to be exhausted, a sleepy handwave.

'Right,' she said. 'But no one's moving from the room until you've worked out some kind of plan. And I'm certainly not letting you touch the cameras until you've done a location recce on your own, so you can prove to me that you're capable of working together without supervision. You'll have to do it in your own time before the next seminar.'

'Bloody hell, Christa. We're not a bunch of nursery school kids,' Justin said indignantly.

'Shut up and listen,' said Rebekah. 'We're not ace movie-makers either.'

'Have you thought what you'll do if you don't get anything new on the Mill site?' Christa asked. 'You can't afford to waste your time completely.'

'Maybe set up location shots and interviews which show the deprivation caused by Gabriel's delay?' said Rebekah. 'At least they'd illustrate the way the college abuses its power.'

'Good. Where on the estate will you start?'

'In the pub – it'll be a doddle,' said Steve. 'We're bound to pick something up there. We'll go at lunchtime tomorrow.'

'And in less than twenty-four hours everyone in Oxford will know what you're about,' Christa said.

'I think we should talk to the kids, quietly, and try to get them on our side,' said Rebekah. 'They've the biggest gripe, and I bet they're well into the Gabriel's Mill site, even though people say it's all sealed off.'

'That's better. And split yourselves into two groups so you aren't too obvious,' said Christa. 'Simply say you're planning to make a student film about the problems of the kids at Gabriel's Grounds. I'm sure I don't need to tell you why it's vital to be discreet. I suggest letting Rebekah and Donna handle the first approaches.'

'So keep your mouth shut for once, Seddon,' said Steve. 'They'll run a mile if they hear you coming on like some upper-class twit.'

'And they'll run a mile from an ugly sod like you,' Justin retaliated.

Christa was becoming bored with their constant bickering.

'I'm not going to tell you again,' she said severely, hearing overtones of Emma in her voice. 'If you can't cooperate, the whole thing's off. My life'd be a lot easier if I simply gave my seminars instead.'

Though Christa still had no faith in her abilities as a teacher, to her amazement the students slowly and somewhat shamefacedly began to settle down. After half an hour they had, with a modicum of prompting, produced a reasonable list of potential opening questions and background shots.

'So now it's up to you,' Christa said, feeling as if she'd just sorted out a rugger scrum. 'See what you can discover, and we'll have a go at filming on the estate next week. And if you've any ideas about being a presenter, Justin, please don't wear that striped shirt. It'll strobe horribly on film.'

'Your mother must worry when you're working abroad,' Miriam said to Christa, who was helping her clear away after a magnificent meal of steamed bananas, roast chicken and groundnut sauce. 'I thank God daily that Wes has decided to stay at home like a sensible man at last.'

At the end of the last class Rebekah had briefly stayed behind to issue an invitation from her parents to supper the following Thursday. Although family gatherings were not Christa's scene, she'd accepted with alacrity, hoping for advance information from Rebekah on the students' activities at the estate.

Wes was still sitting at the supper table while he tried to sort out a maths homework problem for the twins before packing them off to bed. Phil would have received the remark with deadly seriousness, but Wes simply gave his wife an affectionate smile.

They were in a large kitchen-dining room, furnished in an oddly successful mixture of African and English styles. The shelves of the pine dresser were crammed with willow pattern plates, books, a wooden coconut grater, several Makonde carvings, and a brass coffee pot with a scimitar-shaped spout. A magnificent wall-hanging of printed barkcloth was suspended next to a gouache of the sunlit Wiltshire Downs.

'Mum!' said Rebekah warningly, going over to the dresser to fetch the coffee pot. 'Don't get on that old hobby horse again, please. It's up to Christa, not her mother, to decide how to run her life.'

'*Ala!*' said Miriam in Swahili, her tongue lingering on the second syllable with reproving relish. 'My mother's word was law at your age.'

Miriam was short and plump, dressed in a red chenille tunic and grey leggings. Earrings shaped like bunches of silver grapes swung from her ears. Though she was small she quivered with energy from the toes of her high-heeled boots to the very ends of the dark, springy hair brushed back in a halo from her face.

'It wasn't law when you married me,' said Wes. 'I thought your mother would never recover from the shock.'

Another swift smile passed between them, this time full of mutual reminiscence.

'You may say what you like, but children brought up in the West simply don't know what it is to obey,' said Miriam loftily.

The twins, large-eyed and gangly, dissolved into giggles over their exercise books, shielding their mouths with their hands as though they'd heard the remark many times before. Miriam swept a handful of unused cutlery into a drawer, and turned on them.

'*Baas, baas!* We need some peace with our coffee. Upstairs with your homework now, and no computer games until it's done.'

Still convulsed with giggles, the twins trailed from the room, snatching a couple of satsumas from the fruit bowl as they went. Miriam was clearly the rock in the domestic torrent, Christa thought in amused admiration.

While supper, a joint effort, was being prepared, she'd tactfully removed the groundnut sauce in the nick of time from Wesley's ministrations. He'd been so carried away by an account of his exploits during President Clinton's visit to Oxford, that he'd let it solidify into a rubbery mass. She'd also found time to detect and banish an inquisitive white mouse from the pocket of one of the twins, and make some suggestions to Rebekah about her dissertation which were so erudite that in self-preservation Wesley had taken Christa off to his study with a bottle of whisky to watch the Channel 4 news.

'Even the twins are going to know more than me soon. I'm the only bonehead in this family,' he'd said good-naturedly, handing Christa a double measure.

Now, watching Rebekah place the coffee on the table and with a quick hug order her mother to sit down, Christa repressed a pang of envy. It would be difficult not to fit in here, surrounded by an atmosphere of such easy-going but unwavering affection.

'You go and check on the boys, Dad,' Rebekah said. 'Mum ought to put her feet up for a bit.'

'I'll fetch in the whisky too. We may as well make it Gaelic coffee,' said Wes with a grin as he left the room.

'I'm afraid it's a bit of a madhouse,' Rebekah said to Christa.

'I like it,' she replied. 'I don't spend much time at home myself.'

Miriam handed Christa her coffee. 'Wes told me you've just bought a house in Jericho. That's good. Every woman needs a place of her own. Maybe you won't want to go abroad so much now.'

'I doubt it,' said Christa. 'I'm the sort of person for whom everywhere else is home.'

'How interesting that is. But sad too,' said Miriam seriously. 'There's a Swahili poem which says the same sort of thing. Let me see if I can find it for you.'

She started to search the dresser shelves. Rebekah looked up from loading the dishwasher.

'Mum's Ph. D. dissertation was on East African literature,' she said to Christa. 'Just a little something she did to amuse herself while the twins were small,' she added with a wink.

Miriam had discovered the book and was riffling through it.

'Don't be disrespectful, Rebekah,' she said absentmindedly. 'The poem describes the different kinds of household a Swahili girl may have to live in as a bride. Listen.' She found the page, and quoted: ' "The house of the eleventh sort is a house of longing for all that is far away." '

Rebekah looked up from closing the dishwasher door.

'The sub-text being that she should settle down and conform,' she said teasingly.

Miriam clicked her tongue in reproof. 'Don't talk about what you don't know, my child. You aren't married yet. It means you should make the best of what you've got, not search for the impossible.'

Christa expected an indignant explosion from Rebekah, but she simply laughed. 'Searching for the impossible is half the fun. And anyway we can't all be perfect wives and mothers as well as brilliant academics like you.'

'You can if you work at it,' said Miriam severely. 'Nothing's more important than a good family life.'

'Is your mother trying to turn you into a dutiful Swahili

daughter again, Rebekah?' said Wes, as he came back into the room with the whisky.

An argument which would have provoked bitter conflict in Juniper Drive ended with more laughter, and with Gaelic coffees so whisky-laden that they made Christa glad she'd decided not to drive herself home. Only at the end of the evening, as Rebekah waited with her on the pavement for the taxi to arrive, did Christa remember that she hadn't asked her about the location research.

'How did you get on at Gabriel's Grounds?' she said.

Rebekah's eyes shone in the streetlight.

'It was chaos at first – Justin and Steve trying to score off each other, and getting everyone thoroughly pissed off before we'd even started. In the end we told them we were out of it if they didn't shut up. We made Jus buy a big pack of Crucial, and sat around for a bit near the shops just drinking and watching the lads play football. After a while Donna and I got chatting with them, and Steve passed round the Crucial, and suddenly we were all well away.'

'Well done!' said Christa, thinking she could have used Rebekah's diplomatic talents in Bosnia. 'Did you get anything useful out of them?'

'Here's your taxi,' said Rebekah, as a Montego wove down the narrow channel between the residents' cars, and pulled up in front of the house. She opened the door for Christa. 'We'll fill you in on the rest next week,' she said cheekily. 'Didn't you tell us all news is heightened by an element of suspense?'

Christa still had plenty of research to do on her book, but as she sat in the Bodleian Library next day, ploughing through accounts of the Spanish Civil War, her mind kept returning to Mallory's information about the Master.

The weather was making her restless too. Through the window a stiff westerly breeze was tearing the clouds to shreds. Remembering that there was an exhibition at the Ashmolean of the Master's photos of the Waylandsbury dig, she decided to seek inspiration elsewhere, and five minutes later had set off towards St Giles', enjoying her head-on battle with the wind after the Bodleian's scholarly calm.

She had to remind herself to walk sedately up the Ashmolean's marble stairs. The expressions of reverence on the tourists' faces made her want to do a handstand at the top, but as she was about to turn towards the Waylandsbury Room, relief was unexpectedly provided in the shape of Piers.

He was lost in contemplation of Uccello's *Hunt in the Forest*. Mischievously Christa crept up behind him. She remembered the picture from the school trip on which she'd first seen the Waylandsbury Hoard. A mysterious light illuminated the dark encroaching trees. It gave the scarlet-clad huntsmen bearing down on their quarry an extra dimension of menace which had instantly appealed to her teenage mind.

As Christa slipped her arm through his, Piers started in surprise. He'd been so absorbed in the painting that it was almost as if she'd emerged from the forest with the deer. Normally he would have associated Christa with the supremely self-confident hunters rather than their prey, but she still had some of the lost look which had so struck him when she first arrived at Gabriel.

'What are you doing here?' he demanded. 'I didn't know you were into Renaissance art.'

'I came to see the Waylandsbury Hoard. My class may be filming it soon.'

At least her clothes had become sparkier lately, thought Piers. She was brightening the sedate surroundings in very tight Levis, a tomato-red scarf, and a short jacket of supple suede which fitted snugly above her admirably slender hips. For an imprudent moment he considered resuming his adolescent attempts to get her into bed, before deciding that his sex life was already complicated enough.

'I heard you'd persuaded the Master to let your students make a programme about Gabriel. I suppose that's what you were up to at the drinks party. He must have been as pissed as a newt to agree, but well done all the same,' he said.

'And why are you here?' Christa demanded. 'What interests you so much about Uccello's *Hunt*? Or, should I ask, what are the semiotics of the image?' she added mockingly, yet with a relish that made him suspect she might begin to enjoy teaching once she'd got used to it.

'I'm doing a magazine piece on the hunt in art,' he said. 'In the Renaissance the chase was still a symbol of chivalry as well as the ritual demonstration of a noble craft. God knows what the installation artist would do with it today. Probably suspend a stag's entrails in an acrylic cast.'

'Uccello's hunters don't look particularly noble to me. More like a gang of likely lads in fancy dress.'

'It's what I'm always telling you – we construct our own interpretations of what we see.'

'Then come and look at the Waylandsbury Hoard with me. I desperately need another interpretation of that.'

Piers pulled a face.

'Why should you need my help setting up a film? And fourth-century Britain really doesn't appeal. One's heart bleeds for those wretched Romans marooned in the cold and the mud, waiting for the Dark Ages to pounce.'

Christa sent him the challenging look which had inveigled him into some highly dubious exploits in their youth.

'But don't you see the analogy with Gabriel? The Dark Ages could be about to pounce there.'

She made the most horribly accurate observations sometimes, thought Piers. It was a thought he'd been trying to push to the back of his mind for some time.

'Very well then. You'd better tell me exactly what you're driving at, though I imagine it's too much to hope that you might be restrained rather than encouraged by rational comment.'

She tucked her arm under his as they began to walk towards the Romano-British area, their feet echoing on the wooden floor.

'Piers, in complete confidence,' said Christa, 'have you ever heard rumours about the Master passing off someone else's theories as his own?'

'Can't say I have, though some academic supervisors aren't above exploiting their students' lines of thought when their own work begins to look a bit clapped out. Unfortunately there's no copyright in ideas before they're in print. But the Master hasn't published anything of interest for years. He says he's been too busy with college business. Most people suspect he's just dried up.'

'I'm not talking about now, but a long time ago.'

'His last important work was at Waylandsbury. That's practically pre-history in terms of recent developments in research.'

'I *mean* Waylandsbury,' said Christa in a low voice, when she'd waited for a knot of tourists to wander past.

The implications were so enormous that Piers would have dismissed the remark as ridiculous coming from anyone else.

'For God's sake, Christa, you'd better be careful before you start digging into a rumour like that. It's probably just professional jealousy. Where did you hear it?'

'From Mallory Farrar.'

Piers pulled away from Christa and stared at her. His astonishment increased as he saw clear signs of embarrassment. Her skin had taken on the same flush as the terracotta figure of a dancing girl in the display case at her back.

'I thought you were hardly on speaking terms,' he said. 'You were eying each other like knife-throwers at the SCR party.'

Christa, observing a wicked glint of amusement behind Piers' glasses, rushed to defend herself before he jumped to the most ridiculous conclusions.

'I've met him again since then, quite by chance, of course.' Piers was still looking at her so quizzically that she added quickly, 'I'd taken Emma's baby for a walk. It started to rain. Mallory had an umbrella, and he insisted on seeing us back to Jericho.'

'Oho, Mallory now, is it?' said Piers. 'And since when have you let a man order you around? Apart from the dastardly Gareth, of course.'

'It simply occurred to me that if I chatted him up a bit, I might learn some more about the Master. And it paid off, as I expected.'

'This *is* a new departure for you, Christa – taking babies for walks as well as compromising your feminist principles! I haven't been so encouraged for years.'

Luckily they had now reached the Hoard, and its burnished splendour temporarily quietened them both. The room in which it was kept was high-ceilinged, with tall windows of frosted glass, and lined with display cases of oak. Together they wandered round the exhibits, which were set out on deep blue velvet beneath lighting which subtly exposed every detail of the silver-smith's art.

Christa had forgotten that in spite of their magnificence they were very domestic treasures. Even the sumptuous Neptune dish, with its bearded god rising from a stormy sea, had probably been used to serve a Roman risotto of mussels and clams.

It was accompanied by matching sauce boats and ladles, and a set of slender-handled spoons with elegant, elongated bowls. There was jewellery too: intaglio rings of jade and onyx, pendant earrings of pearl, and shining pins for the hair. Christa lingered before a circular silver casket containing scent bottles. Round the base of the domed lid ran the words *Cynthia domina mea est.*

'"I belong to Cynthia". Dear me, what an original *double entendre*,' said Piers. 'Probably her husband's wedding gift.'

'Whereas in reality she would have belonged to him.'

'Come now, Christa. They were probably madly in love. Don't you have any romance left in that battered heart of yours?'

'Not a spark,' said Christa, determined to discourage further forays in this dangerous quarter. 'It's ironic, don't you think, that a chauvinist like the Master made his reputation with the possessions of a woman?'

Piers began to wander round the temporary stands displaying the Master's photos from the Waylandsbury dig.

'I certainly can't see any women here,' he said, pausing in front of the group photo. 'Very territorial, isn't it? He's the lord of all he surveys.'

Christa, in spite of her earlier denial, had been remembering a silver bracelet bought for her by Gareth in Venice during a weekend holiday. Before she left Sarajevo she'd hurled it into the river, to lie beneath the icy water with so many other relics.

She concentrated fiercely on the photo to blot out a memory which still hurt, and as she did so realised that Piers was right. The woman she'd noticed in the *Illustrated London News* had disappeared. She appeared to have been neatly excised from this new print.

'But there was a woman, I'm certain,' she said excitedly.

She dragged the folder containing the copy of the article from her shoulder bag, and opened it on a glass-topped display case.

'Look! On the far left in this print, standing slightly apart from the others. It's exactly the same photo, and it's the Master's own – the credit says so.'

Piers studied it briefly, and shrugged. 'She's probably just a technician. Or a visitor, perhaps.'

'Then why did he cut her out of this later print? There must be a reason.'

'You're letting your imagine run riot now. This is Oxford, remember, not the Balkans.'

'All the same, I'd love to find out who she was.' Christa studied the names of the team beneath the photo. 'I'd been meaning to get in touch with the others. Do you know if any of them are still in Oxford?'

Piers ran his eye over the names. 'I don't think so. And in any case you'll get absolutely nowhere if you ask the academic mafia to spill the beans to an outsider.'

'Someone's already started to spill the beans to Farrar, and he's an outsider.'

'You really think so? A graduate of Gabriel, an honorary D. Litt., opinions so highly respected that even the Foreign Office seeks his advice . . . and of course loaded into the bargain. He's never out of the best-seller lists here or in the States.'

'Are you sure he's loaded? He doesn't seem much of a big spender,' said Christa, remembering the shabby jackets and the frugal breakfast in the market.

'Probably stashing it away for some incredibly PC project like saving a tribe of little green men. And I expect the Master's trying to get him to funnel some of it into Gabriel. Anyway, I think I've spent enough time on this remarkably unfascinating subject. I've got an article to write.' Piers gave Christa a sly glance. 'You're obviously well in with Farrar, so why don't you ask for an introduction to his contact? It shouldn't be too difficult, given your talent for persuasion.'

Christa could think of many things she'd rather do, but when Piers had gone she fished out the magnifying glass she had been using to study research photos, and examined the woman in the photocopy more closely.

She was young, no more than twenty-four or -five, and looked like the stereotypical female research student of the early-sixties with her neat hair and heavy glasses. But her expression wasn't typical. There was a scowling intensity in her gaze as she stood with her head turned slightly towards the rest of the group, as though she longed to be within it yet resented it. It was that expression which made Christa decide to question Mallory again.

Before she went to Gabriel Christa returned to the Bodleian to study the official account of the Waylandsbury dig. It was written by the Master, and there was no mention of any woman researcher. Some further research on her part into the four male post-graduate students working under his supervision led to nothing but frustration.

Mallory wasn't in his rooms in college, but for once the porters' surveillance system, normally a source of immense irritation to Christa, proved useful.

'Dr Farrar? Yes, I did happen to hear him mention he'd be in the Pitt Rivers Library today,' said the head porter, pausing in the midst of a minute scrutiny of the letters he was placing in the fellows' pigeon-holes.

The Pitt Rivers ethnographic collection was approached through the University Science Museum. Christa steeled herself to enduring three museums in one day. The wind, now increased to a gale, was no longer pleasurable. She arrived in the museum's Victorian–Gothic porch in a thoroughly cross and dishevelled state, and stomped past ranks of dinosaur skeletons, trying to avoid the schoolchildren swarming everywhere.

In the lofty galleried hall, virtually unchanged for over a hundred years, where the Pitt Rivers collection was housed, she lingered for a while, fascinated in spite of herself by the seemingly higgledy-piggledy collection of artefacts. Eventually she tore herself away from a case of magic charms, and made for the library on the first floor.

The decor in the room where Mallory was working had been carefully preserved too. It was a symphony of Victorian browns: sober oak tables and bookcases, darker oak floor, yellowy-brown walls, and shelves of books whose leather covers ranged from pale calf to russet Morocco. Sepia photos of early ethnologists, brown-whiskered and brown-suited, looked sternly down at Christa. On the wall a huge circular clock in a mahogany frame ticked ponderously away, as if to remind those working there to fill every minute with endeavour.

Even the letter Mallory was studying at a table near the window was closely covered on both sides in faded brown ink. Enviously Christa recognised the latest in lap-tops in front of him. She'd intended to replace her old one with the same model before her venture into home ownership.

'I need to talk to you again,' she said, firmly ignoring his unreceptive expression. 'I hope you don't mind?'

He didn't reply but indicated a chair next to him, turning sideways to face her and clasping his hands behind his head in a gesture of poorly concealed impatience.

He was wearing a shirt of indigo cotton, the only patch of bright colour in the room. The gesture made its sleeves ride up, revealing the paler inner skin of his wrists, almost as if exposing a hidden, less daunting, self. Round one of them was a heavily incised silver band.

He looked as constrained by his surroundings as she felt, but at least he'd found some way of adjusting to them, she thought. Her gaze wandered through the window to the rooftops outside, where a weathervane was spinning dementedly as if trying to wrench itself free, and she felt an intense longing to be on the move again, to be anywhere but in this room full of past happenings and past lives.

Mallory felt at first as though some wandering spirit of the autumn had been driven into the musty room on purpose to disturb him, but now, following her glance, he became interested in her expression. She sat as if she were one of the gulls balancing on the wind above the roofs, waiting to soar away in the first favourable gust.

He'd been reading Quentin Stannage's letters home: so full of admonitions that his wife must have been glad to see the back of him. Remembering the places from which the letters were written had made Mallory feel restless, and he'd only just settled to his task when Christa arrived. She was probably having as hard a time adjusting to captivity as he was, he thought, and that made him respond less curtly than he'd intended.

'Fire away,' he said, 'as long it doesn't take forever. I want to finish this box of letters before lunch.'

She took a photocopied article from her shoulder bag, and spread it on the table before them. She was so close that he could smell the cool, elusive scent she wore. As he unclasped his hands from behind his head, and leaned towards the photos, his arm brushed against hers. She was wearing a loose truffle-coloured sweater, and he was disconcerted by a sudden intimation of the body beneath. He remembered the baby's hand on her breast, and yet more disconcertingly wanted to feel its warm curve beneath his own hand.

It took all his self-control to fix just half his attention on what she was telling him. His reaction was even more disturbing in that cloistered Victorian room, where eroticism normally only resided between the covers of accounts of courtship rituals.

Most disturbing of all, she was not the sort of woman who usually attracted him. He preferred women who as well as being intelligent, didn't try to conceal their femininity – not someone with thicker skin than an armadillo.

Jesus, he was turning into a demanding bastard, he thought sardonically. His sisters, hopefully producing their capable, conventional friends for his inspection each time he came home, were probably right when they told him he wanted the impossible.

'So you see,' said Christa, breaking into his thoughts in an eager rush, 'the woman's been cut altogether from the print in the Ashmolean.'

'And you think it's a chauvinist plot,' said Mallory, grabbing at the well-worn sarcasm in sheer self-preservation.

She frowned. 'It seems significant, that's all, especially after what you told me by the canal. If she did belong to the Master's team, and if she was the one whose data he stole, he's got every reason to erase her from the records.'

'Have you checked the official account of the dig?'

'Yes, I've just done so. There was no woman on his team. I followed up the four male post-grad students as well. One's dead, and one's on a year's sabbatical looking at temple sites in the Malaysian rainforest, and can't be reached. The other two are now professors at other universities. They didn't want to talk when I rang them, but they did both say they couldn't remember any woman at the dig.'

'Then there's nothing to worry about,' said Mallory absent-mindedly, thinking that her hair was like one of the rumpled bronze chrysanthemums in the fellows' garden.

'I know it seems that way, but I can't let it drop yet. I came to ask you to give me the name of the person who told you the rumour. I'd like to talk to him myself.'

Her request distracted Mallory at last.

'Sorry, but it's out of the question,' he said, thinking with affection of the irascible Gervaise Burford, Emeritus Professor of Gabriel, his own tutor as an undergraduate, as well as the Master's. 'He's very old and doesn't welcome guests.'

Only a chosen few were allowed to disturb his seclusion in a remote cottage on the Marlborough Downs, and even if he did agree to see Christa, he wouldn't mince his words if he considered her arguments unsound. Knowing her capacity for persistence, everything seemed to point towards a potential clash.

Mallory tried to think of an effective way to fend her off. She was looking down at the group photo, frowning at the woman with an almost loving concern, and obviously identifying with her exploitation, if exploitation it was.

Suddenly and irrationally, in spite of all his earlier thoughts, Christa's expression seemed intensely endearing.

'I'll give him a call and ask if he'll talk to you. But I can't promise anything,' he said.

Immediately he was overwhelmed by astonishment at what he'd done. His thoughts scurried around in a way his Confucian philosophy teacher wouldn't have approved of at all. He had to smother this inconvenient and impossible attraction at once. Even more illogically he decided that the only remedy was to visit her on her own ground. The experience was bound to prove the perfect antidote.

'And maybe in return I can take up that invitation of yours?' he said.

Her look of dismay made him certain he'd done the right thing.

'How about tea on Saturday week? I can let you know then if I have any more news,' he went on, handing back the photocopy to emphasise that their conversation had definitely come to an end.

Christa was so startled that she dropped the photo. It glided away beneath his feet. As he retrieved it she could think of no way to put him off for more than a further week or two.

'Of course. Saturday week is fine. Around four?' she said carelessly.

He returned the photo with a half smile.

'Good. I'll see you then.'

As she slipped from the room he was already immersed in the letter again. She might as well not have been there. So much for Piers' fevered imaginings, Christa thought, walking back past the dinosaurs in a state of deep relief that Mallory had only invited himself to tea.

Now all she'd have to produce were an up-market shop cake and some Earl Grey. If he'd come to dinner, she might just have managed a stir-fry, but she didn't relish the prospect of wielding a wok under the critical gaze of someone who was probably an expert at Cantonese cuisine as well as everything else.

12 ∫

After several days of rain which churned the college rugger pitches into mud, the sun made an appearance just in time for the trip to Gabriel's Grounds.

'How did you get on with your research?' Christa asked the students assembled beforehand in the lecture room.

Steve consulted a professional-looking clipboard. Christa waited with amused interest to hear his expanded version of Rebekah's earlier report.

'It was a doddle,' he said. 'Wasn't it, Jus?'

'Yeah, a piece of cake,' said Justin, who had arranged himself elegantly along two chairs, balancing an impressively crammed black snakeskin Filofax on his knees. He looked round at Ted and Mike. 'Wasn't it, guys?' he appealed in his turn, so that a casual listener would have thought it was an entirely male undertaking.

'Which of you men did the questioning, then?' she asked with feigned innocence.

'Well, we didn't actually do the questions. We were more in a directorial role,' said Justin.

He'd taken her advice about his shirt, and was wearing an almost anonymous black bomber jacket, though the designer logo on the breast pocket would probably be singled out at once by the sharp-eyed youth of Gabriel's Grounds.

'We thought the initial approach would be most effective coming from the women,' said Steve.

'The feminine touch, and all that sort of thing,' said Ted, who appeared to have only just got up, and was eating a bacon roll breakfast from a paper bag in a back seat.

'Really?' said Christa, exchanging glances with Rebekah, and noting that Donna was about to explode with indignation. 'So the women succeeded where you didn't? And what did they come up with in their interviews?'

'That's the real break-through,' Justin interrupted. 'We – the women, I mean,' he amended hastily at a look from Christa, 'found two lads among the football players who've managed to get on to the Gabriel's Mill site. They said they collect magic mushrooms there. They've probably got a nice little earner flogging them off in town,' he added in an aggrieved voice.

'What's more to the point is whether they've seen any official activity at the Mill,' said Christa.

'I was about to tell you before Jus shoved in,' said Steve hurriedly, consulting his clipboard again. 'Apparently about a week ago there were some blokes wandering about with theodolites and measuring poles. The lads didn't tell anyone because they wanted to keep their mushroom racket quiet.'

'And it had nothing to do with a community centre,' said Rebekah gleefully. 'I did a tactful check with some of the tenants later on. They've heard nothing about it for months now. Gabriel must be up to something dodgy. Anyway, we've fixed for the lads to take us there this morning, so we'll soon find out.'

'Don't jump to conclusions too soon,' said Christa, concealing her excitement. They had indeed done well, but she preferred to keep them in a level-headed state during the highly unorthodox activities ahead. 'Did you sort out your back-up shots in case nothing comes of the lead?'

'Some general cement jungle views, playground vandalised by the older kids because they've nowhere to go, joy-riders' burnt-out cars, and more or less continuous street football in the shopping precinct,' Steve rattled off from his list.

'Sounds good so far,' said Christa. 'You can splice in contrast shots of the Gabriel playing fields, and some of the more elitist college sports – rowing or fencing, perhaps.'

Ted choked slightly on his roll. The idea of himself as an elitist had probably just occurred to him for the first time, Christa thought.

'How are you going to present the question of your own accommodation?' she asked.

'That's easy. Lots of luscious interiors in the college itself, and especially the SCR,' said Justin.

'Not forgetting your rooms, of course, Justin,' said Rebekah. 'Haute Tudor times the Conran Shop. The viewers *will* enjoy themselves.'

'My flat can show how the other second years live,' said Donna with an unexpected smile. 'Mildew everywhere, and electric points hanging out of the walls.'

'We can get plenty of horror shots at my place,' said Rebekah, who lived with some other post-grads in a narrow boat on the canal.

Christa suddenly felt a hundred years older than the students. They regarded all this as a game, she thought, and longed to be able to approach reporting as light-heartedly again.

'That all sounds fine. So let's get going, and cope with problems as they arise,' she said briskly, before she had more time for doubts or regrets.

'Pity my dad can't afford to buy me something like this,' said Steve, extricating himself from the back of the Mini, which Christa had parked as discreetly as possible across the road from the shops. Four of the students were squeezed into it, and the others had folded themselves like living origami into Justin's equally cramped MG.

'Pity he didn't get his act together, and make some proper money, then. My father didn't have a bean to start with,' retorted Justin, who hadn't recovered from being overtaken by the Mini.

'No one's going to make anything, least of all a film, unless you stop squabbling,' observed Christa acidly. 'Shall we get on with it?'

In the shopping precinct the usual football game was in progress, watched by the usual band of cruising girls. Christa hovered discreetly in the background as the students found their contacts. When both crews were in action, she went first to check on the men, who were filming the footballers.

The presence of cameras had hotted up the game dramatically. Christa allowed the crew enough time to get some sensational footage of the ensuing chaos among the traffic, then moved the filming into the deserted car park behind the shops, to question the players themselves.

She waited until Steve had started extracting enough evidence of wasted energy and thwarted ambition to damn the Master's plans a hundred times over, before moving on to Rebekah's crew, who were interviewing a group of teenage girls.

The one who was speaking now was dramatically unlike the others. Christa had noticed her earlier hovering at the back of the inevitable audience, smoking furiously while balancing a toddler on her hip. The child was pink with health, but the girl had skin like lardy cake, and grease-darkened hair pulled back into a limp scrunchie.

'My mum's chucked me out, so I live with my auntie on the estate,' she was saying. 'She's real good to us, but me and the kid go near mad stuck in the high-rise, with nothing to do but look at the fuckin' birds and the telly.' She threw down the fag-end and ground it into the pavement with her foot. 'Got another smoke, have you?'

Christa silently handed over her cigarette and lighter, miraculously unused for two weeks now.

'Isn't there anywhere here you could go for a break?' asked Rebekah.

'Chance'd be a fine thing! There's no community centre, no mother and baby club like other estates, is there? And the lads wrecked the kiddies' playground because they've got nothing to do.'

With a practised, one-handed movement, the girl shook out a cigarette and removed it from the packet with her lips.

'Can't you go into town?' said Rebekah.

The girl lit the cigarette and scornfully blew out a cloud of smoke.

'What with? The fare's a pound. It costs me a fortune to get to the supermarket as it is. The shops here charge way over the odds.'

'It's a sodding shame the estate can't get what it needs!' said Donna indignantly, when the girl had wandered dispiritedly away.

'Yeah, it is,' said Justin, who'd become oddly subdued as the morning progressed.

The men's crew had finished, and were watching Rebekah's crew at work. Christa eyed him sharply. She'd thought he was bored, but now she wondered if she'd been wrong.

'Made you think at last, has it?' jeered Steve.

'Maybe,' said Justin. 'It's Catch 22 round here, isn't it? Even the little kids are trapped.'

'Well done, Jus,' said Donna. 'You'll be joining the Lib Dems next.'

Her voice was withering, but Justin didn't retaliate. Christa admired him for his admission. She began to think her time at Gabriel might have some use, if it made him look beyond his own moneyed world. Perhaps the college did have some potential for good after all.

When the interviews were over, Rebekah found the two lads who'd offered to take them to Gabriel's Mill. Christa manoeuvred everyone into the chippie for a conference, gathering them round a formica table by a display of lurid orange drinks. The fluorescent lighting made them all appear to suffer from severe iron deficiency, but at least, thought Christa, the sound of Radio Gold and sizzling oil should effectively mask their conversation.

The youths, Barry and Kev, were about sixteen, and wore reversed baseball caps, baggy jeans which made them look like slapstick men, and unlaced trainers with rampant tongues. In spite of their earlier promise, they both now seemed unwilling to talk about their exploits at the Mill.

Christa guessed her presence inhibited them. She was dressed conventionally today, in a sober woollen jacket of loden green, and tailored grey trousers, in case authority had to be impressed. But after she'd bought coffee and plates of chips all round, and hinted that she could get them front seats for an Oasis concert from a friend who wrote a pop music column for one of the Sunday papers, they eventually loosened up.

'Right,' said Kev, the toughest-looking. 'Exactly what sort of info do you want?'

'Just tell Christa here what you told the rest of us last week,' said Steve.

Kev stuffed a chip into his mouth.

'Well, we was having a bit of a lark over at the Mill . . .'

'How do you get into the site?' Christa interrupted. 'I thought it was all sealed off.'

'It is, but the guards are such lazy wankers they hardly ever patrol the fence. Barry and me've made a hole in the wire. We often go through for a bit of a change. We was on the Mill roof the other day, killing ourselves listening to the guards sitting on the steps below – smoking, and on their mobile to the sex line, they were – when a Range Rover rolls up with a load of Mr Bigs.'

While Christa tried not to laugh, Barry, stubbing out his roll-up, took up the story.

'When they'd sent the guards away, they started having a confab. By then we'd hidden behind the chimney, so we couldn't hear much, but they were talking about storing books. It didn't make no sense to us.'

Christa and the students exchanged looks. They were getting some useful information at last.

'Did you catch anything else?' Christa asked.

'No. They didn't stay long. They went off with measuring tapes and clipboards and suchlike. We followed them around a bit, but we couldn't go too near. Then we got bored and came home.'

'Was there a name on their gear?' Christa enquired.

'Can't say I remember,' said Barry indifferently, shaking a line of tobacco into a fresh Rizla.

'How about you, Kev?' Rebekah asked, with a frustrated glance at Christa.

'Maybe there was. I don't go in for reading much,' said Kev.

'Can you show us where they went?' said Christa.

Kev paused in the act of replenishing his chips with tomato sauce, and looked doubtfully at her clothes.

'I guess so, if you're sure you can make it. We might have to bunk off any time.'

'You'd be surprised what I can do,' said Christa with a smile that made him deluge the chips in a ketchup flood.

They approached the Mill site across a stretch of empty ground littered with disembowelled furniture and garden waste. Though Barry and Kev had said the fence round Gabriel's Mill was rarely patrolled, it was still a formidable barrier, with razor wire along the top. The lads ignored a padlocked side gate, and instead pushed through a thicket of dusty, rank-smelling laurel, which ran along both sides of the fence and concealed a neatly cut opening in the wire.

Kev and Barry went through like a pair of ferrets. Christa, the students pressing at her back, squeezed after them, thinking worriedly that though she'd done riskier things in the past, it hadn't been with eight students and a couple of young tearaways in her charge.

The lads threaded confidently through a network of paths between huge banks of bramble and scrub. Most of the site was overgrown, and the Mill, an early nineteenth-century building of brick, was almost derelict with its doors and lofts boarded up, its wheel in a wire cage, and a mill race rushing below a densely coppiced bank.

After filming some general shots, a procedure complicated by Barry and Kev's wanting to have a go, they moved on through the undergrowth and emerged at an approach road with ropes of purple-green brambles snaking across the pitted tarmac. Ahead in a clearing were some newer buildings, a warehouse and small milling works, also boarded up.

'That's where the guards hang out, so don't go too close if you want to film,' Barry said. He consulted a Rolex watch. 'They'll be inside now having their nosh. When you've finished we can slip past easy as wink.'

Although the Master had obviously installed his security on the cheap, and in spite of the lads' reassurance and the boarded-up windows, Christa still felt uneasy. She didn't begin to relax until she'd hustled the students through some rapid long shots, and they were on their way again towards the far side of the open ground.

She was about to disappear into the undergrowth with her charges, when there was a deafening bellow from the office doorway. A guard appeared, tightening his belt.

'Fucking hell!' said Barry. 'Come on, Kev. We're out of here!'

The two lads dived into the undergrowth and were gone almost before Christa knew what had happened. The students uncertainly stood their ground, and Lallie dodged behind Steve.

'Quick, hide the cameras while I distract the guards!' Christa whispered. 'Dump them in the bushes. We'll have to bluff our way out.'

Both guards were now lumbering down the steps, cramming on brass-badged peaked caps vaguely reminiscent of the Los Angeles police. The man at the back was restraining two unmuzzled Rottweilers on a chain leash.

'Bloody hell,' said Justin's voice behind Christa, sounding strangely wobbly. 'Those dogs haven't had any Pal for weeks.'

The guard in front was stomping towards her with his arms swinging like a Japanese wrestler's. His bomber jacket was embroidered with a mailed fist. Christa set off to confront him.

'What on earth do you think you're doing? Remove those animals at once,' she demanded, copying the high arrogant voice she'd heard older dons use on college servants who didn't come up to scratch. 'Can't you see I've got a party of students here? We're on a field trip.'

'Students? Nobody told us nothing about students.'

Beneath the guard's flashy cap and Saddam moustache was a face younger than her own. He was already looking taken aback at her tone. Christa was inspired to more flights of invention.

'You should have received a call from Gabriel this morning,' she said loftily, wishing she dared address him as her good man. 'Possibly your telephone line was engaged. I gather it very often is. One wonders why? Perhaps I should ask your firm to investigate.'

The guards exchanged dismayed glances. She made the most of her advantage.

'I suppose you are at least aware that this is college property?'

'Course we are,' said the leader truculently, though some of his bluster had already disappeared. 'But how do we know you're from Gabriel?'

'This is really most tiresome. Can't you see my ID card?' said Christa, waving it in front of him with her thumb over her name, and hoping he'd be sufficiently impressed by the enormous gold and black coat of arms not to want a closer look.

'What about further documentation?' he said grudgingly.

She made her voice outraged. 'As a fellow of Gabriel Hall, clerical trivialities are not my concern. Any documents the college may have sent to your obviously inefficient employers have no doubt been mislaid.'

'But there doesn't seem much to study here,' said the other guard, now looking more puzzled than militant. 'It's just a derelict old site.'

Christa, suddenly remembering the magic mushrooms, was visited by another stroke of genius.

'Just a derelict old site?' she repeated in scandalised tones. 'It's an area of exceptional scientific interest. My students and I are conducting a botanic survey. There are some absolutely splendid specimens of *Psilocybe semilanceata* round here.'

The foremost guard was beginning to look convinced, but not quite convinced enough.

'How did you get in, then? Why didn't you use the official key to the main gate, like everyone else?' he demanded.

'We prefer to use footpaths in order to do as little damage as possible to the plant life. Naturally we chose to enter by a side gate. Don't you know that all the vegetation within four hundred feet of a road becomes impregnated with toxins from car exhausts?' she said, staring meaningfully at the security van parked outside the mill.

'I still think I ought to get back to the mobile and ask head office to sort things out,' said the guard, looking hugely uncomfortable by now.

'We really don't have time for this kind of incompetence,' said Christa. 'My students work to a strict schedule, and we must complete our survey before development goes ahead. Ancient woodland is a national treasure, you know,' she added.

Very occasionally Oxford style had its uses, she thought, observing delightedly that though the ancient woodland was mostly a scrappy collection of ivy-infested sycamores and pollarded willow, the guard was going to swallow even this pronouncement. She decided to make sure she had the upper hand.

'For that reason I take the greatest exception to the fact that you and your colleague have been smoking here,' she said severely. 'Hundreds of years of growth could be ruined by one careless cigarette.' The guard gawped at her as though she had second sight. 'You'll be extremely lucky if I choose not to inform your head office, because I doubt whether you'll keep your jobs if I do.'

To her delight it worked. A couple of minutes later the two men were slinking back into the mill as if they'd narrowly escaped with their lives.

'Wow! They actually apologised! Nice one, Christa,' said Steve, who up to now had treated her with a slightly derisive respect.

'Yeah, not bad,' said Justin in a stunned voice, looking as if he wouldn't be able to stand many more shocks.

When they'd retrieved the cameras, Christa hustled her charges away along the nearest track before the guards could change their minds. She wasn't at all sure if she could find the way back, but to her amazement Kev and Barry were waiting for them at the next crossing of paths.

'Blimey,' said Kev, 'that was a turn-up. We thought they'd chuck you out, or else call the Old Bill.'

'Thanks for waiting,' said Christa. 'It was really great of you both.'

''S'alright,' said Barry, looking hugely embarrassed. 'We reckoned you'd be well buggered if you couldn't find the way out.'

'We'd better not push our luck too far, but can we just take a look at the site you told us about first?' Christa asked.

'Easy,' said Kev with a confidence she wished she could share. 'It's a clearing at the far side of the Mill. We've made another hole in the wire over there, so we can do a runner any time.'

The clearing seemed as exposed as no-man's-land. It was a huge gravelly area, which at one time must have been used as hardstanding for a fleet of lorries and which supported only a scattering of stunted plants. She'd have to pass them off as rare alpines, Christa decided, if the security men reappeared and found the students lingering on such an unpromising botanical site.

For there was no question of leaving yet. The whole area was marked out with a neat cat's cradle of pegs and black and yellow marker tape, presumably to show the position of the library store itself. It would show up wonderfully on film, and best of all, was printed with a name.

Donna reached it first. 'We've got our lead!' she said in

an awed voice. 'Look, everyone. "Margrave Partners, Chelsea Reach". That's the London construction firm with the flash office tower!'

Christa could hardly believe that their venture had paid off. She watched the students pour across the clearing to examine the tape, blithely flattening the plants in their path. Suddenly she realised her excuse for being there was about to be ruined, and yelled at them to come back.

'You must keep your act together better than this!' she lectured them as they assembled sheepishly round her.

She glanced up at the sky, where the small clouds she'd noticed earlier were gathering into a dark grey mass.

'If you don't start filming right away, it's either going to rain, or those guards'll have second thoughts and reappear. Rebekah, you take your crew and do some long shots. Steve's lot can work on close-ups. And for God's sake, Justin, if you're talking to camera, remember it's more important for the viewers to see the name on the tape than your face.'

This time Kev and Barry obligingly kept watch from the branches of a tree, and the filming providentially finished with the first drops of rain. The students packed away their gear, and back at the shopping precinct the lads were given a pack of Crucial, and assured yet again that their identities wouldn't be revealed.

Christa and the students piled into the cars and made straight for a secluded table at the Turf Tavern where she bought them all a late lunch to celebrate the morning's work. The students were high on excitement, Justin most of all.

'My dad does business with Margrave's,' he said, putting down his lager, and tucking into a prawn sandwich. 'He's bound to be able to fix us an interview with someone on the board. I'm going home next weekend. I'll have a talk to him then.'

'OK, but just a talk at this stage,' said Christa. 'I want to make some enquiries of my own about Margrave's before we go any further.'

In spite of her confident tone, she felt drained. It was ridiculous to have no resilience left after a morning so comparatively low-key, she thought gloomily. In Bosnia she'd kept going for days under stress.

She knew the students wanted to carry on discussing the morning's events with her, yet suddenly the company of Poppaea and a quiet session on Jessie's sofa watching afternoon television held a shamingly irresistible allure.

'I'm off now, but I'll see you all in my room in Bohemia Quad next week,' she said abruptly, cutting across the chatter. 'We'll run through today's footage, and if Justin's father says he can fix an interview at Margrave's, we'll decide how to set it up. But don't forget, no one's to go it alone before then. You've done well so far. Let's keep it that way.'

A few days later Emma was pacing agitatedly around the kitchen at Ethelred Road.

'I told Phil we simply had to get away on our own and take stock of our marriage. I can't go on as we are.'

The stray kitten who'd lately taken up residence had disappeared under the table, sensing trouble. All that was visible was his agitated tail. A pile of ironing had been abandoned, and on the Aga the lid on a pan of potatoes was beginning to dance unheeded over a rising head of steam.

'What did he say?' asked Christa.

Emma had summoned her to too many of these sessions recently. When the phone rang this time, Christa had been cleaning out Poppaea's cage. Though it was a job she hated, it suddenly seemed much more attractive than listening to the usual litany of Phil's defects. Only the remnants of sisterly solidarity had made her drive through the rain-swept streets to Ethelred Road.

'He bloody well had to agree,' said Emma. 'He's dined in hall almost every day this month. The children only see him at breakfast. It's simply not good enough.'

'And where do you plan to go for this rescue operation?'

'I've booked us into a small hotel near Avebury this weekend. It'll be heaven – absolutely peaceful, and we can talk everything out on downland walks.'

It sounded like purgatory to Christa. She couldn't imagine discussing any marriage successfully on a sodden English hillside in a howling gale. Even a package trip to Majorca would be more conducive to reconciliation. Yet as she saw Emma's face smooth out like her ironing at the prospect, Christa felt like rushing off to the Institute, grabbing Phil, and ordering him to make the weekend work.

'Where is he tonight?' she asked.

'At a committee meeting about arrangements for the Founder's Feast next summer. It's a special celebration which only comes up every tenth year.'

'Who's going to look after the children while you're away?' said Christa.

'Noelene. I promised her a week off during the Christmas vacation in return, but it's worth it. Pansy's not too pleased with the arrangement, though. I had to bribe her with a new hat and boots like Chelsea's. She's been so difficult lately. Our rows upset her. That's why we must make this weekend work.'

She returned to the ironing board, sighed, and picked up a shirt.

'Surely Phil's the one who has to make it work?' said Christa. 'You're taking all the strain at the moment. Look at this ironing, for instance. Couldn't he wear drip-dry?'

Emma gave a delicate shudder.

'You don't get the same finish at all. It's a matter of keeping up standards.'

'Get real, Em. No one's going to notice a crease or two these days, except Mrs Slade perhaps.'

'Exactly,' said Em crossly. 'And anyway, Phil has a very sensitive skin. Sea island cotton is all he can wear.'

'Phil, sensitive? That's a good one.'

Christa picked up an avocado from a bowl of ripening fruit, and began to toss it casually into the air like a knobbly green grenade. Emma fought against, and was overcome by, a wave of envy and annoyance.

Briefly she wanted to be free again like Christa, looking wonderful in a loose silk shirt stippled with all the browns of a gypsy-moth's wing, and a pair of immaculate grey jersey leggings. They hadn't come from an as-new shop, like Emma's skirt and blouse. And if her new wardrobe had sent Christa into the red, she'd never agonise about her overdraft. Miserably,

Emma slammed down the iron on the shirt, and hit back in the one way guaranteed to hurt.

'Sometimes you do stupid things for people because you love them. Surely you understand that, after Gareth?'

Christa's shoulders slumped. She returned the avocado to the bowl, looking as miserable as the most green-eyed monster could have wished.

'Yes, you're right,' she said. 'I'd have walked through fire for him.'

Emma felt guilty but better after this admission. She smoothed the last creases from the shirt, folded it and placed it on top of the pile. As she eased her aching back into a chair she thought that in spite of their differences it was oddly good to be sitting here with her sister, discussing the foibles of their men, as they'd frequently done before Christa left home. Even then she'd been alarmingly strong-minded. She'd never wasted time on waning relationships, unlike Emma, who'd taken weeks to disentangle herself.

'If Phil's really so bad, perhaps you should split,' Christa said.

Emma, whose mind had recently been skating round and round the same question, tumbled out the panicky, never quite satisfactory replies she gave herself.

'With two small children on my hands? I couldn't afford a nanny. And I couldn't possibly keep this place going on one salary.'

'It's my guess Pansy'd love to see the back of Noelene. You could get Jamie into a crèche. Or Mother would have him. There's nothing she'd like better.'

'You know perfectly well why I can't leave him with Mother.' She paused, wondering how Christa would take her next remark. 'And I'm not sure I want to leave Phil anyway. Sex with him is still OK, when I'm not too tired. It makes up for a lot. I'm sure you know all about that.'

To Emma's astonishment, Christa blushed.

'Yes, it was pretty good with Gareth. That was one of the problems.'

Emma heaved herself from the chair to untangle a pile of sheets which Noelene had taken from the dryer and not bothered to fold. She couldn't resist another dig.

'I still can't understand how you could let it happen. You know you've always liked to be in charge.' She thrust a sheet at Christa. 'Can you grab one end? It'll be quicker with the two of us.'

As Christa helped to fold and refold the sheet, tugging it taut, advancing and retreating in the familiar domestic routine, she thought about Emma's comment. She'd only been in love once before Gareth, at the start of her career, and her lover wanted complete commitment. The sensation of losing the freedom to control her career had ultimately made her panic and decide never to let it happen again.

From then on she'd been careful to choose men who were sensitive, yet didn't have the ability to dominate, and had discovered she could still run her love-life with satisfaction to all concerned. As a result she'd gone to Gareth's bedroom in the Sarajevo Hilton convinced that she could remain in control.

But once she was in bed with him, the combination of his voice, pouring like warm honey into the crannies of her sub-conscious mind, and the body which took her in a prize-fighter's embrace, affected her like a sledgehammer. Though he'd never harmed her physically, he demanded submission, and with him she'd found domination highly addictive. She didn't realise she'd fallen in love until too late.

She'd come to despise herself utterly for it, for even now she occasionally missed the feeling of total surrender. Emerging from sleep in the middle of the night, grief over Matt's death would still sometimes catch her unawares, and she'd long for the self-annihilating release of sex with Gareth.

When Jamie broke into her thoughts with his regular mid-evening wail from his cot upstairs, Christa found Emma looking at her with a curious expression.

'You have got over Gareth, haven't you?' she asked, in the same bossily maternal tone she used to ask Pansy if she'd finished her homework.

Christa glowered at Emma's back as she went to the fridge to fetch a made-up bottle, and hoped that if she didn't reply, Emma would be sufficiently distracted by Jamie's increasing howls not to notice.

Emma inserted the bottle into an electric warmer, tipped the potatoes into a colander, and returned to her question with the persistence of an automatic number redial.

'*Surely* you wouldn't have anything to do with him again?' she demanded, her eyebrows rising in two horrified arcs. 'You couldn't! It'd be too awful, after the way he's tried to ruin your life. I won't let you. I'd even tell Apollo if I had to.'

Christa was caught off guard by Emma's concern. She sounded just like the elder sister of her childhood, leaping in with all guns blazing to dissuade her from some fascinatingly risky scheme.

'Promise me you won't,' said Emma relentlessly. 'I'll be on the phone to Randall like a shot if you do. I mean it.'

'Stop getting so steamed up, Em,' said Christa with feigned casualness. 'Randall's already warned me off having any sort of communication with Gareth. And I'm hardly likely to encounter him in Oxford. These days it's even less his sort of place than mine.'

Emma looked at her suspiciously. 'But supposing you did?' she persisted. 'Or supposing you went to London and bumped into him there?'

'Then I'd simply walk away,' said Christa airily. 'Just as he walked away from me. Nothing would be easier.'

On the Saturday morning of Emma's weekend break, Christa awoke to grey scudding clouds and near horizontal rain. To keep depression at bay, she decided to decorate the back bedroom. Its yellow Festival of Britain wallpaper, now mellowed to the colour of marmalade, and printed with drawings of vintage cars, had probably been chosen by the adolescent Derek. The royal blue paintwork had not mellowed at all, and the room, unused since his departure from home, was extremely cold.

Christa switched on her fan heater, slotted a reggae tape into the cassette player, and armed with a wet sponge and a scraper began to strip the walls. The process was nothing like the carefree illustrations in her DIY book, for there were layers of older paper beneath the vintage cars. But the heater was breathing out blasts of heat like a friendly dragon, and together with the music and the condensation from the walls soon made the room feel wonderfully like a Caribbean bar. Eventually she became so warm that she changed into a T-shirt and a pair of sawn-off jeans.

By lunch-time she'd ripped away Edwardian roses and Victorian trellis, and managed to clear one wall. She plastered up the cracks with filler, thinking wrily that it was a lot easier than trying to patch up her life. The result so impressed her that she hurled herself at a second wall, only pausing to snatch a sandwich and replace Bob Marley with Sheryl Crow.

Half an hour later she was singing along so loudly that she didn't hear the door bell at first. When she ran impatiently downstairs, Noelene was standing on the step, grasping the hand of a scowling Pansy, whose face was as pink as her clover-coloured cloche. Noelene was dressed to kill in black wet-look jeans and a leopard print sweater. From the parked Volvo came the sound of Jamie's yells.

'Yes?' said Christa unreceptively, sensing imminent trouble.

'I'm really sorry about this, Christa,' said Noelene, 'but I have to ask you a big, big favour. Chel's got a cold and Pansy couldn't go to her house to play. She's been slinging off at me all day.'

'It's your fault if I have!' said Pansy. 'You wasted loads of time after lunch doing your make-up when you'd promised to play chess.'

A look of desperation was settling on Noelene's face. She appealed to Christa again.

'My bloke's coming round to say goodbye in half an hour. He's taking an evening flight from Heathrow. Mrs Holdgate said it'd be OK. I've gotta have some time alone with him. I thought maybe you'd help me out.'

'Sorry,' said Christa, trying to ignore the desperate expressions in front of her. 'Nothing doing, Noelene. I'm in the middle of decorating. I'm not about to look after two children as well.'

'Only Pansy,' pleaded Noelene. 'I can cope with Jamie. He's had some paracetamol, and he'll drop off any minute now. But I'll never get a quiet talk with Jeff while Pansy's in this mood.'

'I hate it when Jeff's there,' said Pansy furiously. 'They sit on the sofa kissing and telling me to go away. I keep waiting for something interesting to happen, but it never does.'

Noelene's blusher became oddly puce. Pansy gave an enormous sniff and gulp.

'Please, please, let me stay to tea,' she muttered. 'You promised I could visit you, remember?'

Thinking that she must be totally losing her grip to allow Pansy to get round her with such ease, Christa capitulated.

'All right. But I want you back here to collect Pansy by six, Noelene. I can't do your job indefinitely.'

'No sweat, Jeff's train goes at half-five,' said Noelene, her complexion slowly returning to a less alarming hue. 'And don't worry. You've got a great touch with kids.'

'Pity I can't say the same for you,' said Christa *sotto voce* to Noelene's departing back. She was already halfway down the path on her three-inch heels.

Pansy dragged off her jacket and shook her hair free from her hat before skipping into the sitting room.

'It's like a doll's house,' she said, looking round in rapture. 'I *love* the bluebells, and the ship on the rug, and the dear little china dogs, and the squashy sofa and *everything*!'

She pirouetted on the rug before trying a few bounces on the sofa. It responded nobly, only emitting the minimum of twangs. Poppaea, whom Pansy hadn't yet noticed, was not impressed.

'Mind your manners, please!' she squawked from her perch, performing an outraged sideways dance of her own.

Pansy rushed over to the cage.

'A parrot, a real parrot! Can I hold it on my arm?'

Christa grabbed Pansy's finger just as it was about to poke through the bars.

'Not yet. Sometimes she bites. Next time, when she's more used to you,' she said, already conceding another visit, but disarmed by Pansy's admiration for the decor Emma had so despised.

'What's she called?'

'Poppaea. A Latin name like your second one.'

'She's got a lovely red tail like a centurion's cape. We're doing the Roman legions at school, you know. Shall I tell you about them?'

Christa cast around desperately for a diversion.

'Wouldn't you rather see upstairs?' she asked.

In the bedroom Jessie's satin eiderdown sent Pansy into further raptures.

'Even Chel's mummy hasn't got a beautiful nightie case like this,' she said, stroking it tenderly. She draped herself over the quilt. 'And your bed's exactly like Princess Perfect's. Can I stay here for the night?'

'Perhaps, when I've finished decorating the spare room,' said Christa. She wasn't up to sharing her bed with anyone yet, least of all a hyperactive five year old. 'Come and look.'

Pansy was enchanted by the half-stripped wallpaper. She pulled off several long experimental strands, and garlanded them round her neck.

'Can I help? Please, please let me. The paper makes such a lovely hissing noise when I tear it away.'

Again Christa found herself giving in, but after Pansy had been enveloped in an old T-shirt to protect her clothes, she proved a surprisingly dedicated assistant. It didn't take long to finish the whole of the second wall. Pansy surveyed it with deep satisfaction.

'It's almost ready for the new wallpaper now,' she announced. 'Can I come with you to choose it?'

Christa's cautious reply was lost in the sudden pealing of the front door bell. Pansy was across the room before it had stopped.

'I'll go,' she said importantly. 'It's probably someone selling poppies.'

'Tell them to wait. I'll be there in a minute,' said Christa, making for her bedroom. Her sleeves were soaked with water from the sponge.

Pansy hurtled downstairs. Christa peeled off her sweatshirt, grabbed the brown silk shirt from the back of a chair, pulled it on, and got to the top of the stairs before hearing a voice which made her freeze.

Poppy sellers never sounded like that. Mallory had arrived for tea. She'd forgotten about his visit, she'd forgotten the cake, and she'd now have to entertain him with Pansy monitoring every look and word.

13

Mallory had walked over to Jericho with the coldest of cold feet, and at first, when Christa's front door swung open, he thought he'd made some hideous mistake over the house as well.

A small girl stood in the hall wearing a T-shirt which reached to her knees, dusty jeans, pink suede boots with trailing laces, and a necklace of what appeared to be wallpaper round her neck.

A hostile green gaze inspected him, and made it very clear that he didn't come up to the mark.

'Where's your box of poppies?' she demanded.

'I don't have any,' he answered meekly.

'Then not today, thank you,' she said, and started to close the door.

'Hey, hold on.' He inserted his foot in the doorway just in time. 'This is Christa's house, isn't it? I've come to tea. Look, I can prove it.'

He held out the contribution he'd bought on impulse en route. Her expression improved remarkably as she read the name of the pâtisserie on the box.

'The *Maison Blanc*,' she said in reverent tones. 'Yummy, scrummy.'

She opened the door again, and made a ballet dancer's curtsy.

'*Entrez, Monsieur, s'il vous plaît. Ma tante arrivera toute de suite.*'

Trying not to laugh, Mallory stepped into the hall. This must be the other Holdgate child, and equally impossible to ignore.

'*Comment vous appellez-vous?*' she demanded.

'My name's Mallory Farrar,' he said with a smile, as he put the cake box on the hall stand.

'*Moi, je m'appelle* Pansy – Pansy Laetitia Holdgate.'

The confident way she shook back her hair reminded him strongly of her aunt.

'Do you like my new boots?'

She thrust a foot forward for his inspection.

'*Formidable*,' he said gravely. '*Vous êtes une vraie minette.*'

'What's a *minette*?'

'Look it up,' said Mallory, his attention diverted by the appearance of Christa on the stairs, long legs bare below frayed shorts, and wearing a pair of white woollen socks with her boots which made her seem schoolgirlish and sexy at the same time. It was a distracting combination.

'Mummy always wears a dress when guests come to tea,' said Pansy, casting a censorious glance at the same legs as Christa arrived breathlessly in the hall.

'I'm so sorry,' she said to Mallory. 'We were decorating, and I completely forgot your visit.'

She tried to appear suitably apologetic while running her fingers through her hair, which had been rumpled by the rapid change of clothes. Fragments of wallpaper fluttered to the floor. No wonder he was staring at her, she thought.

'Do come into the sitting room,' said Pansy, addressing Mallory in her most gracious voice, and clearly deciding that the grownups had lost their wits. 'We've got a parrot *and* a real fire.'

'A Master's wife in the making, if ever I saw one,' said Mallory to Christa with a grin, as Pansy flitted past them.

'I don't think matrimony figures much in Pansy's future plans,' said Christa, going ahead of him into the sitting room.

She was surprised at this deployment of charm in spite of her forgetfulness. He was clearly on his best behaviour, dressed formally in a new jacket with chinos and a navy shirt. His eyes, now taking in the room, were the colour of a winter sea above the jacket's grey-blue tweed. Emma would have been in raptures, Christa thought.

'Me and Chel are going to have motorbikes and work for Pony Express when we grow up,' said Pansy.

She danced over to the parrot's cage.

'Look,' she said to Mallory. 'Isn't she lovely? Her name's Poppaea. One of my names is Latin too.'

'So I gathered,' Mallory replied.

Pansy sent him a suspicious glance before returning to the parrot.

'She's supposed to know lots of different languages, but she won't speak them to me,' she said wistfully. 'And I've only learned French.'

Poppaea was stomping up and down on her perch, regarding the male intruder with a jaundiced eye.

'Wipe your boots, wipe your boots!' she squawked.

Pansy's face lightened. She burst into fits of giggles, covering her face with her hands, and peering at Mallory through her fingers.

'I inherited Poppaea with the house,' said Christa, thinking with some pleasure that he was undergoing a baptism of fire, 'but she used to belong to someone from Gabriel.' She summoned up the name Jessie had mentioned. 'A Dr Jephson, I think.'

'Jephson?' Mallory turned to Pansy with a serious expression. 'He did an excellent translation of the *Thousand and One Nights*. Perhaps we should try Arabic.'

He went closer to the parrot. '*Shikamuu*,' he said.

Poppaea almost fell off her perch in excitement.

'*Marahaba, marahaba, marahaba!*' she screeched.

Pansy was transfixed. She gazed at Mallory in admiration.

'That's brilliant! Truly, truly humungous! Isn't it, Christa?'

'Yes, of course,' she said faintly, realising that her ally was about to go over to the other side.

'Will you teach me some Arabic? Will you teach me now, this minute?' Pansy asked Mallory. 'The special writing too?'

'After tea, maybe,' he said, with an amused glance at Christa.

'Quickly, then,' said Pansy, grabbing her hand. 'Let's put the kettle on. It's got a whistle, you know,' she informed Mallory. 'And we've a dear little jam pot like a cottage with the roof for a lid. You'd better make some toast, Christa, then we can try it out. You don't have to worry about a cake. Mallory's brought us one from the *Maison Blanc*. What sort is it, Mallory?'

'*Tarte aux fraises*. Is that all right?'

'Strawberries, my favourite!' said Pansy. 'Do come along, Christa. We haven't got all day.'

Mallory had taken one of the easy chairs, and stretched out his legs to the fire. He regarded Christa with a lazy smile.

'Better do as you're told,' he said. 'It seems we're in the hands of a higher power than ours.'

The room was extremely quiet after Pansy's departure with Noelene. She'd produced a flood of social chit-chat during tea, eaten most of the toast and two large slices of tart, and afterwards learned a dozen Arabic phrases with dazzling ease.

Mallory was as patient as he'd been with his seminar. And yet, Christa had thought, watching him at the table initiating a heavily breathing Pansy into the mysteries of Arabic script, he most certainly didn't give the impression of a passive observer of life. His tall, lean frame looked as if it should have been on horseback dashing across some far-flung steppe.

He returned to the fireside chair on Pansy's departure. To Christa's dismay he showed no sign of leaving. The curtains were drawn, the fire had sunk to a glowing mass, and Poppaea had been extinguished beneath her serge cover in a thoroughly over-excited state. The remains of tea still lay on the table. The glaze on the tart shone like a smaller fire beneath the light of a single lamp.

Suddenly Christa didn't want him in the room any more. His presence disturbed her now Pansy wasn't there as a buffer between them. She wondered whether to clear the table, and decided it was too obvious a ploy. But when she hit upon offering him some whisky, hoping he'd recognise it as one for the road, she found the bottle was almost empty.

Her housekeeping had caught up with her again. The only other alcohol in the house was Jessie's home-made wine. In desperation she fetched a bottle of dandelion cordial from the pantry, filled a couple of glasses and carried them into the sitting room.

'Jessie, the old lady who lived here before me, made this,' she said, giving him a glass.

Mallory held the cordial to the fire. It was the colour of topaz. He sipped it cautiously. His eyebrows rose.

'The real stuff,' he said. 'It's got a kick like arrack.'

Christa took the chair opposite him. She tasted the cordial too, and as it caught in her throat like a fiery sigh, a picture came to her of Jessie hobbling about her garden painstakingly gathering the ragged blooms.

Mallory, who'd been meaning to leave as soon as decently possible after Pansy's departure, found himself unexpectedly at ease. He watched Christa's face change. Her expression was as transparent as the cordial, very different from Caitlin's thousand masks which had once intrigued him so.

'You liked Jessie?' he said.

'She made the best of everything,' said Christa. Her gaze went to the photo on the mantelpiece. 'A bit like Matt, except that bad luck got him in the end.'

'Matt Brady, your cameraman? You were very close, I think?'

'Yes,' said Christa. 'We were good friends. Just friends, in spite of what some of the tabloids implied. Not that I let them worry me,' she added.

He guessed from the throwaway comment that they'd bothered her a good deal.

'They've certainly worried me lately,' he said. 'At one stage I thought I wouldn't have a single reader left.'

'You mean because of Caitlin Trevor? I interviewed her once.' She looked at him levelly. 'I have to say I liked her a lot. She seemed so at ease with herself and life. But I suppose that's exactly how the public sees Gareth, too,' she added, almost to herself. 'Anyway, things are getting better for me now. I hope they will for you.'

The candour of her smile was as unexpected as a tree in January bursting into leaf. Mallory, who'd just managed to keep himself afloat after the shipwreck of the affair with Caitlin by refusing to explain or complain, was caught off balance yet again.

He reminded himself sternly that like Caitlin she was a professional communicator, and no doubt equally skilled at establishing a rapport. It would probably vanish when he told her his news.

'I'm afraid I haven't been able to fix your meeting with Gervaise Burford,' he said. 'He's only just come out of hospital. He broke his hip.'

She bit her lower lip, the struggle with disappointment evident on her face. 'Then I'll just have to think of something else, I suppose. Poor old chap. Is he all right?'

'He's doing well, but he's not in the sunniest of moods. He gave me a huge bawling-out for disturbing him.'

She gave him a quick, slightly shamefaced look. 'Sorry. Thanks for trying, anyway.'

Mallory made another involuntary concession. 'I can always ask again later. How's the film coming on?'

'Some of the students need to realise they're not potential Louis Malles. Otherwise, they're pretty good.'

'You really ought to attend meetings of Governing Body. If you're right about Gabriel's Mill, the Master's quite likely to slip by a fast one over the development of the site.'

'I know I should, but at the moment the prospect of dining in hall is quite bad enough. I must put in an appearance soon. Sometimes I feel as if I'm trapped in some wonderfully comfortable gilded cage, where all the other occupants are perfectly content not to look through the bars.'

'Not all. And they can't stop you thinking what you like. Someone, I forget who, called it the final freedom.'

'It's only half a freedom, if you can't express your thoughts.'

She left her chair and went impatiently across the room to check a window which was rattling in the rising wind. The supple fabric of her shirt seemed to flow against her body. The incandescent heap in the grate collapsed with a sliding hiss, as if disturbed by the repressed energy in her step.

She returned to pile more fuel on the embers, and stayed kneeling on the hearthrug, letting the tongs rest in the hearth as she watched the rebirth of the fire. The room was very quiet apart from the wind and the coal's occasional splutter and crack, but there was no awkwardness in the silence.

'Don't you miss the world outside?' she asked, still gazing into the flames.

'I miss the desert. The sand sea, the Arabs call it. The dunes are like huge smooth waves which never break.'

He preferred to get down what he'd seen on paper before talking about it. Comments, however sympathetic, usually took the edge off his first impressions. Yet talking to her didn't have that effect. If anything, it made the memories more vivid.

'I've never had time to go there, and I missed the Gulf War,' she said, continuing to gaze at the burning landscapes in the fire.

'It scares some people when they can see nothing but the dunes,' he said. 'It's like being a swimmer in mid-ocean.'

'I should like that.'

Her voice was wistful. She'd be good to travel with, he thought unexpectedly. Not like Caitlin, who, when she'd flown out to meet him at the end of his journey, had insisted that he attend her as closely as a courier on a package tour. That was when things between them had started to go wrong.

'You have the time now,' he said to Christa. 'Why don't you try somewhere not at war for a change?'

'Maybe I should,' she answered dreamily.

A sudden spurt of flame back-lit the loose folds of her shirt, and again he received a tantalising glimpse of the curve of a breast. Her head was bent, the firelight now throwing into relief the nape of her neck.

He couldn't resist running his fingers lightly against the direction of the short, scissored hair. It offered a delicious silky resistance to his touch, and he wasn't too startled by what he'd just done to notice there was a very slight delay before she shivered and pushed his hand away.

'Why did you do that?' she demanded angrily.

'Attraction of opposites, I suppose,' he said, trying to turn it into a joke.

'Right. We're opposites, so don't even think of doing it again. I've had enough of emotional disaster.'

The edifice of coal she'd so carefully constructed shifted slightly over its glowing base. A smouldering cinder rolled towards her. He flicked it back into the fire, moving so swiftly that it had no time to burn his hand, and found himself kneeling by her on the rug.

She gave him a furious glance, and started to jab at the coals with the tongs, dislodging a brilliant shower of embers into the ash below.

'"Born to trouble as the sparks fly upwards",' he quoted lightly. 'But maybe we both know enough by now not to get burnt.'

She threw down the tongs with a clatter, and crossly shifted her stance to face him.

'That's one of the oldest lines there is,' she said.

In spite of the bravado her voice sounded uncertain. The firelight was gilding her skin and hair. It had been an afternoon of doing what he didn't want to do, but he could still stop this – he must stop it, he told himself.

Almost involuntarily he stretched out his hands and laid them over her breasts. They were like fruit warmed by the sun, yet for all her response she might have been some effigy at a shrine. The contrast unsteadied him even more, and he risked leaning forward to touch her mouth with his.

There was no reaction, just a continuing stony inertia which made it impossible to decide whether she was scared, or in some emotional impasse.

Tentatively he moved his lips over hers, and this time produced an only too explicit response. Her mouth compressed and hardened, warding him off as if she'd chosen to use his love-making as a trial of strength.

He put his head back to look at her, playing for time while he tried to grapple with disappointment and an even more irrational impulse to go on.

'I'm not into arm-wrestling of any sort,' he said drily.

Christa's face burned at the remark. After her experience with Gareth, she had been desperate for Mallory to understand she intended to remain in charge. She'd waited for his tongue's brash intrusion into her mouth, for a groping hand to move to her groin, but it hadn't happened.

His hands remained where they were, as if he were waiting for her to make some sign. She wanted and didn't want to push them away. The way he was touching her made her feel valued again. She closed her eyes, desperate not to betray herself.

'This doesn't have to be a fight, you know,' she heard him say in a quiet voice.

He moved his hands just once, slowly down and up, sliding them across her nipples almost thoughtfully, as if he were learning a sexual braille. She wanted to think as well, to work out what was happening to her, but she couldn't.

Instead she covered his hands with hers, and let his lips map her throat and the line of her jaw, travel across her eyelids, explore the soft skin behind her ears, as though he was still trying to imprint her on his mind.

Gareth's foreplay had simply been a means to obtain any consent, however token, before overwhelming her. Sex with him was like being caught up in some huge ship's propeller, which afterwards flung her aside, and yet towards whose blades she always swam again.

Mallory's love-making was totally different, and yet strangely it was reducing her limbs to water. Her body lost its resistance. Slowly, with one of his hands now on her back, and the palm of the other beginning to graze her nipple in the most delicate and delicious of abrasions, she slid to the floor.

Gareth would have been already hanging over her and ripping open his flies. But Mallory was lying by her side on the rug, her head in the crook of his arm, and with immense deliberation one-handedly undoing the buttons on her shirt. It was strange to see the blond hair falling in a straight sweep, and the disciplined, ironic mouth so close to her, instead of Gareth's wiry black pelt and his restless lips demanding instant access to every part of her body and mind.

He freed one breast and gathered it in his hand. With his tongue he laid a warm path round the tender tissue of the areola, then gently blew on it a long, lingering breath. She had never known that such a small gesture could arouse such sensitivity. Her body screamed for him to take her nipple in his mouth, and yet if she let him, it would mean that she'd once more begun to give herself into another person's power.

As if wrenching herself from a perfect dream, she struggled to a sitting position, trying to ground herself in reality by concentrating on the ordinary, familiar contents of the room. She began to do up her shirt, discovered she'd buttoned it crookedly, and almost weeping with frustration, tore at the offending fastening.

'Don't,' he said. 'Let me.'

He was treating her like a child, she thought, because she'd behaved like a child. She should have stopped things much, much earlier, as she'd always been able to do before Gareth.

She glanced up at Mallory as he fastened the final button. His face was expressionless. Anger, or even scorn, would have made her feel better, and made it easier to banish him.

She desperately needed to have her house to herself, to forget this had ever happened, to continue putting together the jigsaw puzzle of her life which she'd feared for a moment he might scatter again.

'You'd better leave,' she said. 'I told you it was no good. At least you have to believe me now.'

Abruptly she got up and went to the table, carefully avoiding his gaze. She began to stack the tea-things, clashing the crockery together and tipping the cutlery into a noisy heap.

Through the clatter she heard him go into the hall. She waited for the front door to slam, but his footsteps returned. She looked up and saw him standing in the middle of the room, casually winding a long grey scarf round his neck. Equally casually, she slid the remains of the tart on to a smaller plate, breaking the fragile pastry into crazy paving.

'There's no need for that,' he said. 'You've made the sub-text very clear. You've obviously got far too much unfinished emotional business to make any relationship work.'

She rounded on him furiously.

'Don't talk about me as if I'm some bloody postmodernist book. There's plenty wrong with you as well. You're a living monument to wounded male pride. At least I'm trying to rebuild a normal life!'

He tucked the end of the scarf into his jacket, and walked towards the hall. At the last minute he looked back at her.

'Hasn't it ever occurred to you that your concept of the normal is decidedly odd? Think about it,' he said.

It was ridiculous, Christa raged to herself as she tipped the strawberry tart into the waste bin, to have this reaction to what the most radical feminist would scarcely call date-rape. She washed up in a turmoil of suds and indignation, and went upstairs to shut the back bedroom window, which had been left open to dry the walls.

She leaned out before she closed it. The rain had stopped. The smell of the canal, a watery mixture of sweetness and decay, hung in the damp air, overlaid with the faint aroma of hops from a nearby brewery. A ginger cat, briefly illumined in the light from the window, stalked through the autumn wreckage of Jessie's dahlias. Her senses felt so aroused that she fancied she could hear its pads on the rotting leaves.

The stillness reminded her of what Mallory had said about the desert, and she suddenly, perversely, wished she could have been with him there. She'd always been too busy reporting on the drama of life to linger anywhere, but he seemed to have a way of deriving pleasure from normally unregarded things which she would have liked to learn. Still more perversely, she now wanted to read his books.

But she wouldn't, she told herself firmly. She was going to forge on in her own way. To prove it, she shut the window, and went downstairs to phone one of the fellows she'd met at the drinks party. He'd implored her to visit him in his rooms to see his first editions. They were probably the academic equivalent of etchings, but he was good-looking and very bright, and she needed to reassure herself that she could spend an evening with a man and remain entirely and amicably in control.

As she was leaving the house in response to his eager invitation to come round at once, the phone rang again.

'Yes?' she snapped unhelpfully, in case it was Mallory ringing to apologise.

'Christa!' said Emma's voice. 'I'm calling from the hotel. I wanted to say thanks for having Pansy. I've just spoken to her on the phone. She had a wonderful time.'

'Yeah, we seemed to do all right,' said Christa non-committally, knowing from the suppressed curiosity in Emma's tone exactly why she'd called. 'How are things on the blasted heath?'

Emma's voice flattened slightly. 'Phil got his feet wet this afternoon. He thinks he has a cold on the way. But the hotel's perfect. Pure eighteenth-century. They even heat the beds with a warming pan.'

'Wonderful,' answered Christa, thinking she'd prefer the more reliable services of an electric blanket if she had to share a bed with Phil.

'Pansy said Mallory Farrar came to tea. I could hardly believe it,' said Emma unflatteringly. 'How did you manage to get him round to your house?'

'I didn't manage anything. He more or less invited himself. He'd helped me over some research, and I couldn't refuse.'

'Pansy was quite charmed. Are you going to see him again? I'd jump at the chance, if I were you.'

'No, I am not! For God's sake, Emma, keep your fantasies for yourself. You'd better get back to Phil and the warming pan right away,' said Christa, slamming down the phone.

On the way to her next seminar, Christa passed Blackwell's travel shop. The siren-song of the books on display had made her so restless when she first arrived that she'd taken to avoiding it. But today she had some time to spare, so she wandered in, telling herself sternly that there was no need for childish subterfuges anymore.

Once inside she leafed scornfully through Mallory's book on India to assure herself that it couldn't possibly be the modern classic described in the blurb, and became completely hooked. As a result she left Blackwell's with it under her arm, and only five minutes to spare before her class.

In spite of being late, she was delayed again by a headline on a newsagent's stand in Holywell Street. The previous night Howl had set fire to a meat farmer's fodder store, but hadn't realised there were animals in the shed next door. The account was accompanied by horrific photos of barbecued cattle.

It was typical of Howl's lethally amateur activities, Christa thought, as she hurried on along Holywell Street, only half aware of the pedestrians ahead of her. Because she was so preoccupied she didn't realise till only a few yards away that one of them was disturbingly familiar, stubby and broad-shouldered with a rolling gait powering through the passersby.

Christa instantly slowed down, and her stomach lurched with relief as Eileen turned to the left down Mansfield Road. When she got to the crossing herself, and peered cautiously round the street corner, the speeding figure was already a safe distance ahead. Yet although it vanished almost at once along another side street, Christa worried for the rest of the way to Gabriel, wondering if Eileen was turning her attention to the city centre again.

*　　*　　*

Christa's students, who'd been waiting on the stairs, crowded into her room. She'd tried to make the atmosphere as unacademic as possible, with a casual arrangement of chairs facing a monitor, and editing equipment set up on a side table. Newspaper clips of the best in recent reportage were tacked to the walls, and she'd invested in an electric percolator which produced coffee capable of rousing the dead.

Only when they'd run through the footage shot at Gabriel's Mill, and she'd taught the students how to use the editing machine, did Christa go on to the next part of the investigation, though Justin had been bursting to tell her his news for the last forty minutes.

'Did you get anywhere with your father's contacts?' she asked, putting him out of his misery at last.

'No sweat,' he answered eagerly. 'It turns out he goes to the same health club as Sir Jeremy Margrave himself. My dad mentioned it to him in the massage room, and he said OK to an interview right away. It's been fixed for next week at the Margrave Tower. What's the matter, Christa? It's great news, isn't it?'

'Not necessarily,' she said brusquely. 'If you remember, I told you to ask me first.'

Not in her worst moments had she thought they'd be invited to interview Sir Jeremy himself, or Sir Jerry as he was known. He couldn't have been a worse interviewee for an amateur. She'd never encountered him personally, but she remembered seeing seasoned reporters return from talking to him so shattered that they only just had the strength to crawl into the nearest pub.

She knew from her recent research into Margrave's that his initial millions had been made in the early eighties converting warehouses into fashionable flats. He'd moved on to redeveloping industrial sites, asset stripping as he went, and now ran a construction empire with its own architects who specialised in designing buildings to enhance the corporate image. According to a journalist friend, he'd never lost the manner acquired in his first job with a firm of notoriously unscrupulous estate agents, where, he was fond of boasting, he'd broken all commission records.

'What's wrong with going straight to the top?' Justin demanded.
'It's a fantastic chance.'

'Any of the other partners would have been an easier subject.
He's the sort of guy who enjoys putting people on the hook.'

'He wouldn't do that to the son of a friend.'

'He'd do it to his own son if he felt like it.'

'It's bound to be OK if my dad's set it up,' said Justin truculently.

Christa hoped for the sake of the other students that he was
right, though every instinct told her he wasn't. However, it
was too late to pull out now. They'd just have to make the
best of it.

'If you're interviewing someone of that calibre, you can't all
pile into his office,' she said, looking round the class. 'In any case
I don't have the funds for fares for everyone, so I'm afraid half
of you will have to stay here and carry on with local work.'

'I'm not interested in helping a bastard like that get air time,'
said Steve. 'There was a piece about him in the *Clarion* recently.
His firm's got a really dodgy record on work-force safety.'

'I'd love to go,' said Annabel breathlessly, batting navy blue
lashes at Justin. 'Shot-lists are such fun.'

'Then you'd better make them legible and accurate, otherwise
it'll be a waste of your fare,' said Christa, who'd spent some time
trying to marry Annabel's happy-go-lucky scrawls to the footage
shot during the previous class.

'I've got an eights practice next week, so I have to be here,'
said Ted.

'London really gets to me. The pollution's worse than Oxford,'
said Donna. 'And if I stay we can set up some shots of my flat.'

'I'll help you,' said Lallie.

Christa knew Steve could direct them standing on his head. She
wasn't so certain about her own charges, apart from Rebekah,
though Mike had turned out to be an art-house movie buff
with an instinct for handling a camera. She could only hope
the seriousness of the occasion would sober the students enough
to hold together as a team when they arrived in London the
following week.

Initially Christa's assumption was correct. The Margrave Tower's galleried central atrium of glass and arching steel ran from floor to roof, exposing the hurrying occupants like the cross-section of a termites' nest. It was dominated by an enormous chandelier, a descending spiral of aluminium down which pulsed a stream of dazzling neon light. The students, gazing at it from the entrance hall, were for once struck dumb.

Christa was not so impressed. She hated the way the tower reduced its inhabitants to insignificance. To her surprise she found herself thinking almost affectionately of Gabriel. At least its rambling buildings were on a human scale.

Briskly she brought everyone back to earth.

'Right, now we've got the go-ahead from security, you'd better do some establishing shots of the entrance hall first. Since Justin's interviewing Sir Jeremy, he should do a stand-upper to camera here to establish his presence in the Tower. Remember to set up the shots so people aren't milling about behind him.'

A stand-upper, or report direct to camera, needed above all a self-assured, fluent presenter. Christa doubted if Justin had ever had a confidence problem in his life, but she was still dubious about his ability to present his surroundings rather than himself.

To her pleasure he remembered her lecturing, and performed surprisingly well. The only problem was that he knew it, and when the filming was over tried very hard to dissuade her from accompanying them to the actual interview. He manoeuvred her to one side as they waited for the high-speed bullet-shaped lift which served only the penthouse floor.

'Why don't you put your feet up in that brasserie over the road, and we'll report back to you the moment we've got it in the can?' he said, smiling at her as if she were an elderly aunt who'd been shopping too long. 'My dad's given Margrave a brilliant spiel about us. We'll be fine on our own.'

'I'm glad you think so,' said Christa, who would rather have interviewed a great white shark. 'But it's my job to get you all back to Gabriel in one piece.'

'Please, Christa,' pleaded Rebekah. 'We did all right at the trial run, didn't we? And it is meant to be our own effort. Sir Jerry'll think it's really wet if our lecturer comes too.'

Although Christa remembered how she'd hated to be over-directed in the studio, and though Rebekah was producing, and

Justin had a written and well-rehearsed list of questions, she knew it was too risky to relent.

'Sorry, but no. You may even find you're quite glad I'm around. And for God's sake, Justin, don't let Sir Jerry overawe you. It'll be exactly what he wants, but if you're persistent and polite, you can't go wrong.'

Her misgivings were reinforced by Sir Jeremy's personal assistant, a tungsten-faced woman of forty something in a grey pinstripe suit with arrow-sharp revers. She was unimpressed by the gaggle who'd descended on her employer.

'I hope you realise how lucky your students are,' she said to Christa. 'Sir Jeremy normally only gives interviews to professionals. You'd better go in right away. He's very strict about timekeeping.'

That's all we need for a thoroughly unrelaxed interview, thought Christa wrily, as the PA pressed a button and connecting doors slid aside to admit them to a lofty marble-floored room whose windows looked towards the private gardens of Buckingham Palace.

So this was the latest in executive sanctums, Christa thought, taking in the long, low sofas covered in white silk, and the Hokusai woodcuts on the wall.

Two Bonsai pines, larger than any she'd seen outside Japan, grew in tortured layers from what appeared to be genuine Satsuma pots. They stood on either side of a desk of black lacquered oak at which sat Sir Jerry, in a suit even more precisely tailored than his PA's, gold fountain pen poised above a pile of faxes, looking as if he was about to pose for the cover of *Life*. The image makers had obviously been hard at work.

'Good morning, Sir Jeremy,' Christa said sweetly, determined to grasp the initiative. 'It's extremely good of you to agree to this interview. May I introduce everyone?'

As she ran through their names he turned on them a pair of tinted spectacles through which it was impossible to assess his gaze, though he did manage gracious nods all round.

'I know you're short of time, and we're quite ready to begin,' she concluded breezily. 'I expect you'd prefer to stay where you are. It's a most impressive setting.'

'Just a moment,' he said, in a voice from which all regional

giveaways had been carefully ironed out. 'You haven't introduced yourself. That won't do, will it? At Margrave's we're all
friends.'

First round to him, she thought.

'I'm the team's academic supervisor,' she said, 'here simply to
lend an occasional hand.'

'You mean you're their teacher? Fred Seddon said nothing
about that.' He switched his gaze back to the students, who were
lined up on a sofa. 'These kids are too old to have a nanny round
them all the time. It'll be much more fun for us on our own.'

The students stared at Sir Jeremy like a bunch of chickens
wondering whether to cross the road.

'I knew you'd agree,' he said confidently, pressing a switch on
his intercom.

A strident beeping, guaranteed to ruin the hearing of anyone
who didn't instantly respond, filled the air. He smiled blandly as
it drowned Christa's protests, and almost before she knew what
had happened the PA appeared, grabbed her arm and virtually
frog-marched her from the room.

'I just hope they're up to it,' the woman said waspishly when
she'd released Christa in the outer office.

'I've every confidence in my students,' she answered in a
cold voice.

She sat down and began to leaf through a glossy pile of
architectural magazines, trying to control her fury. The PA didn't
bother to offer her any of the coffee simmering in a percolator
by her side, but instead launched into a caustic telephone conversation with a government Permanent Secretary who wasn't
producing the right information fast enough. She'd only just put
down the receiver when Sir Jerry's secret weapon beeped again.

The PA shot like a race-track hare into his room, and reappeared
with a smug expression.

'He wants you to go in. There's a problem, as I expected, and
I advise you to sort it out fast. He isn't pleased.'

When Christa returned the students were still lined up on
the sofa facing Sir Jeremy. He'd removed his glasses and was
regarding them like a particularly obsessive topiarist deciding

where to make the next cut. Dobermann eyes set in a synthetic orange-brown tan switched in her direction.

'These poor kids haven't been properly briefed. No wonder they're all at sea. Fred Seddon should have warned you that I always want to see the questions first. And I prefer to choose who interviews me.'

Justin was as white as the sofa he was sitting on. 'You didn't tell my father you wanted to see the questions, Sir Jeremy. And I assumed you'd like me to do the interview as you knew my dad.'

Sir Jerry gave an unsympathetic laugh. His thinning hair had been blow-dried into a brittle mesh across his scalp.

'Didn't you say you were studying economics? Haven't you learned never to assume anything in business at that college of yours?'

Sir Jerry was running true to form, thought Christa. Any moment now he'd be telling them he was educated in the university of life. If he let the interview continue at all, the next step would be to power them into filming a monologue on his rags-to-riches career, and in twenty minutes he'd send them away with nothing but a lesson in self-advertisement.

'This is the first time my group has interviewed someone of your calibre, Sir Jeremy,' she interposed smoothly. 'They're very aware of the privilege, and very anxious not to lose this chance.'

He leaned back in his grey leather chair, basking in the flattery like a lizard on a stone.

'I'm sure they are. I'm usually paid for my time, Miss – Miss – what's your name? You never said.'

'Miss Keith,' said Christa, deliberately not giving her first name.

Luckily he hadn't recognised her so far. He probably got his news straight from an agency, and kept his television for the latest pulp videos from the States.

'I thought you were all Doctors of Philosophy at Oxford. Spindoctoring, now, that might be a useful degree.'

He laughed at his witticism, careful not to display too much bridge work.

'My students simply want to get a general profile of you and the firm, and the projects you have in hand,' said Christa. 'They know you're at construction's cutting edge.'

'That's true enough,' he said, beginning to looking slightly mollified. 'And so I should be, considering the salaries I pay my staff.'

He ran a considering glance along the row of students.

'All right, let's get on with it.' He consulted a massive gold and platinum watch. 'You've got exactly twenty minutes left. And I'll have that one there to do the interview.'

Christa felt her stomach lurch with apprehension as she followed the line of his jabbing finger. It was directed straight at Annabel.

'You mean Miss Fairfax,' she said smoothly. 'I think you'll find she'd rather not. She prefers the production side.'

'I'd love to do it. I don't mind a bit,' said Annabel brightly, completely oblivious of Christa's and Justin's frantic warning glances.

'There you are then,' said Sir Jerry. 'And I'm always happier with blondes.'

He cast a disparaging look at Rebekah which made Christa remember a piece she'd read in one of the broadsheets about his overseas company's exploitation of African labour.

'Very well, then, we'll go ahead. Will you set things up, Rebekah?' said Christa in desperation, mentally hearing the minutes ticking away, and deciding they had to enter the mine-field whether they liked it or not. There was still a chance that Annabel had been paying attention while the questions were rehearsed in class.

'I'd rather someone else did it,' said Rebekah coldly, staring at Sir Jerry with utter disdain.

Christa had every sympathy with her for refusing to direct the interview, but it meant she now had to deal with two cases of wounded pride.

'Then you'd better take over, Justin,' she said, thinking that it might at least go some way towards making up.

To his credit, Justin kept his head. He carefully positioned Annabel, checked Mike's camera angle, and retired to a spot where he could signal to her unseen by Sir Jerry. Christa, taking refuge behind a huge temple gong, was joined by Rebekah, now demoted to the shot-list.

Sir Jeremy knew all the interviewee's tricks. He deployed a mixture of patronage and slick bonhomie on Annabel, using her Christian name, and urging her to call him Jerry. Instead of firmly addressing him by his title, and steering him towards the development of the Mill site she allowed herself to be dominated completely.

He consistently ignored her questions, replacing them with ones of his own, and so confused her that by the time they were within two minutes of the end of their allotted time, she hadn't once mentioned the real reason for the interview.

Behind Sir Jerry's back Justin held up a sheet of paper with 'Gabriel's Mill' scrawled on it, and made vigorous winding-up motions with his other hand.

Annabel's eyes widened in startled surprise, but she made a feeble effort at last.

'It's been absolutely fascinating talking to you, Sir Jeremy,' she said, managing to catch one of his very few pauses. He was able to go longer than a Sumatran pearl-fisher without drawing breath. 'There's just one more point. Would you be able to confirm that Margrave's has been working on a proposal for a library store on land owned by our college at Gabriel's Mill? We're all desperately interested, because we've an idea that the old store in town might become student accommodation.'

If ever there was a soft-bellied question, that was it, thought Christa resignedly. It begged for a denial.

Sir Jerry stared blankly at Annabel. 'I can't imagine where you picked that one up. The sooner you put it out of your pretty head, the better.'

He shot his cuff and once more looked ostentatiously at his watch.

'I think that's just about it, in any case,' he said. 'You're a lucky young lady to have had so much of my time.'

Christa willed Annabel not to let the subject drop, to ask again in such a way that he had to give a direct reply, but she simply allowed the interview to die in a welter of effusive thanks.

'It's been a pleasure,' said Sir Jerry blandly. 'I always like to help the young. Do send me a copy of your tape.'

*　　*　　*

'Wasn't he sweet?' said Annabel nervously, gazing at the exasperated expressions round her as the lift began to shoot smoothly towards the ground.

Justin, suffering severely from loss of face, rounded on her at once.

'You fuckwit! You total dumbo! You've ruined the whole bloody thing. And Christ knows what he'll say to my dad!'

Annabel burst into floods of tears, and cast herself into the arms of the startled Mike.

'I did my best, I did my best!' she wailed. 'Don't let him be so horrible to me!'

She hadn't stopped sobbing when they reached the entrance hall. Justin was still white-lipped, Mike looked deeply embarrassed, and Rebekah was clearly only just restraining herself from remarks even more cutting than Justin's.

It had been agonising for Christa too, watching someone else kill an interview she knew she could have carried off, but she was determined that Sir Jerry shouldn't win.

'Listen to me, Annabel,' she said in a voice which produced an instant pause in the waterfall. 'I know it was tough for you in there, but no professional film crew can afford to carry a quitter. So either you get yourself together while we have an early lunch in the brasserie over the road and try to work out some way of rescuing things, or else you go straight back to Oxford. Which is it to be?'

Annabel looked up from Mike's chest.

'Rebekah quit,' she gulped. 'You're not angry with her.'

Christa just kept her temper.

'There's a huge difference between a racial insult, and what was said to you. So make up your mind. Will you stay, or go?'

Annabel slowly disentangled herself from Mike, gulping and wiping blue smears from her face.

'I'm sorry. I want to stay,' she said in a tiny voice.

'Jesus, you've actually got her to turn off!' said Justin in awe. 'And do you really think we can still save things, Christa?'

'It's amazing what a meal and some wine can do,' she answered, though she had no idea what their next move would be.

14

An hour later, amid the thirties decor of the brasserie, and encouraged by two bottles of Chardonnay and mountains of designer pasta, the students were looking happier. Christa felt worse. From her seat on a banquette against the wall she had a perfect view across the crowded tables to the long chrome-railed bar. The room was crammed with media people and young business executives, all busy exchanging gossip, pushing their entertainment allowances to the limit, and making her horribly homesick for her other life.

'Brilliant *fettuccine alle vongole*,' said Justin, moving a heap of discarded clam shells to the side of his plate, and pouring himself more wine. 'So, what's the revised plan of campaign?'

He looked at Christa expectantly.

'I was hoping you'd tell me. After all, this is meant to be your project.'

'No way will my dad fix us another interview when he hears how I messed up on this. Anyway, it's useless getting on to the other directors now. That bastard Margrave will already have tipped them the wink.'

'Maybe we need to find a mole,' ventured Annabel, glancing at Christa as if she expected her suggestion to be shot down in flames. Though her make-up had been repaired, there was clearly still a large hole in her self-esteem.

'That's not a bad idea,' said Christa, producing the beginnings of a smile from her at last.

'Yeah, not bad at all, Annie,' said Justin kindly, 'if only we knew how to find a mole in the first place.'

'I used to have a friend who did temping at Margrave's, but

that was ages ago,' said Rebekah, absentmindedly tearing apart a poppyseed roll.

Her hair was braided into a topknot threaded with beads of jet, and she'd shrugged off her red fake-fur jacket to reveal a skinny black ribbed sweater. She was trying not to be distracted by stares from an extremely personable young executive at another table where some kind of celebration party was going on.

'Very helpful,' said Justin. 'Why does Flash Gordon over there keep giving you the eye?'

'Probably wondering why I'm sitting with a no-no like you,' said Rebekah. 'Do you have any contacts in temping agencies, Christa?'

The same thought had already passed through her mind and been rapidly dismissed.

'I do, but even if we found an agency with employees at Margrave's, it wouldn't let them talk to us. It'd be too scared of losing the account.'

'We could try the office cleaners, but we'd have to hang around till they came in tonight,' suggested Mike.

'Cleaners wouldn't know how to access electronic files,' Justin objected scornfully.

'You must be joking,' said Rebekah. 'I've got a friend at the LSE who funds herself by cleaning the flats of Hooray Henrys like you.'

'Pack it in, will you? Save your social conscience for that smarty-pants friend of yours. Looks like he's coming over.'

The executive had given up trying to make contact from a distance, and was advancing towards them.

'Hi, Rebekah! Don't you remember me? Tony Kitembe?'

Rebekah's face broke into a smile of recognition at last.

'Tony, of course! I didn't recognise you without your dreadlocks. Come and join us. Meet Tony, everyone. We were at Cambridge together, and his dad came out of Uganda at the same time as mine.'

'Well, well,' said Tony, after further introductions all round, 'this calls for some fizz, I think.'

Though he'd exchanged an enthusiastic Rasta handshake with Rebekah, the accent in which he ordered champagne was pure public school.

'So you're all at Gabriel,' he said, as the wine waiter bustled away. 'What are you doing in the wicked world of commerce, then?'

'We're making a video as part of a media studies course. Christa here is our supervisor.'

Tony, who possessed the enviable looks of a Benin bronze, had been sneaking more puzzled glances at Christa. His face cleared. 'Of course – Christa Keith! I couldn't place you at first. You've changed a bit as well. Those reports you did from Bosnia were brilliant. How come you're teaching now?'

'You could call it R and R,' said Christa. 'And what have you been doing since Cambridge, Tony?'

She'd meant simply to deflect further questions about herself, but got as an extra the enjoyment of seeing Justin's stunned expression as Tony gave them a run-down on his star-studded career since graduating.

'So when I'd finished my year at Harvard Business School, I decided to do corporate accountancy and go for the money-bags,' he concluded. ''Fraid I never had as developed a conscience as you, Rebekah.'

'You jammy sod,' she said. 'And after all those Socialist Worker demos we went on together.'

'Yeah, I haven't done badly so far,' he said. 'Forty K a year, and a company BMW.'

'Jesus!' said Rebekah. 'Where do you get that sort of hand-out?'

'Margrave's. You know, the construction firm. It's just over the road. But they've been tight-fisted with their bonuses lately, so I'm moving on to something better. This is my last day, in fact.'

An enormous hush fell over the rest of the table, interrupted only by a waiter popping the champagne cork, and placing the bottle in a bucket of ice.

'Tony,' Christa said to him with a smile she didn't often employ, 'pour yourself a very large glass of champagne, and let Rebekah tell you how you may be able to square your social conscience after all.'

The other people in the brasserie were starting to filter away, and the waiters had begun to reset the tables for the evening wave of customers as Rebekah wound up the sorry tale of their interview with Sir Jerry.

'So you see, he gave us one hell of a run around, and yet we got nothing,' she said.

'That's not unusual,' said Tony with a grin. 'But I still don't understand why the development of the Gabriel's Mill site should bother you so much. Aren't the students pleased with the idea of better accommodation? And what's it got to do with my conscience?'

Without telling him their real motives, Rebekah had tried very hard to find out if he knew that Margrave's was involved in the development. But though he'd made a lot of sympathetic noises about the interview fiasco, he'd been maddeningly cagey so far.

Rebekah turned to Christa with an enquiring look.

'Shall I go ahead?' she asked.

Before Gareth, Christa would have believed the intuition which told her Tony could be trusted. But now she hesitated as a garish picture of the ruin of all their careers if he let them down floated through her mind.

'What do the rest of you think? It's your decision as well,' she said to the other students.

'Go ahead, Rebekah. It's fine by me,' said Mike quietly.

'And me,' said Annabel.

Justin was having a tussle with his baser instincts. There was a long pause while he scowled into his untouched champagne, and irritably scored the table cloth with his knife.

'Yeah, OK by me too, if you really want to trust a *nouveau*,' he said at last.

Rebekah smiled at Tony. 'Take no notice. His dad's the biggest *nouveau* of all.' She leaned forward confidentially. 'Now I'm laying us all on the line with this information, Tony, so I'm counting on you to help out. Boy, will it make you think!'

Tony's face slowly lost its easy geniality as he listened.

'Christ! That's a pretty nasty tale. I'd no idea of the background to the scheme.'

Rebekah pounced triumphantly on the remark.

'You know about the proposal, then?'

'Oh, yes, of course. I haven't worked on it personally, but one of the cost accountants asked me to look over the figures. It seemed a bloody good investment as far as Gabriel and Margrave were concerned. The second stage of the development will definitely incorporate an up-market shopping mall. Now you've told me all this, I'm even gladder to be getting out.'

'I knew you hadn't really changed!' said Rebekah, beaming at him. 'You're the same old Tony.'

'Jesus, here we go! Why don't you just bring on Mantovani, and be done with it?' said Justin in disgust.

Christa hastily took over the conversation.

'The students wouldn't want better accommodation at the expense of the estate. We're trying to expose Gabriel's plans, but we need some sort of firm confirmation that they exist,' she said to Tony. 'Would you be able to get us a copy of the proposal?'

He shook his head decidedly. 'No way. It'd mean doing the dirty on the cost accountant, and he's a friend. I don't want to get him fired.'

Rebekah's face fell. 'But you're our only lead so far.'

'I knew this wouldn't get us anywhere,' said Justin with satisfaction.

Christa jumped in again before open warfare broke out between Justin and Rebekah.

'Would you be willing to confirm on camera that this project is already under way, Tony?'

He considered, frowning. 'I'm not so sure. Margrave could give me a hell of a lot of grief, even when I've gone.'

'Supposing we guaranteed you anonymity?' said Christa. 'We could set up an over-the-shoulder shot from the rear, so your face wouldn't be seen as you talked. If we filmed outside, and focussed on a background of the Margrave Tower, your figure would be fuzzy anyway.'

'What about my voice?'

'We can copy the sound-track and distort it if you like? It won't matter as long as we've got the original.'

'Please,' pleaded Rebekah. 'If you agree, I'll invite you to the Shrove Tuesday Feast next term. You'd meet masses of influential old Gabrielites, all loaded. Think of the contacts you'd make!'

'With people like Jimmy Judd? No, thanks.' Tony grinned at her. 'But I wouldn't mind a spot of contact with you again. OK, I must be crazy, but I'll do it.'

'Great!' said Rebekah, responding with a smile like a sun-lamp. 'I knew you wouldn't let us down.'

'Just make sure you film it somewhere discreet, for God's sake. There's a quiet square with a good view of the Margrave Tower a couple of blocks away. The fewer people who see me doing this, the better.'

Christa went to her room in college the following day feeling unusually contented. In spite of the frustrations she'd enjoyed steering her group towards success.

She also looked with a kinder eye on her surroundings as she crossed King's Quad. Though the college's foundation had been funded by Henry VIII plundering the monastery coffers at the Reformation, it hadn't proceeded to glorify Mammon like the Margrave Tower, and still didn't give that impression in spite of all the Master's efforts.

She'd only just arrived in her room, and was viewing the first shots from the London footage, when she was further surprised by a phone call from her father.

'Your mother went to a group therapy session yesterday. Though I still don't think your way of persuading her was right, it does seem to have done the trick,' he said happily. 'She's too stubborn to ask you herself, but it'd mean a great deal to her if you went to tea this afternoon. I'll try to get home early too.'

Christa's pleasure at the news even stayed with her as she studied the footage of the Sir Jeremy interview, whose only merit was that it could be spliced with devastating effect into Tony's revelations. After an hour of poring over it, she went to make herself some coffee and found she'd run out of her favourite Colombian blend.

Borrowing from Mallory was out of the question, though she knew he was in his room. She'd heard the sound of a sitar through his closed door as she came up the stairs. But if he was listening to music it meant she could safely have coffee in the SCR.

Again she didn't have her usual feeling of alienation as she crossed the King's Quad, where students were drifting off to lectures in other parts of town. Normally she dodged past them, impatient with their gossip about missed essay deadlines and plans for the next college bop. But recently she'd given a talk to the Junior Common Room on her experiences in Bosnia, and as students waved at her she realised she was getting to know them at last.

The SCR was almost empty, except for Leda, sitting by the fire with her coffee and a cigarette. She was as immaculately turned out as ever, but she looked tired. She beckoned Christa over.

'Come and join me,' she said. 'I could do with a diversion.'

Christa sat down, thinking that the tranquil room, whose furniture and ornaments had slowly accrued through the centuries, couldn't have been less like the Margrave penthouse suite. She was startled to realise she'd begun to feel more at home here too.

'Trouble with Governing Body?' she asked, telling herself that though she hated taking Mallory's advice she really should observe the workings of this legendary beast.

'For once it's the least of my problems. I've just spent an hour with the local CID. We're having more problems with Howl.'

'But I thought they'd lost interest in you and were going for cattle farmers instead?' said Christa.

'Not entirely, I'm afraid. They've turned their attention from the Institute itself to the property of staff. At the moment they're conducting a nuisance campaign: wrecking gardens, slashing car tyres, pushing nasty little offerings of excrement through letter-boxes. I'm sure you know the scene.'

Christa grimaced. 'Not very imaginative. And horrible to be on the receiving end.'

She remembered Eileen's juggernaut progress down Holywell Street and thought that the woman must be more than a little mad. She was gladder than ever that she hadn't followed up her allegations against the Institute.

'It's especially unpleasant for staff with families,' Leda said.

Christa wondered if Philip had been affected. She'd heard nothing from Emma since the country weekend, so perhaps they'd escaped.

'The CID seems to think Howl's activities are fairly amateurish compared to some organisations, but there's a chance they could develop into something worse – arson attacks on homes, letter bombs, that sort of thing,' Leda went on. 'We're all going to have to be a lot more careful about personal security until Howl is finally sorted out. I really don't have time for this kind of thing, but I'll have to find it somehow, and so will the staff.'

'You must,' said Christa gravely, remembering her many professional encounters with terrorism. It had been hard enough to take when she wasn't personally involved.

Up to now she'd always scrupulously respected journalistic confidences, but at Apollo she'd had Randall to back her up, and her own family hadn't been embroiled. Though she was inclined to agree that Howl's activities were non-professional and disorganised, the remotest prospect of Pansy or Jamie being harmed was too horrible to contemplate. She began to think she might have to tell the police about her encounter with Eileen and Paul.

She was almost glad when Mallory's unexpected appearance in the common room diverted her thoughts. His eyes travelled over her impassively as he took his coffee and the *Independent* to the opposite end of the room. She forced her attention back to Leda, who was giving her a curiously diagnostic look.

'How's the film going?' she asked. 'But perhaps I shouldn't enquire too closely.'

'You've heard about it?' Christa was surprised.

'The Master himself told me. He seems delighted with the idea of some publicity for Gabriel. I'm pleased the students are going to have an official voice at last. Well done.'

'Did he say if he'd got his side of it set up?'

'I gather he's collecting some heavy guns among the alumni. He's planning to astonish you.'

'The plan is mutual,' said Christa, longing to tell Leda the real purpose of the film.

'The project's obviously suiting you, anyway. You've looked much better lately. But don't rush yourself. Getting over what happened in Bosnia may take longer than you expect. How are things with your parents?'

Christa remembered she'd given Leda a brief description of

the problems at Juniper Grove during their drive back from the Institute. Though Leda hardly commented at the time, it must have been filed away in her physician's mind.

'I'm going to see my mother this afternoon. She's started group therapy at last.'

'That's brave of her.'

'It'll make a huge difference to my father and sister if it works.'

'And to you, I think,' said Leda quietly.

'Not so much. I've been away from the family for a long time.'

During the whole of the conversation Christa had been aware of Mallory's presence, even at the other end of the room. Now, to her consternation, he came with his coffee towards a desk just a few yards away, giving her a grave enquiring glance as he sat down.

His insensitivity was incredible, she thought, pointedly blanking out her own expression, and returning her attention to Leda, who was beginning to gather up her briefcase and jacket.

'Sorry this has been so short,' she said, 'but I've a meeting at eleven.'

'I'm going too,' said Christa, hastily finishing her coffee, and keeping her eyes firmly fixed on Leda's back as she accompanied her from the room.

Leda paused at the door to adjust her scarf. 'I hope you enjoy your afternoon. I'm off to persuade the Dean that the Student Counselling Service needs rather more than tea and sympathy from volunteer faculty wives.'

She glanced towards Mallory, who'd just begun a letter at the desk, and then at Christa. 'Remember, don't be too hard on yourself. It'll come back, you know.'

'What will?' asked Christa.

'Letting people near you again,' Leda said with a gleam of amusement as she hurried away.

Leda's enigmatic remark was still occupying Christa as the Mini crawled in a long line of cars towards Botley. The medical profession was much too inclined to play God sometimes, she told herself crossly. Just because Leda knew a thing or two about post-traumatic stress, it didn't make her another Dr Ruth.

From these thoughts it was a short step to more unsatisfactory memories of Mallory's visit to Jericho. Their only merit was to distract her so thoroughly that for once she arrived in Juniper Grove relatively unruffled by the awfulness of the traffic.

Today Alice opened the door. She was wearing a new dress, Crimplene again, but at least in a nineties style. There was another surprise too. Pansy, a frilled apron down to her ankles, clung to Alice's hand, and behind her Emma, still in her teaching clothes, was emerging from the kitchen along the hall.

'Christa, darling! Come in quickly, before the warmth escapes,' said her mother. She smiled fondly at everyone. 'How lovely to have all my girls with me once more.'

Christa caught Emma's eye, and just managed not to laugh.

'We're putting hundreds and thousands on the fairy cakes,' announced Pansy, dragging Alice back to the kitchen. 'Quickly, Grandma. The icing mustn't get too hard.'

'I shouldn't think there's another house in Botley where fairy cakes are still being made,' said Christa. 'Why is Pansy here, Em? I thought you weren't going to bring her again.'

Emma looked sheepish.

'I decided that perhaps I'd been a bit unkind, especially since Mother's made this effort with the therapy. And Pansy seems to have got over the incident in the shop. She said she wanted to come.'

'Has Mother told you how she got on at the clinic?'

'Not yet. I didn't like to ask in case I rocked the boat in some way. But I'm sure she'll mention it now you're here.'

In the sitting room Jamie, on a blanket and rubber sheet to protect the pristine carpet, was attempting four-point press-ups, watched fondly by Conrad.

'Isn't he a marvellous little chap?' said Conrad, when he'd greeted Christa. 'He's a strong look of my grandfather, the county cricketer, you know. Did I ever tell you how he made a century for Suffolk?'

Christa placed herself in the least upholstered chair, and flicked through a copy of the *Lady*, while Emma dutifully listened to the story they'd heard scores of times. She'd just got to a letter about remedies for iron mould when Pansy, guided by Alice, proudly pushed the tea trolley into the room.

'Look at my cakes!' she said, grabbing the plate and dancing up to Christa with it. 'They're even scrummier than the one Mallory bought you.'

Alice made an agitated swoop towards the cakes, rescuing them as they were about to descend on the carpet.

'Go and sit next to Mummy, Pansy, like a good girl, while I pour out the tea. We don't want any accidents today.'

Pansy flung herself on the sofa, slumping against Emma and pouting. As Conrad went into the usual routine with the occasional tables, Christa prayed that her mother wouldn't take up the reference to Mallory's visit.

Her luck was out. Alice lifted the teapot in its eau-de-nil cosy, and said in a voice saturated with maternal curiosity, 'Pansy mentioned earlier in the kitchen that you'd had a friend to tea, Christa. Have you known him long? Do tell us more.'

'Yes, do,' said Emma wickedly.

Pansy bounced upright again. 'He's *très, très* brill, Grandma. Even Noelene said he was a hunk. He knows ten languages – ten! He's teaching me Arabic. And he said Christa had to do as she was told!'

'Now that really is promising,' said Emma. 'Don't you think so, Mother?'

'Yes, I suppose so, dear,' said Alice, casting a nervous glance at her youngest daughter. 'Perhaps you'd like me to invite him to a family supper, since he's taken such an interest in Pansy?'

'Let's keep a sense of proportion about this, for heaven's sake,' said Christa, trying to sound unconcerned. 'He's already been to dinner with Emma and Phil. Personally I've had more than enough of him.'

'I haven't,' said Pansy.

'He does sound rather nice, I must say,' said Alice. 'What a shame you've taken such a dislike to him, Christa.'

Now a strong note of suspicion tinged her voice. Christa gave herself a stern reminder that she was there to celebrate her mother's triumph, bit back the retort she burned to deliver, and meekly started to hand round cups of tea.

Providentially Jamie chose this moment to heave himself on

to his hands and knees and crawl six inches before collapsing back on the rug. By the time he'd been coaxed to do it at least ten more times, Conrad had photographed the proud moment for posterity, and Alice had recounted in hideously embarrassing detail her own children's first attempts at propulsion, tea-time was over at last.

Conrad went upstairs looking for some old photos. Jamie sat on his grandmother's lap, red-faced and over-excited. Pansy, by contrast, had become steadily more silent, and was kicking mutinously with her heel at the carpet.

'Be careful, darling, please,' said Alice, dragging her attention from Jamie. 'You're going to ruin the pile.'

'I want to do something as well,' said Pansy. 'I want to do my goblin dance.'

Emma paled. Pansy's goblin dance had already wreaked havoc at Ethelred Road.

'Not today, Pansy,' she said. 'Perhaps in the garden sometime, when summer comes.'

Alice dropped a kiss on the baby's head. 'Ask Grandpa to have a game of Snap with you, Pansy, when he comes back.'

'Snap, yuk! Chel and me like liar dice best. We're going to Las Vegas when we grow up.'

'Stop showing off,' rapped Emma. 'Grandma would simply prefer you to do something quiet.'

Pansy's eyes roved frustratedly round the room in search of alternative entertainment. Christa was wondering whether it would make things worse if she offered to teach her poker, when Pansy's gaze fell on the display case of Alice's cherished thimbles.

'The thimbles, Grandma! Please, please, let me play with them, just this once. I'll be careful, truly I will.'

Christa could see the struggle on her mother's face as her desire to control her surroundings overcame her desire to please Pansy.

'No, darling. I'm sorry. They're too fragile, too precious.'

'But all I want to do is hold them and look at them,' said Pansy, her face becoming as pink as her boots. 'Mummy lets you hold Jamie. It's just the same.'

'It's not the same at all,' said Alice, beginning to look almost as agitated. 'I'm much, much older than you.'

Tears began to roll down Pansy's cheeks.

'I'm allowed to hold Jamie too, and I'm much, much younger than you,' she wailed with devastating logic. 'You love your horrid old thimbles more than me. I'm never, ever coming to see you again!'

'Really, Mother, you might have let her look at them,' said Emma indignantly, as Pansy stormed into the hall, where she could be heard kicking the stairs between violent outbursts of sobs. 'We'll have to go home now, or she'll make herself sick. I only hope I can calm her down before she gets in the car.'

Alice's face was flushed as Emma left the room

'What a fuss about nothing,' she said, not looking at Christa, and bouncing the baby energetically on her knee. 'What an enormous fuss, wasn't it, Jamie?'

Christa was feeling almost as upset as Pansy, but she'd become increasingly suspicious of her mother's unwillingness to discuss the therapy session, and was determined to find out what had happened before she made her own departure.

'Pansy's got a lot of adjusting to do at the moment,' she said. 'I'm surprised you don't understand. After all, you're having to cope with new things as well.'

'Emma was an angel when you were born. She adored looking after you.'

'How did the clinic go?' Christa asked, certain that she was being deliberately misunderstood.

'Oh, quite well,' said her mother into the back of Jamie's head. 'Your father took me shopping afterwards, and I bought a new dress.'

'So I see. Did you like the psychotherapist?'

'Yes, yes,' said Alice rapidly. 'She was a little too informal, perhaps, but very nice all the same.'

Christa began to relax.

'And how about the other people there?'

'Some of them were rather odd, but they seemed pleasant enough.'

Alice stood up and hoisted Jamie on to her hip.

'Shall we go and see if Pansy's better now, young man?'

Christa still didn't entirely trust her mother. Her account of the therapy session had been remarkably bland.

'So you felt it was a success?' she persisted.

'Your father thought it was a big step forward. It's not fair to interrogate me like this, Christa.'

Alice began to move purposefully towards the door.

'And you're going again next week?' said Christa.

Alice didn't reply. Christa leaped up and caught her free arm just as she was about to whisk herself and Jamie to safety. His face creased in protest at the abrupt movement.

'For goodness' sake, do you have to be so awkward?' chided Alice. 'No wonder Jamie's difficult with you. You don't like your auntie giving you nasty sudden shocks, do you, darling?' she cooed at him.

'Answer me, Mother.' Christa's temper was beginning to fizz. 'Are you going again next week?'

'No, I am not, if you must know,' said Alice in an irritable voice. 'Once was quite enough. I'm much too old for public soul-searching, and for being told what's wrong with me by a girl of Emma's age.'

'I'm sure it wasn't like that.' Christa could hardly contain her exasperation. 'Leda Lennox told me the clinic has an excellent reputation. You're condemning it before you've given it a chance.'

'It has helped me, because I was able to go shopping afterwards. I've done what you wanted, I feel better, and I don't need to go again.'

'So you'll visit me and Emma without having to drag Dad along? You'll go to London on your own to see those plays you used to love? Tell me that, and I'll be satisfied.'

'Well, perhaps not right away, but I'm sure I will in a month or two.'

'You got Em and me here under false pretences, and you know it!' Christa erupted.

The skin in the V neck of Alice's dress was mottled with patches of red. 'It's a difficult time of life for me. It's not always easy to cope.'

'Exactly! So you need help, and if you don't stop kidding yourself you can manage without it, it'll soon be too late.'

Alice assumed her wounded expression, clearly expecting the usual cycle to begin once more: guilt and resentful apology on Christa's part, followed by tearful, heartfelt, yet empty promises of her own.

'Jesus, Ma, there's no point in this, is there?' Christa said, all the anger unexpectedly draining from her. 'We've been through it a hundred times before, and you never, ever change. I'm going home too.'

'Please yourself. You always do,' said Alice in a trembling voice, clutching Jamie like a life-belt.

In silence they went into the hall where Emma was zipping a sulky, tear-stained Pansy into her jacket, and in silence Christa pulled on her own coat. Emma, sensing the tension, looked up enquiringly at Christa, but she was already halfway through the front door, unable to bring herself to say goodbye.

Outside it was dark, and beneath the street lamps the verges were already touched with frost. Christa waited by the Mini as Emma stowed the children in her car. She closed the door, and came over.

'What's up?' she asked. 'Have you and Mother had a row as well?'

Rapidly, her breath clouding the air, Christa told her what had happened.

'The whole outing's been a disaster all round,' said Emma. 'I really thought Mother was going to make it this time. I've decided not to go again with the children. I shall feel awful, but anything's better than having Pansy make another scene over those wretched thimbles. Not that I blame her, in a way. Mother's positively anal about them.'

She gave Christa a hug. The gesture was oddly comforting.

'Cheer up,' she said, and added mischievously, 'at least you've had the most gorgeous man in Oxford to tea.'

'Thanks a bunch,' said Christa derisively, but hugging her back all the same.

As she waited for Emma to return to the Volvo so that there was more room to move the Mini, she remembered her conversation with Leda.

'Hang on a moment!' she called, dashing over to Emma while

she fumbled with the lock in the driver's door. 'Has Phil said anything to you about Howl today?'

'Has he not! He rang at lunchtime, and told me the CID had spoken to all the Institute staff.' Emma glanced into the car to make sure Pansy wasn't listening. 'We haven't received any of Howl's latest offerings yet, thank God, but we're now supposed to look out for letter bombs too. It's bloody worrying with small children to think of, and I've quite enough problems as it is.'

'Didn't Phil mention anything about the car?'

'He said we have to keep it locked in the garage at home, not in the drive, so it can't be tampered with.'

'You will do that, won't you, Em? Don't ever forget,' said Christa.

'I'm not likely to,' said Emma, pulling up her collar and staring at Christa with worried, serious eyes. 'I just wish the police would get this sorted out. I can't understand why it's taking them so long. Howl seem such an amateurish lot in some respects.'

Christa glanced into the back of the car, where Pansy had decided to read *Tintin* to a drowsy Jamie, and tried not to think of them as mangled human wreckage.

'Sometimes the amateurs are the most dangerous of all,' she said. 'Please be very, very careful.'

Emma got into the driver's seat and let down the window.

'I've told you, I will be. But I'm inclined to agree with what Phil says. Howl's simply trying to intimidate us.' She turned on the ignition, and put her head out of the window to deliver a final remark before revving away. 'Anyway, what's all this concern for your family, Christa? You'd better take care too. It sounds as if you might be getting fond of us after all.'

After a reluctant visit to the police with her information about Howl, Christa was glad to immerse herself in teaching and writing for her book. The remaining weeks of term were spent helping her group edit the London footage and film more local interviews.

By the end of November the shops were submerged in tinsel. The general assumption that the only place for any right-minded person to spend Christmas was with the family drove her to book a holiday in Morocco instead. It was worth going into the red, she decided, to avoid the gathering Emma had planned.

Howl had mercifully ceased its postal activities, at least for a while, Emma and Phil were in a state of stand-off over their marital disagreements, and Alice was preserving an injured silence. Conrad sometimes called in on his way home from work, ostensibly to wait for the rush hour to die down, but in reality, Christa guessed, to have a break from Juniper Drive.

By the final week of term, the Bodleian was one of the few places in Oxford unaffected by Yuletide frenzy. At 8 p.m. on a bitterly cold night Christa felt she'd read enough about Vietnam. She decided to head for home via a cheering pub supper in the Eagle and Child, but first made a swift detour through the deserted streets to fetch some books from her room at Gabriel.

When she left there, Mallory's door was standing slightly ajar, and casting an inviting crack of light across the stone stair. She had just finished his book and made the embarrassing discovery that many of their views were remarkably alike. If she hadn't already met him, nothing would have stopped her pushing open the door and going in to talk.

Though Gabriel was never very warm, tonight it seemed like a hothouse compared to the temperature outside. Christa wound her scarf more snugly round her neck, and pulled on the beret from the pocket of her Sarajevo jacket.

The wind made her eyes water and whipped at her scarf. She paused at the end of Jowett Walk to tuck it into her collar. To her right along Mansfield Road another lone walker was ploughing through the wind, also wearing a scarf, wound so tightly round the head that it looked like an Arab burnous and only the eyes peered out.

Again the rapid, rolling stride, and the way the walker's shoulders strained against the jacket covering them, were frighteningly familiar, and this time Christa, in the Rasta beret she'd worn at the meeting with Howl, was instantly recognised. Eileen's head went down like a gun-dog, and she set off towards her at a fast, soundless run

Christa jammed her shoulder bag under her arm and tore off

to the left towards Holywell Street, praying there'd be some other pedestrians there. Unusually it was almost empty. She looked back, saw Eileen catching up on her fast, and bolted across the road.

Desperately she thought of jettisoning the cumbersome bag of books, but her name was in some of them, and if Eileen discovered her real identity she'd be in worse trouble. She began to rush towards Longwall Street, where she could see traffic passing, and heard one of the books fall to the pavement behind her.

Frantically she snatched it up, glanced back towards Eileen, and saw through wind-blurred eyes that a group of cyclists had suddenly emerged from New College in a wobbling, uncoordinated crowd which filled the road. Eileen was poised almost gibbering with frustration on their far side, forced to let them pass.

Christa dashed on, turned right into Longwall Street, narrowly missed annihilation by a lorry, and dodged into the grounds of New College through a side gate which was open for once.

As she cowered in the freezing dark behind a tree trunk, praying that Eileen's squat figure wouldn't appear, some strange trick of her overwrought senses made her think of the *Forest Hunt*. She really was at bay now, she thought grimly. She had no illusions about what would happen if Eileen found her. She was clearly intent on retribution for not following up Howl's information, and the severity of it would depend on whether she knew Christa had gone to the police.

She'd run though several highly unpleasant scenarios in her mind and was shivering with cold by the time she realised she'd shaken Eileen off, temporarily at least. As her heart stopped pounding, and her legs returned to a more solid state, she decided to risk going back to Gabriel to call a taxi from the safety of the porters' lodge.

Cautiously crossing Longwall Street, and scuttling along beneath the high wall after which it was named, Christa felt as exposed as a target in a fairground rifle range. Her fear didn't begin to recede until she reached a projecting gateway where the road veered, and she knew she was about to see the distinctive shape of Gabriel's clock tower outlined against the sky ahead.

At the exact moment she relaxed her watch a figure hurtled across the road, and hit her like a flying sandbag from the side. As Christa reeled she was pinned to the wall by a pair of iron forearms clamped across her chest and neck.

It felt as if a press was crushing the breath from her lungs. Eileen's face hung over Christa like an eclipsed moon, her eyes craters in a slit of pallid skin, and Christa caught a whiff of sweaty, unwashed hair.

'I knew it was you the minute I saw the nignog cap.' Eileen's voice was no longer controlled, but strident with success. She increased the pressure on her arms, using them like pistons to emphasise her words. 'You broke your promise. You grassed on us, you bloody, fucking slag!'

Christa had been beaten up once before, at a border post by an official who'd been so drunk that most of his blows didn't land, and those that did had little force. Matt had diverted him with a fistful of dollars and hauled her back into the Land Rover suffering more from damage to her pride than anything else.

This was very different. As she gasped for breath, feeling like a half-strangled chicken in Eileen's grip, she thought dazedly that having force used against her by another woman was even more horrible than the violence itself.

'I grassed because things changed. You started on the families of the Institute staff,' she croaked. 'If you threaten children you deserve everything you get.'

Through bleared eyes she saw over Eileen's shoulder that the road was empty still. If only the lights at the junction with the High would change, and release a stream of friendly traffic in her direction, she might just have a chance of escape.

'You wasted our lead,' Eileen said. 'Wasted our time and a sure bet, because we know something dodgy is happening at the Institute. We've had another tip-off from abroad.'

She poked her face closer. Christa began to feel sick. Her head swam and her legs had become like spaghetti again, but through the buzzing in her ears she heard the faint roar of accelerating traffic. The road was well-lit, and Eileen was bound to be seen.

Eileen heard it too. She cast a quick glance over her shoulder at the lights of a string of cars just starting to appear, then back at Christa.

'You're lucky,' she said. 'But I'm telling you, don't ever mess with us again. If I catch you sniffing round Howl even once after this, I'll send the heavy squad to sort you out.'

Eileen released her grip, and just before the car lights reached them, swiped the knuckles of her open hand across Christa's face as deliberately and powerfully as a backhanded drive at a tennis ball. When the lights swept by she'd already plunged into the darkness on the other side of the street.

Christa slid down the wall to the ground, and slumped with her head on her knees, waiting for waves of faintness to recede. Blood trickled down her chin, and her face felt as if she'd run into a tank.

Eventually she looked up, managed to control the swirling sensation the movement caused, and saw that the road was empty again. None of the drivers had stopped for her, but perhaps that was a good thing, she decided hazily. If she'd been hauled off to hospital, and the press had got wind of the incident, Randall would never have believed it was a chance mugging.

She investigated her face with her fingers, found a large area of swelling round one eye, and a minor cut on her upper lip caused by a ring, but nothing worse. She hauled herself up, and began to walk unsteadily towards Gabriel, keeping to the wall for support, and looking for the side gate into the fellows' garden.

When it finally appeared, the world swam alarmingly again as she searched for the key. Inside the garden she collapsed on a stone seat, waiting for the giddiness to settle. She had to reach her room. There she'd make herself some very strong coffee, and call a taxi on the mobile phone which she hoped was still in her bag.

By the time she got to Bohemia Quad she'd almost seized up with shock. She managed to stagger into a ground-floor bathroom to wash her face, but the spiral steps of the stair and the state of her legs combined to defeat her completely. She sat down, dropping her bag beside her. She'd forgotten that the step narrowed towards the central pillar, and the bag slithered and bumped down the stairs, scattering half its load of books before landing at the bottom with a heavy thud.

Slip sliding away, she thought hysterically. Things always slip away from me.

The Paul Simon tune beat with maddening persistence in her mind. She rested her head against the cold stone wall, and waited for the courage to go on.

15

When Mallory heard the noise outside his room, he'd just taken up his sitar in an effort to stop himself thinking, not about Caitlin, but Christa. She'd stayed in his mind with burr-like tenacity over the last few weeks.

It hadn't helped to see her recently in the quad being chatted up by a retinue of younger dons. And worse still, strolling arm in arm with Piers Gurney, obviously deep in the sort of friendship between a man and a woman which he'd so signally failed to establish with her himself, and which in any case he'd stopped believing could exist.

He listened again. There was now absolute silence. But the noise had sounded very like something or someone falling, and one of the oldest dons lived in the rooms opposite his. Reluctantly he put down the sitar and went to investigate.

A figure was huddled on the stairs below him, a figure wearing a striped beret. He knew who it was at once. Christa had been wearing the beret the first time they met.

At the sound of his step she slowly turned her head. Her right eye had almost disappeared. There was an angry graze across her cheek, and a cut in her upper lip.

'Jesus!' he said in horror. 'You look wrecked. What happened?'

'Someone leaned on me,' she said with an attempt at a grin so obviously painful that he almost winced in sympathy.

She got up, holding on to the wall. There was blood on her jeans. She looked down towards the books at the bottom of the stair, and swayed. Any moment now she's going to join them, he thought, hurriedly moving to help her.

'It's OK. I'm going to my room. I can manage,' she said.

'Like hell you can. You'll break your neck in that state. And what are you going to do when you get there? One-eyed first-aid?'

'My first-aid's pretty good,' she said with a lop-sided smile, and suddenly subsided on the stair again, her pallor becoming a delicate shade of green. 'If you don't let me get on, I'm going to throw up at your feet.'

'Go ahead. You're not climbing those stairs. Either you rest in my room for a while, or I ring for an ambulance now.'

She leaned the uninjured side of her head against the wall, and closed her eyes. Her face, unlit by her blue, direct gaze, looked exhausted.

'I didn't know you were into resuscitation as well,' she said with another faint smile.

Taking this to mean agreement, he retrieved her bag, somehow got his arm round her and hoisted her into his room. She needed to lie down, he thought, but the bedroom was the usual college ice-box, and in any case she'd probably refuse to go anywhere near his bed.

She might well object to the sofa too, but at least it was near the fire. He manoeuvred her on to it, shoving a pile of papers and his sweater to the other end.

'I'm going to the common room for some brandy and ice,' he said. 'Swear you won't move while I'm away?'

Christa didn't answer, but settled back with a sigh, her eyes still closed. She heard him shut the outer door, a sign to visitors not to intrude. Gradually her head felt less like a gyrating top, and she began to concentrate again on the external world.

She could see a glow against her lids, though only a little on the swollen side, and hear the uneven hiss and pop of an elderly gas fire. There was a faintly exotic scent in the air, something she couldn't quite place, and she risked opening her eyes.

She sat at one end of a couch covered with rough, unbleached cotton and a jumble of cushions whose colours reminded her of southern France. A sitar was propped in the other corner like a pot-bellied guest.

In front of her stood a low sandalwood chest scattered with opened mail. The wooden floor, polished to a deep gloss by generations of scouts, was uncarpeted, apart from a magnificent Kelim rug before the fire, and the mullioned windows were curtainless. As usual the gas fire lurked in the back of an impressive fireplace, this time of carved Tudor stone. On the wall above the chimneypiece a line of Urdu script had been painted in flowing black strokes, and above that was tacked an Indian saddle-cloth of gold and red silk.

Other than books, the shelves covering the longest wall held only one clue to the occupant of the room: a bronze winged head with a prophetic stare. The furniture, including a solid oak refectory table which served as a desk, was the college's, and everything else could be packed in the chest or a trunk. If Christa had never met Mallory, she would at once have summed it up as the room of someone on the move, and of someone in whom a love of beauty and asceticism was fascinatingly combined.

Her inspection, which had taken some time because her brain seemed to be working in slow motion, was interrupted by Mallory's return with a bottle of cognac, glasses, some ice cubes in a plastic bag, and a college table napkin. He put the brandy and glasses on the chest, and neatly wrapped the napkin round the bag of ice.

'Here, put this on your eye,' he said. 'It's probably too late, but worth a try.'

Gingerly she held it to the afflicted eye. He sat down at the other end of the sofa and gave her an appraising stare.

'You need to see a doctor,' he said.

'I don't. It was just a slap, and I've washed the cut. It looks worse than it is.'

'Some slap. Is your sight OK?'

'Of course, or I'd have gone straight to casualty. I'm not a complete fool,' she said, wishing he'd stop behaving as if she were potentially brain-damaged, and offer her some brandy before her self-control went again.

'Who did it?'

'Howl,' she said. 'A woman as well. That's not happened to me before.'

'I thought you were going to let the Howl investigation drop.'

'I was. But when they began to harass the families of the

Institute staff I decided to tell the police what I knew. The woman I had the run-in with was one of the people I'd interviewed. She recognised me in the street, though luckily she still doesn't know my real name. She thought I'd let them down, and I had in a way. I broke a confidence.'

The coherence of her explanation seemed to reassure him enough to pour her a glass of brandy. She felt like an avalanche victim seeing the St Bernard arrive. The situation was made doubly embarrassing by the memory of the tea-party fiasco, which, though neither of them had referred to it, was as present as a home movie projected on the wall.

'You ought to tell the police about this incident as well,' he said.

'What could they do? They had no one fitting the descriptions of the people I'd seen on their files, and it was hard enough persuading them not to tell Apollo what I'd been up to as it was.'

To her horror she heard her voice waver. The police had not been pleased by Christa's delay in telling them about her contacts with Howl. Though she knew it had been a reasonable decision at the time, they'd made her feel irresponsible, and she'd found herself longing for the back-up she would have got from Randall and Matt.

'Calm down. It was only a suggestion,' he said mildly.

She took another gulp of brandy, placed the parcel of ice on the chest, and tentatively explored her face. Her eye felt less swollen, and her lip more so.

'God, what a mess,' she said.

'Some people like the Lolita look.' She stared at him suspiciously, but his face was completely straight. 'You're going to have a colourful eye soon. As colourful as your career,' he went on.

'You sound as if you don't approve.'

'You've got to admit you approach life at a fairly fast gallop.'

'I'm not going to take up Zen, if that's what you're about to suggest.'

'A small application of Zen might not come amiss, all the same.'

He went to the fire and stood with one arm resting along the chimneypiece, glass in hand, looking at her as though he was trying to translate some tangled piece of verse. The easiness of his pose was completely unself-aware, she thought. Gareth in the same place wouldn't have been able to resist a baronial stance.

'You weren't exactly detached in the covered market,' she said more moderately.

'That was a one-off. I'm no Schwarzenegger.' His voice was dry. 'I meant that you should try coming out of the fast lane now and then. You might find there were other things to enjoy.'

Though it was something Christa had also been thinking about lately, Mallory was the last person she wanted to point it out. Whenever they were together they always seemed to engage in this useless sparring dance, this sequence of meet and retreat which invariably left her feeling unsettled and unsure of herself.

There was no point in putting up with it, even in the interests of first-aid. She'd have one more glass of brandy, and then go, even if she had to crawl to the porters' lodge.

'Is the bronze head Greek?' she asked. The classics were always a safe subject at Gabriel.

'It's a copy of Hypnos – the dreaming god.'

'What does the writing over the fireplace say?'

'Roughly translated, "I am a traveller in my own land." Anything else?'

She smiled, though her lip felt as if she'd been to the dentist.

'Do you really play the sitar?'

'A little.'

'Would you play now?' she asked, thinking that it would at least let her enjoy the brandy in peace.

His smile again reversed the dance. 'You want a rest from homilies? All right. But I warn you, I'm a learner.'

He came back to the sofa, propped one leg under him, and balanced the sitar against his other knee.

'Perhaps a winter *raga* would be best,' he said meditatively. 'A *raga* explores a mood.'

'What sort of mood?' she demanded.

'Stop looking so suspicious. Its meaning depends on you.'

He bent his head over the sitar, plucking a series of experimental notes from the strings before he began. The shape of the instrument and his pose made it seem as if he was listening to a living thing. The *raga* itself, once she'd realised that it wasn't going to evolve formally like a European tune, satisfied her in the way that the pattern of a snowflake could make her think both of its own perfection and the sculpted drift of which it would form a part.

As a final fan of notes slowly vibrated into silence she was still lost in the music. When Mallory looked up and caught her expression, it was as though a rushing, irrepressible stream had unexpectedly broadened into the tranquil waters of a lake. He wondered what had made her so reluctant to reveal this other self. He didn't think it could have been just the experience with Gareth Hyde.

'You look as if you heard the *anahata nada*,' he teased her. 'It's the inner sound, which only the gods hear.'

'Perhaps,' she said slowly. 'Did you play like that for Caitlin?'

'Sometimes.'

'What really happened between you?'

The directness of the question startled him. He couldn't help a sardonic tone entering his voice.

'More information gathering?' he enquired.

'I just wanted to understand. Don't forget I've met her, and now I know you . . .' she hesitated. '. . . now I know you better, it seems odd that things should have gone so wrong.'

He shrugged, thinking that however he described the relationship, she was bound to give it a feminist slant.

'I felt Caitlin wanted to own me. And I don't just mean sexual fidelity. She wanted to transform me into something I wasn't.'

'Perhaps it was because she made movies, because she was accustomed to having a vision of how she wanted things to be,' Christa said. 'For creative people sometimes real life becomes muddled with the imaginary.'

He was startled by her perception, though he should have expected it from someone who was such an acute observer of everyone except herself.

'You mean I didn't want to become Caitlin's construct? You're a postmodernist after all.'

She didn't answer, but gave him a gently mocking smile which goaded him into another question.

'Anyway, let's not talk about Caitlin. I've managed to exorcise her at last. Since this seems to be true confessions time, what made you become involved with Gareth Hyde?'

Her face clouded. Again he didn't expect her reply.

'It was a reversal of your situation. He's the only man to have possessed me in the way you said Caitlin wanted to possess you. He was like a drug you know you should give up, but you never quite can. I felt slightly – mad all the time I was with him.'

Her voice was husky. Damn, he thought. It wasn't fair to have asked her that.

'But you've escaped the enchanter,' he said lightly.

'I hope so.'

The deadness of her voice made him feel even more of a heel.

'How about a spring *raga* next?' he said in desperation.

He plunged into the opening notes before she could object. His mind wasn't on the music as he played, but on what she'd just said. Though it seemed incredible after the way Hyde had behaved, he wondered if she still had ambivalent feelings about the relationship.

Mallory was so preoccupied that he played the middle section twice. When he finally looked up she was asleep, lying sideways among the cushions, her hair curtaining her eyes. The swollen lip made it seem as if she'd been crying. It was still more unsettling to imagine her in tears. He told himself he'd been crazy to come on to her as he had at her house, when they both needed space more than anything else.

He went into the bedroom to fetch her a blanket before setting off for a long session in the common room. If she was still asleep when he got back, he'd simply shut himself in the bedroom, leaving her a note to let herself out. Nothing would send her away faster than the cold of his rooms in a December dawn.

Christa woke to Boanerges striking eight. A blanket had been put over her, but the air was cold against her face. It felt better this morning, and when she sat up the room remained reassuringly stationary.

The sitar occupied the dent in the cushions where Mallory had been sitting, and the door to the bedroom was firmly closed, but a note bearing her name was propped against a brandy glass. Though the terse message inside made it very clear that he wasn't to be disturbed, she felt uneasy that she hadn't thanked him in person. She decided to go downstairs to the bathroom again, thinking that he might be up by the time she returned.

Shivering over the washbasin, she drank some water from her cupped hand, for she was thirsty as well as ravenously hungry. As she dried her face on a roller towel, she studied herself in the mirror. The injured eye was acquiring a yellowish-purple tinge, and her swollen lip made her look like a nymphet.

It reminded her of Mallory's comment the previous night, one of several she would rather not have remembered. To her annoyance he seemed to have gained a certain moral ascendancy.

The thought still rankled when she returned to his room. She paused while looking for a pen to gaze at the closed bedroom door. He was so maddeningly self-assured, she thought, so certain she wouldn't invade his privacy, yet he'd had no scruples about invading hers at Jericho.

She scribbled a note as crisp as his, and impelled by some impulse of devilment, cautiously lifted the heavy iron latch on his door. She'd leave the note right by his bed, making it insultingly clear that she'd found nothing to tempt her there.

The door swung inwards noiselessly. The curtains were slightly open, so that she could see across the room a college wardrobe and chest of drawers, whose top was strewn with loose change, a discarded tie and the brandy bottle. Next to an iron bedstead flecked with patches of peeling paint stood a dented zinc trunk bearing a Discman and a spidery-armed reading lamp.

Mallory was asleep on his side, with his head towards her and an Indian cotton quilt pulled loosely up to his waist. Above the quilt he was naked, the flat dawn light clearly defining a brown arm and shoulder, and some impressive musculature.

She stole over to the trunk, and placed the note where he couldn't fail to see it. He stirred slightly but didn't wake. Impelled by a further mischievous impulse she knelt down by the bed to look at him more closely. It was perfectly fair, she reasoned. He'd had hours to study her last night, and God alone knew what further damning judgements he'd made.

What she could see of his body was drop-dead gorgeous, an

opinion no doubt shared by many women before her. Wickedly she considered further retribution, toying with the idea of sliding beneath the quilt while he was still half-asleep, and then enjoying his reaction as she made a rapid exit. But though he'd had no compunction about arousing her, she scorned prick-teasing, and unfortunately, however hard she tried, she couldn't quite equate his love-making with that.

Dark gold stubble blurred the line of his jaw. His long mouth with its notched upper lip had an engaging tilt even in sleep. Looking at it, she couldn't resist taking a very small revenge after all. Softly she placed her lips against his.

His skin had the spicy, male smell she'd begun to forget. He sighed, and as he began to surface from sleep his mouth opened under hers, and moved questingly upwards. Again she was startled by the strength of her response when she'd thought she was in complete control.

Though his eyes were still closed, his hand found her shoulder. 'Caitlin?' he said drowsily.

The single word shocked her. It made her feel Mallory had been playing her along out of curiosity, just to see what made her tick. And if that really was the case, her response meant she'd again made a fool of herself. In her heart of hearts she knew her reaction was disproportionate, but she couldn't completely control it. She had to find out if he still wanted Caitlin after all.

His hand moved to the nape of her neck. His eyes flew open. He stared at her incredulously and touched her swollen lip.

'That was nice. Or did I dream it?' he said.

'You didn't dream it. And I didn't dream what you said afterwards.' She tried to sound nonchalant. In spite of everything she wanted to kiss him again.

He smiled lazily. 'I hope it was complimentary. You look terrific with that Lolita lip. How about more?'

Though his hand caressed her cheek in a way which made her melt, she forced herself to move back.

'You said Caitlin's name when I kissed you.'

His hand became still. 'And what's so wrong with that?'

'You told me you'd exorcised her.' She was unable to keep back the bitterness in her voice.

He emerged alarmingly fast into full alertness, hauling himself up on one arm to stare at her.

'I was half-asleep. I was dreaming, for heaven's sake, and I certainly didn't expect to wake up and find you almost in my bed.'

'I wasn't almost in your bed,' she retorted. 'I was simply saying goodbye.'

He gave her a long, level look.

'Really? All right, then, you've said it, so why don't you go?'

Impatiently she ignored the question.

'You still miss Caitlin, don't you? I need to know the truth.'

'What the hell is this about? Why this sudden possessiveness? All I've ever offered you is friendship, nothing else, and you know it.'

'Me and Caitlin and how many others?' she asked derisively, trying to cover her hurt and confusion.

'That's rich, coming from someone who's probably spent her whole adult life chucking men.'

'At least I never dumped my lover in the shit.'

He was only too awake now, staring at her with narrowed eyes, and looking as unpredictable as an armed Scud.

'You bitch. You encouraged me to talk about her, you seemed so fucking concerned, and all it's led to is this.'

She leaped up and rushed to the end of the bed, clutching the rail as she yelled back at him.

'Don't dare use that sexist word on me! I didn't once encourage you. You were the one who homed in like some phoney Freud, who made me confide in you because I thought you'd been through the same mill, when you were still hooked on Caitlin all the time!'

He sat up, white with fury. Beneath her anger and humiliation was a cold, unpleasant delight that she'd at last made him lose his self-control.

'I've already told you! I'd been dreaming of her, for God's sake! Can you control your dreams as well as everything else? It'd take more than Freud to sort you out. I doubt if you're capable of making a normal emotional connection with anyone.'

She refused to let him see how much the comment hurt. It's not true, it's not true, she thought frantically as she forced herself to walk with deliberate slowness away from the bed, suppressed tears burning her bruised eye. She turned at the door, knowing he was hardly likely to streak through the college in pursuit.

'I wouldn't want a connection of any kind with a hippie throwback like you,' she flung at him. 'You can keep your pitch for those literary groupies of yours!'

In the sitting room she snatched up her bag, wrenched open the doors, and shot down the staircase, almost losing her footing on the steps.

As she went through the main gate, the porters' minds were clearly working like fruit machines over the combination of her black eye and early departure. They were probably wondering which of the fellows had slept with her and then beaten her up.

The thought made her laugh to herself all the way to South Parks Road, but once safely in a passing taxi she was hard pressed not to cry. She had an irrational feeling that she'd lost something, but couldn't decide what, however hard she tried to analyse herself.

In the run-up to her holiday, Christa tried to hammer out ideas for the television debate, for she planned to let the students loose on the shooting script next term. As she worked, she kept thinking anxiously that she still didn't have the extra evidence against the Master which would conclusively finish his reputation off.

Though she'd read every bit of literature available on the Waylandsbury dig, and had even discovered a couple of labourers who'd worked at the site, there was still no clue to the identity of the mysterious woman.

She certainly wouldn't get any more help from Mallory. He was spending a lot of time with an awesomely intelligent and attractive female don from Lady Margaret Hall. Christa frequently heard their laughter coming from his room. She retaliated by embarking on a high-profile flirtation with a visiting marine biologist who looked like a Bay Watch guard. She'd decided to soothe her wounded pride by letting it develop into something more, until his love-making during a preliminary encounter turned out to be even less imaginative than that of the squid he studied.

Christmas in North Africa revived her, and she came home with a deep tan. Though the weather which greeted her was so cold that it made her think there'd be barbecues on the Thames before long, her little house, now central heating had been installed, was marvellously warm.

For the rest of the vacation Christa stayed at home in a delicious fug, curled up on the sofa with her lap-top, working her way steadily through her research notes and Jessie's stock of home-made wine. Sometimes in the evening Miss Harker appeared for a word-processing lesson, for Christa had volunteered to guide her into the electronic age.

Occasionally she went to the cinema in Walton Street, or to the Eagle and Child for a gossip session with Wes. She was longing to tell him the real plan behind the documentary, but Rebekah had implored her not to, in case it upset Miriam.

Her father, calling in on his way from work soon after her return, was diplomatic about the family festivities. He'd arrived looking more stooped and weary than usual, with flakes of snow on the shoulders of his herringbone tweed coat.

As Christa installed him before the fire and went to fetch his whisky and water, she felt she was getting old as well. In the summer she'd be thirty-two, and all she had to show for those years was a wrecked love-life and a wrecked career. The last wasn't her fault, but Mallory had given her some uncomfortable thoughts about the first.

Damn him, she thought, pouring herself a double whisky instead of a single, and rattling the pretzels into a bowl so sharply that some of them bounced on to the floor.

'How did Christmas go?' she asked, sitting opposite her father.

'We went to Emma's. She cooked a magnificent dinner. But your mother was a little too helpful, and Phil wasn't helpful enough, so things became somewhat strained, especially between Emma and Phil.'

Christa was surprised. Emma had returned from the country weekend in a Pollyanna-ish state of optimism about her marriage which had lasted right up to Christmas.

Conrad tapped out his pipe in the coal scuttle, and began to refill the bowl with the pungent tobacco which he was only allowed to smoke in the garden shed at home.

'I'm worried about them,' he said. 'Phil doesn't seem to realise just how tired Emma is. They're still overstretched financially, though I've done my best for them. Apparently Phil's mother isn't in a position to help.'

She never was, thought Christa. The dowager Mrs Holdgate lived alone in a huge house in Golders Green. Her only pleasures were trawling round Harrods and Peter Jones, and complaining about how hard it was to live on an investment income of thirty thousand a year.

'If only things had been different, your mother could have taken the pressure off Emma by having the children during part of the holidays,' Conrad continued.

The wind was howling outside. Christa heard a thin spattering of hail on the window pane. It made her want to take the next plane back to Morocco. She sighed without knowing it. Her father puffed out a cloud of smoke.

'And how about you, Christa? When you and Emma were doing so well I felt I'd succeeded at parenthood if nothing else. Now I think I've failed at everything. I couldn't even get a job I was tailor-made for.'

'Have you heard that Tom Carver's moving to a post at a bigger library in Cambridge at the end of the year? Apparently his wife's very ambitious for him and pushed him into it,' Christa said, hoping to divert her father before he realised she hadn't replied and before he went into a tail-spin of gloom. 'You should try for Gabriel again. You might be lucky this time.'

'Yes, I'd heard. But I won't be lucky while the Master's still in charge.'

'The interview isn't till June. A lot could happen before then,' said Christa, thinking of the debate. 'Leda's got most of the younger staff on her side, and we've several new fellows this term.'

Conrad gave her the canny look which had always preceded some irritatingly perceptive remark about her behaviour as a child.

'We?' he said. 'So you're thinking of yourself as part of the college now. That's an improvement at any rate.'

'For heaven's sake, Dad, it was just a figure of speech. Promise me you'll re-apply. There are other reasons why I think you'll have a good chance this time, but I can't tell you about them yet.'

He smiled at her. 'Then I suppose I must, if I want to continue to enjoy my visits here. But it'd take a miracle to get me the post.'

Half an hour later, watching him set off for home, Christa longed to banish his resigned expression. It made her even more determined to thwart the Master. She'd just have to hammer again at the doors of the Waylandsbury academics who'd refused to talk to her before.

When term began, the agenda for the first meeting of Governing Body for once held a potentially promising item. It was listed as 'Bohemia Bequest'.

Nothing would have kept Christa away. She knew the land at Gabriel's Mill had been part of that bequest, though there wasn't a word about the item in the accompanying sheaf of notes, and it was tucked away at the agenda's end. It must refer to what had been discussed by the accommodation committee last term. Not even the Master would dare set the development in motion without keeping Governing Body informed.

The meeting took place in the college committee room above the SCR. Its huge mahogany table was capable of seating fifty with ease, though today it held only half that number. The windows hadn't been opened for centuries, judging by the stuffy air, and the logs in the firebasket were layered with dust.

Above the fireplace was a pensive head and shoulders portrait of the Bohemian Queen. Shelves containing leather-bound runs of past minutes lined the walls, and in a corner a locked glass-topped case covered with a green baize curtain displayed the original document of the Bohemia Bequest. Christa studied the yellow seal-studded parchment through the glass before the meeting began.

'Does anyone ever get to handle this?' she enquired of Piers, who'd accompanied her.

'Only the senior college officials. It's like Holy Writ as far as they're concerned.'

Piers turned his attention from the stiff black lines of script, and focused on Christa instead. She was a great deal easier on the eye, wearing beneath her gown a sleek pinstripe trouser suit and black patent ankle boots which, with her short hair and scarlet-glossed lips, gave her the ambivalent look of a night-club entertainer in thirties Berlin. Those dons with AC/DC tendencies must be thoroughly rattled, he thought.

Her black eye, which she'd flaunted for several days as nonchalantly as a new shade of eyeshadow, provoking much scurrilous conjecture among the younger fellows, had faded, but her scent, Vent Vert he guessed, haunted the stuffy, formal room. She was altogether a disturbing presence.

He'd made a bet with himself that she wouldn't stay at the meeting longer than an hour, but to his surprise the minutes lengthened into one and then two hours, and she was still by his side. A butler glided in with Lapsang tea and shortbread biscuits specially made for the college by some Highland cottage industry, and Miss Harker stopped taking the minutes to preside over the cups.

The two hours became three. Piers longed to leave, but he was determined to find out why Christa was indulging in such a lengthy bout of masochism.

Oddly enough, Farrar had stayed as well. He too brought a marked charge to the proceedings, wearing one of his unstructured Italian suits which, Piers thought enviously, needed the physique of a surfer beneath them to look really effective. Leda, usually a rallying voice of liberalism, was absent because of some crisis at the Institute, but every so often Farrar dropped a pointed remark into the discussion which led the newer dons to vote against the Master, who was perceptibly not amused.

Eventually the younger fellows began to filter away, drawn by the call of quality time with their offspring. There were now only two items left on the agenda. Piers flicked his gaze knowledgeably over them, and groaned to himself.

The next, listed as 'College Linen' could go on for another hour, and the last, 'Bohemia Bequest', looked deceptively simple but had similar potential for inflicting death by tedium.

The Master, still perfectly dapper at the head of the table, showed no sign of flagging. He picked up the agenda.

'*Res duodecima*,' he intoned in Latin. 'Item twelve: "College Linen". The replacement of individual linen hand towels in the

SCR gentlemen's cloakroom with paper towels or an automatic hot air machine. I'll run through the salient points in the accompanying memorandum from the Domestic Bursar.'

'Pity,' Piers whispered to Christa. 'I was hoping for something with a little more of a frisson, perhaps to do with sheets, weren't you?'

Christa stifled a laugh as she riffled through several pages of a learned paper on the possible methods of drying sensitive academic hands. The SCR ladies' cloakroom was a claustrophobic converted cupboard with a threadbare towel on a rattling roller.

'Do you really have individual towels in your loo?' she whispered back.

'Stacks of them, all embroidered with the college coat of arms, and nothing but the best huckaback, my dear. Not to mention brass taps, polished every day, and mahogany seats on the thrones. Don't even begin to tell me what yours is like. I can guess.'

Christa suppressed another giggle, looked up, and caught Mallory's gaze fixed repressively on her. Loosening her shirt collar in a slow provocative gesture, she stared back in a way designed to infuriate. He frowned and looked away.

'What's going on?' whispered the ever alert Piers. 'You and Farrar have been trying to turn each other to stone all afternoon. Don't tell me he was the one who gave you the black eye?'

'Don't be so childish,' Christa snapped.

'Takes one to know one,' said Piers with an affectionate smile, which Christa was glad to see produced another frown from across the table.

She emerged from yet another re-run of the scene in Mallory's bedroom to hear the Master say, 'So the majority vote is to stay with individual towels. An excellent decision, in my opinion. Standards have to be maintained.'

'But only for the men, of course,' said Christa in a low voice. So far she'd avoided any open comment during the proceedings in her impatience to get to the final item.

The Master smiled vaguely in her direction, and glanced at his watch, as everyone else except Mallory had been doing surreptitiously for the last half hour. He looked round the table at the college officials, a handful of tortoise-like senior dons, and the few younger fellows who remained.

'We still have a quorum, and so I'll proceed to the last item, the Bohemia Bequest. We need spend only a very short time on it before adjourning for pre-prandial sherry in the SCR.'

'Perhaps I could say at this point, Master,' said the Bursar, 'that the college's portfolio of investments based on the remaining funds from the Bequest is performing extremely well. The market is particularly buoyant just now.'

'Only what I should expect, in such capable hands as yours, my dear Bursar,' purred the Master. 'However, I don't wish to talk about investments today, but rather to devote myself very briefly to one of the leases connected with the Bequest.'

Christa glanced at Mallory, saw he was watching for her reaction as well, and looked hastily away.

'May I hazard a guess that you are about to refer to the somewhat knotty question of Gabriel's Mill?' the Dean asked, his chair pushed well back from the table to accommodate his enormous bulk.

Christa was already getting the impression that this exchange had been rehearsed. She risked another glance at Mallory. His gaze briefly locked with hers again.

'The lease of Gabriel's Grounds for development as a housing estate was most unfortunate in the first place,' the Bursar interposed. 'It's not at all a suitable association for the college. I've always been against letting the tenants benefit from the Mill site.'

'I'm delighted that's the general feeling among us,' said the Master. 'I rather expected it to be.'

'Not so fast,' said Mallory. 'I don't think that's the general feeling among the majority of fellows at all.'

'Really, Dr Farrar? You do surprise me. The fellows have been well aware that this item was on the agenda. If you are correct, why have so many left the meeting?'

'Because the agenda did not state the specific content of this item,' Mallory said coldly.

The Dean burst into a diversionary fit of spectacular coughing, dabbing his eyes and clutching his chest.

'Perhaps you'd be good enough, Master, since we are rather

short of time, to let us know your thinking on the subject,'
said the Bursar, interposing a practised save through the Dean's
wheezes.

'And perhaps you'd be good enough, Miss Harker, before we
go any further, to record my objection to this oversight in
the minutes,' said Mallory. 'Then those not present will know
exactly what's going on.'

As Miss Harker wrote agitatedly in her shorthand notebook,
Christa could scarcely believe that Mallory, whom she'd considered an arch sitter on the fence, had emerged so openly into
the fray.

'Nothing is going on, Dr Farrar, as you put it,' said the Master
irritably. 'I was about to point out that Professor Saltash, though
the most delightful of men, unfortunately chose to ignore the
Zeitgeist of the early eighties.'

'Some people would call that fortunate,' Christa interrupted.

The Master gave her a patronising smile.

'Our former Master did not anticipate the increase in student numbers, nor the explosion in property values during the
eighties,' he continued, ignoring her remark.

'So I take it you've hit upon one of your splendid compromises,
Master,' said the Bursar.

'That is not for me to say.' The Master smirked. 'However, I
can tell you that the accommodation committee has sanctioned
a small feasibility study on ways of using the Mill site other than
developing it for the benefit of the estate.'

Judging by its lack of surprise, the old guard had been lobbied
beforehand. Sycophantic murmurs of approval went round the
table. The sprinkling of younger fellows moved uneasily in
their seats, but seemed unwilling to cross swords with the
Master without their absent colleagues' support. Even Piers
kept cravenly quiet.

'I thought you'd be pleased,' said the Master. 'The matter has
been delayed far too long. I'm certain this is what Professor
Saltash would have wished if he were with us now.'

Christa was about to protest when Mallory forestalled her.

'I doubt if even you, Master, can claim a direct line to the
dead. Professor Saltash would have fought to the last ditch any
suggestion of breaking his promise to Gabriel's Grounds Estate.

He would never have wanted the college to connive in creating a social underclass.'

'I agree with Dr Farrar,' said Christa, amazed at herself. 'And I must add that I've been disturbed to detect signs of an underclass even here at Gabriel. I'm sure the newer dons have been struck by it too.' She stared meaningfully at them, trying to shame them into support. 'That's worrying enough, without the college fostering it in the world outside.'

'Your feelings do you credit, Miss Keith, but there's no need for such melodrama, I assure you. It isn't the way we do things at Gabriel,' said the Master. 'I've merely suggested an informal marshalling of the facts, so that we know exactly how we stand before we proceed.'

'Proceed where?' asked Mallory. 'I see no need for the college to proceed anywhere except in the direction of Professor Saltash's promise.'

'You're jumping the gun, Dr Farrar. There can be no possible objection to a presentation of the facts. It's in the best liberal tradition. Nevertheless, since you have reservations, I shall sound the opinion of the board. And though you are welcome to speak, Miss Keith, may I remind you that as neither a tenured fellow, nor the possessor of an honorary doctorate from this University, you cannot vote at meetings of the Governing Body of Gabriel?'

Christa watched sardonically as the Master's gaze roved round the table like a fox transfixing a coop of hens.

'*Nemine contra?* No one against, except for Dr Farrar? Exactly as I thought. Then since we are running a little late, I shall bring this meeting of Governing Body to a close.'

'Hold on a moment,' said Mallory. 'I'd like to know the exact wording of what Governing Body has agreed to.'

'Why, simply to consider informally at some future meeting whether to adhere to Professor Saltash's somewhat quixotic undertaking, or to proceed in the direction of one of several rather more sensible options which will be relayed to Governing Body after the opinion of experts has been consulted.'

A miracle of inexactness, thought Christa, which could easily be concealed in an agenda under the heading of 'Any Other Business'.

'Since this is a question which clearly affects the whole ethos of Gabriel, it should be discussed at our next meeting, as a separate item,' Mallory said.

He did his own visual tour of the faces at the table. Christa was unwillingly impressed to see it produce a noticeable lessening of tension in the younger dons.

'I agree,' said a tutor in philosophy, whom Christa had never heard utter a syllable up to now. 'Some things are more important to the college than financial gain.'

'An excellent idea,' chipped in the oldest don, who'd suddenly woken up after slumbering like Alice in Wonderland's dormouse for most of the afternoon. 'Cut the waffle for a change. This meeting has gone on far too long. It's sherry time.'

'I think most of those here agree with me on this point at least, Master,' said Mallory, again glancing round the table, and producing a clear majority of assenting faces.

'Very well, very well. You've made your point, Dr Farrar,' said the Master testily, closing with a snap the leather-bound covers of the college regulations which lay before him. 'Then since there's no more business, I shall bring the proceedings to a close.'

Christa guessed that the last thing he now wanted was more dissenting voices.

'Before you do, I should like it officially confirmed that this resolution will also appear in the minutes,' said Mallory. 'I've noticed several omissions recently. Not Miss Harker's fault, I'm certain,' he added with a smile in her direction.

'How very odd. There must have been some error in the photocopying machine. Naturally the resolution will appear,' said the Master as evenly as a speaking clock.

While Miss Harker, now redder than the porcelain rose at the neck of her blouse, scribbled a final shorthand note, the Master made a swift exit accompanied by his flunkeys. Mallory strolled after him, accompanied by most of the remaining fellows, who all at once seemed remarkably anxious to talk to him in private.

'Wow! Some meeting!' said Piers in an undertone to Christa. 'The Master's definitely rattled.'

'No thanks to you,' she retorted. 'Why didn't you speak out against him as well?'

'You didn't seriously expect me or any of the tenured fellows to commit academic suicide?' he demanded indignantly. 'Because that's what opposing the Master means, unless one's absolutely certain of the majority's support. It's different for you and Farrar, swanning off at the end of the year.'

Christa was too busy thinking about her plans to soothe Piers' injured feelings just yet. The next meeting of Governing Body wasn't until mid-May. By then, if all went as she hoped at the debate, at best the Master would no longer be Head of House, and at worst most of his moral authority would have gone.

Nevertheless she still needed to gather more damning evidence against him, for if he were able to arrive at the meeting with his authority intact, she doubted if even Mallory could prevent the Master from developing the Mill site as he wished. It would be a hard task, for though the Waylandsbury academics who were available had grudgingly consented to speak to her at her second attempt, she'd learned nothing useful from them

'You shouldn't be so snappy with your old friends,' said Piers, gathering up his papers in what Christa now realised was a serious huff. 'Otherwise I shan't tell you some news I picked up from the Bursar over tea. You might be sorry if I don't.'

It was probably a trifling piece of college gossip, Christa thought, but Piers was the last person she wanted to hurt, and so she tucked her arm placatingly through his as they went down the stairs.

'All right, I'm sorry already,' she said. 'I know it isn't easy for you just now. What's this hot news of yours?'

Piers stopped halfway, and turned towards her, his eyes glinting in the way which meant she wasn't going to like what he said.

'You'll be seeing another old friend soon. Gareth Hyde is to be one of the Master's personal guests at the Founder's Feast.'

16

Only years of controlling her emotions when the chips were down enabled Christa to turn aside Piers' revelation with a joke.

'So?' she said indifferently. 'I got over Gareth months ago. Now I'm away from Apollo there's nothing more he can do to me, and he's not worth the effort of revenge.'

'I wouldn't be too keen to see such an old flame again, all the same.'

'That's your bad luck. You sound as if you want to upset me, Piers,' she snapped, hurrying faster and faster down the wide oak staircase, her gown billowing out in her wake.

'You must feel a tiny pang of worry, at least,' he said, catching up with her at the bottom of the stairs.

Christa turned on him in a swirl of black cloth.

'Stop needling me, will you? I told you, Gareth means nothing to me now. What does bother me is why the Master asked him in the first place, and why he accepted.'

'Didn't you tell me he was a graduate of Gabriel? He's got every right to attend.'

'He disliked Oxford as much as I did. He couldn't wait to leave. It was another of the things we shared.'

She was silent for a moment, remembering Gareth's ruthless impersonations of his tutor's stammer, which had made her helpless with laughter at the time and ashamed of her enjoyment when she met the kindly old scholar in person. She suspected now that Gareth hadn't liked Oxford because there were too many other people around brighter than himself.

Her annoyance began to subside. She looked cautiously about

her for eavesdroppers, but they were alone in the lobby which led to the SCR.

'You know, if it didn't seem so paranoid, I'd almost believe the Master invited him specifically to get at me,' she said.

Piers added his gown to a line of others hanging from their pegs like roosting bats.

'No conjecture's too far-fetched where the Master's concerned,' he replied, fishing a diary out of his jacket pocket. 'The Feast's near the date of your debate, isn't it? Yes, the very next day, according to this.'

'Jesus, then I'm not paranoid at all!' said Christa, sitting down in a hurry on a very hard Tudor bench. 'The Master's definitely trying to rattle me!'

'But you've just said Gareth doesn't bother you,' Piers observed wickedly. 'So let's have a drink and forget about it.'

Christa was so furious with herself for her reaction, and so perturbed by it, that she knew she wouldn't be able to present an unruffled face to the common room. She muttered an excuse about some urgent work, which Piers plainly didn't believe for a minute, and hurried away.

When she climbed the stairs to her room, Mallory's door was closed. He was probably enjoying the adulation of his fan club in the common room. It was another excellent argument against joining Piers for a drink.

Christa tore off her gown, and chucked it in a corner. She knelt on the window seat and pushed open the latticed casement, taking long steadying breaths. Above the rooftops a new moon was rising into a dusky blue sky. In the sheltered quad beneath, drifts of early paper-white narcissi were beginning to unfold in flowerbeds only lightly touched by frost.

She'd leaned out of this window in the same way many times before. When she first arrived it had been with a sense of desperation, a longing to escape. But now she realised that the tranquil atmosphere, the feeling of being independent yet not alone, had grown on her. The thought of meeting Gareth again anywhere was bad enough, but not here. She could imagine him swaggering through college, carelessly deciding where to bestow his sexual favours next, stamping his personality everywhere like the marks of sweaty fingers on polished wood.

Lamps were beginning to glow in other rooms not curtained yet. A student she knew was brushing her hair, sweeping it back in flowing strokes, before going to dine in hall. And the Dead Sea Scrolls expert was hunched by his desk-lamp, poring over some ancient script.

The air was chilling rapidly, but as always the scene had calmed her. Too much was at stake to allow herself to be disturbed by Gareth again. She hugged her arms about her shoulders, and firmly told herself that when she saw the new moon before the Feast it would be a lucky one.

A few days later, just as Christa had shaken a top-hat of snow from the milk on the front step and brought it inside for her breakfast coffee, the phone rang.

She knew it could only be Emma at this early hour. Snow had set in again, and she was probably ringing about some crisis to do with the car. Phil was particularly stingy about sharing it during the cold weather. Several times lately Christa had ferried Noelene and the children to and from their various activities.

'Sorry, Em, I can't do any chauffeuring today. Don't you remember, I told you the Mini was having an MOT?' she said briskly into the receiver, thinking with pleasure of the leisurely breakfast she was about to consume.

'I didn't forget. Phil's left me the car today and taken the bus to Gabriel.' In spite of this concession Emma's voice was unsteady. 'Noelene and Jamie are walking Pansy to school – she loves the snow. But I desperately need to talk. Can you come round?'

Christa glanced out of the window towards the road, where cars were crackling cautiously along icy ruts, and last night's snowfall already looked like a veil of dirty lace.

'Can't you talk to me on the phone? I haven't eaten yet, and it's Alaska outside. Anyway, don't you have school today?'

'You don't understand. This is serious. I'm not going to school. My life's in bloody ruins.' Emma's voice was beginning to thicken with tears.

Christa gave up the idea of breakfast. Emma so rarely made dramatic announcements about herself that something must be very wrong.

'Hang on, and I'll be with you in half an hour,' she said.

Christa trudged towards Emma's house beneath a blank, copper-coloured sky. Yesterday's snow had partially thawed before freezing again beneath last night's fall. In Ethelred Road a gang of truant boys had made a slide in the rutted ice down the middle of the street, and were competing to see who could perform the longest run.

Christa dodged a snowball lobbed in her direction, and turned into Emma's drive. Drifts lay against the garage doors. Pansy had drawn a face on the snow-covered bonnet of the Volvo outside.

As Christa went through the back door, stamping her clogged boots on the mat, domestic chaos met her eyes. A tower of washing-up teetered in the sink, and Jamie's bib, smeared with baby muesli and raspberry yoghurt, lay on the floor amid a scattering of plastic toys.

Breakfast bowls gluey with congealed porridge had been pushed to one end of the table. At the other Emma stood by a wicker laundry basket, sobbing quietly while she sorted unironed clothes. She was still in her dressing gown, and her hair trailed round her tear-stained face like ivy on a funeral urn.

'For God's sake, Em, what's happened?' Christa demanded. Only a major crisis could have loosened her sister's grip on domestic routine.

'Phil wants a trial separation!' she wailed, thumping herself down on a chair and burying her face in a snowy vest. 'He wants to leave us and go to live in Gabriel! How could he be so selfish?'

Very easily, thought Christa, who was not at all surprised. A year ago she would have said it aloud, and congratulations would have been her first impulse. Now she found herself aching for Emma, who unlike herself didn't have any get-out, who was stuck with the children and a financial scenario which could hardly be worse.

'The children need their father,' Emma gulped, raising a scarlet face from the vest. 'Pansy's such a handful, and I couldn't go to work without Noelene. We can't afford to pay for her salary and Phil's accommodation in college.'

'What brought all this on? Has he found someone else?'

'Nothing so dramatic,' said Emma, with a huge quivering sigh. 'Sometimes we have meals a little late when I'm delayed at school, and occasionally Jamie gives us a bad night. Phil says that and worrying about the mortgage have made his irritable bowel worse. Apparently it's affecting his research. He says he must have some peace.'

'So what are you supposed to do?'

'Phil says I should give up my job while Jamie's so young, and we should move back into a smaller house. He says he'll give me till the end of this term to think about it, and if I don't agree he wants a divorce. But it's not fair, it's not fair! I love my work, and I love this house!'

She plonked her elbows on the table, and burst into more despairing sobs. Christa filled the kettle and switched it on. Nothing was going to be possible till Emma stopped crying, and even less was possible until she learned not to let Phil bully her.

'Come on, Em,' she said, sitting down beside her, and putting an arm round her shaking shoulders. 'This won't get you anywhere. You bet Phil isn't sobbing all over the Dean. Right now he'll be having a soothing time bonding with his buddies over coffee and *The Times* crossword in the SCR. If you go to pieces you simply play into his hands.'

'But I'm sure he meant it,' hiccupped Emma. 'He's never said it before.'

'Balls! He knows which side his bread is buttered. Where else would he get room service like yours? If he moves into college he'll have to iron his own shirts, and he knows he'd get a huge black mark from the Master's wife if he asked for a divorce.'

'Do you really think so?' said Emma with a watery smile.

'Of course I do,' said Christa, crossing her fingers and praying her assessment of Phil was correct. 'What's more to the point, do you really want to stay with someone who gives you all this grief?'

'I love him, Christa. You still don't understand. He can't really help how he is,' said Emma earnestly. 'His mother's always treated him as though he's the centre of the world, and that makes it hard for him to adapt when the children have to come first. But he does try, truly he does. He couldn't have been sweeter on that country weekend.'

'Big of him, especially as the children weren't there,' said Christa, wondering how she'd feel stuck with a forty-year-old Peter Pan, and having to remind herself firmly that Gareth was just as much a Peter Pan in his way. She'd been ready to hang on to him indefinitely if he hadn't jettisoned her. 'Anyway, why can't Phil ask his mother to help out if the mortgage situation's giving him so much stress?'

'He has, but she's said no.'

Emma discarded the now sodden vest, and distractedly took up a blouse instead.

'I hate to say this,' she went on, 'but I think she wants our marriage to fail, then she'll have Phil to herself. She's probably terrified that if she gives us money, I might get some of it if we split. But I don't want us to break up.' Tears were again spilling down her cheeks as she twisted the arms of the blouse into a knot. 'I couldn't bear it.'

Christa longed to tell Emma to cut her losses and let Phil go, yet the memory of her own misery in a similar situation once more made her hesitant. She couldn't encourage Emma to go through it too, not before all the remedies had been tried.

'Then you'll have to stand up to Phil. If he discovers you can be as bossy as his mother, he'll probably knuckle under, just as he does with her. There must be some financial solution if we think hard enough. But women do survive alone, you know,' she couldn't resist adding. 'Look at Chel's mother.'

Emma wiped her eyes on the blouse. 'I'd rather not,' she said with a shaky grin. 'She always makes me feel so inadequate. I think I'd rather look at you.'

'Me?' said Christa, rushing to switch on the kettle now she sensed the worst of the crisis had passed. 'I'm not much of an advertisement for success – hardly on speaking terms with my mother, and junked by the only man I've ever wanted. I wouldn't call that effective life management.'

She dumped a double dose of coffee in the cafetière, and began to clear away the porridge bowls while the kettle boiled.

'I think you've done pretty well since you came here,' Emma replied. 'You've got a house, and you've got Pansy eating out of your hand, not to mention your admirers at Gabriel, who are legion according to Phil.'

'I'm sure he doesn't approve, even if you do,' said Christa
acidly, though the unexpected praise warmed her, for Mallory's
criticism still rankled.

Suddenly, as she made the coffee, she wanted to tell Emma
about it, to be reassured that he was entirely and pig-headedly
wrong.

'I've got critics at Gabriel as well,' she said, taking the cafetière
to the table with some milk and the only unwashed mugs she
could find, both adorned with nursery rhymes. 'I was accused
recently of being incapable of making normal emotional connec-
tions. Do you think it's true?'

Emma fished out a tissue from her sleeve, blew her nose, and
frowned while she considered.

'That's fairly harsh. I suppose you won't tell me who said so?'

'No, I won't. But it was someone whose opinion most people
respect. It worried me a bit,' Christa ended lamely, astonished at
what she'd just said. 'Have you had any breakfast, Em? Let me
make you something to eat.'

'Don't change the subject,' said Emma, beginning to revive at
the twin prospects of coffee and giving sisterly advice. 'No, I don't
think it's true, though you often do your best to make it look that
way. If this mysterious someone was a man, are you sure you
weren't playing hit and run?'

'Of course not!'

Emma eyed Christa severely.

'Well, not much, and he started it,' Christa said.

Emma began to laugh.

'And how much provocation did you give him? At least he
seems to have got through to you. Maybe you should stay around
next time.'

Christa started to laugh as well, partly from relief that Emma
seemed to be back on an even keel, partly to conceal her own
unease.

'There won't be a next time. I've definitely blown that one,'
she said offhandedly. 'Why don't I fix us some bacon sandwiches?
Then we'd better think of ways to mend things between you and
Phil, if that's really what you want.'

After breakfast Emma, still looking wan, but more positive at least, went to have a shower. She'd been persuaded to talk to Phil about converting the sub-basement, now used as a playroom and store, into a flat which they could rent to visiting academic staff. Christa, busy washing up, felt as if she'd just set up the reconciliation of two unpredictable heads of state. But the best thing about her session with Emma had been re-establishing the rapport between them which had been missing for so long.

When Emma returned she was in her school clothes, with her hair neatly pushed back beneath an Alice band, and weighed down with the usual bags of exercise books.

'I'm going to work after all,' she said. 'My first class isn't till eleven. I shall feel so guilty, otherwise. If I don't turn up some other poor soul will have to stand in for me.'

'The sooner you learn to stop feeling guilty about everything, the better,' Christa teased her. 'All right, you carry on. I'll just finish the tidying, and let myself out.'

'What amazing domesticity!' said Emma, coming to her side. Unexpectedly her arms went round Christa. 'Thanks, for everything. I really mean it.' She smiled mischievously. 'Who knows? If you carry on this way, we might even not quarrel any more.'

Christa tried to conceal her pleasure with a joke. 'Hardly likely. Get yourself off to school, Em, do, before we start hearing the heavenly choir.'

When Emma had gone, Christa put the last of an army of mugs in their appointed place, wiped the draining board, and hung up the towel. She'd been quite virtuous enough for one day, she decided, beginning to put on her boots. She'd just finished lacing them, when it struck her that she hadn't heard the Volvo pull away. Perhaps Emma was still scraping off the snow, she thought idly, and then felt a lurch of terror as she realised what that meant.

The car had been out all night, and Emma, her mind blissfully occupied with thoughts of the enormous rent she and Phil would get for the flat, could so easily forget to check it as she'd been warned. Christa tore into the hall. As she did so she heard the car door slam shut.

Desperately she ran outside. Emma caught sight of her in the driver's mirror, and waved her hand gaily in farewell.

'Don't, Em!' shouted Christa. 'Don't switch on, for God's sake! Not before you've checked the car!'

Emma couldn't hear. She turned the ignition key. Christa's heart missed several beats. The car chugged harmlessly into life and moved down the drive. Oblivious of the arctic wind whipping though her sweater, Christa rushed to the gate to check its progress down the street.

A backwash of relief began to overwhelm her when it had safely progressed halfway. Emma was obviously feeling more confident about the icy surface of the road, for she accelerated, and as she did so, caught sight of Christa from the corner of her eye. In the second that she turned her head for a last wave, a boy on a sledge, propelled by another at his back, came hurtling towards the car.

As though in a dream, Christa heard the brakes screech and saw the car swerve. It missed the sledge by inches, skidded in a wild zig-zag along the road, juddering on the rutted ice, and slammed head on into the trunk of a tree.

In the grim lull after the sound of grinding metal and shattering glass, snow floated down from the branches in a bizarre second fall. The boys were already running away. Christa tore into the road towards the Volvo, her feet slipping on the ice.

The car was still relatively intact, though glass from the windows lay like frosty confetti all around. Emma, only half in the seat-belt as though it hadn't been securely clipped in place, was slumped unconscious over the dashboard, with blood slowly welling through her hair. Her Alice band was tangled in the steering wheel.

Christa wrenched at the door handle, but it was jammed. Sobbing with frustration, terrified in case the petrol tank ignited before she could get Emma out, she dragged at the door again and again. Still it didn't budge.

After seconds which seemed like hours she suddenly realised the key was still in the ignition. Roughly winding her arm in her scarf, she put it through the jagged window frame, and turned the key to off.

Frantically she began to search for a pulse in Emma's neck. The skin was clammy and cold, exactly as Matt's had been. I'm going to lose Emma as well, Christa thought desperately. I'm going to lose my sister just when we were getting to know each other again.

A woman was hurrying towards her from a house over the road. She had a first-aid box under her arm and snow crunched under her authoritative, determined step.

'I've sent for an ambulance,' she shouted in a ringing North Oxford voice. 'I saw it all. I'm Neighbourhood Watch!'

Just as Christa had given up hope she felt a pulse spring against her touch, a very faint pulse but most definitely there. She leaned against the wrecked car, trembling with shock. The woman was bearing down on her like a hospital ship.

'Then why the hell did you let those boys sledge here in the first place?' Christa snapped, and began to laugh hysterically, overwhelmed by joy that Emma was alive, and terror that she might still die.

The hospital was nothing like the one in which Matt had been treated. Emma, severely concussed, lay in intensive care surrounded by every life support machine known to science, and ministered to by a huge team of attendants. Yet she looked appallingly like Matt, her face as white as her hospital gown, her closed eyes sunken in their sockets, and her nose prow-like as though even the flesh of her face had retreated in shock.

Christa waited while X-rays and a scan took place, and left urgent messages everywhere she could think of for Phil. After coffee in Gabriel he'd gone to a meeting in London, but hadn't arrived there yet.

A specialist appeared to tell Christa that Emma had a hairline fracture of the skull, with no apparent complications, but he couldn't give a firm prognosis until she regained consciousness. His refusal to commit himself terrified her, though the nurses told her that it was standard practice at this stage. She longed to be able to talk to Leda, who was away in the States for a week.

Noelene had risen impressively to the occasion, and volunteered for twenty-four-hour duty with the children for as long as necessary. Christa's parents, both looking years older, arrived at the hospital within half an hour. Her mother, in a frenzy of anxiety, talked and fussed non-stop, and eventually had to be taken home in tears. Christa by this time was quietly frantic too, for Emma's condition hadn't changed.

In the mid-afternoon Phil turned up at last, his neat hair for once disarrayed, his coat buttoned awry, and generally in such a state of shock that he scarcely noticed Christa, who hadn't left Emma's side. As he bombarded the charge nurse with questions, Christa discreetly melted away, thinking wearily that at least the accident had made him think about Emma instead of himself.

She felt intensely isolated, just as she'd done after Matt's death, and when she got back to Jericho flung herself into an orgy of cleaning, trying to make herself so tired that she couldn't think. As she grimly scoured the oven, and scrubbed the scullery floor, she remembered how often she'd seen her mother do the same when she was upset.

By the time dusk fell, and she'd dug over half the vegetable plot as well, there was still no change in Emma's condition. In desperation she was about to go round to the nearest off-licence for a bottle of whisky, when the front door bell rang.

Pansy stood on the doorstep, accompanied by Noelene. She was sucking her thumb and clutching Emma's old doll. Her eyelashes were spiky with tears, her face red and swollen.

'What's happened? Where's Jamie? Is something wrong?' demanded Christa, at once fearing some further disaster.

'No worries. He's asleep at home,' said Noelene soothingly, though she was looking more than a little frayed herself. Her blonde curls had lost their bounce, and there was a hole in her tights. 'A mate of mine's keeping an eye on him. But poor little Pansy here's feeling really choked. She wouldn't eat any supper, or go to Chel's overnight.'

Pansy started to cry. 'Everyone's being too nice to me! I know it means Mummy's going to die. Daddy hardly spoke to me at supper, and now he's gone back to the hospital!'

'Right on about her daddy, I'm afraid,' said Noelene. 'This has really screwed him up. He looked flaked out. But Pansy needs to talk to someone, and I can't get through to her. I thought . . .'

Noelene's voice trailed away on a suggestive rising note. And though Christa hadn't felt so exhausted since the night Matt died, and was fit only for whisky, bed and oblivion, she made herself issue the invitation expected of her. She even, in a further fit of altruism, lent Noelene the Mini until Phil was able to get a replacement car.

Pansy wandered forlornly round the sitting room, trailing the doll by its skirt, when Noelene had gone. The grate was empty, and Christa hadn't yet laid a fresh fire.

'It's not nice and homey like it was before,' Pansy said, slumping dejectedly on to the sofa, and wiping her eyes with the doll's petticoat. 'Mummy is going to die, isn't she? Daddy won't even let me see her.'

Christa sat down beside her and took her hands. They were miniature versions of Emma's, long and slender and very cold.

'The crash made her very tired. That's why she's taking a long time to wake up. The nurses say she'll probably be fine when she does. I think we should believe them, don't you?' said Christa, trying to sound convincing.

Pansy nodded doubtfully. Christa cast round for a diversion.

'Would you like to help build the fire? There are lots of newspapers and sticks outside. And you can light it, if you like.'

A faint glimmer of interest appeared on Pansy's face.

'With real matches? But I'm not allowed.'

'With real matches.' Christa searched for more ways to lift the gloom. 'Then maybe we could fetch a Chinese takeaway – chopsticks and fortune cookies too.'

Pansy brightened a little more. 'I'm not allowed Chinese food either. Mummy says it has too much MSG.'

'You're allowed to do anything you like in a crisis.'

'Are we really in a crisis?' said Pansy, looking impressed in spite of herself.

'You and me both, kid,' said Christa in a Bogart voice. 'So let's stick together and see this thing through.'

Pansy's wobbly giggle made Christa feel unexpectedly better too.

'Can I sleep in your bed? And choose a video to watch with the takeaway?' Pansy asked.

'Of course. And maybe afterwards you'd like to try a hand of poker or two. Only you have to promise not to tell Mummy when she wakes up.'

*   *   *

When Christa got to the hospital next morning Emma's condition was unchanged, and she was glad she hadn't phoned to enquire about her before walking Pansy to school. The nurses were still optimistic, encouraging her to talk to Emma, but the hospital staff had been optimistic at first about Matt, too. After half an hour of holding Emma's limp hand, anxiously scanning her unconscious face, and trotting out futile childhood reminiscences, Christa couldn't bear it any more.

She stopped briefly in the hospital entrance hall to brace herself with vending-machine coffee for the bus journey home. As she sat there amid the bland decor designed to tranquillise, and watched an ornamental windmobile revolve uselessly in the grounds outside, Phil walked through the automatic door. Though his expression was dour he had returned to his usual dapper self, briefcase in hand, as if fitting Emma into his schedule between far more important things.

Christa jettisoned the coffee and went to waylay him. His face became even more dour as he saw her approach.

'Emma hasn't changed, Phil. But the nurses are hopeful, all the same.'

'You've been to see her already today?' he said, sounding mortally offended.

Oh, God, thought Christa wearily, he's trying to compete even over this. Emma might be right about his sense of inferiority, but it seemed incredible that he should regard her as a threat just now. Nevertheless she did what Emma would have wanted and tried to placate him.

'I was so worried about her that I came straight over when I'd taken Pansy to school.'

'You bloody well deserve to be worried,' he said angrily. 'Emma only had the crash because of you. It was your fault.'

'My fault?' echoed Christa, moving to one side as a man in a wheelchair, both legs in plaster casts, came spinning by. She wondered if Phil could be suffering from delayed shock.

'Yes, yours. From what the police tell me, I gather you went to see her just before the accident. I can guess exactly why. You were encouraging her to leave me. Otherwise she would never have missed seeing that sledge, nor driven off without properly fastening her belt. But of course, on the iciest day of the year, you filled her head with so much loony feminist rubbish that she forgot to concentrate.'

Christa thought dazedly that Phil must be putting on this masterly display of double-think in order to make himself feel less guilty.

'How dare you make such an accusation from so little evidence? Why didn't you ask me what happened before you spoke to the police? I was there, for God's sake.'

'I prefer my information to be reliable,' said Phil loftily. 'All I can hope, Christa, is that this accident will at last have taught you not to interfere in our marriage. Can't you realise that Emma's not like you? She has responsibilities, children to think of. How do you suppose they'd manage without her?'

Christa's self-control disappeared in a wave of anger, distress and incredulity.

'You expect them to manage without *you*!' she hurled at him. 'That's what Emma was concerned about, not anything I said to her. You're a bully, Phil. You're bloody lucky Emma's stayed with you this far.'

Christa was shouting now. A cleaner, swinging an industrial polisher like a flying saucer across the floor, looked at them curiously.

'And what do you or I matter at the moment, anyway? Emma's recovery is the only important thing. Why don't you stop blaming everyone except yourself, and go and see her? You're an idiot as well. She loves you, and when she wakes up she'll want you there, though God knows why after the way you've behaved.'

Phil looked dumbfounded. She ignored his call to her to come back as she hurried through the doors into the harsh winter brightness outside. A bus for the city centre was about to leave. While it rattled through the suburbs she sat on a back seat going over and over what Phil had just said, and in spite of the vigour of her self-defence, fighting off an irrational feeling of guilt.

By the time Christa started to walk up Walton Street she was almost crying, partly for Emma, partly for herself. She felt she was never going to get her life together again. As tears began to run down her cheeks, she slipped along a side alley into the disused graveyard of St Sepulchre, where she could regain her self-control unobserved.

The entrance path, through the arch of a Gothic gatehouse, was lined with sombre ranks of juniper and yew. It petered out in a semi-wilderness, bounded on two sides by the brick ramparts of the ironworks, which were camouflaged by the spreading tracery of some ancient beeches. Headstones stuck up like the arms of drowning men from clumps of withered grass, and brambles surfed across half-obliterated plinths. All around lay disintegrating reminders of Victorian sentiment: celtic crosses, cracked slabs adorned with crusader swords, marble angels with chipped noses and faces streaked with algae like green tears.

There had been an overnight thaw. In the sunshine the more sheltered parts of the graveyard were comparatively warm, though the wind was raw. From the ironworks came a faint clanking and thumping which provided a bizarre background timpani to the song of a wren in the depths of a cypress tree.

In a far corner someone was moving about stealthily among a group of laurels. It was probably another fugitive, a junkie perhaps, looking for somewhere quiet to shoot up, Christa thought, picking her way between headstones towards the beeches. Mast crunched like praline beneath her feet, and snowdrops had spread in thick clumps among the grass.

She sat down on a raised tomb, wiping her eyes with a ragged paper handkerchief she'd found in her pocket. The cold of the slab struck through her jeans. Nearby on a dilapidated pedestal stood a broken-handled urn, almost overgrown with ivy trails. It made her remember so vividly Emma's face the morning before the crash, and the motto on the base of the pedestal was so impregnated with Victorian gloom that she again wanted to cry.

As she squeezed her eyes shut to keep back the tears, she heard other footsteps crunching beneath the trees. She looked up, and saw Mallory walking towards her. Too late she remembered that he'd once told her Quentin Stannage was buried here.

'Go away,' she said, her voice rough with crying, and buried her face in the handkerchief, waiting to hear his footsteps depart.

Nothing happened. She peered round the handkerchief and saw him sitting on a tomb opposite, the collar of his sheepskin jacket turned up against the cold, steadily watching her.

'I heard at Gabriel about Emma's accident. I'm very sorry. You must feel wrecked.' He hesitated. 'What's the latest news?'

'How should I know? The hospital staff keep giving me a lot of rubbish about how she's comfortable and improving, when she hasn't even regained consciousness yet.' Christa scrubbed furiously at her eyes. 'And stop staring at me. I wish you'd go and find your explorer, or whatever it is you're doing here.'

At first when Mallory had seen Christa she was so motionless that she seemed like some Victorian statue of grief. Yet there was no resignation in the pose, just a stoical endurance so obviously painful that in spite of all the earlier rejections his automatic response was to comfort her.

'Don't be so hard on yourself. If the staff say she's improving, you should believe them,' he ventured.

There was a long pause while she appeared to digest this advice. She put away her handkerchief, and unexpectedly smiled, like a pale sun mirrored in water.

'I told Pansy more or less the same thing. But it's not only that.' She hesitated, pushing at the beechmast with the toe of her boot. 'Phil said it was my fault.'

'Why on earth should he think so? I understood the car skidded on ice.'

'It's a long story. I probably shouldn't tell you, but he'd threatened to leave Emma if she didn't give up her job and agree to move to a smaller house. I was with her before the crash, and during it as well.' She hesitated again, and he saw her hands clench on the edge of the tomb. 'It reminded me of when Matt died. I knew I couldn't bear to lose Emma too. I almost thought I couldn't cope.'

She sighed, huddling further into her jacket.

'The feeling shook me a bit,' she went on, with another attempt at a smile. 'But anyway, that's beside the point. Phil thought I'd been advising Emma to get a divorce, upsetting her so that she didn't concentrate on her driving, when all the time I was helping Em to think of ways to keep the marriage together. It was so – so bloody unfair!'

Christa in the role of marriage guidance counsellor, and reactionary marriage guidance counsellor at that, was a development indeed. Mallory wanted to laugh, and yet the increasing wretchedness in her voice was making him want to hold her too.

He went and sat next to her, telling himself he was mad

to run the gauntlet of rejection yet again, that he still had time to walk away. But he couldn't. She kept reminding him of the snowdrops at his feet, their delicately streaked flowers gleaming among thickets of grey-green spears. He was now more certain than ever of the innate sensitivity behind the barriers she put up round herself. It was worth one more try at getting through to her.

'I told you, I want to be alone,' she said, glancing apprehensively sideways at him.

'If you're determined to be the Garbo of Jericho, I can think of better settings than a burial ground.'

A smile had begun to lift the corners of Mallory's mouth. Christa stared at him in distrust, hearing the amusement in his voice.

'I like it here,' she said, thinking irritably that this was no time for a tease. 'It suits my mood,' she added grandly. 'Go away.'

She began to pluck at an ivy shoot clambering up the side of the tomb, so that she wouldn't have to meet his gaze.

'All right. But just stop throwing punches and listen to me first.' His voice wasn't amused any more. 'If I do walk away this time, that's it. I won't offer again. And you need to realise no one can take on the whole world without help.'

'For God's sake, you make it sound as if I'm seriously screwed up,' she said truculently, though her mind rushed to her worries about being unable to function professionally any more.

'Not yet. But you will be if you don't let people back into your life. You've made a start with Emma and the children. Now you could try with me as well.'

The ivy came away in a series of tiny, Velcro-like rips. Her legs were so cold they felt numb. She got up, and began to walk about while she struggled with her thoughts. Mallory had almost echoed Leda's advice to her, yet it was very hard to have to admit, even tacitly, that she needed to change. She turned to face him by the beech tree, feeling horribly unsure of herself.

'How could that work? You're just as screwed up.'

As she said the words, she knew they weren't true. In spite of his experience with Caitlin, he had an acceptance of life she would have liked to learn. He was tough, but though it was an odd word with which to describe a man, there was a sweetness about him too.

He came over to her and took her hand.

'Maybe,' he said lightly. 'So perhaps we should try some mutual analysis?'

Deciding was made even more difficult by the physical attraction that had returned as he sat by her side. Though she was cold and weary, his touch was starting to affect her like a shot of adrenalin. The surroundings made a biblical phrase come into her mind. She would like to lie with a man again. And it could be so good with Mallory. Everything could be so good.

As the bell of St Barnabas, a few streets away, chimed out the half-hour she put her free hand in the opening of his jacket. She could feel his heart thudding beneath his shirt.

'All right,' she said in a voice she couldn't make quite as flippant as she wanted. 'Let the therapy begin.'

He steadied her head in his hands against the smooth trunk of the beech, and began to kiss her. She slipped her fingers between his shirt buttons, and found bare skin.

His breath drew in sharply as he felt the cold. She undid a button and ran her hand over his ribs. They were as warm as rippled sand. She loosed another button, slid her hand downwards, and found a soft pathway of hair beneath his belt. She began to release the buckle

Abruptly he stopped kissing her.

'Jesus, no, not here.'

'Don't you like it?' she enquired mischievously, looking at him through half closed eyes. She slipped her hand round to his back, down his spine to the hard, muscular curves at its base, and heard his sharp intake of breath. He caught her wrist and pulled her hand away.

'What do you think? But I don't want to have our first fuck to an audience, alive or dead.'

'An audience?' She looked away, momentarily puzzled, and saw a line of fascinated faces at a window in the ironworks. She began to laugh. 'I see what you mean. Your place or mine?'

He kissed her hand as he fastened the buckle of his belt.

'Yours. It's closer,' he said.

*   *   *

Christa didn't remember much of the walk to her house, except that they went so fast the pavement seemed to run away beneath them.

The temperature indoors was tropical after the graveyard, but she felt cold again as they climbed the stairs. In spite of her lightheartedness at St Sepulchre's, she had the illogical feeling that this was going to be some sort of test. She must control herself, try to be detached and unemotional, so that he wouldn't know she cared if it went wrong.

She rushed round to the far side of the bed, and with her back to him rapidly began to take off her clothes. Miraculously, she'd made the bed before leaving the house, but the curtains were still drawn. A faint light filtered round the edges, and when she glanced sideways at the dressing-table mirror she could see Mallory still standing by the door, looking at her.

Hastily she dropped the last of her clothes on the floor like a swimmer determined to get the first plunge over as fast as possible.

'I'm ready,' she said to the watcher in the mirror.

It had taken Mallory a few moments to adjust to the decor, which reminded him of a setting for newly married bliss in a pre-war Ealing movie. With its faded wedding photo and sagging mattress where the dents of two bodies were plainly visible, the room had such a strong character of its own that it seemed almost as if a third person were present.

The fact that Christa hadn't altered it seemed at first a good sign, to confirm his feelings about her other self. But now her behaviour was rapidly changing the whole affair into a transaction. If she really was regarding things that way it would be a disastrous start. Yet the figure in the looking glass was pale and enticing as an underwater nymph, and once he'd taken off his own clothes, he wasn't sure if he'd be able to hold back a second time around.

'I'm ready,' she said again, as if he were a doctor about to produce a speculum.

He went over to her and took her in his arms. Her breasts were soft and full against his chest. In spite of the warmth she was shivering, and when she put her own arms round his neck and kissed him almost desperately, it began to dawn on him that the tough, devil-may-care Christa had simple stage-fright.

He began to kiss her back while manoeuvring her on to the bed, then tore himself away and began to undress, watching her all the time in case she suddenly took flight.

In the subdued light her skin seemed to have absorbed some of the dusky hue of the coverlet. Her nipples were a deep enticing red as if they'd been rubbed with carmine, the soft skin around them like the petals of a poppy. And the shadow between her legs reminded him of the charcoal smudge at a poppy's heart.

As he unbuckled his belt, the room was so silent that he could hear his own breathing. He had to force himself to slow down all his movements in an urgent attempt at self-control.

In the silence, and only too aware of what appeared to be Mallory's sudden reluctance, Christa felt as exposed as someone lost in no-man's-land. She wondered if he'd been put off by some aspect of her appearance, or whether he knew of Gareth's comment about her using sex as a security blanket, and had thought better of it.

This was all a huge mistake, she told herself, wishing she could sink through the bed and disappear. If only he'd stop standing there and looking at her. The end of the bed concealed the lower half of his body, so she couldn't see if he was aroused, but from the continuing silence something had clearly turned him off.

Damn him, she thought, why should I meekly wait as though I'm some sultan's most junior wife? She turned over abruptly and buried her face in the pillow, counting down deliberately from ten as if waiting for a cue, saying to herself that if he didn't respond by the time she got to zero, she'd tell him the whole thing was off.

She reached three, and was already in despair, when she felt him lie by her side. His hands began to caress the arches of her feet, move slowly along her calves and thighs, and up to her shoulders in long tender sweeps which made her feel as if her whole body was sinking slowly and luxuriously into warm water. Gently he turned her over to look at him. She pulled his head down to meet her lips. He took her in his arms, and as their bodies fitted against each other, she knew he was aroused.

She was still so programmed by Gareth that she automatically tried to spread her legs. But Mallory didn't let her. Instead one hand returned to her back, and as he kissed her he moved his fingers lightly across the base of her spine, producing sensations there she'd never known existed.

'Mmmm – wonderful – more,' she murmured, with a last attempt at reason as his kisses progressed to her throat. 'Is this tantric sex?'

He raised his head to look at her, and she saw the gleam of his teeth in a lazy, tender smile.

'If it were we'd have to wait six months before moving on. I haven't reached a high enough state for that.'

'So assuming you'd waited six months, where would you go next?'

'Here, and here, and here,' he said, his lips tracing a path from the hollow of her throat to her breasts, then to her navel.

'And last of all,' he went on, 'the truly enlightened yogi would pass through the dark gate.'

She curved her legs round his back and drew him to her again.

'And what would he find there?' she asked as she felt him enter.

'The lotus heart, the source of being,' he said, and as he began to move inside her she embarked on a willing immolation which, when its pulses overwhelmed her, became as never before a dying into life.

17

When Christa awoke, the St Barnabas clock was striking three. She felt deliciously languid. It was nothing like the aftermath of sex with Gareth, which always left her mentally and physically depleted.

Though the side of the mattress where Jessie's errant husband used to sleep was empty, the bedroom door was ajar, and she could hear the sound of the shower. The thought of Mallory's body under the running water was almost too tempting to resist, until she suddenly remembered Emma.

She sat bolt upright, and praying that the fates wouldn't punish her for so comprehensively forgetting her sister, snatched the old thermal vest from under the pillow, pulled it over her head, and rushed downstairs.

In the sitting room she couldn't remember where she'd put the phone, and Poppaea didn't help by bursting into cackles of manic laughter at her frantic search. Eventually she found it lurking beneath a newspaper in one of the fireside chairs. Though she'd banked up the fire before going out that morning, and it was glowing satisfactorily through the wire mesh of the guard, she shivered as she waited for the call to go through.

It took forever for the ward to answer. Then the charge nurse had to be found, enquiries made to establish Christa's identity, and case notes consulted. She felt sick with worry. The scent from a bowl of hyacinths on the sideboard seemed to suffocate her. Hurry up, hurry up, she screamed soundlessly into the mouthpiece, certain that Emma was worse, and they were working out how to relate the news.

Eventually someone picked up the phone with a clatter at the other end.

'Your sister's regained consciousness. Everyone's delighted with her progress, though she's still got some way to go. She won't be returning home for a few days yet, and she'll have to take things very easily at first.'

As the call finished, the arm holding the phone fell limply to Christa's side. It was as though she'd had her birthday twice in one day. The earlier release of making love, combined with this latest gift, took the final clamps off her self-control. Silently she began to weep as if she'd been told Emma had died.

When Mallory, now dressed, and puzzled by her absence, came downstairs in search of Christa, he found her standing by the fire in floods of tears and wearing a garment that looked like a penitential shift.

Gently he removed the phone from her hand, and put it on the seat of a chair. He took her in his arms, bracing himself for the worst.

'What's happened? Is it Emma?' he asked.

'She's woken up, and I'm so happy, and so lucky, because now I have you both.' Tears were still pouring down Christa's face. 'I know it's bloody, bloody silly of me. I know I'm going on like one of Apollo's soap opera queens, but I just can't help it.'

When they'd left St Sepulchre's Mallory had been anticipating an affair which would probably last till the end of their time in Oxford, and then burn itself out. But he hadn't suspected their love-making would affect him so profoundly. She'd displayed another self which, though he'd guessed at its existence, was far more sensitive, more intuitively tender, than he'd dared hope. And now this open declaration of her feelings was going to force him to think about things in an entirely different way.

'There's nothing wrong with showing how you feel,' he said gently.

She wiped the back of her hand across her eyes. 'I hate unloading on anyone, and especially you. I can't bear to be like my mother. It's what she does all the time.'

'I doubt very much if you're like her,' he said, torn between amusement and concern. 'She's agoraphobic, isn't she?'

'You know?' said Christa, staring at him in astonishment.

'Emma told me a bit about it at that dinner party last year.'

'What did she say?'

'Nothing much, just that it had been difficult when you were young.'

'It's difficult now,' Christa said. 'I've given up attempting to get through to her.'

He hesitated. This wasn't the time to cross more thorny ground, but he remembered how he'd felt when his father died.

'Perhaps you have to try a different line of approach,' he said. 'Just don't give up entirely. You might regret it later.'

They would clearly have to talk more about their families at some stage. But not now, while there were more important things to do, and while she was wearing nothing but that odd garment whose ravelled edge only just covered the top of her thighs, and which was so worn and thin that he could see her nipples through the ribbed cotton.

'I think you should get dressed,' he said, kissing Christa in a way that made Poppaea rattle the cage door furiously with her beak, and let loose a spate of Arabic. 'If you don't, we shall have to risk sea-sickness on the hearth rug again, and Poppaea already disapproves.'

Christa smiled.

'I've gathered that. What's she saying?'

'It's unrepeatable. Old Jephson must have done most of his research in Cairo brothels. Get dressed, and if you have some eggs, I'll make you an omelette for lunch before you go to see Emma.'

She reached up and put her arms round his neck.

'I'm never sea-sick,' she said. 'And I'd rather have you instead of lunch.'

A week later the snow was gone, and more signs of spring had tentatively begun to arrive at Gabriel, bringing with them beguiling wafts of sweetness from behind sombre garden walls, powdering the grey willows with sunshiny pollen, and applying pale pink blusher to the cherry trees in the fellows' garden. Christa felt equally transformed, and could no more conceal her happiness than the celandines along the banks of the Isis could stop their flowering. Emma, though still in hospital, was improving daily, and Leda had returned and provided additional reassurance that she'd make a full recovery.

Christa felt intuitively that the Master would not be pleased by her affair with Mallory, and wanted to keep him in ignorance until after the debate. Mallory, now away in London on a book promotion, had been sleeping at her house, but she knew it was almost impossible for anything to stay secret in Oxford for long.

On her way to the seminar in which she intended to discuss the set-up for the debate with her students, she called on Piers to return a borrowed book. He appeared to have had an impromptu supper in his room the previous night, for his waste-paper basket contained two empty bottles of college Chablis, and some take-away cartons. He was working through a pile of essays, with Mehitabel snoozing in his lap, and looked considerably hung-over.

'Half my first years can't spell,' he grumbled, 'and the other half still haven't started to think for themselves. God alone knows why I chose to teach. I recently met someone who graduated with me, and he's earning twice as much swanning about the world selling software. He's got a PA like Sharon Stone as well.'

'You know Sharon Stone's not your type,' said Christa.

'I'm not sure what's my type. That's the problem. Anyway, spring certainly seems to be in your step these days. Farrar's been looking a lot less lean and hungry too, and I hear you've been seen dining *à deux* in town. Do you think it's wise?'

Mehitabel jumped down from his knee and padded towards Christa, heading for her more comfortable lap. Christa decided there was no point in trying to hide the affair from Piers.

'I'm so happy I don't really care if it's wise.'

She did indeed look blazingly happy, Piers thought, feeling markedly past it in comparison. At a drinks party the previous night he'd met a ravishing young medic, very slim, with cropped auburn hair and skin like ivory, who, after he'd given what he thought was an excellent performance in bed, had asked him in unpleasantly clinical terms if he was sure he had his sexual orientation sorted out.

'Then if you're pleased, I am,' he said sourly.

'Don't be such a kill-joy, Piers. You can't imagine how good things are just now.'

Yes, I can, he thought gloomily.

'But it's not exactly a marriage of true minds, is it?' he observed out loud.

'What the hell do you mean by that? You're such an intellectual snob sometimes.'

'I simply meant that *au fond* your interests aren't the same. You don't really feel alive unless you're dicing with death. That's how you get your kicks. He's more the sort of guy who observes life. I reckon that's what went wrong between him and Caitlin Trevor. She needed to be where the action was too. If you decide to stay with him, it'll be a huge change for you.'

Christa was silent, her hands in Mehitabel's fur. At the moment she couldn't bear to face the possibility that Piers' casual assessment might be true. She hadn't talked about the future to Mallory yet, or about Gareth, because she'd decided it was too early to get on to such dangerous ground. So much had happened recently which she was still trying to understand.

'Perhaps I'm changing from how I was,' she said slowly. 'Mallory grounds me. It sounds like cheap magazine psychology, I know, but it's true. I don't feel tied by the relationship, but – sort of calm and centred.'

'Been getting at you with his Eastern schmooze, has he? And some *Kama Sutra* thrown in too? I wish I had a line like his.'

'No, he hasn't.' She blushed. 'Well, not exactly.'

'And what'll happen when Gareth turns up? You're not going to turn a hair, I suppose?'

'No, I'm not.'

'I'll believe it when I see it. Farrar's going to be like a red rag to him. It's my bet Gareth will do everything he can to show he's still able to make it with you. You never could resist a challenge, and I can't imagine Farrar being particularly impressed if you do try to even the score with Gareth.'

'Pack it in, Piers,' said Christa, losing her temper as he voiced all the worries she'd so far managed to suppress. 'Didn't you make it yourself last night? You're just jealous.'

'Maybe I am. But I also don't want to see you hurt again. That's why you'd better come down off cloud nine and start thinking ahead.'

Christa walked over to her seminar mentally continuing the argument with Piers. He would try to spoil a beautiful day, she thought crossly. As she walked down the corridor, she pushed the subject from her mind. Nothing was going to divert her from the documentary. Her professional instincts were too strong, and she had the responsibility for its success squarely in her hands. Yet the documentary was another subject she hadn't discussed with Mallory, guessing he would approve even less if he knew about the risk she'd taken at Gabriel's Mill.

Luckily Christa's students were too keen to grapple with the actual presentation of the debate to notice anything different about her. Rather than using the Great Hall, where the butlers hated having to move the massive tables and benches outside, she'd got permission to film in the chapter house, once part of the former abbey.

It was an octagonal building, with a roof supported by pillars which branched into a fan-vaulted ceiling like a petrified forest. A weak winter sun shone fitfully through the arched windows. The students had dispersed themselves on a stone bench against the wall. Their voices bounced from the empty surfaces.

'What about the sound?' asked Steve, who had his feet up on the bench and was eating an orange.

'We'll hire a professional for the day to wire the place up. It's in the budget. You've all got enough to do already, and the sound levels must be balanced properly. The seating and equipment will absorb some of the echo,' Christa said.

'At least the windows aren't stained glass, and it won't be dark in the evening at that time in May,' said Rebekah, her red jacket bright against the grey stone, as she walked about surveying the interior. 'We'll have plenty of light.'

'Not enough,' said Christa firmly. 'It'll need to be improved with floods from high up. That means hiring a sparks as well, and some scaffolding, so you'd better start working on the Bursar for permission now. He's probably fussier than the National Trust about potential damage to the building's fabric.'

'I hadn't realised there was going to be such a huge amount to do,' Justin complained. 'And if we don't count the Easter vacation, the debate's only a few weeks away.'

'At least it's before Eights Week, so we shan't miss any partying,' said Annabel, who as usual was sitting as close as possible to him, though Justin himself seemed to be concentrating more these days on Rebekah.

'You're lucky. You've a lot more time than a professional television crew,' said Christa. 'And the debate's going to take place after dinner, so the establishment should be in a tolerant mood.'

She'd made herself sound encouraging, though she'd begun to feel uneasy now that the event was getting near. In spite of what Piers had said, the relationship with Mallory seemed to be taking the edge off her need to prove herself. But she had no intention of letting the students down. For their sake, if not for her own, she had to pull everything together and make the debate work.

'What's the best way to set up the floor?' Rebekah asked, busily scribbling on a clipboard.

'A semi-circular arrangement of chairs for college staff and the public, and students on the stone seat round the wall behind them,' Christa answered, forcing herself to concentrate on the practicalities of the set. 'Then the audience can face the two panels across a central arena. It'll give the cameraman and presenter plenty of room to move about. You must work out the other details for yourselves.'

'I'll ask my dad to get Dreaming Spires' publicity people to handle the tickets for the public,' said Rebekah.

Christa reminded herself to make sure Stacey and Glenn got seats. Glenn in particular could be replied upon as a doughty champion for the rights of the estate, and it would help if the students invited some parents too.

The Master had already sent her a note saying he wished to be the last to speak in the summing up. She intended to reply with a formal schedule for the proceedings, and to get his written agreement to it. The timing of the various stages in the debate had to be perfect for the students' video footage to produce the maximum effect. The less scope he had for manoeuvre, the better.

In the meantime she was still trying to get ahead with her investigation into the Waylandsbury Hoard. Mallory had managed to fix a meeting with Gervaise Burford the following weekend, so she might make more progress then.

Emma was still in hospital. She'd improved enough to conduct a coherent conversation, but was having difficulty remembering the events of the twenty-four hours before the crash.

When Christa went to visit her after the seminar she'd been moved to an ordinary ward and was sitting by her bed in a towelling dressing gown she'd had since the sixth form. Her hair was tied back with one of Pansy's ribbons. Next to her was a showy arrangement of carnations and lilies, much too big for the hospital vase.

'Who's the admirer?' Christa asked.

'Phil. He brought them last night,' said Emma, looking bashful. 'He's been marvellous since the crash. It sounds awful, but I really don't quite understand why, especially as I've just remembered that horrible row we had before the accident. It's almost as though someone's said something to him about our marriage.'

'Probably Dad. He's been worried about you both,' said Christa, trying to conceal her surprise. She'd never thought Phil would take her tirade to heart.

'Father was here yesterday after work. He never mentioned it. But he did have one piece of good news. Mother was so upset about not being able to help with the children that she's started to attend the clinic again.'

'We've all heard that one before,' said Christa drily.

'It'd be marvellous if she could help, even if it's only later on. Noelene's feeling the strain, and I'm not going to be able to do much for a while. I was wondering if you could do me a big, big favour tomorrow, and have Jamie for the day, so she can get a proper break?'

Christa was in such a state of euphoria over Emma's recovery that she would have agreed to almost any request, but by the following afternoon she'd decided that self-sacrifice had its limits.

Jamie, face the colour of a runner-bean flower, blue eyes open just wide enough to make sure he had Christa's full attention, had been screaming for an hour almost non-stop.

He'd behaved like an angel all morning, playing contentedly with his toys while she dealt with a pile of mail and responding to her cuddles with dribble-wreathed smiles. But after lunch he'd become an infant monster again, and was now in such a frenzy that he shuddered with rage as he wound himself up for each new howl.

Christa, at first certain she was being treated to a masterpiece of histrionics, was beginning to wonder if he was about to have convulsions. An adult in such a state would have had a coronary long ago.

She dared not ring Emma at the hospital for advice. The slightest hint of something wrong would probably give her an instant relapse. Christa felt so desperate that if Mallory had been around, she would even have consulted him in the hope of gaining some insight into the infant psyche.

Thinking of Mallory made her remember what he'd said to her about her mother. Since she'd learned Alice had resumed group therapy, she had been wondering if she should make another effort in that direction. Now, in such an extremity, anything was worth a try. She grabbed the phone and punched in the number.

'Ma, it's me, Christa. I think there could be something wrong with Jamie. I'm not sure what to do,' she gabbled, too anxious to choose her words.

Luckily she'd captured her mother's attention dramatically enough for her not to interrupt while she relayed the whole sorry tale of her own inability to cope.

'The trembling's getting worse. Do you think he's going to have a fit?' she concluded in desperation. 'I have to get him calmed down before we go to fetch Pansy from school.'

Alice didn't sound at all surprised.

'It sounds to me as though he's missing Emma.'

'But I can't stop him! And he's gone a really awful colour!'

'You used to as well, when you were annoyed,' said Alice placidly. 'Babies often do. You'd better bring him straight over.'

• Willow Tickell

'I can't. The Mini frightens him. It's too noisy.'

She hoisted Jamie with one arm further up her shoulder. She was now faced with a crisis at both ends, for his nappy was soaking and she suspected he'd freak out completely if she tried to change it as well as take him for a ride.

'He's too worked up to take out anyway. Please, please, Ma, come over here!'

'You know I can't, not without your father,' her mother faltered, the confidence draining from her voice.

'I'm desperate, Ma! I swear I'll come to tea on Sunday, dinner even, if you'll only try, just this once.'

'Don't ask me, please. You don't know how guilty I feel when I have to say no.'

'Just ring for a taxi. For Christ's sake, you'll only have to walk down the garden path on your own, and Em said you'd started therapy again.'

'But I might not feel well on the way, and the taxi driver might not understand.'

'Look, Ma, it's not for me, it's for Jamie.'

'I can't, I can't,' came her mother's eternal wail, and in despair and exasperation Christa switched off the phone.

Half an hour later Jamie had finally sunk into exhausted silence, but only as long as Christa held him clamped to her while she walked up and down. She'd been forced to wrap his nether regions in a towel rather than risk a nappy change.

As she was wondering whether she dared attempt it now, the latch on the front gate clicked. She looked out of the window, expecting more junk mail, and almost dropped Jamie in astonishment. Her mother was trotting up the garden path in her sensible court shoes and sensible belted coat, with a brown velveteen beret like a bean bag perched on her curls. Mary Poppins herself could not have been a more welcome sight.

'You made it! Well done! But where's the taxi?' Christa said as she opened the door to the accompaniment of Jamie's renewed squalls. 'Did it drop you up the road?'

'I got out in Walton Street.' Alice's voice was wavery but distinctly proud.

'You walked from Walton Street? On your own? That's marvellous!'

• 368

Normally after such a sortie Alice would have been on the point of collapse. Instead she was taking off her coat and hat, patting her curls into place, and looking vastly pleased with herself. She hung her handbag over her arm, plucked Jamie from Christa's arms, bustled into the sitting room and sat down with him in a fireside chair.

Christa subsided on to the sofa feeling as if the US cavalry had arrived. She watched in awe as her mother lovebombed Jamie with baby talk which reached new depths, even for her. To Christa it sounded as good as a Mozart duet, and within five minutes it had reduced Jamie to wide-eyed, blissful silence.

'I stopped in Walton Street to get him this,' said Alice, searching in her handbag. 'It should do the trick, but it'd probably be best if we didn't tell your sister.'

She produced a blue plastic dummy with a teat which would have pacified Oedipus, and inserted it into Jamie's mouth. Within two more minutes his eyelids started to droop.

'Poor little soul,' said Alice. 'He's been missing his mummy. Emma was still feeding him herself once a day, you know.'

'You're a genius, Ma,' said Christa. 'And even more of a genius to get here on your own. I'd almost gone under. You don't know how glad I am to see you.'

Alice was blossoming by the minute, and for once made no attempt to find fault with Christa's maternal or domestic abilities. She didn't interfere in the kitchen while tea and biscuits were produced, didn't cavil at the absence of home-baking, and amazed Christa by saying she liked the house.

When tea was over, and Alice had been unable to resist transferring the now slumbering Jamie from the sofa back into her arms, she seemed so at ease that Christa suddenly decided to ask a question she'd wanted to know the answer to for years.

'Ma, don't tell me if you'd rather not, but do you have any idea what started your agoraphobia off? I can't believe it was really just a general inability to cope with life.'

Alice looked at Christa, then down at Jamie. She sighed.

'No, of course it wasn't. But it was too painful to talk to you and Emma about it at the time, and I felt you were too young.' She gave a rueful smile. 'But perhaps I should tell you now. You're certainly old enough, and they keep telling me at the clinic that I shouldn't bottle things up.'

'So what happened?' said Christa, holding her breath and praying Jamie wouldn't wake.

'Do you remember you and Emma going to stay with your grandmother in Southwold when you were very small?'

'Yes, of course. I must have been about four,' said Christa, who remembered the visit partly because of the titanic clashes she'd had with her disciplinarian grandmother, partly because she felt her mother didn't want her any more.

'You went there because I was ill. I'd had a very bad miscarriage. I was terribly upset. Couldn't bear to talk about it to anyone except your father, and that's when I started to have this irrational fear of going out. It wasn't your fault, of course, but when you came back from Southwold, you seemed to have grown away from me, and that made everything much worse.'

Alice had kept her eyes on Jamie while she talked, but now she looked up almost as if she expected a reprimand rather than sympathy. The look seemed infinitely pathetic to Christa.

'Oh, God, Ma, I'm so sorry. It must have been terrible for you,' she said rushing over to hug her impulsively, and making Jamie stir and begin to wake up. 'If only you'd known how much Emma and I missed you! And when we got back, you were so strange and withdrawn. I suppose I naturally turned to Emma instead.'

'If only you'd been old enough to tell me how you felt,' said her mother sadly, with her cheek against the top of Jamie's head as she rocked him. 'I suppose I've been trying to make you need me ever since, but it's been in the wrong way.'

They talked for a very long time, in a way Christa never remembered talking with her mother before. They stopped only when Christa suddenly realised she'd have to fetch Pansy from school. She still felt penitent. She'd never realised quite how much her mother wanted to be told she was needed. Now she suddenly saw another way to help her by luring her out again.

'Come and meet Pansy from school with me. I'm having her till six, then Noelene's picking both children up. She's been missing Emma so much, and she'll be thrilled to see you.'

Pansy was even more thrilled to be sworn to secrecy about the dummy.

'Jamie can't help being such a baby, I suppose,' she said, skipping along by Alice's side in a new hat of sky-blue denim with daisies round the brim. 'And Daddy says Mummy mustn't have any worries just now. Will you come and see me in the school concert next week, Grandma? I'm playing the piano. My piece has two minor keys.'

'Why don't you, Ma?' said Christa. 'Live dangerously for once. It's the event of the year.'

They were walking home via Walton Street to buy chicken-burgers and Pop Tarts for tea. As they passed Stacey's salon Pansy suddenly gave a squeak of joy.

'It's the hairdresser's where Chel's aunty works! And look, there's Chel in the window waving at me! Her mummy sometimes leaves her there after school. Please, please, let's go in.'

Christa thought how slow she'd been not to have realised Chel was Stacey's niece, though Stacey had never referred to her by name. Pansy was already pushing open the door. Christa glanced quickly at Alice, who seemed to be holding up remarkably well, and followed her in with the buggy.

After everyone had cooed over Jamie, Chel, a hugely self-possessed child in rose-printed leggings and a pink sweat shirt, her blonde fringe in a plastic roller and each finger nail painted a different shade of red, carried Pansy off to watch Stacey's assistant, Diane, putting highlights in a client's hair.

Christa introduced Stacey to her mother, and as they chatted saw with amusement that Stacey was sizing up Alice's neat grey curls.

'You've got lovely hair, Mrs Keith, so thick and wavy. Some of my clients would kill for it. Have you ever considered a warm ash rinse? And a style with a bit more movement?'

'I don't really think I'm a warm ash sort of person,' said Alice, glancing doubtfully at Diane's client, whose hair had just been wrapped in foil and left to marinade.

Pansy, catching the conversation, came running to join them.

'Please, please, let Chel's aunty do it for the school concert. You'll be the best grandma there.'

'Your bone structure's perfect,' said Stacey. 'It seems such a shame not to show it off.'

Christa could see Alice beginning to weaken, and realised that Stacey and Pansy between them were on the verge of accomplishing more on the maternal fashion front than she and Emma had ever been able to achieve. Before Alice had a chance to retreat she added her own contribution.

'Why don't you have it done the morning before the concert? Then we can lunch together before going on to the school.'

'You and me? Lunch?' said Alice, obviously in the grip of severe temptation. 'I suppose in that case I might manage it.'

As Stacey hurried off to fetch the appointments book, Christa reflected with amusement that her mother's thought processes were as visible as the working of a glass-encased clock. Lunch together meant her younger daughter all to herself, and a perfect chance to enquire into her future plans.

But for once the prospect didn't irritate Christa. Like a filter on a camera lens, the relationship with Mallory seemed to be affecting her whole outlook, softening the way she looked at everything.

'We'll meet at Brown's,' she said to Alice, adding firmly to make sure she didn't backslide, 'I'm sure you can there get on your own.'

'I think I might even manage that too.'

'Of course you will. You've done brilliantly today,' said Christa, giving her mother's arm a squeeze of approval which made her colour with pleasure.

Christa hadn't seen Stacey for a while, and when the appointment was made, and Pansy had dragged Alice off to look at the window display, she asked her if she was still going to meetings of the Peaceable Kingdom.

'Yes,' Stacey said, 'though Glenn doesn't really approve after that business with Howl. But I have to do something to help the cause, and we've had a bit of a shake-up on the committee lately so it's livelier than it was. We've got something quite big coming up soon.'

'What's that?' Christa asked, more out of politeness than any real interest. From what she'd heard of the Peaceable Kingdom so far, it seemed to have very little pulling power.

Stacey looked round furtively to make sure no one could hear. 'On May bank holiday we're having a march and a public meeting in St Giles'. You mustn't tell Glenn. It'll be very orderly and well-organised, but I don't want him to know.'

'Won't he ask where you're going?'

'He won't be around. He's working with some mates on a self-help project over the holiday. They're building their own homes on a site in Summertown.'

'Supposing he sees your picture afterwards in the papers or on TV?'

'There's not much chance of that. We've been so low key up to now, the media just aren't interested. Dreaming Spires and the local press have better things to go to on a bank holiday.' Stacey hesitated, then said without much hope, 'I suppose there's no point in asking if you'd cover it?'

Christa smiled at her. 'Afraid not. I'd love to have a go at reporting again, but I must keep on the straight and narrow till the end of the year.'

Christa hadn't been aware that Mallory owned a car until he insisted on using it at the weekend, refusing to cramp his legs into the Mini for too long. And when a dark green Mercedes coupé turned up outside her house she didn't at first associate it with him.

'I thought you weren't into modern methods of transport,' she teased him as he stashed away her holdall in the boot.

'I'm not. But if I've got to have a car, I prefer one that doesn't break down and doesn't hang about on the motorway.'

'A Volvo would fit that bill just as well,' she teased him, wishing the Mercedes were hers.

He closed the boot and held out the keys.

'Would you like to drive?'

'You only asked me along as your chauffeur?' she said, taking them.

'Stop stirring things up. I can't think of anyone else I'd trust with it. And you're so much prettier than Emery, anyway.'

She smiled as she slid into the leather driving seat. Emery

was the Master's chauffeur, and had as much facial charm as a warthog. Driving towards the ring road she remembered Gareth's attitude to his Citroën, which he saw almost as an extension of himself and drove like an Exocet. She had spent journeys with him in a state of over-stimulation which had been characteristic of their whole relationship. When Mallory took the wheel after a village tea, he drove in such a relaxed way that she fell asleep and didn't wake till they were pulling up outside Gervaise Burford's house.

It was a rambling old vicarage of flint and brick, set in the lee of the Marlborough Downs. The housekeeper, Mrs Canynge, a woman in her late-sixties with her hair in a steel-grey crown of plaits, and wearing a suit like a horse blanket, treated Christa with reserve. She clearly preferred having Mallory to herself. This was made even more apparent when she showed them their rooms, which were at opposite ends of the house.

'Professor Burford's still having his nap,' she said to Christa before leaving her, 'I'm sure you're tired too, so don't bother to hurry downstairs. Dr Farrar and I are old friends, and we shall have plenty to talk about.'

When she'd left to take Mallory to his room, Christa went over to the window and opened it. The garden backed straight on to the downs, and was bounded by a flowering blackthorn hedge, whose faint almond scent mingled with the more pungent smell of sheep cropping the downland turf. She could hear lambs bleating and somewhere the murmur of a stream.

It was a very English scene, whose every detail she now seemed to take in with new eyes: the tiny, acid-green leaves bursting from blackthorn twigs, the scalloped edges of yellow lichen patches on the window sill, the raindrops shining in the fresh spring grass. Everything seemed to be heightened since this relationship with Mallory began.

As if in response to her thoughts she heard the door open, his footsteps approach, and felt his arms come round her beneath her breasts. She leaned her head against his chest.

'Mrs Canynge seems determined to keep us apart,' she said. 'Do you think you're up to midnight pathfinding along all those corridors?'

'I'm certainly not up to facing Mrs C in her hairnet and

dressing gown. Last time I was here she was crashing about all night making cups of Ovaltine.'

'Then you'll be less traumatised if you stay here with me?'

'Much less traumatised,' he said, turning her round and kissing her. 'And I think we should take a quick nap too. Just to make sure your bed fits us both.'

They dined in some style, at a table adorned with silver candelabra and heavy lace mats. The food, copious amounts of Lancashire hotpot, followed by stewed rhubarb and custard, was served on Royal Worcester plates.

'Château Lafite. Wine experts say it should be drunk on one's knees,' said Gervaise, pouring Mallory another glass of a velvety claret.

Arthritis had skewed his fingers sideways, and the swollen knuckle joints bulged like marbles beneath the papery skin. His head, on which the fine white hair grew to meet a neatly trimmed beard, had sunk almost to his chest, but his eyes in their hollow sockets were as alert as a young man's.

He'd taken a liking to Christa, thank heaven, thought Mallory, not that it would have been hard for anyone, even so venerable, to be attracted to her. Her skin had a faint peach flush in the candlelight, and she wore a green dress from which her neck and head rose like a flower. Luckily she hadn't tried to impress him with the latest media gossip, or a description of her work in progress, as Caitlin, on her only visit here, slightly in awe of him and very slightly contemptuous too, had tried to do.

Christa wasn't afraid. She listened to him, stuck to her opinions, and occasionally teased him gently as he hadn't been teased for years.

'Mallory tells me you're interested in Vernon Slade's past,' Gervaise said to her, when Mrs Canynge had gone to make the coffee. 'Why, exactly?'

'Because he's misusing his power. And because it's easier for me to try to undermine that power than an outsider.'

'A laudable ambition, but not easy to fulfil. His talent for manipulation should never be underestimated. I can remember his reign as president of the Gabriel JCR in his final year.

Disastrous. The atmosphere became so snobbish that an under-graduate from a state school tried to commit suicide. Everyone was greatly relieved when Slade went off to the other place for his higher degree.'

'Did you have much to do with him at the time of the Waylandsbury dig?'

'No. He was teaching at another Oxford college then. Old Professor Saltash blocked every appointment he tried for at Gabriel. If Saltash had been alive at the time of Slade's election, he'd never have become the new Master.'

'Mallory told me you'd heard a rumour that he stole someone else's data to locate the hoard?'

'A Gabriel post-graduate – he died last year, alas – working on the dig with this other person implied as much to me afterwards. He was upset because Slade had tried to undermine him too – hinted that he wouldn't be recommended for his degree unless he allowed the major part of his own work on the dig to be writ-ten up under Slade's name. I advised him to confide in Professor Saltash, who quickly sent Slade off with a flea in his ear.'

'Do you remember the name of the other person who was supposed to have located the hoard?'

'I was never told it. And I visited the dig so long ago that I really can't recall any of the other people there, except for Slade of course. My brain isn't a hundred percent these days.'

'You were there?' said Christa. Mallory could hear the excite-ment in her voice.

'Yes. This used to be my parents' house. I expect you know the dig took place on the downs near here. I was interested to see the set-up, though it was just as I expected.' Gervaise unhooked his stick from the back of his chair, and began to heave himself creakily from his seat. 'I usually take coffee in my study after dinner. It's a warmer room. Perhaps you'd care to join me?'

Mallory went to help Mrs Canynge wash up, while Christa accompanied Gervaise on a slow progress into a book-lined study where a log fire crackled in the grate. He subsided into a sagging armchair and sat there like an elderly gnome while Mrs Canynge, now looking much happier with Mallory captive in the kitchen, appeared briefly to place coffee, a bottle of malt whisky and glasses by his side.

Christa, trying not to watch his gnarled hands shakily splashing whisky into the glasses, took a chair opposite him and made a quick inspection of the room. Sharing the wall with some amateur watercolours of English cathedrals were photos of what appeared to be classical sites visited in Gervaise's youth. A collection of fishing rods and walking sticks was stashed in a Greek amphora. Behind the door hung a mac with a lining of perished rubber, a pair of binoculars and an old Leica.

Christa was beginning to feel sleepy in the warmth. Her gaze moved idly over the books. On a top shelf was a row of photograph albums, their spines dated in white marking ink.

'I was somewhat snap-happy in my younger days,' Gervaise said, following her gaze, 'and unfortunately I could never bear to throw my efforts away.'

'Might you have taken some photos of the Waylandsbury dig?' she asked, suddenly alert as she realised the implication of this remark.

'I really can't recall. It was in sixty-two, wasn't it? Why don't you have a look?'

Christa heaved the 1962 album down in a cloud of dust. When she'd stopped coughing she took it over to a table lamp, and began to leaf carefully through the pages. The photos were firmly stuck in place, but each one was captioned neatly in ink. To her delight, almost at the end of the album, she struck treasure trove of her own, in the shape of six photos of the Waylandsbury dig. And in the final one, again standing on the edge of a group, as if shy, or marginalised, or afraid, was the young woman she'd seen before.

Gervaise studied it for so long with a large tortoise-shell-handled magnifying glass, that she was almost bursting with impatience by the time he spoke.

'Do you know, I can't remember a thing about her. I'm so sorry not to be able to help.'

Sighing with frustration, Christa retrieved the album and studied it again.

'Do you have a photocopier here?' she asked.

'Good heavens, no. But if you want a copy, you're most welcome to borrow the album. Mallory can return it when he visits us next. Or you can, if you're with him. I hope you will be. Is that what you intend?'

Christa, still absorbed by the photo, was startled by the question. She looked up to find him watching her as if he knew her thoughts.

'I'm not sure what either of us intends,' she stalled.

'You're shocked because I'm so direct. That's one of the privileges of old age, my dear. It was a bad business for him with the Trevor woman. They weren't compatible, but neither saw it until it was almost too late, and then she was too selfish to let go gracefully.'

Christa was dismayed by this damning assessment of the unfortunate Caitlin. He obviously demanded the highest qualities in a potential partner for Mallory, qualities she wasn't at all sure she possessed.

'So you think I'm right for him?' she countered.

'Very possibly. Sometimes the unlikeliest matches work the best.'

Amusement began to triumph over her dismay.

'And am I not allowed to ask if he's right for me?'

'Only you can decide that. Neither of you may be capable of making the necessary concessions in any case. Personally I could never do so, though I regret it now.'

Christa, still trying to digest this rather too accurate pronouncement, was overcome with relief when Mallory returned to the room.

'Ah, there you are,' Gervaise greeted him. 'We've had a most interesting little chat, and Christa has found a photograph which may well be of some use.'

'I hope Gervaise didn't grill you,' Mallory said to her in an undertone, passing her chair to fetch himself some coffee. 'He's inclined to forget that new guests aren't students up for a viva.'

'We were talking about Waylandsbury,' she replied, anxious to prevent further enquiries. 'Could we go there tomorrow? I'd like to see for myself where the hoard was found.'

The sun was warm in the lee of the whale-backed long barrow which had reputedly once held the bones of Wayland, the Saxon smith-god, and where a fleeing Roman household had buried its treasures. No trace of the dig remained now above the smooth turf, apart from an English Heritage plaque on a sarsen stone to show where the hoard had been found.

Christa's head rested in the crook of Mallory's arm. The grass beneath them was soft and sweet-scented. A meadow pipit soared into the sky, spilling out trills of song across the valley below, where meadows lay in chequers of chocolate-coloured earth, vivid green winter wheat, and blue-grey kale. She couldn't remember when she'd last felt so peaceful, yet her talk with Gervaise still nagged at the back of her mind.

'Did you come here with Caitlin?' she asked. 'Gervaise said you'd brought her to see him.'

There was a long pause. 'So that's what he was talking to you about,' Mallory said eventually. 'I only brought her here once. She didn't want to stay long. Caitlin's an urban creature at heart.'

'Part of the Katherine Mansfield film was set in Cornwall. She must have adjusted to the country on location. I wish you'd tell me what went wrong?'

He glanced sideways at her as if trying to gauge her reaction in advance, and then sat up.

'All right, but I'm not too proud of my part in it,' he said, his gaze now fixed on the view. 'We'd arranged that I'd fly on to Delhi at the end of my trip and meet her for a holiday there. She'd always been attracted by the idea of India, and had a plan for a film based on one of Kipling's stories.'

'Sounds like a good idea, from what I know of her work.'

'I thought so too. But it was her first time in the developing world, and she was so thrown by the dirt and the poverty and the bureaucratic delays that we had to come home. She's a highly organised person, and in India she felt out of control. It does affect some people that way.'

'So it meant the end of her film, presumably. Poor Caitlin,' said Christa softly, remembering how frustrated she felt herself when a pet project fell through.

'Her reaction had enormous implications for our future. I'd known that because of her work we couldn't be together all the time, but I'd always assumed she'd enjoy travelling with me between movies. To make things worse, when we got back to London a fax was waiting for her with an offer of work in the States on a Spielberg film. Obviously it was an offer she couldn't refuse, but she expected me to make my base in Hollywood with her from then on. I couldn't face living indefinitely in LA. Because she'd already waited for me for a year, she saw it as a personal betrayal. Neither of us would compromise.'

Gervaise's words came back vividly to Christa.

'What were you both going to do before this happened?' she asked.

'Marry, stay here while I wrote the Africa book, and Caitlin set up the Kipling film. She'd originally been enormously enthusiastic about it. It was one of the things that made her so attractive, and such a good fund-raiser. But when India in its reality threw her, she unfortunately transferred that enthusiasm to LA.'

Christa sat up, feeling cold. The meadow pipit was still singing, the sun was still on the grass, but the story sounded too like a possible scenario for herself and Mallory.

'The same sort of thing might happen to us, you know,' she said.

Mallory put his arm round her again. He hadn't meant to discuss their future so soon, knowing it would be a subject full of pitfalls.

'Perhaps,' he said. 'But you're not like Caitlin.'

'I am in one major respect. My career's just as important to me, and I go where it takes me.'

'Haven't you ever thought that you'd like to make your own decisions about where you go, and how much depth you give your reports?'

He'd phrased the question with care, wanting to avoid the slightest coercion and scared of inhibiting the change he sensed had been taking place in her.

'Unfortunately I can't choose where wars are going to happen, or how soon the next one will break out.'

'But are you sure you're content to do that for the rest of your career?'

She pulled away from him, and began to pluck at a clump of grass, bending her head so that her hair slid forward and he couldn't see her face.

'That's a loaded question,' she said. 'Does it mean you think I shouldn't?'

'I've a feeling you might be ready to try something different, something ultimately more satisfying, once you realise you don't need to keep proving yourself. And I'm not saying it just because I love you, and it would be more convenient for us.'

'And how about your need to disappear for months, if not years, on your own? That wouldn't be convenient for us either.'

Her voice had become increasingly wary. He knew that if he was going to ask for changes from her, she had as much right to expect similar changes from him. Again he longed to tell her how much his father's death had jolted him, but decided it could sound like emotional blackmail.

Instead he said carefully, 'The last trip was too long. I didn't realise until my father died that the quest was becoming more important than reality. And I've discovered I like teaching. I thought I'd try more of it at Gabriel next year, between shorter trips. You might enjoy going with me on some of them.'

'Doing this new, fulfilling work you've suggested for me, I suppose. And exactly what form would it take?' Her voice, though dry, to his intense relief sounded less hostile now.

'You could do your own freelance reports, on anything that interested you. You've got the contacts to market them, and there's an endless supply of stories in the developing world.'

Christa abruptly got to her feet, scattering blades of grass. The vivid colours in the fields below were being absorbed by the shadows of racing clouds. She wished Mallory hadn't said what she'd been thinking increasingly herself over the last few weeks. To go freelance would be a huge gamble, but to do it with him would be an even greater commitment to a different way of life.

'I'm not sure,' she said. 'And no one would give me a commission at the moment anyway. My professional reputation's at rock bottom.'

'If your work's good enough, someone will take it.'

'I can't. It's too soon. I think it's best if we just call the whole thing off.'

Abruptly she turned and began to hurry away down the long, flinky path which led to the valley, telling herself in panic that it was much too early to make any choice, especially when Gareth was about to reappear in her life. She'd lost her nerve again, and this time over Mallory as well as her work.

Caught off guard by Christa's impulsive departure, Mallory watched her hurtling along the narrow path, ignoring flints and tussocks of grass, her hands stuck in her pockets, shoulders set against him and the world. Suddenly her stubbornness infuriated him.

He caught up with her and grabbed her hand, forcing her to slow her pace to his.

'For God's sake,' he shouted at her, 'why won't you accept that you don't know everything about yourself?'

She turned towards him, the wind whipping her hair across her face. Her expression was so wretched that he forgot to be angry. He took her in his arms, wrapping them round her so that she couldn't run away.

'It's all right, it's all right,' he said, into the silken softness of her hair. 'Just stop panicking, and let's give this one more try. How about coming away with me in the Easter vacation? I've had an invitation from some friends in Cornwall. Just a trial run, no strings attached?'

Already she was less tense. As he felt her beginning to relax, he risked a joke.

'My friends have a boat. There's nothing like making love in a bunk to test a relationship, you know.'

There was a very long silence, followed by an encouragingly penitent laugh.

'Sounds interesting,' she said. 'How could I possibly refuse?'

18 ∫

When Christa returned to Oxford from Cornwall there was no time for further investigations into the identity of the mystery woman on the Waylandsbury dig. The holiday had been so good that she'd stayed much longer than she intended. The debate was scheduled for the first Friday in May. She'd given the students another chance to pull out at the beginning of term, but they were still determined to go ahead, so it was now even more vital to make a success of things.

As Christa surveyed the chapter house just before the porters opened the main doors to usher in the audience, she thought it probably hadn't seen such a potentially explosive gathering within its walls since Tudor times. She was standing in a gallery behind a fretted stone screen, where abbey visitors had once been able to monitor the deliberations of the monks, and which was now being used as a control centre. Rebekah, the producer, and Annabel, her assistant, armed with the shooting script, a monitor, and the radio microphone which linked them to the production team on the floor, were sitting at a trestle table with a perfect view of the entire chapter house.

The Domestic Bursar had produced two enormous banners of blue silk, painted with the gold leopard and silver lily from Gabriel's coat of arms. They'd been artfully draped to disguise the lightweight scaffolding supporting the floodlights.

As planned, chairs arranged by the porters in semi-circular rows faced two low tables on a dais. Behind one stood the Master's canopied and velvet-cushioned seat, formerly the abbot's throne, which was flanked by leather chairs borrowed from the college library for his special guests.

The porters, spurred on by hefty tips, had produced from the store a splendid set of ebony and gilt neo-Gothic chairs for the table at which the student panel would sit. Steve was going to head the panel, supported by three of Gabriel's leading lights in Union debates.

Privately Christa thought Rebekah would have been better in Steve's role, but she'd declined the honour.

'I'd love to, but no thanks,' she'd said. 'My mother's going to be in the audience. She'd instantly suspect I still had hankerings after a reporter's life. And anyway, if I were on camera it'd give the Master more ammunition. He could point out that I'm obvious proof of the college's non-chauvinist, non-racist principles.'

The centre of the chapter house now formed a circular arena where Justin, as presenter, would coordinate proceedings. On one side Mike was operating a fixed camera on a tripod, and at the other a large-screen monitor had been set up on which everyone could see the video footage. Donna, with the second camera, would move about as Ted, the floor manager, directed her.

At the moment he'd just finished dashing around with Lallie, his assistant, checking everything worked. Wires snaked across the flagstoned floor, and the floodlights had already taken any chill from the air. On a cue from Rebekah he signalled the porters to admit the audience. The heavy wooden doors were flung open, and people began to throng in, bringing with them the scent of roses from the quad outside.

Christa felt nervous in a way she hadn't done since Bosnia, as students, chattering like roosting starlings, crammed on to the hard stone bench around the wall and into the back rows of seats. According to Rebekah, ever wilder rumours had been circulating among them about the content of the debate.

She was hugely relieved to see Stacey and Glenn in the front of the audience, which had a good leavening of people from less rarified parts of the city to balance a large contingent from North Oxford. Wesley and Miriam were there too: a mixed blessing, for though Wesley would, if all went to plan, relay the news of the Master's downfall to the Dreaming Spires newsroom, he would view the proceedings with a mercilessly professional eye. Justin's father, whom she'd met earlier, was also a mixed blessing, boasting about his son in a voice like a public address system.

Mallory, only just returned from another promotion tour, had not yet appeared. They'd talked very little about the debate, and Christa sensed he was still unhappy about the media involvement in her investigation. But Leda, newly arrived from the Institute, came to the gallery especially to wish them luck.

'I think it's safer that I don't know what you're planning, but I'll be rooting for you from the floor,' she'd said, before leaving to take her seat among other members of the university in the audience.

'And here's Dr Gurney at last,' said Rebekah eagerly, as footsteps sounded again on the gallery stair. 'Now we shall really know what we're up against.'

The Master had threatened to fire any of the office staff who divulged the names of his guests before the debate, but Piers had promised to rush ahead of them after dinner to let Christa know their names.

'I've been listening to the biggest load of reactionary rubbish you've ever heard from the Master's team. But I'm afraid he has a run of aces, all the same,' said Piers, arriving out of breath at the top of the stair.

'Just get on with it, will you?' Christa said impatiently, worried that they'd appear before Rebekah could brief the floor crew.

'Well, for starters, Berkeley Greene.'

'God, that prat,' Rebekah groaned.

He was an art historian who ten years earlier had presented an immensely popular TV series on treasures of the British nation. He'd traded on his success to turn himself into an elder statesman of the arts. Though he was lampooned mercilessly by the young turks of the art world, middle Britain adored his reassuringly old-fashioned courtesy and the mellifluous voice which made his platitudes sound like extracts from the writings of Ruskin or Morris.

'At least no one under forty's going to take him seriously, but he does have a hell of a lot of clout. And I'm afraid there's worse to come,' said Piers. 'The Master's corralled Ceridwen as well.'

Christa began to feel as worried as Rebekah looked.

Ceridwen was a rock star who lived in a story-book manor house in the Cotswolds, and was devoted to the cause of conservation. She was so popular that the more impressionable of her followers tended to believe anything she said. All her opinions were pre-packaged for her, usually by her personal trainer, but tonight, no doubt, by the Master.

'At least she's an intellectual lightweight,' Christa said, trying to brace Rebekah. 'Justin and Steve'll run rings round her.'

'I doubt if they'll run rings round Sir Gregory Thomas,' said Piers.

'The physicist? The Nobel prize-winner?' Rebekah's voice was dismayed. 'God, we're going to have work hard to convince him.'

'Exactly,' Piers said. 'He has an international reputation, and masses of gravitas. He'll make the Master look good just by association. Anyway, I'm off to find a decent seat before the rest of the fellows turn up. I wouldn't miss this for anything.'

'Blimey, that's quite some line-up,' said Rebekah nervously, when Piers had gone, and Christa had given Justin and Steve a rapid briefing on the perils to come over the radio mike.

'None of them will be able to deny your video evidence,' said Christa. 'It's all there, for everyone to see.'

She'd half expected the Master not to follow the schedule he'd been sent, but at exactly ten to eight he entered the chapter house with his guests. A ripple of excitement went through the audience. He was followed by his usual retinue of older fellows. The younger ones, including Phil, were as usual at this hour fulfilling the demands of quality time.

At the last minute Mallory slipped in, and took a place at the back by a pillar. Christa was glad to be concealed from his distinctly unimpressed gaze.

The Master, a gracious smile stretched across his face, was wearing his usual dress at unofficial college events – the gown of some Middle European honorary doctorate, a magnificent ermine-bordered garment with sleeves of viridian silk which he draped like wings over the arms of his chair.

'So good of you to honour a student gathering,' Christa heard him say in his high, penetrating voice to his companions. 'I trust you'll make allowances for them.'

Berkeley Greene, in a velvet jacket, looked like an elderly seducer in a drawing-room comedy. He was sitting on the Master's left, his thick silver hair brushed back from a bland, well-fed face. To the Master's right, Ceridwen, black hair streaming across the shoulders of her white satin suit, smirked at the audience. Next to her the Nobel prize-winner, a spare, craggy-faced man with a distant expression, looked thoroughly out of place.

Ted gave the audience a five-, two- and one-minute warning, and vigorously quietened persistent chatterers with flaps of his hands. There was no opening music, for that would be dubbed in later, but on Rebekah's cue he started the debate exactly as Boanerges began to strike eight.

'Go for it, son!' bellowed Mr Seddon, bursting with pride as Justin, in a high-revered pinstripe suit, strode confidently into the centre of the arena.

'Welcome, everyone,' Justin said, gesturing expansively to the audience and keeping admirably calm. 'We're here tonight to discuss what Gabriel Hall stands for, and where it's heading. But before we begin, I should like to express the students' gratitude to the Master for his broad-mindedness in agreeing to this public debate.'

'That's right, Jus,' muttered Rebekah, as the Master beamed an acknowledgement. 'Get him well buttered up before he's roasted.'

'Although many of the students have lately begun to differ from the college establishment,' Justin continued, after he'd introduced the members of the panel, 'this doesn't mean they're ungrateful for the benefits Gabriel is able to offer them. These benefits are shown admirably in the official publicity film – part of it will be screened now, as an introduction to the establishment point of view in this debate. Later you'll be seeing video evidence filmed by the students of a rather different aspect of Gabriel Hall.'

A frown had appeared on the Master's face at the last sentence, but was rapidly replaced by an expression of smug self-satisfaction as a shortened version of the official video, activated by Justin with a hand-held remote control unit, rolled smoothly on to the public monitor. By the time it finished, all except the most conservative members of the audience looked as if they'd undergone death by chocolate. The fellows were trying to register interest in something they'd seen too often, and among the students beer cans were being surreptitiously produced.

'You'd better let the Master loose with the celebs before everyone dies of boredom,' Christa said to Rebekah.

'And now,' Justin said, smoothly picking up his cue on the radio mike, 'I call upon Professor Slade to lead his distinguished team in giving us their vision of the role of Gabriel Hall in the modern world.'

'Which I am particularly delighted to do, in view of the quite unfounded misapprehensions which seem to have arisen lately,' said the Master, rising from his canopied chair.

As he endlessly droned on about the need to maintain the high standards and caring traditions of Gabriel, gesturing with his silk-draped arms to emphasise his words, he gave a strong impression of speaking *ex cathedra*. Luckily Justin had learned a great deal from the disaster of the Margrave interview, and allowed him exactly five minutes before deftly moving on to the official guests.

The audience, who'd again been showing signs of strain, revived as Ceridwen in her enticingly husky voice expressed the same sentiments, but far more attractively, with much tossing of her hair, and crossing and uncrossing of her silver-stockinged legs. Luckily Berkeley Greene, who'd drunk too much Jubilee sherry, and was looking like a sleepy guinea-pig, dispensed only a few platitudes, mostly recycled from his TV documentary. And the Nobel prize-winner, whose mind still seemed far away, delivered the briefest of appreciations of his undergraduate days at Gabriel, before mentally returning to bosons and quarks.

Even so the students were looking particularly restless. A slow walk-out on their part could be disastrous, thought Christa, triggering the departure of the Master and his side-kicks as well.

'Next we come to something very different,' Justin said, 'a student video report on their view of Gabriel, the first part of which will focus on accommodation for second years and female post-graduates. Steve Drew, chairing the student panel, will provide comments as it's shown.'

Steve, using the remote control to freeze the footage when he wanted to emphasise a point, revealed himself as even more of a television natural than Justin. His laconic, razor-sharp comments soon had most of the audience eating out of his hand.

The footage had been made into a devastating indictment of the establishment, mixing interviews with the poorer students, cinéma-vérité shots of their sub-standard accommodation in town, and wickedly edited contrasts with the life style of the fellows and those second years who, like Justin, had managed through parental influence to stay in college.

It captured everyone's attention as firmly as a Quentin Tarantino movie. The parents in the audience were clearly horrified by the revelations. Several mothers screamed at a blood-curdling shot of a rat running across the kitchen table in Rebekah's narrow boat.

In the brief silence as the first part of the video ceased, the Master and his supporters among the fellows in the audience looked stunned. The Dean's wheezing filled the chapter house like the sound of someone trying to inflate an airbed.

'So you can see why we students feel as if the establishment really doesn't give a toss about us, why so much of what goes on in Gabriel at the moment is nothing but top dressing,' Steve went on rapidly, before the Master had come round sufficiently to speak. 'However, we know we're well off compared with some of the community outside. So in the second part of our presentation we want to show the problems among the under-privileged of Gabriel's Grounds Estate, also caused by the college's reluctance to share its wealth.'

The Master leaped up from his chair, flapping his arms like semaphore flags.

'I really must protest. Gabriel's Grounds Estate is most definitely not within the remit of this debate,' he protested.

Justin produced from his pocket the letter in which the Master had agreed to the terms of the interview.

'You did confirm, Master, in this letter, that each side should have twenty minutes to present its video evidence with complete freedom of comment. You and your supporters have been given that privilege. We've only had half our time. Surely you must agree that it's in the best tradition of Gabriel that we should have our full say too?'

'Shame, shame!' shouted the students, scenting an advantage, and drumming their feet delightedly on the stone floor. 'Let our video go on!'

Miriam, who was still bursting with indignation over the shot of the rat, jumped up, brandishing her scarf like a banner.

'Maskini! Mwizi!' she hurled at the Master. 'We put our children's lives in your care, you make them live with vermin, and then you try to deny them freedom of speech!'

'Shut up, Mum, for God's sake,' muttered Rebekah. 'There are plenty of rats in Mombasa too.'

As Wes hauled Miriam back into her seat, Justin's father, sensing that his son could be about to lose any further opportunity to shine, bellowed out, 'Aye, let the young ones have their say. I've not put good money into this college to see it misused.'

The Master, eyes popping with fury as he realised he was on the point of losing one of the college's most valuable benefactors, subsided into his chair, and angrily motioned Justin to continue. A great cheer burst from the students.

'Quickly! Cue the Gabriel's Grounds piece!' Christa said to Rebekah. 'We've got to get it rolling before the Master changes his mind!'

This time the audience was riveted, and especially by Rebekah's interviews with the young single mothers on the estate. When the video ended Ted was almost unable to control a spontaneous outburst of clapping and comment. Leda was frowning with concern, and Christa could see Stacey only just managing to restrain Glenn from a public outburst.

Justin rapidly resumed his grip on the action before the Master had time to forestall him.

'I'm sure, Professor Slade, you'd like to start our panel discussion by explaining exactly why the college has chosen to ignore both the needs of its students, and its promise to the Gabriel's Grounds Estate. After that we'll hear what the other members of the two panels have to say, and at the end there'll be a chance for the audience to air its views.'

The Master had already resumed his usual hard-boiled expression.

'I'm delighted to be able to explain,' he said. 'The Governing Body of Gabriel holds the welfare of its students and of the less privileged in the highest regard. Both these matters have been exercising our minds for some considerable time, and will, I am confident, very soon be resolved to the satisfaction of everyone concerned.'

'But what does "very soon" mean, Master?' Steve broke in. 'As many of those here know to their cost, time moves slowly at Gabriel.'

'I very much hope that something will be settled by the time I retire as Master, at the end of this academic year.'

'And how will it be settled, exactly?' Steve pressed.

'That, I'm afraid, it would not be in the interests of anyone to reveal. There are various delicate negotiations still taking place.'

'I don't understand,' Steve persisted. 'Why should negotiations be necessary to fulfil a simple promise?'

But though Steve and his team worried the Master like a pack of terriers in the discussion that followed, they were unable to produce anything more specific. Berkeley Greene and Ceridwen, taking their cue from the Master, were infuriatingly sheep-like. Sir Gregory, clearly a man of few words, asked one or two questions the Master was only just able to field, but otherwise confined himself to making notes in the back of a diary.

Christa was beginning to worry at their lack of progress.

'This is becoming too much of a cliff-hanger,' she said to Rebekah. 'Cue Justin to wind up the panel debate, and let's see if the audience can get a better response from the Master.'

Donna and the hired sound man, in trainers so that they could move silently around the chapter house, nobly tried to keep up with infuriated questions from the floor. These the Master again stonewalled, with a masterly lack of commitment. The fellows, many looking ashamed but clearly sensing they'd be in deep trouble if they made any comment, were silent. Of them all, only Leda spoke up.

'I consider it disgraceful that Professor Saltash's promise has not yet been carried out,' she said, in a clear voice which carried all round the chapter house. 'I have every sympathy with the students and the estate, and when I take over as Master I promise to do everything in my power to restore the good reputation of Gabriel.'

Glenn's patience had run out. He leaped up, arms folded across his chest, muscles bulging through his jacket sleeves, looking ready to flatten the Master.

'That's all very well, but I'm a member of the tenants' committee at the estate, and we need a specific reply now about if and when the Mill site is going to be developed for our benefit. It's ten years since the last Master died, and since then Gabriel has given us nothing but bullshit.'

Both Mike and Donna trained their cameras on the Master for his reply. It felt as if the whole chapter house was holding its breath.

'As I've already said, this problem will be resolved by the time I retire as Head of House. I feel it's not unreasonable to ask you to restrain yourself and your colleagues until then, Mr . . . er . . .'

'And what does that mean on the bottom line? Yes or no? I'm warning you, Professor, there's a lot of unrest, a lot of ill-feeling on the estate. You've only seen a small part of it on the students' video. You're bloody lucky it hasn't turned into violent protest yet.'

Some of the students started a slow handclap. Ted signalled to them furiously to keep quiet. Steve leaped into the fray again.

'The students would be a lot happier too if they could have an unequivocal undertaking about these problems, Professor Slade.'

'That seems fair to me, Master,' said Sir Gregory, who had up to now continued to sit like an Easter Island statue.

'Frankly I too must say I'm a little surprised that this has been allowed to drag on so long,' said Berkeley Greene, ever anxious to keep on the side of an audience.

'I guess I have to agree with the students too,' said Ceridwen. 'My heart's always been with kids from every walk of life. I'm nothing but a big kid myself, and I was brought up on an estate. Come on, Prof, make everyone's day, commit yourself. Because that's what this world is about, commitment, isn't it everyone?'

She raked the audience with a smile like a searchlight.

'It seems everyone here wants a firm undertaking from you, Master,' said Steve.

'Very well. Naturally I cannot undertake anything without the approval of Governing Body, but I do give this assurance – that the matter will reach a resolution at its next meeting, which is only two weeks away.' He looked at his watch. 'By my reckoning, we have twenty minutes left, Mr Drew. I suggest that you proceed with all speed to the summing up. Our distinguished guests must be wanting refreshment, and I'm not anxious to subject them to a moment longer of this farrago than necessary.'

'We haven't nailed him!' said Rebekah distractedly. 'I'm going to have to cue Justin to use the Gabriel's Mill footage and the Margrave interviews.'

'Just as you wish, Master,' said Justin. 'Instead of a formal summing up of their case, the students have chosen to show a final piece of film. And after that you and your panel will, as requested, have the last word on behalf of the college. Steve, will you introduce your video?'

'Sure thing,' he said, turning easily to the audience. 'The Master implied that nothing has been settled yet, but I think other conclusions will be drawn from what you're going to see next. Watch it, and decide for yourselves.'

Even the Master sat goggle-eyed as the activities of Margrave's planners at Gabriel's Mill were damningly revealed. Wes had stopped laughing and was frantically making notes. Mallory grew increasingly grim-faced. When Tony's evidence, spliced brilliantly for contrast with the Sir Jerry interview, provided the final *coup-de-grâce*, the Master looked as if he'd been struck by the hand of God.

At the end of the video Glenn didn't even wait for Justin to call for an official reply. He shot out of his seat, shaking a huge fist at the Master.

'You double-crosser,' he shouted. 'You've kept the estate on a string for ten bloody years. Gabriel honour? Gabriel fair play? It's just a fucking con. Get out of this one if you can, Professor. Go on, speak up, we're all waiting to hear you!'

'Speak, speak, speak,' the students round the wall began to chant, leaping on to the stone seat, joining raised arms and swaying like a football crowd. Christa grabbed the radio mike.

'Calm them down, Ted! The Master's got to be heard. He has to condemn himself.'

Ted strode around the arena, making damping down gestures with his arm which were finally heeded.

The Master, ashen but still worryingly resolute, got up, this time without a single grandiose gesture.

'Ladies and gentlemen,' he said, 'I am as shocked and distressed as you by what I've just seen. As I said earlier, this matter has been discussed at meetings of the relevant college committee, but I had no idea that anything said then would be taken further without the agreement of Governing Body. However, if I remember correctly, an approach to Margrave's was mooted at one stage by the Dean.'

Christa felt like a climber suddenly encountering a precipice between her and an almost-attained peak. The Master was about to blame everything on Dr Anstruther, who'd fallen back in his chair, speechless with asthma and shock.

'Though I'm sure he had the college's best interests at heart,' the Master drove on relentlessly, 'I can only assume that he unwisely went ahead on his own initiative. Perhaps, Dean, you could confirm that that is so?'

'Jesus, this is horrible,' said Christa, remembering Piers had told her the Dean owed his promotion to the Master.

She felt she was watching a living sacrifice, as Dr Anstruther, purple-faced, wheezing like a pair of broken bellows, sweat beading his forehead, hauled himself out of his chair to face his accuser. He was scarcely able to stand. Miss Harker, who'd been sitting nearby, rushed to his side.

'Isn't it true, Dean,' said the Master in his most impassive voice, 'that you took matters into your own hands, from the best of motives I'm sure, and asked Margrave's to draw up this pilot scheme?'

'He's not well, Master!' said Miss Harker frantically. 'He needs help. Call an ambulance, someone!'

'My God, this is public crucifixion of the wrong guy,' said Rebekah in awe.

'Yes, yes, I take full responsibility,' the Dean wheezed, and collapsed back in his seat, his hand clutching his chest, while Miss Harker anxiously loosened his collar and tie. 'I'm sorry. I apologise to everyone here for a most misguided act.'

'Just as I thought. And perhaps you'd be good enough to

confirm that matters were taken no further than the pilot scheme that the students have so providentially revealed?' said the Master relentlessly.

'Yes, yes, nothing further was done!' puffed the Dean, his lips blue, and his chest labouring like a runner's at the finishing post.

'Just as I thought, so I trust that the audience will not force me to put a very sick man through any more of this ordeal. In the interests of his health, I shall forgo my summing-up and trust that everyone here will regard the matter as closed. I most certainly do, and deeply regret that I ever agreed to take part in this farce.'

He swept out of the Chapter House, bearing Berkeley Greene and Ceridwen with him, and accompanied by his deflated retinue, who were obviously wondering if his axe was about to fall on any of them.

The audience burst into a hub-bub of conjecture while the Dean, barely conscious, was supported away into the fresh air to await an ambulance. Annabel had already rushed off to congratulate Justin. The students were conducting an indignant meeting among themselves, Wes was finishing his notes, Glenn had gathered a band of North Oxford sympathisers and was offering conducted tours of the estate, and Miriam was filling in Justin's father on more of the Master's iniquities.

Christa stared at Rebekah, still stunned by the ruthless way the Master had sacrificed the Dean.

'That was wonderful television,' she said slowly, 'but at a huge cost. I'd never have allowed you to go ahead if I'd known this would happen. The Dean's not evil, just weak. He didn't deserve to be destroyed like that.'

'I agree,' said Rebekah, fanning her flushed face with the script. 'But at least our footage can be edited to make a fabulous competition entry. And the Master won't dare take it out on us now it's all in the public domain, and the parents know what's going on. We've made people think, which is what we wanted, surely?'

Christa, watching the audience begin to disperse, didn't answer. Mallory was talking gravely to Sir Gregory. She'd have to go down to the floor to supervise the clearing up, and she wasn't looking forward to his comments. She'd expected to present him with a triumph, but instead the Master's reputation was still intact, though only just.

She was furious with herself for not having come back earlier from Cornwall to pursue her investigation into the Waylandsbury dig. Now she had less than two weeks before the meeting of Governing Body in which to find more evidence to discredit him.

Mallory, still talking to Sir Gregory, surreptitiously watched Christa deal with the porters' grumbles while they cleared the room. Though she was moving about with her usual confident, springy step, she was carefully avoiding his gaze.

He also had been going through a maelstrom of emotions. He was deeply disturbed by the public humiliation of the Dean, which had helped no one except the Master, and the debate had reinforced his suspicion that Christa would be unable to give up the all-absorbing pursuit of a confrontational career. But most of all, he was full of misgivings about the imminent arrival of Gareth Hyde.

Christa still hadn't mentioned it, though she must have seen the guest-list for the Founder's Feast posted in the common room. The subject was so inextricably tied to Matthew Brady's death that he hadn't wanted to hurt her by asking outright how she felt about Gareth now. Yet he'd never forgotten that Christa had once said Gareth was like a drug she couldn't give up.

When Sir Gregory had departed for the Master's Lodge at last, Mallory went to join her. She looked at him warily.

'If you're going to say I told you so, I'm not interested,' she said. 'I still think we were right to hold the debate.'

'I was going to say I've missed you,' he answered, kissing her. 'It's a wonderful evening. Why don't we walk by the river, and eat afterwards in town?'

She was so wrong-footed by this approach that he managed to get her to the riverside path at the edge of the deer park without argument. There they were comparatively private, apart from a couple of punts drifting along the stream whose occupants were interested in nothing but themselves. He took her hand.

He sensed a resistance in it, and knew she was still on the defensive. She'd been stealing glances at him, as if trying to assess his mood.

'So, are you pleased with the way the discussion went?' he asked.

'Of course I'm not. It didn't give me pleasure to see the wrong person destroyed, or the wrong side lose.'

'Do you have to think of it in those terms? It's not a war.'

He hadn't meant to sound critical, but realised too late that he did. She pulled her hand away and thrust it into the pocket of the linen jacket she was wearing with her jeans. He sneaked a glance at her. Her expression was mutinous.

'I'm well aware of went wrong,' she said, turning to face him under a beech tree whose newly unfurled leaves were a vibrant green in the last rays of light. 'But I still believe it was better to have done it than not at all.'

'All the same, I don't think you should take things any further.'

She stared at him, her face pale and intense beneath the rustling leaves.

'Not go on! But that negates everything I've tried to do so far, everything the students have risked!'

'You've all risked quite enough. The Master knows exactly what you're up to now, but you have no way of knowing what he's planning behind the scenes. The only way to get at him really effectively is through the corridors of power. I've been talking to Gregory Thomas. He has a lot of influence here. I gave him a full run down on what's going on, and he's agreed to help. I can pull a few other strings too.'

She looked depressingly unreceptive.

'But that's so risky, so vague. If the Master gets this past the next meeting of Governing Body, too many people will suffer. And he still doesn't know I'm investigating the rumour about the Waylandsbury Hoard.'

Mallory thought bleakly that he might have known she wouldn't give up that particular wild goose chase.

'Look, I didn't especially want to get involved, but I will, if it keeps you out of it,' he said. 'Leave this to me, and I swear I'll stop the Master, but in my way.'

It would mean lobbying, manipulating, asking for and calling in favours, everything he most disliked, but he was desperate for her to agree. It would prove she wasn't irrevocably hooked on the buzz of confrontation.

She hesitated, but her hand came out of her pocket and took his again. They began to walk on. On the other side of the river, the Gabriel deer raised their heads from the grass, and gazed at them with huge mild eyes as they passed.

'If you let me take over and try to get him removed quietly, there'll be no danger of destroying Gabriel as well as the Master. If everyone's forced to take sides in public and Leda inherits a totally demoralised and discredited college, it'll take years to rebuild its reputation.'

'Maybe you're right,' she said slowly. 'But I'm not sure if I can let this go. It's important to me. Because of the way Matt died, I need to prove I can accomplish something really big again.'

He put his arm round her, feeling an enormous rush of relief that she'd admitted this much to him.

'But not by flinging yourself into more confrontation and destruction. You're trying to prove yourself the wrong way.'

She rested her head against his shoulder. 'Maybe,' she said, again refusing to look at him. 'I'm not sure. I'll think about it.'

They'd moved into a green tunnel of pleached limes as they walked on. She stopped to kiss him, like a child who was trying to impress with her good intentions.

'We have to talk about Gareth as well,' he said. 'You must know he's coming to the Feast. I need to know what his visit's going to do to you.'

There was another long silence. It was almost dark beneath the trees, and the path and the river were deserted.

'It won't do anything,' she said, twining her arms round his neck like the branches above them, and punctuating her words with more kisses. 'With you around I shall hardly notice he's there. I'll prove it to you now.'

Mallory gave up. He couldn't resist her in this mood, though he knew she was using the most basic ploy of all to get out of a straight answer. Or rather, he could have resisted, but suddenly didn't know how he'd cope if she admitted Gareth Hyde still had a hold over her.

At least she looked more glamorous than when she'd seen Gareth last, Christa thought, surveying herself in the cloakroom mirror before entering the common room for drinks before the Feast. She'd bought a dress which had wiped out a week's salary, a clinging garment of black silk crêpe, long-sleeved and almost ankle-length but slit at one side to mid-thigh. With it she wore high-heeled sandals and a choker of jet.

Christa had made love to Mallory by the river out of sheer desperation, and bitterly despised herself for doing so. Afterwards she'd found an excuse for him not to come back to Jericho with her, the first time she'd deliberately excluded him, and she thought wretchedly that Gareth had already begun to spoil things.

She would have liked to avoid the Feast altogether, but that would have made Mallory even more suspicious. As it was, he'd suggested they went to it together and she'd had to make another excuse, knowing she needed to be alone when she met Gareth.

She'd deliberately chosen to arrive as late as possible, and when she entered the common room it was already thronged with fellows and guests. The windows were open, and more guests were wandering about in the garden, admiring the collection of old-fashioned roses for which it was renowned.

At first Christa had no time to look for Gareth. She was too busy receiving the congratulations of an encouragingly broad cross-section of fellows on the revelations in the chapter house. The Master, from whom she'd expected anything from veiled intimidation to a formal complaint to Jimmy Judd, behaved as though the debate had never taken place, and she began to realise Mallory's assessment of his character was right.

He was a consummate diplomat. He guessed, not without reason, that she'd exhausted her fire-power, and at the moment saw no point in wasting further energy on her. He was saving his resources for the now all-important meeting with Governing Body.

When she was alone again, Christa took a glass of sherry

from a passing butler, and began to scan the guests. She was looking for Gareth's prize-fighter's shoulders among the men's dinner-jackets, and trying to pick up the deep, distinctive timbre of his voice.

At first, almost with a sense of disappointment because she'd psyched herself up so much for the meeting, she thought he wasn't there. But then she caught sight of him near the fire-place, blatantly chatting up Ceridwen who along with the other panellists had been invited to the Feast. He looked as piratical as ever, his tight-curled hair gleaming above his swarthy face, wearing a black shirt and white tuxedo which made him seem ridiculously Hollywoodish but more sexy than any other man there.

Any other man apart from Mallory, that was, Christa thought distractedly. He was deep in conversation with Leda by the bay window, cool and self-contained in an evening suit most definitely not from Beverly Hills, his blond hair darkened to gold in the evening light, his long, quirky mouth so different from Gareth's.

Christa felt dizzy as she contemplated the two of them, as if she were being forced to choose between creatures from the dark and light side of the moon. Her gaze went back to Gareth. He suddenly caught her eye, and sent her a long hot look which gave her the same feeling of sickness and excitement as a visit to the Chamber of Horrors as a child.

'Animal magnetism at its most obvious,' Piers commented acidly in her ear. 'One understands, yet doesn't understand, what women see in Hyde. We've just had a fascinating little chat, and as far as I can discern his brains appear to reside mainly in his balls.'

Christa giggled and felt slightly better.

'Farrar's just been talking to him about Rwanda. He wiped the floor with him verbally,' Piers continued. 'I got the impression that he'd have liked to beat the hell out of him physically as well. Have you spoken to him yourself yet?'

'No, thank God, and I don't want to. That's why I've arrived so late, and once dinner's over I shan't wait for coffee. With luck I won't have to speak to him at all.'

'I thought you'd rather relish a confrontation.'

'Then you thought wrong. I don't intend to give him that pleasure.'

'Good heavens, can this be the Christa we know and love, practising restraint at last? Farrar must be having an influence on you. But you're a bit over-optimistic. I presume you haven't yet seen the placement for dinner.'

Christa stared at him in dawning horror. She'd had no opportunity to study the plan pinned discreetly to the common-room notice board.

'You're sitting next to Gareth Hyde,' Piers announced, looking delighted at the consternation he'd caused.

'But I can't! Who could have done this to me? Don't tell me – Mrs Slade!'

'Wasn't it rather naive to expect otherwise after the way you got at the Master in the debate?'

Christa ignored him, trying frantically to think of some way out. The butler had just appeared in the doorway with the brass gong which heralded dinner.

'Swap places with me, Piers,' she said. 'You must. I won't get through it otherwise.'

'Sorree. Any other time, but not today. I'm next to Ceridwen. You couldn't possibly expect me to pass up a chance like that. Why don't you ask Farrar? I'm sure he'd love to defend your honour.'

As the gong sounded Christa realised she'd have to tough things out. Though it was infinitely tempting to appeal to Mallory, and she knew how much it would please him, she couldn't off-load her problem on him now.

Sticking close to Piers, as she hadn't done since first going to primary school in Emma's care, she progressed with the other guests into the Great Hall. It was the first time she'd attended a formal celebration there. The students had been relegated to an earlier meal, and the heavy oak tables were arranged in a horse-shoe setting in the body of the hall.

Paintings of past Masters and benefactors stared down quizzically from the panelled walls. On the tables branching candelabra illuminated gleaming cutlery, sparkling crystal, the glossy folds of damask napery, and magnificent silver salt-cellars shaped like Triton shells. At the top table, in front of the Master, was the famous Gabriel centrepiece: gilded figures of the Muses holding up a garland of white tea roses and heliotrope from the fellows' garden.

When Christa found her seat, Gareth hadn't yet taken his place on her right. Mallory was sitting two places away on the opposite side of the table, where he could see every nuance of her behaviour, but she couldn't easily speak to him.

It was, no doubt, another of Mrs Slade's sadistic little ploys, she thought. She looked away hastily to find out who was on her other side, and discovered Tom Carver there. Mrs Slade had probably done that to annoy her as well, but at least he'd be quite happy to drone away at her all evening, so that she need only address the briefest of remarks to Gareth.

Though the hall, always chilly, was warmed by a blaze of logs in the massive stone fireplace, her skin crawled with gooseflesh as she sensed Gareth sitting down by her side. She heard him pull up his chair, smelt the scent of Aramis, and was suddenly bowled over by a flood of memories.

She looked across the table, saw Mallory gazing at her, and was briefly steadied. There was another reprieve as they stood to hear the chaplain say grace, but all the time Gareth's bulk seemed to loom over her.

'You're looking well, *cariad*,' he said, the moment their chairs had scraped back into place. The deep Welsh voice which used to seem so attractive now sounded utterly false. 'How's life?'

The casualness of the enquiry made her forget every resolution to ignore him.

'Don't *cariad* me, you bastard,' she hissed at him, as a butler slid a plate of asparagus *Maltaise* in front of her. Luckily the table was wide, but she was terrified in case Mallory heard their conversation. 'How dare you turn up here? You as good as murdered Matt, and my reputation too. Wasn't that enough for you? You're bloody lucky I didn't have the money to take you to court.'

'You don't look much of a victim to me,' said Gareth, his brown eyes fixed on her in amusement as he slapped butter on a piece of roll. 'You seem to have landed on your feet all right. And I was bloody upset at the way you went for me in that Heathrow interview.'

'*I* went for *you*! How about the lies you'd spread about me?' Christa was already nearly speechless with fury.

He picked up a piece of asparagus and crammed it into his mouth, chewing with huge gusto, lips shiny with sauce.

'They were true, you know. I did you a good turn getting you away from Bosnia. You were played out. The big time was too big for you. In another month you'd have been dead as well as Matt.'

'For Christ's sake, surely you must feel some responsibility for the way he died? And for what his sister had to go through. She adored him, and he was her only family.'

He smiled at her mockingly. 'It was your decision to risk the front line, not mine.'

'It was your decision to ditch me. Don't even try to deny it to my face.'

'Yeah, OK, it was.' Gareth took a gulp of Chablis as though it was water. 'Quite frankly, I thought the relationship was beginning to stifle us. You were getting so bloody involved. I did try to warn you, but you didn't want to listen. Calm down and get on with your dinner, like a good girl, and let's talk about something else.'

Christa was almost incandescent with rage by now, but she retained just enough command of herself to glance again at Mallory. The expression on his face, of profound concern mixed with a fury of his own which looked as though it too was only just being controlled, scared her as she'd never been scared before.

With an enormous effort she deliberately turned her back on Gareth, and in a voice which sounded more like a croak, managed to ask Tom Carver about his new job. It was the hardest thing she'd ever done in her life, but mercifully Gareth's attention was instantly monopolised by Mrs Carver on his right, and Tom Carver was more than happy to maunder on indefinitely about his future plans.

Christa could scarcely touch the smoked sturgeon which followed, or the rack of lamb *poivrade*, but by the time raspberry mousse with a marsala sauce arrived, and Gareth hadn't spoken to her again, she began to feel slightly better and realise her ordeal was coming to an end. Mallory, now chatting to the Senior Tutor, looked more relaxed too.

She'd just decided she could try a little of the mousse, and had put a spoonful in her mouth, when to her horror she felt Gareth's hand on her thigh in the slit of her skirt. His fingers began to trace the light, persuasive circles which had always been his secret signal to her that he wanted to leave and go to bed.

She almost choked and hurriedly put down her spoon. As she grabbed a glass of water, Gareth's fingers began to move upwards beyond her stocking top, kneading her skin, gently pinching it and raking it with his nails. Luckily his hand was concealed beneath the vast damask dinner napkin which lay in her lap, but Mallory was staring at her with a frown.

Frantically she tried moving her leg away, but still Gareth's hand progressed onward, reaching the lace edge of her pants, until one sly finger infiltrated the crease of her groin. This time she felt the awful Pavlovian response, a response she didn't want, of desire mixed with loathing. She couldn't understand how it was possible to have the two feelings at the same time.

In utter desperation she put down her glass, slid her unused dessert fork under the napkin, and jabbed it violently into his thigh, trying to look as though she was doing nothing more radical than brush a crumb from a lap.

She heard his sharp intake of break as his hand was hastily withdrawn. Casually she resumed her dessert, though the mousse trembled in the bowl of the spoon. She felt him incline towards her, so close that his lips touched her hair.

Mallory was so still and tense that he scared her. His eyes had deepened to a very dark blue, as they always did when he was aroused.

'So you still care,' Gareth said, with a low, intimate laugh which made several people look in their direction. 'I thought you might.'

'You're the last person I'd care for now,' she hissed back desperately. 'I loathe you. Back off, will you, for Christ's sake?'

She couldn't help glancing at Mallory again. Gareth intercepted the look, and she remembered too late that he was like a homing device when he sensed competition.

'You protest too much, *cariad*,' he said. 'Aren't you getting enough of the right stuff from your frosty friend over there? You always were a babe who needed a good seeing to.'

'Sod off, Gareth. I won't tell you again. Next time you'll have the fork where it really hurts. I've a good mind to do it anyway. Someone should have years ago.'

'OK, OK, there's no need to lose your rag,' he said lazily. 'And with an old friend too, one who's brought you a special present as well.'

'I don't want any more presents of any sort from you.'

'You will this time. It's Matt's St Christopher.'

Christa stared at him. Matt's sister had given him the St Christopher medallion which he always wore, and after his death she was desperate to have it as a keepsake. But it wasn't round his neck when he arrived at the army hospital, and Christa had always assumed it'd been lost somewhere in the front line.

'How did you find it?' she asked wonderingly.

'I was back in Bosnia recently, covering the UN peace operation. It had been found by someone at the Hilton. Matt's name was engraved on the back. The chain was broken, so it must have fallen off there. The manager asked me to see it got to the next-of-kin.'

'For God's sake, Gareth, give it to me. It means so much to Matt's sister. She was terribly upset because it had disappeared.'

'I thought you might be pleased,' he said with a complacent smile. 'But it's in my room, I'm afraid. I'm staying in college. How about coming along to collect it before we have coffee in the SCR?'

Again Christa's skin crawled with cold.

'You can't be serious. You bring it here.'

'Surely you're not scared to be alone with me again?' he taunted her. 'You said you loathed me. So prove it. Come to my room. Otherwise you're not getting the St Christopher.'

Christa shot a glance at Mallory. He was deep in conversation again. She could easily pretend to go to the cloakroom, and disappear for ten minutes or so. She had to, both for Matt and herself.

'All right,' she said recklessly. 'As soon as dinner's over, I'll meet you in Cloister Quad.'

19

Gareth had a guestroom on the first floor of Cloister Quad. It was sparsely but adequately supplied with some uninspired modern furniture, prints of college scenes, and a chest of drawers on which was prominently displayed a saucer for the scout's tip on the guest's departure.

It would be well-earned after Gareth's stay, thought Christa. He was dramatically untidy. Wherever he went, underpaid overworked hotel maids, charmed by his flattery, daily restored order only for it to be immediately destroyed again. In his wake shirts spilled out of drawers, discarded clothing was flung on the backs of chairs, and jackets dangled lopsidedly from wire hangers looped over wardrobe doors.

This occasion was no exception. Three empty beer cans, a bottle of whisky, a plastic toothmug, cigarettes, and an empty bag of salted nuts occupied the bedside table. Half the nuts were scattered over the carpet. Pages of the *Gorgon* were strewn round an armchair, and a sodden towel lay on the window seat.

Gareth went over to the bedside table and picked up the mug and cigarettes, waving them at Christa.

'Drink? Smoke?' he said. 'You need to lighten up, *cariad*.'

'Just give me the St Christopher. That's all I need. I don't want to spend a moment more than I have to with you.'

Gareth sat down on the edge of the bed, which was already in a chaotic state. He couldn't take the shortest of naps without subjecting sheets and pillows to a radical work-out. Casually he poured himself a large slug of whisky, and lit a cigarette.

Christa was so wound up that when the smoke hit her nostrils she felt like a junkie deprived of a fix.

'Come on, you bastard, stop playing about, and tell me where the St Christopher is.'

Gareth leaned back against the pillows and thumped his legs on to the bed, inflicting further devastation on the coverlet. He put down the mug and left his cigarette to smoulder on the bare wood of the bedside table.

Insolently, lazily, he pulled off his tuxedo, and dropped it on the floor. His bow tie followed, and keeping his eyes on her like a male stripper, he pulled the buttons of his pleated dress shirt apart.

'I had the chain mended. It's here,' he said. 'You'd better come and get it.'

She could see the medallion half hidden in the pelt of hair on his chest. It seemed obscene for him to be wearing it instead of Matt. She felt sick again and sat down heavily on the end of the bed, thinking with grim humour that it'd serve him right if she threw up over his patent leather shoes.

'Why are you still trying to destroy me?' she asked. 'Surely you've done enough?'

'Not destroy you. Just finally bring you to heel. You were always a stroppy bitch. That was your attraction – and your problem.'

'I didn't have any problem, Gareth. You were the one who was all screwed up, only I didn't know it. You had my love, but you're so greedy it wasn't enough. You couldn't handle my success, so you had to have my career too. And now I'm rebuilding my life, you're jealous again. That's why you want to cut me down to size.'

'Rebuilding your life, are you? In this backwater? Wasting your life, I'd say.'

'A lot of good things go on here which someone like you couldn't even begin to appreciate,' retorted Christa.

Gareth looked at her curiously.

'Don't tell me they really matter to you, this tinpot place and its tiny concerns? You must be losing your grip.'

'If you find it so boring, why did you bother to come at all? You've always said how much you hated Oxford. Was it just out of spite?'

'Give me a little credit, pet. As it happens I've got a rather juicy assignment for Metro here on Monday. Something hush-hush, not the sort of thing I usually do but potentially big. You'd love it. What a pity I can't take you along.'

Christa wondered if he was making up the assignment to needle her, then forgot about it entirely as he delivered his next taunt.

'Your place is in the real world, with real men, not people like Farrar. I can see he's got the hots for you, but he's not your type. You need excitement, and you won't get that on the hippy trail.'

'Excitement like being framed? Excitement like the death of my friend? Mallory's the best thing that's happened to me for years.'

'Stop kidding yourself. You need someone who can keep you in order, and you know it.'

'That's the only sort of relationship you understand, isn't it?' she said scornfully. 'Because it's the only sort of relationship with a woman you're able to have. I'm sorry for you, Gareth, because you miss so much. I miss nothing of what I had with you.'

'Not even the sex?' he said lazily, keeping his eyes on her. 'Not even the tiniest bit?'

He was such an exploitative bastard, she thought, crushing a sneaking, queasy worry that perhaps he was right. She had to get out, to get the medallion and go.

'All I want from you is Matt's St Christopher,' she said, sizing up the distance between them and the length of the chain. She wasn't going to get it over his head without making herself very vulnerable.

'I've already told you. Come and get it.'

His eyes were lively, dark, shining, like a fox waiting to spring.

'You'll have to lift your head so I can take the chain off,' she said.

'You'll have to kiss me first.'

There was no alternative. He was too strong for her to risk a surprise attack. She bent down, and put her lips on his. Gareth's breath was heavy with whisky and tobacco smoke. She felt as though she was cheapening everything she'd shared with Mallory.

One of Gareth's hands raked through her hair, dragging it over her face as he pulled her towards him. The other hand shot into the front of her dress and pounced on a breast, kneading it roughly through the silk of her bra. She waited for her usual helpless, excited response, and instead felt nothing but revulsion. The heat of his body, his smell, the crudity of his approach, now disgusted her.

She grabbed the chain, gathering the two strands together, and flung herself backwards with her full weight. The chain snapped. He cursed as she dragged it away.

She made for the inner door, wrenched it open, dashed through, and slammed the outer door back in his face before rushing away down the stairs. Once outside she tore along the cloister, turned into King's Quad, and took a short cut across the sacred grass. As she did so she cannoned into Mallory, who was coming in the opposite direction just as fast. He must have been looking for her in her room, she thought hysterically.

He grabbed her arm, staring at her through narrowed eyes which had become such a dark blue that they were almost black.

'You've been with Hyde, haven't you? You couldn't keep away, even after what he did to you.'

The contempt in his voice made her feel like a tart. She suddenly realised how she must look, with her hair falling over her face, and her dress off one shoulder, but there was no time to answer, for Gareth's footsteps were pounding nearer and nearer. Mallory released her arm as though throwing it from him.

Gareth's face, flushed with whisky and the numerous glasses of wine he'd drunk during the Feast, took on an expression of gloating triumph as he realised the depth of Mallory's fury.

'Couldn't keep her, could you?' he taunted. 'Christa wants a real man, not a wanker like you.'

He staggered slightly before steadying himself. Christa hadn't realised quite how drunk he was, and when drunk Gareth loved stirring up a brawl.

Mallory was watching him with a tense stillness she'd seen only once before in the confrontation at the covered market.

'Why not let Christa make up her own mind what she wants?'

he said. 'If she knows, that is,' he added with a look in her direction that froze her.

'She doesn't need to,' said Gareth. 'There's no contest. There never was. Because she still wants me.'

His voice was getting louder. Several windows were open above them, and students' heads were starting to pop out. Christa thought despairingly that the situation was rapidly acquiring all the characteristics Mallory most loathed and Gareth most loved.

'What do you think I've been giving Christa while you've been sounding off with those other back-numbers in the SCR?' Gareth went on. His voice was now as loud as a tabernacle harmonium. It echoed through the quad. 'A good shagging, and that's what she knows she'll always get from me. So I'm taking her back, and you, buster, won't lift a finger to stop me, because basically you don't have the bottle.'

Heads were appearing all round the quad. Christa couldn't bear it. Gareth was making her feel like a bitch caught between two dogs. For the first time in her life she contemplated running away, but he clamped a sweaty hand round her wrist.

'Come on, pet, let's get back to where we left off,' he slurred.

'Leave her alone,' said Mallory, beginning to move towards Gareth.

'It's all right. I can deal with him. He's just drunk. And he's lying, anyway,' said Christa frantically, realising that the unbelievable was about to happen. Mallory was prepared to fight in public with Gareth.

Gareth let Christa go and swayed in Mallory's direction.

'Come on, boyo! Let's be having you!' he shouted, and launched a sledgehammer punch at Mallory's head.

Mallory ducked so fast he seemed like a flying shadow. He whirled round, and with his arm held rigidly across his body, rammed his elbow upwards into Gareth's ribs.

Gareth gasped, staggered back, and recovered himself. He lashed out with another blow. Again Mallory dodged, and landed a sideways kick like a tomahawk just above Gareth's knee.

Gareth swayed backwards, and toppled into the fountain in the centre of the quad. There was an enormous splash. A sheet of water rose into the air. He emerged clinging to a dolphin, was too drunk to heave himself out, and slowly slid back into the water, where he sat swearing and spitting out bits of weed.

A huge wave of applause went round the quad. Christa looked up and saw students hanging out of the windows, cheering and wolf-whistling. Her legs felt like left-over pasta. She couldn't have run away if she'd wanted to.

Mallory was stony-faced as he returned to her. He took her arm, and propelled her towards Bohemia Quad and their stair. On the landing by his room he finally let her go.

'I hope that's enough public exposure for one evening, even for you,' he said in a voice which made her wince.

'It wasn't like Gareth said, it wasn't, I swear!' said Christa frantically. 'He had Matt's St Christopher. It was in his room. I had to go there to get it back. Look!'

She held out her clenched hand and unfolded it, showing him the medallion in her palm and the broken chain. He still looked totally unimpressed.

'Don't you remember I told you how much Matt's sister had wanted it?' she said in desperation. His expression thawed slightly.

'How did Hyde get hold of it?' he asked

'It was left with the manager at the Sarajevo Hilton. I had to get it. Matt's sister had so little to remember him by. For God's sake, try to understand.'

'You really think Matt's sister would have wanted the St Christopher at such a price? And you could have asked Randall to deal with it, in any case.'

'Stop being so bloody logical!' she burst out. 'Can't you see it was something else I needed to do? In a very small way it helped to atone for Matt's death. I had to prove I could handle Gareth as well, that he didn't have any hold over me any more. And he doesn't. He tried to make love to me, but it was loathsome. I couldn't bear it, especially after you—'

She broke off, unable to continue, shaking with reaction. Mallory's face relaxed. He sighed, and took her in his arms.

'Hyde's right about one thing,' he said. 'You take a hell of a lot of dealing with. All right, I understand why you did it, but this sort of thing is no good for either of us. It just sets you off on another cycle of self-destruction, and makes me act in a way which I hate. It's not much of an achievement to beat up a drunken yob. And karate isn't meant to be a form of punishment.'

She rested her head against his chest, still unable to speak, just wanting to wind down and be with him. As always she felt the sense of safety to which she could never quite surrender entirely.

'Now isn't a good time, but soon we have to talk this through properly, you know,' he said.

Christa felt almost helpless with relief that she hadn't lost him, and that she wasn't going to have to talk about their future just yet. At the moment she didn't have the energy to discuss anything. She wondered how she'd cope with front-line reporting. Since meeting Gareth again she'd become convinced she had to go back to it. Mallory would have to understand that it was the final step towards restoring her self-esteem. In the meantime, live for the moment, she told herself. Don't think about next month or next year. Just enjoy this while you've got it.

Next day was Sunday, and Mallory had to visit friends in London. He wanted Christa to go with him, but she pleaded tiredness, which was only partly true. She knew she'd feel uneasy until Gareth left Oxford. His reference to a special assignment was nagging at her.

Some big story must be about to break if Metro TV wanted a reporter of his reputation on the spot. But according to local radio nothing unusual was coming up in the city on the following day, apart from the Peaceable Kingdom demo which was bound to be a milk-and-water affair. And she didn't like to interrupt Wes's scant leisure time to see if he could provide any clues.

By mid-morning she was so restless that she decided to go into town and look around. She saw nothing untoward until she was walking along St Giles' on the way back. A couple of lads were moving rapidly along the kerb ahead, one keeping watch while the other tried the handles of parked cars. As the look-out saw her, she realised the boys were Barry and Kev.

'Christa! How're you doing?' said Kev delightedly, when she'd caught up with them.

'Fine,' she answered, trying not to look amused at their complete lack of guilt. 'And I won't even begin to ask what you're up to here.'

'We've got a living to make, same as everyone else,' said Barry, as seriously as if he were running a chain of used car lots. 'And in any case we're doing a bit of general sussing-out as well. We've got something important coming up.'

They both looked so cheerfully ruffianish that her spirits rose, and on an impulse she decided to offer them a drink at home. It'd get them away from the cars, and divert her thoughts for an hour or so.

Their reaction to her house amused her even more. They made a thorough inspection of the premises, told her exactly where villains – in which category they luckily did not seem to include themselves – were likely to get in, advised her to buy a Dobermann, and offered to get her a better video recorder.

'So,' said Christa, when they were settled on the sofa with cans of lager and cigarettes, 'what's this "something important" you've got coming up?'

The two lads looked questioningly at each other. Barry shifted a large wad of chewing gum from one side of his mouth to the other.

'It's big,' he said. 'And in your line of work as well. What's it worth if we tell you?'

All at once Christa wondered if this could be connected with Gareth's assignment.

'What did you have in mind?' she asked.

'A coupla tickets for another concert, say Pulp this time?' suggested Kev.

'Done,' said Christa, hoping her friend would be able to come up with the goods again. 'Go ahead, let's hear you.'

'Well,' said Kev, 'the lads from Gabriel's Grounds have organised a fucking big march tomorrow in St Giles', alongside the Peaceable Kingdom demo. It's to demand our rights from Gabriel. Kids from all the city council estates are going to be there, and those guys Steve and Jus, who were at the Mill with you, are bringing in the students as well.'

Barry lobbed his empty lager can into the coal scuttle, and reached for another.

'We're going to take the police and everyone by surprise. By the time the fuzz tries to stop us it'll be too late. We've heard Howl's joining the demo too. They're coming into the open at last because they're pissed off with the Institute.'

'It'll be a right old ding-dong, and no mistake,' said Kev with relish.

Christa's mind was racing. A march involving students, unemployed youth, the Peaceable Kingdom and Howl had huge potential for trouble. No wonder Metro wanted Gareth there!

She felt utterly frustrated at her inability to compete while he snatched such a scoop from under her nose. The more she thought about it, the more tempted she was to cover the demo herself. Her teaching year was almost over, her book was almost finished, and she hadn't put a foot wrong yet as far as Randall was concerned. As she'd expected, the Master had made no complaint to Apollo about the debate.

If she could just get Wes to join her, she was certain she could do a better coverage than Gareth – a coverage which would prove to Randall that she was still able to deliver the goods, and provide her with a trial run for returning to work.

As soon as the lads had gone, Christa called Wes. This was more important than his holiday. He was in the garden, but came to the phone good-naturedly enough when summoned by Miriam.

'Hi, Christa. Want to come round? We're having a barbecue.'

'Listen, Wes,' she gabbled, 'could you go somewhere you can speak to me alone?'

'I am alone. I'm in the study. Miriam's gone back to the garden. What's happened?'

She blurted out everything she'd just heard, and what Gareth had told her the night before. There was a long excruciating silence.

'We'd heard nothing of this at Dreaming Spires,' said Wes eventually. 'Thank God Rebekah's away. She had an invitation to spend the weekend at Tony Kitembe's home, otherwise I'm certain she'd be in the thick of things. What are you going to do? Tip Randall off, I suppose, so Apollo can be there too?'

The poorly concealed regret in his voice spurred Christa on.

'I've got to cover this myself. Gareth's involved. It's a personal challenge. I can't pass it up. And I want you to be my cameraman. Please, Wes. It could be the free-lance scoop of the year for you, and it's a way of restoring my reputation again.'

There was another long delay while she heard Wes put down the receiver, go to close the door, and come back again.

'I daren't let Miriam hear this,' he said. 'Town and gown, Howl and the Peaceable Kingdom – what a mix! It'd be fun, but dangerous too with those maniacs from Howl about. And some of the youngsters from Gabriel's Grounds are fairly crazy characters too. I'm supposed to be leading a quiet life these days, for the sake of Miriam and the kids.'

'We've always been fine in the past, and you know we make a great team.'

'Well, as it happens, Miriam won't be here tomorrow,' he said. 'She's taking the twins on a day trip to London, so I can sort out my tax and expenses in peace. Do you know who Metro's cameraman is?'

'No, but probably Ace Kelly. Gareth usually teams up with him on the few UK stories he does these days.'

'Kelly! He's a really nasty bit of work. It'll be a pleasure to cut him out.'

'So you'll do it?' said Christa in elation.

'Yes, I'll do it,' said Wes. His voice became serious. 'But have you thought this through properly for yourself, Christa? If we don't pull it off, and Randall gets to know what you've been up to, you'll be in big trouble again. I can easily ask someone from Dreaming Spires to go with me if you want to change your mind.'

'I don't care,' said Christa. 'I've decided it's a risk I must take.'

'All right then. It's your decision, of course. I'll have to go now or Miriam will wonder what's going on, but meet me this evening around eight in the Eagle and Child and we'll get tomorrow sorted out.'

As soon as Wes had rung off, Christa called Stacey to tell her she was covering the demo after all, and to warn her about Howl. To her surprise the Peaceable Kingdom had already heard the news.

'The committee's certain it's just a rumour. Howl's never come into the open before. They don't work that way. We're not going to cancel our plans because of them.'

'You know I wouldn't be covering the demo myself unless I thought it was much more than a rumour. You're crazy to go on with this,' Christa protested, increasingly alarmed at the prospect of Howl on the rampage among the Peaceable Kingdom's pacifist and hopelessly ineffectual ranks. 'I've promised not to give any details, but I've heard other groups are coming in on the march too. They'll flatten you.'

'We reckon we have a duty to show the public there's another way to support animal rights beside Howl's.'

'What about Glenn? You promised him you'd have nothing more to do with Howl. He'll be furious if you get mixed up with them again.'

'I'm too far in now. I can't let the Peaceable Kingdom down,' said Stacey stubbornly.

As Christa rang off she decided it was no good worrying any more about Stacey. She'd just have to try to keep an eye on her in the fray. But it was harder than she'd expected to push to the back of her mind the thought that she and Wes were both about to break promises too. Mallory certainly wouldn't approve, but luckily he wasn't returning to Oxford until Monday evening when the demo would safely be over.

Mallory missed Christa even more than he'd expected. All the time in London he was conscious of a nagging worry that he should have tried to solve the impasse of their future before he left. He'd wanted to demonstrate by his absence that he trusted her over Gareth Hyde, but he didn't trust Hyde himself. In the end his anxiety and longing to see her became so great that he decided to return early on Monday morning.

When he walked across King's Quad towards his room, where he intended to leave his bag before going to Jericho, there was an unusual air of activity for so early on a holiday. Students were standing about in groups, talking excitedly but falling strangely silent as he passed, and in one group what looked like placards were hastily concealed.

The porters sensed something was going on too, for they kept dodging out of their cubby-hole to keep an eye on things. It was quite obvious that the students weren't preparing for anything as innocuous as an early-morning run.

To his further surprise, and initial delight, he encountered Christa hurrying purposefully down the last few steps of their stair. She too had an air of suppressed excitement about her, which he was beginning to recognise meant she had something on hand. Her clothes were unusual as well, for what was already a warm and sunny day. She was wearing a leather jacket, a pair of battle-scarred jeans, and heavy boots.

Her expression when she saw him combined pleasure and defensiveness, but he was so pleased to see her that he didn't bother to analyse it.

'I came back early because I missed you,' he said between kisses. 'How about a day on the river? The weather's perfect.'

'Mal, I'm so sorry, but I can't. I've promised to help Wes with something today.'

She was almost stammering. He couldn't understand why she sounded so nervous. He slipped his hands under her jacket. She felt different too, tense and keyed up.

'Has something happened while I've been away? Did you have another run-in with Gareth?'

'No, no, not Gareth, nothing to do with him,' she said, trying to pull herself free. 'I must go, really. Wes will be waiting.'

He tried to take her hand, but it was clenched round her pocket tape-recorder. Suddenly he began to connect her behaviour with that of the students.

'You're up to something, Christa. I know all the signs. Could it be the same thing that's making the students high so early in the day?'

She didn't look at him. His heart sank.

'It's just a small demo,' she said. 'The students are joining some of the kids from Gabriel's Grounds and a few other groups in St Giles'. Wes is filming it. I thought it'd be fun to go along.'

'That sounds like a recipe for a whole lot of trouble to me. Who are these few other groups?'

'Just the Peaceable Kingdom,' she said, trying to dodge past him.

'You said a few. Who else?'

'And Howl maybe. That's all.'

'Howl? Have you gone completely mad? You promised Randall you wouldn't get involved.'

He'd wedged his back against the wall, using his arm as a barrier across the stairs to block her way. She had her back to the opposite wall. Her hair was falling into her eyes. She pushed it back impatiently. Her hands were shaking. She saw him looking at them, and shoved them into her pockets. She looked beautiful, vulnerable, and utterly determined

'Stop being so bloody judgemental,' she hurled back. 'It's my decision and my life.'

'I was under the impression that it was beginning to be our life, that we were going to make joint decisions.'

'We are, I promise, just as soon as I've done this,' she said passionately. 'It's hugely important to me. Gareth's going to be there. He talked about a special assignment on the night of the Feast, but I didn't connect it with the demo until yesterday.'

'For God's sake, Christa, that's all the more reason for you to stay away.'

'But don't you see, he thinks it's going to be his scoop? I know Wes and I can produce a better report. It means getting my own back on him, proving I can produce the goods as a professional again, both to Randall and myself.'

Mallory just managed to hold on to his self-control. Nothing he'd been saying to her over the past months seemed to have got through. Everything he'd thought she'd learned seemed to have been forgotten.

'You're not thinking straight. You're simply playing into Gareth's hands once more. You haven't got the back-up of a studio, he doesn't fight fair, Howl are a bunch of maniacs, and heaven knows what other lunatics may turn up once there's a riot in the offing. Because there will be a riot, if Howl's involved. And what about Wes? You told me he'd promised his wife to stay away from trouble. He'll be your responsibility, just as much as Matt was.'

Christa tried not to admit he was echoing much of what she'd said to Stacey.

'If you loved me you wouldn't stop me,' she said, fiddling with the case of the tape-recorder, unable to meet his eyes. 'I need to prove myself.'

'It's because I love you that I'm trying to stop you. You don't have to keep riding the wall of death to be happy. There's more to life than that, but for some reason you won't let yourself find it.'

He was again forcing her to think about things she didn't want to think about yet. His gravity made her realise he was about to demand a final decision from her. She couldn't give it, not now, when such a huge prize was within her grasp.

'So what do you think I should do instead?' she demanded furiously. 'Present breakfast-time chat shows, I suppose?'

She knew she was being grossly unfair to him, but she was almost frantic with conflicting thoughts.

'We've been through this before. You know I don't. There are plenty of issues other than war which wouldn't turn you into a burnt-out case.'

'All right, all right,' she said, 'I'll think about it, I promise, but not now. I have to do this first. You've got to understand.'

He looked at her for a long time, and then silently lowered the arm barring her way. Panic began to race through her.

'There'll always be something you have to do first, won't there?' he said gently. 'If you go ahead with this, we're finished, because I can't take seeing you turn away from everything that really matters.'

She felt sick as she realised he was forcing her to choose.

'I'm asking you for the last time – don't go to the demo,' he said. 'Let's try to sort things out instead.'

'I will sort things out, I promise,' she said, frantic with frustration. 'But afterwards, not now.'

He thumped the side of his fist against the wall. When he took it away she saw the skin was grazed and raw. He let his arm fall to his side, and kissed her very gently.

'You're never going to stop kidding yourself, are you?' he said, and stepped back to let her pass. 'Goodbye, then, and look after yourself, since you won't let anyone else do it for you.'

As Christa headed towards the demo she couldn't believe she'd again lost the most important person in her life, and that this time she'd been the one to walk away. She tried to persuade herself that when Mallory saw her report on TV, he would understand why she'd had to do it. He was going to be in college for another four weeks. She still had plenty of time to make him see things her way. But none of her brain-washing worked, and by the time she arrived in St Giles' she was desperate for the adrenalin rush of confrontation which would help her forget him.

The war memorial was next to the graveyard of St Giles' church, on a wedge-shaped site where the Woodstock and Banbury roads merged. From here the concourse of St Giles' stretched for more than four hundred yards to the Martyrs' Memorial and the church of St Mary Magdalen, before er ling at Broad Street.

The sky was a clear blue, and tulips and forget-me-nots swayed in a light breeze round the memorial site. Teenagers from other city estates were lounging about in the graveyard with their placards, and tanking up with lager while waiting for the contingent from Gabriel's Grounds. Passers-by, attracted by the air of something about to happen, had begun to gather quietly round the memorial as well.

The atmosphere felt more like that of a festival than a demo, and though two police cars outside the Institute of Mathematics were keeping an eye on things, their occupants didn't look particularly worried so far.

Wes had parked his long-wheel base Volvo, with its heavy roof rack on which he could stand to film, on a yellow line by the grassy space between the graveyard and the war memorial, trusting in his Press sticker to keep him there. He was sitting smoking in the front seat, the latest in cameras by his side.

'Hi,' he said, as she slid in beside him. 'The light's great today. Everything's looking good so far. What do you want to do first? A piece to camera before things get too busy?'

It felt strange to be reporting again, but Christa's voice was perfectly steady as she stood with a shot of St John's, Balliol and the Martyrs' Memorial stretching away at her back, and detailed the grievances of all those she expected to be involved, apart from Howl. She wouldn't refer to them until they actually appeared. As always the problem was to keep the piece short as

well as fair. Unless they were very lucky, they couldn't expect
more than a few minutes' air time at the most.

When she had finished she climbed with Wes on to the
Volvo's roof. Tourists and shoppers were slowly swelling the
crowd round the war memorial, and students had begun to
flood out of St John's and Balliol.

There was no sign of Ace Kelly and Gareth yet. Christa
decided they were probably having a bracer in the Eagle and
Child. Traffic was still getting through, but at half its usual speed.
An ice-cream van turned up, and parked at the foot of the war
memorial, where it started to do a roaring trade. Christa was
beginning to wonder where the demo had got to, when the
sound of music at last began to float in their direction.

'It's the kids from Gabriel's Grounds!' said Wes, swinging his
camera in the direction of the Woodstock Road. 'It looks as if
they've hijacked a truck.'

An articulated lorry was crawling in their direction, a monster
placard fixed to the cab roof with the words 'Justice for Gabriel's
Grounds' in lettering a foot high. Bunches of scarlet helium bal-
loons were tethered to the trailer at the back. They surrounded
an exuberant amateur steel band and a mass of youngsters
brandishing cheerfully mis-spelt placards, and yelling slogans at
the crowd. The holiday seemed to have put everyone in a
carnival mood.

Many more teenagers were boogeying in the road round
the truck between handing out leaflets to anyone who'd take
them. The supporters from the other estates started to pour
out of the churchyard and mass round the truck too, almost
completely halting the rest of the traffic going to and from the
Woodstock Road.

'Looks OK at the moment,' Christa said to Wes, 'but there are
some real hard cases out there, believe me. I'd better go and talk
to them before the animal rights people arrive and things start
to hot up.'

They plunged into the crowd, and had just done a series of
interviews when a very different kind of music began to drift
from the direction of the Banbury Road. As Christa and Wes
scrambled back on top of the Volvo, an orderly vanguard of
mainly middle-aged, middle-class Peaceable Kingdom protestors

appeared, four abreast, carrying placards whose slogans were written in perfect italic script. They were headed by a sturdy North Oxford matron singing 'All Things Bright and Beautiful' in a booming contralto voice.

Behind them Christa spotted Stacey, trailing along with a younger, less coordinated gaggle of Peaceable Kingdom protesters. They were mostly parents accompanying children dressed as animals and holding lopsided placards adorned with runny powder paint. Some of the youngest children in buggies were holding pet mice and rabbits in cages on their laps.

Next came a contingent of travellers, accompanied by a large number of characterful dogs and several goats. And right at the back of the column was a solemn band of Buddhists from an ashram in Norham Manor, complete with bells and saffron robes, who appeared to have attached themselves to the march by mistake.

'Should be interesting if Howl turns up among that lot,' said Wes to Christa with a grin, when she'd finished interviewing the Peaceable Kingdom. 'What I want to know is where Gareth's got to? How about doing a recce, before more police turn up? They must have sent for help by now.'

Christa slipped away, pushing with some difficulty through the throng. The traffic had ground to a standstill at the war memorial end of St Giles'. In the distance she could hear the sirens of police cars trying to enter from Broad Street. More crowds of holiday shoppers, attracted by the sound of the steel band, were pouring in from that direction too.

It was hard to see anything in the crush, but as she battled along she eventually spotted Gareth, sitting in a flashy four-wheel-drive in the parking area outside Pusey House. Ace Kelly, who according to Wes had been fired by his previous employer for rearranging corpses into more photogenic attitudes in Chechnya, was above him in the branches of a plane tree, filming the crowd.

Gareth was talking earnestly to a bunch of skinheads, handing out twenty-pound notes from the car window as lavishly as free samples. She couldn't risk being seen by going nearer to check, but she had a strong suspicion he was bribing them to stir up trouble.

By this time police reinforcements had got through and cleared a way for official transport down the centre of St Giles'. She could hear the sound of more music from the far side of the street, and struggled across to find out what was happening there.

The students from Gabriel, late as usual, were emerging from a side alley near St John's, led by the college jazz band, and singing a highly scurrilous song about the Master to the syncopated tune of 'Gaudeamus Igitur'. They were unable to get anywhere near the war memorial, and headed off towards the Martyrs' Memorial instead, where they set up their public address system and festooned the monument with placards.

Christa dived into the Lamb and Flag pub to buy some sandwiches and cans of beer for herself and Wes. When she got back to him the Gabriel's Grounds supporters were taking it in turns with the Peaceable Kingdom to address the crowd through their loud-speakers.

By this time it was very hot, and the air was full of dust. Several elderly tourists had collapsed and been rushed off by paramedics to ambulances now lined up at the entrance to the church. The more cautious among the Peaceable Kingdom supporters had retreated to the comparative calm of the graveyard where they'd set up an impromptu crèche for their children and animals.

'We could do with a second camera, but we'll manage,' said Wes happily, when they'd returned from a sortie to the Martyrs' Memorial to interview the students from Gabriel, and he was changing camera batteries in the Volvo.

'It's turning into one hell of a crowd,' said Christa. 'There's no sign of Howl yet. I wonder if they've thought better of it.'

In the graveyard a full-scale bop was now taking place to the sound of the steel band. So far the good-natured, carnival atmosphere prevailed. The proceedings had been handled with a most Oxonian restraint by every one concerned, but as Christa and Wes were sharing their sandwiches back on top of the Volvo, they saw riot police pile out of black vans at the entrance to Little Clarendon Street, and line up awaiting orders.

'Jesus, look at that!' said Wes. 'They must be expecting big trouble any moment now.'

Christa knew it had already arrived. Through the tumult she'd caught the heavy beat of a bass drum and a noise she hadn't heard since leaving Bosnia: the sound of marching, booted feet.

Almost falling off the Volvo roof in her effort to crane across the crowd, she saw a huge, solid phalanx of dark-clad marchers, those at the front in skull masks and bearing Howl banners with a logo of a snarling wolf, advance towards them down the centre of St Giles. By sheer weight of numbers they'd taken over the whole of the emergency access.

At their head, preceded by a drummer thumping out a single insistent funeral note, marched Eileen, recognisable at once to Christa by her characteristic gait in spite of her mask. She was holding up a wooden cross as tall as herself, to which was nailed an effigy of a crucified chimp. On either side of her silent figures carried placards bearing the words, 'Stamp out torture at the Tucker Institute'.

'My God, how Grand Guignol!' said Wes, zooming in on the effigy.

Christa didn't answer. At first she couldn't understand where the sound of marching boots was coming from, for the Howl supporters all wore soft shoes, but now its origin had become horribly clear.

'Stop a moment, Wes!' she said urgently. 'Look who's marching behind Howl. It's the Saxon Front!'

The Saxon Front was a neo-Nazi organisation which the police had only just kept under control over the last few months. It had targeted only London and Birmingham up to now. An awed silence fell over the crowd as its members, hulking swaggerers with military haircuts, in black leather and swastika-emblazoned T-shirts, powered their way like a human tank through St Giles', lustily singing the 'Horst Wessel' song.

'Nazis in Oxford of all places!' said Wes, clamping his eye to the camera again. 'Why the hell isn't anyone stopping them?'

'Someone is, and it's going to be a disaster!' said Christa frantically. 'Look in front of them!'

Suddenly, out of nowhere, the band of Buddhists had appeared, walking straight into the marchers' path, chanting and ringing bells, completely unperturbed by the oncoming horde as if bent on self-destruction.

The temptation was too great for the Saxon Front. The 'Horst

Wessel' song abruptly ceased, and they fell on the saffron-robed monks. At the same time Howl made a dive for the Peaceable Kingdom, the Gabriel's Grounds contingent and the students piled in on the Saxon Front, and the youngsters from other estates happily entered into whichever punch-up was most accessible.

A colossal free-for-all ensued, raging back and forth across St Giles', while the onlookers tried desperately to get out of the way, and Christa and Wes filmed as close as they dared.

Stones and bottles hurtled through the air. The Gabriel rugby team, storming through the scrum, managed to divert Howl from the Peaceable Kingdom with a series of flying tackles. Christa, doing a piece to camera on the very edge of the fray, and hardly able to make herself heard above the din, had to be snatched away by Wes.

By this time they'd been pushed back almost to the car. A splinter group from the Saxon Front was trying to get control of the Gabriel's Grounds' truck. The ice-cream vendor had fled from his van, which was now occupied by estate youth hurling iced lollies and cans of fizzy drinks at the neo-Nazis. Most of the Peaceable Kingdom had managed to retreat in a state of outraged shock to the safety of the churchyard.

Wes was still filming, and Christa had just dodged a flying can, when she saw Stacey standing in floods of tears at the churchyard gate. She rushed up to her and hurried her inside, terrified she'd be injured if she stayed where she was.

'I had to phone Glenn,' sobbed Stacey. Her hair was tumbling over her face, and there were streaks of raspberry ripple on her white denim jeans. 'I had to tell him to call in his mates. The brickies and the scaffolders are the only people who can stop this lot now. He was so mad, I don't think he'll ever speak to me again.'

'It's OK, calm down,' Christa shouted at her over the din. 'The riot squad must be going to move in. Just stay here. Glenn'll be even more wild if you get hurt.'

Christa had lost Wes in the crowd, but somehow fought her way back to the Volvo, and clambered on top. Scanning the swaying mass, she made out a long line of police with riot shields at last fanning across St Giles'. Someone shouted that mounted police were coming in from the Broad Street end. At the same time a flash of scarlet caught her eye and she saw Wes slumped against the foot of the war memorial, blood pouring from a gash on his forehead.

She slid down from the car roof, wrenching her ankle as she dropped the last few feet, fought her way to his side, and half carried, half dragged him into the churchyard. He collapsed in the shelter of the wall, his head in his hands, blood running through his fingers, down his wrist, and falling in huge splashes on to his chest.

The blood on his T-shirt affected her as though she'd been hit herself. He looked so like Matt. Suddenly she thought of Miriam and the children, and the consequences for them if Wes died. Her legs almost buckled as she frantically asked herself how she could have let him take the risk.

She fell on her knees next to him, examining the gash with shaking hands, expecting to see the gleam of bone, terrified he had a fractured skull. When she found it wasn't nearly as bad as it looked, she almost fainted with relief.

'Jesus, Wes, I thought you'd had it as well as Matt.' Christa was close to tears. 'I don't think I can take much more of this.'

Wes had discovered his handkerchief and clamped it to the wound. The fabric was reddening rapidly. His precious camera was still safely under the other arm. A paramedic had already begun to move in their direction.

'For Christ's sake, you can't go to pieces now,' he said shakily. 'I'm no good like this, but if you hang on for another half hour, I reckon we'll have the whole thing in the can. You've got to take the camera and get out there. We can't afford to miss the crisis point.'

He pushed the camera towards her. 'Go on. I've not risked divorce to lose the best part of this. The camera's easy, a real honey. You can practise on me first. We need some more injury shots.'

Taking the camera, Christa did as she was told, while the paramedic hovered anxiously behind her. She was feeling sick with reaction and memories of Bosnia when she again plunged into the crowd. It had thinned considerably, and foot police were mopping up and arresting every stray activist in sight.

But between the Martyrs' Memorial and Balliol, the mounted police were only just keeping the remnants of Howl and the Saxon Front at bay. They were trying to move from St Giles' into Broad Street so that they could march towards Gabriel.

Christa climbed over the railings of St Mary Magdalen graveyard at the back of the memorial, and clambered into a laburnum tree, helped by a bunk-up from Kev who'd been hiding behind a tombstone from the police. She settled the camera comfortably on her shoulder. A leafy branch hid her from Ace Kelly, also filming the scene from halfway up a Balliol drainpipe across the road.

She was so near the horses that she could smell their sweating flesh and the leather of their harness. Though they were jittery, they were still under control. But at the exact moment she trained her camera on them, someone lobbed a firecracker under their legs, and the line began to seethe in a restless, rearing commotion of hooves.

She took her eye from the viewfinder to see where it had come from. Below, a few yards to her right, was an underground public lavatory, the subject of much student folklore, and the haunt of flashers and tramps. She nearly fell out of the tree as she recognised Gareth lurking at the top of the steps, calmly lighting firecrackers, throwing them from behind over the heads of the mounted police, then bobbing down unseen into the well of the lavatory entrance.

All her earlier suspicions were verified. He was deliberately trying to orchestrate the riot, to stir up more violence to enhance the dramatic impact of his report. Christa knew that if she filmed him in the act, no TV company, not even Metro, would ever give him work again. He was so sure of himself that he never bothered to check his surroundings as she coldly and carefully recorded his every move. She even got shots of him when he'd barged his way across the road to direct Ace Kelly.

Gareth had done his work well. The line of mounted police began to falter. For a moment it looked as if the mob would break through. Christa, exhausted by the physical and emotional demands of the day, braced herself to move on.

But there was no need. Suddenly, erupting into the heart of the struggle from Broad Street, Glenn and a posse of builders appeared, wearing hard hats and using pieces of hardboard as riot shields. Roaring an Oxford United football song, they descended like JCBs on the Saxon Front and Howl, and proceeded to demolish them.

Christa was able to use the last of her footage and her energy on shots of the severely battered activists, including Eileen and the leader of the neo-Nazis, being hoovered up and bundled into riot wagons by the police. Then, determinedly escorted by a scowling Glenn, she limped back up St Giles' to rejoin Stacey and Wes.

By tea-time St Giles' was back to normal again, apart from a litter of discarded placards and broken glass.

Christa had just watched a motor-bike courier take off for Apollo with Wes's footage, already roughly edited at a local post-production studio. Randall, warned by Wes to expect it, didn't yet know about Christa's part in the report.

She guessed Gareth and Ace were driving with their footage straight to Metro to catch the mid-evening news, and would soon be in the company bar, gloating over their achievement while it was edited. They'd think they'd scooped the field, for she was certain they hadn't seen her and Wes, and no other TV crews had appeared.

Wes himself, his forehead adorned with butterfly plasters, had gone home to do some fast talking to Miriam before his exploits appeared on the screen, and would no doubt be given a lecture and cosseted to death. Stacey had already been scolded by Glenn, and then enfolded in a bear hug and borne away. The Gabriel's Grounds youth and the students, most of whom had escaped arrest, were celebrating in pubs all over town.

When Christa got home, aching from the buffeting of the crowd, she collapsed into Jessie's chair. Instead of savouring an imagined picture of Gareth's face when he saw the Apollo news, for he always recorded rival reports on his video, and of Randall's when he saw her footage, she felt deeply and painfully alone.

She had no one to celebrate with. Emma was having a long weekend in the country with Phil, and even her parents, making the most of Alice's new mobility, were away visiting relations in Suffolk.

She desperately needed company. She needed to forget the recurring memory of Wes's face and shirt covered with blood, and the thought that Miriam could have been a widow, and Rebekah and the other children fatherless. She needed to push away the truth she didn't want to acknowledge: that covering the riot had brought with it none of the usual psychological boost.

She didn't even feel better when Randall rang, ecstatic over the report. He told her she'd be hearing about reinstatement very soon, and said he was sending a crew down to Oxford the following morning to interview her about her triumph over Gareth. He also promised to get Jimmy Judd to fix any objections by the Master to her report.

'This'll put you right in the picture again, Christa. You're bloody lucky you brought it off. I'd have fired you if you hadn't, but I can't tell you how glad I am things have worked out for you, and that Gareth's been nailed at last. Make sure you watch Apollo's nine o'clock newscast tonight.'

Even the sight of her own footage, of Wes's brilliant camera work, of Gareth's downfall, failed to cheer her. Eventually she felt so wretched that she decided she must go to Gabriel and see Mallory, though it would mean admitting she might have been wrong.

But when she climbed the stair to his room, still aching in every joint although she'd had a bath, there was a note in his handwriting tacked to his outer door.

'Mallory Farrar will be away until further notice. Students may collect their essays from the Senior Tutor's office.'

She tore down the stairs, across the quad and into the Porters' Lodge.

'Dr Farrar? Where did he go? Do you know when he'll be back?' she demanded breathlessly.

The porter turned his attention from the portable television tucked away in a corner.

'My, your TV report really put the cat among the pigeons, didn't it, Miss Keith? But I have to admit I'm glad. Things were getting to a pretty pass here. Our young ladies and gentlemen ought to have made themselves heard long ago.'

Christa was too wound up to notice this concession.

'Dr Farrar! Where is he?' she asked again, in a fever of impatience.

'Took off for India this afternoon, he did. He's doing research in some big library in Delhi before he starts his next book. If he's not back by the end of term, he asked Fred and me to send his luggage on.'

20

Christa slept late next morning, and was woken by a film crew from Apollo hammering at the door. After the screening of her report on the riot, Metro had been forced to fire Gareth and issue a public apology. The crew had brought an armful of newspapers, which were full of his disgrace. By the time she'd done the piece for Apollo, the tabloids were queuing up for her reaction as well, and Kitchener Road was full of press cars.

It should have been one of the sweetest days of her life, yet it wasn't. By going away, Mallory couldn't have signalled more clearly that the possibility of a reconciliation did not exist, but Christa still missed him with a deep, longing ache. She kept trying to persuade herself that she was far better off alone, free to manage her life exactly as she wished. Randall was certain to offer her an assignment just as hazardous, and with her newly enhanced reputation, even more lucrative than Bosnia, but her usual excitement at the prospect of danger just wouldn't kick in.

Eventually, rather than stay miserably at home, she decided to go over to Gabriel to collect her mail. There she found the porters in their element. They'd been turning away more of the media all morning. Her group had sent her flowers, and when she went for coffee in the SCR, people queued up to congratulate her. Piers asked her out for a celebratory drink in the evening, insisting that she dine with him afterwards in hall. Only the Master said nothing, giving her instead a frosty nod, but Christa felt safe from his disapproval at last.

After coffee she went to her room, and lethargically began to sort out the contents of her shelves in preparation for her departure. While she was doing so she found Gervaise's photo album, and thought guiltily that she must send it back.

Several of the photos had come adrift from their grey sugar paper pages, perhaps as a result of the damp Oxford atmosphere. When she checked through, more fell from the Waylandsbury section. She found some glue in a drawer, and began sticking them in. The last one was of the Waylandsbury group. She studied it regretfully, wishing she could have solved the mystery before she left Gabriel, and turned it over to apply the glue.

She was astonished to see on the back a brief pencil note: 'Waylandsbury Dig, 1962'. Then came the Master's name and those of the male research assistants and their colleges, neatly jotted beneath each other, and at the bottom of the list 'Violet Quinn, Gabriel Hall'.

She got out her magnifying glass, and studied it again. There was no mistake, even through a film of crusted paste. She put the photo in her pocket, and rushed over to the Dean's office.

Miss Harker was perusing the *University Gazette* while having a sandwich lunch at her desk. She'd blossomed in the absence of the still-convalescing Dean, and had prevailed on the Bursar to replace her ancient typewriter with a word processor which had become her pride and joy.

'I must congratulate you on a splendid piece of reporting yesterday, my dear. I found it so reassuring that our students were once again publicly demonstrating for the rights of others. They haven't done that for the last ten years.'

Christa tried to look modest while more praise was heaped upon her.

'Do you have a list of the post-graduate students at Gabriel in 1962?' she was able to ask eventually. 'I want to track down the address of a Violet Quinn. I thought it might be interesting to do an article on early women students for the college magazine.'

'What a good idea. There should be a list in our archives in the Bohemia Room,' said Miss Harker. 'Normally you'd need the Dean's permission to consult them. But since I'm in charge at the moment, there won't be any problem.'

The particular file Miss Harker was looking for was on a top shelf in the darkest corner of the Bohemia Room. She descended the library stepladder bearing a venerable box-file crammed with papers, and dumped it on the committee table.

There she proceeded to go through its contents with maddening thoroughness, reminiscing as she did so, until Christa was ready to scream with frustration. But she knew from their instruction sessions on the word processor that it was no good hurrying Miss Harker.

'Ah, here we are!' she said, after treating Christa to a long description of the 1962 Gaudy feast, which had been distinguished by the chef tipping a roast boar's head into the Master's lap. 'Now who was it you wished me to look up?'

'Violet Quinn,' said Christa, almost dancing with impatience.

'That name rings a bell, for some reason,' said Miss Harker, running her finger down the yellowing page of a student list. 'Yes, here we are. She registered as a D. Phil. student in 1960, but left two years later without completing her degree. *Aegrotat*, a note says.'

'Doesn't that mean she left on medical grounds?' Christa asked, wishing she'd done a refresher course in Latin before coming to Gabriel.

'Yes. And it also means we can find out more about her, because there should be an *aegrotat* file somewhere as well.'

After Miss Harker, now severely out of breath, had plodded up and down the steps several more times, the file in question was finally located.

'There's only a medical certificate and a forwarding address here,' she said, when she'd studied the contents minutely. 'But I remember a little about her now. Violet Quinn was the first female doctoral student at Gabriel. She lived out, of course, for there was no accommodation for ladies in college then. Sadly the strain of her work became too much for her, poor soul. Her failure was particularly unfortunate because it made the fellows reluctant to admit other female post-graduates.'

'What does it say on the medical certificate?'

'"Nervous debility", which could mean almost anything. But it seems to have had a happy ending of sorts. Apparently she married, because her name on the forwarding address has changed to Violet Whittingstall.'

'Where did she go?' Christa demanded excitedly, thinking that at last she was making some progress.

'Too far away for you to speak to her in person, my dear. Australia. Cairns, in Queensland, to be precise. I'll write the address down for you, but there's no phone number, I'm afraid.'

Christa's spirits had sunk so low at the prospect of trying to track down someone who lived on the other side of the world, and who had probably moved several times anyway, that she almost didn't bother to ring international telephone enquiries when she got home. When she did, the operator could find no one of that name in Cairns.

'But there's a Dr Frederick Whittingstall in a place called Ross Bay. He's the only one in the Queensland directory.'

Christa dialled the number, thinking that it would be late-evening in Australia, and if this Dr Whittingstall was Violet's husband, he'd be in his mid-sixties now, and possibly addicted to early nights. But she didn't have any time to spare with the meeting of Governing Body only a week away.

Dr Whittingstall had clearly been in bed. He sounded irritable and suspicious when he answered the phone.

'Yes, my wife is called Violet,' he barked. 'But she's asleep. Can I take a message?'

'My name's Christa Keith. I'm phoning from England, and I need to speak to her very urgently. Couldn't you please wake her up and at least ask if she'll talk to me?'

'You'll have to ring at a more convenient time. Don't you realise how late it is?'

'Just tell her it's about Gabriel Hall and the Waylandsbury dig. I desperately need some information about her part in it.'

There was a momentary silence, during which Christa could hear Dr Whittingstall breathing like an enraged dragon.

'I can tell you now, she'll have no wish to talk about that,' he thundered. 'Who are you exactly, anyway, and what do you want this information for?'

'I'm a fellow of Gabriel myself,' said Christa. 'Believe me, Dr Whittingstall, I've no wish to upset your wife in any way.'

'Then in that case you'll get straight off this line. She'll never talk to you about Waylandsbury or Gabriel. They've given her enough grief already,' he snapped, before slamming down the phone.

Christa tried the number again, in the evening, before meeting Piers. The first time the doctor put the phone down on her. The second time Violet herself answered, and was just able to say apologetically that she really didn't want to speak, before Dr Whittingstall broke into the conversation and cut her off. The third time all Christa got was an answering machine.

She slumped on the sofa in frustration, and wondered what to do. Though Violet sounded potentially reasonable, her guard-dog of a husband wasn't going to let Christa get anywhere near her on the phone.

If she could just see Violet in person she was almost certain she could persuade her to talk. The only way to do that was to fly to Australia, and fast. She knew it was an enormously long shot. The fare would wipe out her bank balance again, but her most recent visa hadn't quite expired, and if the trip was a success the expense would be more than justified.

When Piers asked Christa to his room for a nightcap after dinner, she accepted. Though she suspected he'd ask her questions she didn't want to answer, and though she still had to pack for the flight she'd managed to book for the following day, she couldn't face going back to Jericho to think about Mallory.

The window was open to the warm summer's evening. In the distance Christa could hear students playing tennis, snatching some exercise between revising for exams. A slender, crop-headed person in fencing gear smiled from a new photo on a bookshelf. 'Love from Max' was scrawled across one corner. Copies of Piers' latest book, *Ghostly Machines: the Zeitgeist of Adaptation, Simulacra and Cultural Commodification*, sat half unpacked in a cardboard box on the floor.

'Congratulations. You've finally got the SCR at your feet,' said Piers, pouring her a measure of the lethally potent vodka he'd brought back from a British Council trip to Russia in the Easter vacation.

He dislodged Mehitabel from his chair, lit a cigarette and surveyed Christa. He was feeling more optimistic about his own life. The *Times Literary Supplement* had given his new book what was, for academe, a rave review, and he'd started an affair with a young Cambridge don, met recently at a conference, whose intellectual and sexual gymnastics he found eminently satisfying.

Christa, on the other hand, who should have found life at the moment more than satisfying as well, looked, now they were alone and she'd stopped acting, almost as depressed as when she'd sat in the same chair eight months ago.

'The Master isn't at my feet,' she said gloomily. 'I wish I could be sure of nailing him at the next meeting of Governing Body. I'm taking a quick trip to Australia tomorrow to see someone who might help.'

'Good heavens! Isn't going to the other side of the world somewhat excessive?' Piers teased her, longing to know what she was up to, but knowing he'd get short shrift if he enquired outright.

'No, it isn't. And don't bother to ask me any more about it because I'm not telling you. You're just like Mallory, so bloody negative sometimes.'

Piers held his breath. So far she'd slapped him down each time he mentioned Farrar.

'He never approves of anything I do,' Christa went on, 'so we've decided to split.'

'Really?' said Piers, not daring to risk a less non-commital remark.

'He thinks I've changed since I came here, that I'm hanging on to some unnecessary attachment to conflict which isn't good for me. He thinks I'm capable of higher things,' she added with a wry grin.

'It does take an odd kind of pathology to make it one's whole way of life,' said Piers, deliberately trying to stir her up so that he'd learn more.

'Thanks for nothing,' said Christa, her head bent over Mehitabel who had already jumped on to her knee and was treading out a place in her lap.

'His pathology must be rather odd as well. People of his sort have usually had a dysfunctional childhood. The urge to travel is often a subconscious need to get away from smothering parents or siblings. It's no different from the way you keep needing to prove yourself.'

'I never thought I'd hear someone as bright as you trotting out ersatz psychology. Most people have had a dysfunctional childhood in some way or another. And anyway, Mallory's almost too grown-up.'

'OK, if he is, it means he's worked through the hang-ups, so perhaps you should have listened to him.'

'Perhaps I shouldn't listen to you,' she said. 'Give me another drink and let's talk about something else.'

She sounded so irritable that Piers knew he'd got through to her. He was seriously fond of Christa, he thought, as he reached for the vodka. Though no one would be more delighted than himself if this trip to Australia led to the final overthrow of the Master, he didn't want to see her casting herself on the rocks yet again. But whether she'd ultimately grab the lifebelt was quite another matter.

Thirty-six hours later, bleary-eyed with jet lag, and jittery from numerous cups of coffee to keep her awake, Christa drove into Ross Bay late at night in her hired Moke. She checked in to the first motel she came across, a white concrete box which turned alternately red and blue in the pulsating light of its neon sign.

The night air, which was full of the sound of tree frogs, had cooled down considerably since her arrival at the airport, though she was still glad of the enormous electric fan in her room. She set her alarm for seven the following day, took a couple of sleeping pills, and fell asleep to the sound of its blades whirring like a hummingbird's wings.

It was still whirring busily when she woke. She had a shower, grabbed a quick breakfast of fresh pineapple, toast and coffee, and discovered from the receptionist that Dr Whittingstall was a semi-retired psychiatrist. He still saw a few patients at an office in town every morning between ten and one.

At ten-thirty Christa set out for the Whittingstalls' house. It was a typical Queenslander bungalow of white-painted clapboard, set on stilts and built among palms, its shady verandahs hung with bougainvillaea. Rainbow lorikeets and sunbirds flitted through the lush greenery surrounding it. She guessed the back garden must run down to the ocean, for behind the sawing of cicadas she could hear waves breaking on the shore.

Christa had pored over Violet's photo a hundred times. Though the woman who opened the door was more than thirty years older and grey-haired, it was almost like meeting a long-lost friend. And yet Christa got an impression of some radical change of personality – a change she didn't for the moment have time to work out.

'Mrs Whittingstall?' she said.

The woman nodded, looking puzzled. She wore a simple cotton beach dress and rubber flip-flops.

'I'm Christa Keith. I phoned you a couple of days ago.'

Violet Whittingstall looked astonished now.

'But that was from England,' she said. Her voice was still predominantly English, with only a faint Australian accent. She'd put on more weight since the photo was taken, and the sun and late middle age had lined her face.

'I came over especially in the hope of talking to you. I know it must seem a huge intrusion, bursting in on your privacy like this, but I urgently need your help.'

'You're right, it is an intrusion,' said Violet firmly. She was regaining her equilibrium fast. 'I know you want to talk about the Waylandsbury Hoard, and I appreciate that you've come a long way, but it was a difficult time for me which I'm sure you'll understand I don't want to relive. I've let that part of my life go.'

The woman had an immense serenity. That was the difference about her, Christa suddenly realised. She no longer looked as if she was battling against the world.

'I understand exactly how you feel,' said Christa in desperation, as Violet started to close the door, 'because I can guess the real reason why you left the dig. Unfortunately Vernon Slade is now Master of Gabriel, and he's doing his best to ruin the college completely. He has to be stopped. You're the one person who can help.'

Violet shook her head, though she'd at least let the door swing open again.

'Even if your guess were correct, I'm not interested in exposing Vernon. I could have been once, but not any more.'

'I understand that too,' said Christa, desperate to keep her talking after this half admission of the truth. 'But now others are being defrauded by him, and not just students. Won't you please let me tell you what's going on, then you can judge for yourself?'

The heat had increased considerably since the early morning. Christa felt dizzy with stress and a deep fatigue, more emotional than physical, which had persisted ever since the riot and Mallory's departure. She steadied herself with her hand against the door frame.

Violet hesitated.

'You look played out,' she said. Her frown was replaced by the same look of concern Christa had seen a hundred times on her mother's face. 'All right, if it's so important to you, you'd better come in and tell me more. But you don't know how lucky you are. My husband's gone to Cairns for the day, or there wouldn't be any question of my talking to you.'

The sitting room had floor-length windows, so that the garden and a glimpse of dazzling white beach and blue sea seemed an extension of the house. The sound of the ocean filled the room with a constant background presence.

'Go on to the verandah,' said Violet. 'I'll fetch some iced coffee.'

The decor was a mixture of antipodean and English country house. There were cane lounging chairs, a chintz-covered sofa, some tapestry stools, driftwood carvings, aboriginal paintings and prints of old Australia, but they were all insignificant against the view which beckoned through the trees. Christa sat down, and with half her attention on the sea, began to rehearse her story while she waited for Violet to return.

The coffee jug was empty by the time Christa had concluded the story of Gabriel's Mill and her long-running battle against the Master.

'So that's why I have to stop him,' she said, putting down her empty glass on a raffia mat. 'If I don't, he'll succeed in yet another huge fraud, as well as retiring with his reputation unblemished.'

'And what do you personally get out of it?' asked Violet, who'd been sitting composedly in her chair, and listening almost without comment.

'Me?' said Christa, taken aback by the question. 'I get the satisfaction of revealing the truth.'

'If there's one thing I've learned as a doctor's wife, it's that the truth can be a double-edged sword.'

Violet rested her elbows on the arms of her chair, and leaned her chin on her clasped hands. She sighed.

'All the same it seems I'm going to have to tell you about Waylandsbury. But first you have to promise me that the information won't be made public. If you want a confrontation with the Master, it must be done in private. I can't subject my husband and children to the media attention that would surely follow a public exposure.'

Though the threat of public exposure would have greatly strengthened Christa's hand, she had a strong feeling this self-possessed woman would tell her nothing if she didn't comply. In any case she had no right to upset Violet's life again. She decided she'd just have to find a way of getting the Master on his own at the meeting of Governing Body, perhaps during the break, so that he had no chance to prepare a defence.

'Very well, I promise,' she said. 'I undertake to confront the Master privately.'

Violet settled back in her chair, her eyes on the skein of surf breaking on the shore. Her hands lay loosely in her lap as if she were consciously trying to relax.

'I'd gone to a women's college for my first degree before I started to work under Vernon Slade, and had very little confidence in my ability to attract men. I was longing to get to Oxford because I had dreams of emotional as well as intellectual fulfilment there. But as you've found out, Oxford doesn't always come up to expectations.'

As though it was impossible to stay entirely relaxed, she picked up a piece of tapestry from a side table and began to work on it as she talked. She was certainly attractive now, thought Christa. Like Leda, the sort of woman whose depth of understanding drew people to her.

'When we began work on the Waylandsbury dig, Vernon was investigating it as a neolithic burial site, but I began to suspect a Roman treasure could be hidden there,' Violet continued. 'I got on the trail by finding a reference in the margin of the single remaining page of a lost Anglo-Saxon chronicle in the Gabriel library. There was a lot of exclusive male chumminess among the rest of the Waylandsbury team, and only Vernon seemed interested in my theory. He encouraged me to go on.'

Christa listened, enthralled, as Violet revealed the details of her long hunt for more clues in libraries and museums throughout Europe.

'Eventually I had all the evidence I needed to persuade Vernon to try a different line of approach. By this time I'd started to sleep with him. My academic and emotional life seemed to be coming together at last.'

She let the tapestry rest for a moment, her eyes on the sea again.

'I was so naive. I showed Vernon my data, confident he'd give me full credit if we discovered what I expected to find. To my horror, he poured buckets of cold water on my discovery, in a way that Oxford academics can do only too well. He made me feel useless intellectually, and to cap it all, a few days later ended our affair, saying I'd become unbalanced by my obsession with my theory.'

She picked up the tapestry again, and Christa could sense her tension in the way she stabbed the needle through the canvas.

'I couldn't cope. I fell apart, and ended up in hospital. That's when I learned to do this.' With an ironic expression Violet held up the tapestry. 'But luckily a young Australian doctor, in Oxford on an exchange, was in charge of my case. I slowly got better. We fell in love, married, and at the end of his stay I went back to Australia with him. Soon afterwards news broke of the discovery of the Waylandsbury Hoard.'

'How could you bear it?' Christa asked, even more astonished by now that Violet had done nothing to reveal her part in it. 'I'd have been so angry, so determined to get my work recognised.'

'I was expecting my first baby. Pregnancy has an amazing way of taking one's mind off other things.' She picked up a framed photo on the side table of herself with three small children, and smiled at it before going on. 'My husband thought it would be bad for me to re-open old psychological wounds, so I never challenged Vernon. When the children went to school, I switched to anthropology and did a doctorate on aboriginal culture. I got a job which satisfied me completely, and as the years went by, what Vernon had done meant less and less. Now I hardly ever think of it.'

Christa said goodbye to Violet after a simple lunch of grilled tuna, salad, and home-baked bread. In her bag she had a letter from Violet to the Vice-Chancellor, accompanied by a photocopy of her research notes on the location of the treasure. Luckily they were dated, and annotated by the Master with crushingly dismissive remarks. Christa felt certain the threat of sending the letter would make him drop his plans for Gabriel's Mill. He would never know of her promise to Violet.

In spite of this she felt curiously flat as she drove back in the sweltering heat to her hotel. For some reason the success of her trip and the prospect of a final reckoning with the Master weren't turning her on at all. Normally, with time to spare after an assignment she would have been meeting local media people, rushing about getting ideas for more stories, and generally squeezing the last drop of opportunity from a new locale.

Instead she moved to a beach hotel, went for a swim, and afterwards slept through the rest of the afternoon. In the evening she sat for a long time on the shore, thinking of what Violet had told her at lunchtime about the aboriginals and their way of life.

As she listened to the breeze in the palms, and watched the moon make a pathway of shifting silver across the sea, she tried to subdue a continuing, insistent desire for Mallory, and for the time to explore this huge, fascinating continent in a different, more leisurely way. But she'd blown that, she firmly told herself, and rather than endure more useless introspection she went to her room, took two more sleeping pills, and set her alarm for the early-morning drive to Cairns Airport.

Christa couldn't imagine anything going wrong this time with her plans to overthrow the Master, but once back in Oxford she spent the day before the meeting of Governing Body trying to find out the likely outcome of the vote on Gabriel's Mill.

As Leda lived in college, Christa had hoped to get her opinion in the common room before dinner. But the porters said that lately she'd been working during the evenings on some branch of her research at the Science Museum, and would probably eat in town. Christa guessed she must be interested in the biological specimens stored in the basement there.

One of the security staff let her in by a side entrance to the museum. He led her through the dimly lit main hall where skeletal dinosaurs stalked forever beneath a canopy of cast-iron foliage, and pointed her in the direction of an imposing Neo-Gothic doorway.

The room beyond the door was a monument to Victorian scientific endeavour. An immense mahogany cabinet whose ranks of display cases were filled with specimens of butterflies and shells stood against one wall. In a corner a stuffed dodo lurked. Across the lintel of the fireplace was carved a Greek inscription, which reminded Christa uncomfortably of Mallory and that first night in his room.

Leda was sitting at a table in her white lab coat, writing some notes.

'Christa! It's good to see you at last,' she exclaimed. 'I've been trying to track you down. I wanted to tell you what a huge effect the debate and your reporting of the riot have had on Gabriel. People are starting to think about the real purpose of the college again, and a lot of that is due to you. You've every right to feel very proud of yourself.'

'Other people helped too,' she said, feeling absurdly pleased all the same. Leda's good opinion meant more to her than anyone else's at Gabriel. Except perhaps Mallory's, she suddenly thought. 'You've a splendid room here,' she went on, rapidly changing the subject. 'What's the inscription over the fireplace?'

'It really belongs to one of the curators. I'm allowed to use it temporarily in the evenings. The inscription is Greek, part of the Hippocratic Oath. Where have you been, anyway? Celebrating? You look shattered.'

'It's jet-lag, not a hang-over. I've just come back from Australia.'

Leda raised her eyebrows.

'Was this a trial run before re-entering the professional fray? Apollo must be anxious to get you back after your report on the riot.'

'A trial run of sorts,' said Christa nonchalantly, who'd been trying not to think what she'd say when Randall phoned. 'I came to ask how you think the voting's likely to go on the Gabriel's Mill issue tomorrow?'

Leda looked serious. 'By my reckoning your recent activities have persuaded about a third of the older fellows to desert the Master. I've done some discreet lobbying myself, and brought a few others round, but at the moment the vote appears to be on a knife edge. I tried to persuade Gervaise Burford to come along, but he refused point blank. Apparently he's vowed never to attend a meeting while Vernon Slade's still the Master. And unfortunately Mallory will be away – unless you've heard anything to the contrary?'

'No, nothing', said Christa shortly.

'I left a telephone message for him at his contact address in Delhi when I realised how close the voting was likely to be. Unfortunately he was out of town and no one knew when he'd be back.'

'Putting as much distance between us as possible,' Christa said bitterly.

'I presume things didn't work out for you. I'm sorry. May I ask what went wrong?'

'I don't know.' Christa tried to look unconcerned. 'I suppose we simply see things in different ways.'

'How do you mean? I'd have said you were very alike. Both constantly searching for something – knowledge or the truth. People of that sort often look so far ahead that they don't realise things to do with themselves are in front of them all the time.'

'We didn't think alike about my work. Mallory thought war reporting was wrong for me, that I should try something else.'

'And do you still believe he's wrong?'

Leda's voice was kind but insistent.

'I don't know any more,' said Christa miserably, unable to tell her a direct lie. 'But it's too late now, even if I did change my mind.'

Leda got up, gathering together her notes.

'Are you going home after this? Let's have a drink together at the Lamb and Flag first, and if you'd like to, you can tell me about it. I've just got to check something in the specimen store, but if you don't mind waiting I'll be back in fifteen minutes. There's a kettle in the corner. Make yourself some coffee.'

The fifteen minutes stretched to thirty. Christa, spending them alone with the dodo and her thoughts, became increasingly faint-hearted at the prospect of confiding in Leda. Though part of her wanted to, she wasn't sure she could take what she might hear. She also had a nagging, instinctive feeling that this was something she must sort out for herself. In the end she decided to find Leda and, pleading tiredness, say she'd decided to go straight home after all.

The museum was decidedly eerie in the gathering dusk as Christa went in search of the security guard to ask the way to the specimen store. She finally located it in the basement, down two flights of stairs and along a short corridor. There was a notice on the sturdy oak door saying: 'Strictly no entry without permission. Experiment in progress'.

The guard had told her to hammer on it to attract Leda's attention, but to her surprise it wasn't locked, and she was able to go through into the store.

It was a small windowless room, crammed with jars of preserved specimens on tiers of wooden shelves, with narrow passages leading between. Leaning in a corner was the knobbly backbone of an ostrich, taller than herself, and on shelves against one wall rows of skulls grinned down like relics from a Sicilian charnel house. They were enough to put off any but the most intrepid trespasser.

Apart from these macabre inhabitants the room was empty, but it led into another. On her way to the connecting door Christa passed jars containing specimens of brains. Their convoluted folds gleamed palely through the glass, and she wondered if Leda was using them in her meningitis research.

In the next room reptiles, most of the colour leached from their skins by formalin, were coiled neatly into more ranks of jars. Leda wasn't here either, but there was another connecting door, which led to a further room. This was occupied mainly by specimens of fishes, and an assortment of oddities which included a jar of baby moles, their tiny pink paws only too visible against their dark fur, pressed against the glass as though trying to get out.

Christa hastily looked away, and headed for a door at the end of the store, whose heavy oak planks were studded with wrought-iron nails. On it was another notice prohibiting entry. She pushed, and it opened soundlessly.

A distinctive smell greeted her, one she remembered clearly from the Institute, a smell of ammonia and bark litter. There was an unusual sound too, someone singing in a low voice. She ventured in, and saw a sight infinitely more astonishing than anything in the other rooms.

Leda was sitting in an old-fashioned wooden office chair with a towel spread across her lap, and a baby chimpanzee with enormous eyes and wispy fur clinging to her as she rocked it to sleep. By her side was an empty feeding bottle. She was totally absorbed in the little creature.

A cage similar to those Christa had seen at the Institute, containing bark shavings, a nest of towels, and a large furry toy monkey, presumably a surrogate, stood in one corner. The room itself was a small basic laboratory with a work bench and a Belfast sink. It was impossible for anyone to look in through the small frosted-glass window set high in one wall. The room might have been designed for concealment.

Christa's involuntary exclamation of surprise made Leda look up. Her strong, confident face sagged.

'How did you get in?' she said in a voice breathless with shock. 'Oh, God, the outer lock of course. I remember now. It didn't catch properly the other day, but I thought it was just a temporary fault.'

Christa sat down on a lab stool, and looked at Leda. For once in her life she was at a loss for words. The risk Leda was taking was colossal. She could get years in prison for importing a wild member of an endangered species. On top of that she'd ignored quarantine, and must also be experimenting without Home Office permission.

'So Howl was right after all,' she said at last, too winded to think of a subtler comment.

Leda stroked the baby chimpanzee's head. Its eyes were beginning to droop just like Jamie's.

'Yes, but Yatima here only arrived via Germany two weeks ago. I'd been waiting a long time for her.' She smiled ruefully.

'It's rather ironic that I didn't mind the delay because it meant you were likelier to discount Howl's suspicions. I was actually more afraid of your investigations than theirs. You're a lot more professional.'

Christa went over to look at the infant more closely. Her tiny stomach was distended with milk, and the forefinger of the hand not clinging to Leda was plugged firmly in her mouth.

'How old is she?' she asked, still feeling stupefied by her discovery. If she'd ever looked up to anyone, it was Leda. She'd regarded her as a model of probity. And, oddly enough, perhaps because Leda wasn't attempting any kind of cover-up or self-justification, in a way she still did.

'Just a few months. She's an orphan. That's what her name means in Swahili. She wouldn't have survived in the wild.'

'She's so perfect,' said Christa, feeling sick at the thought of experiments on such a tiny creature. 'What have you been doing to her?'

'Just taking blood samples, and a few other small but vital tests. Nothing traumatic, I promise you. I've already got most of the data I wanted. She's going to a private zoo in Ireland soon, where I'll be able to visit and keep an eye on her. It's a good place as zoos go, and with luck she'll be able to breed when she's mature.'

Christa's brain had begun to work properly at last. More implications of her discovery were crowding in on her. If she'd discovered what Leda was doing during the course of a profes-sional assignment, she would have felt bound to report it to the police. If she went ahead and did so anyway, it would mean the certain end of Leda's medical career as well as a possible prison sentence. It would also mean she'd never succeed the Master.

'Jesus, Leda, how could you do it?' she groaned, clasping her hands to her head in frustrated despair. 'How could you have risked so much?'

'Easily,' said Leda in a quiet voice. 'Surely you haven't forgot-ten those children brain-damaged by meningitis in Bosnia? It's worse even to see a child die. The data I've got from Yatima has already radically advanced my research.'

'All the same, I don't see how I can let this go. If only you'd locked the door,' Christa said desperately.

'Of course you must make your own moral choice about what to do. I shouldn't dream of trying to influence you. But knowing you as I do, I don't suppose there'd be much point in trying anyway.'

Her dignity was as breath-taking as her self-control. Christa felt near to tears. She wanted to scream that it wasn't fair, that she shouldn't have this hideous dilemma forced upon her.

'I'm sorry,' said Leda. 'You're the last person I'd have wanted to land with this, especially when you've already been through so much.'

Christa wished Leda would stop being so nice. It made the decision harder still.

'How do you manage the logistics of keeping Yatima here, anyway?' she asked, trying to stall for time.

'Betty helps during the day. I give Yatima a very mild sedative at night, mixed with her milk. This room is almost sound-proof, and I have the only key. Very few people come into the rest of the store, apart from the curator.'

'But you're so scrupulous, so – so honourable. I still can't quite take it in,' said Christa weakly, thinking that it was typical of Oxford to present her with a moral choice like this.

'I must admit it's the first time I've seen you completely at a loss,' said Leda with a faint smile. 'Come on, Christa, tell me what you're going to do. I'd like to prepare myself. Unfortunately I can't lock you up like Yatima.'

'I wish you could. Then I shouldn't need to make a choice.'

'There'll be no recriminations from me, whatever you decide. But I would like you to think very hard what it'll mean to the meningitis research and the Institute.'

The infant was asleep. Leda got up, carried her over to the cage, and with infinite tenderness settled her in the nest of towels. She checked the water supply before carefully padlocking the door.

Because of Leda's calm impartiality, because she still hadn't pleaded or threatened or panicked, Christa had the sensation that she was more in charge of the situation than herself.

'However I choose, one of us is going to suffer,' she said miserably. 'If I don't report this, it'll be the first time I've deliberately concealed the truth from the public. I've got to have time to think. In any case, whatever I decide to do must wait until after the meeting of Governing Body tomorrow. You have to be free to vote against the Master's proposals for Gabriel's Mill.'

Though Christa took the last of her sleeping pills, she hardly slept that night. Leda had unfailingly supported her, and knowing what she was putting Leda through by the delay made Christa feel like a torturer.

Yet she had always prided herself on her professional integrity. To jettison it would feel like self-betrayal. It was the sort of ethical problem Gabriel's philosphers loved to discuss over their port, but which was so hideous in real life.

The morning brought no relief. She was still agonisingly undecided, and had the additional problem of the meeting of Governing Body that afternoon to deal with as well. When she went into the common room for coffee, it was clear that intensive lobbying was still going on. Fellows she scarcely ever saw had turned up for the day, and negotiations were obviously set to continue through pre-lunch sherry and the meal itself.

She ate some sandwiches by the river while again trying to make up her mind over Leda. Eventually her continuing indecision drove her to the Bohemia Room, where she was the first fellow to arrive.

It seemed an almost full house was expected, for the already large committee table had been extended with several leaves to accommodate over forty places. Miss Harker, in a new navy blue suit worn with a ruffled blouse, trotted round it setting out pristine sheets of blotting paper. Down the middle of the table were ranked the traditional silver inkstands and quill pens which appeared at every official meeting.

Piers was the next to arrive, just as Christa had managed to wrest open a window and let in a refreshing waft of twentieth-century air.

'You were crazy to miss the fun at lunch,' he said. 'The place is thick with rumours. The Master's playing his cards close to his chest. He was whipping people off for one-to-one sessions in the garden between coffee and lunch. I hope your secret weapon is a good one, but you'll find there's an interesting surprise coming your way, in any case.'

'Not another, for God's sake. Stop being so gnomic. I'm not in the mood for it.'

'All will be revealed in due course. I can hear the vanguard staggering up the stairs now. Some of the older fellows had so much sherry they're almost legless. They'll probably spend the whole meeting asleep.'

'As long as they wake up in time to vote on the right side, I don't care,' said Christa, studying the agenda for the twentieth time.

The ratification of Leda's appointment and the future of Gabriel's Mill were the last two items, apart from Any Other Business. A confidential detailed proposal for the development of the site had accompanied the agenda, and Christa wondered how the Master had managed to justify it to his cronies in the interval between the document's circulation and the meeting.

Now she too could hear the Master's pedantic voice outside, accompanied by the querulous voices of the older fellows, and the wheezing of the Dean, who had finally returned to work. When the Master appeared he looked so supremely confident that she began to wonder if he had a secret weapon of his own.

By two minutes to two nearly all the fellows had arrived, but Leda was still missing. More unpleasant conjectures flitted through Christa's mind. Perhaps this was the surprise Piers meant. Perhaps Leda had ducked out already, and the Master was going to announce her resignation at the meeting.

When at one minute to two she heard Leda talking to someone on the landing outside, Christa felt as though the archangel himself had appeared. But a moment later a man's answering voice made her stomach contract. Mallory had unexpectedly returned.

When Leda walked in her face was grave, but she was as self-possessed as ever, wearing a scarlet suit which perfectly set off her striking helmet of hair. Mallory had a splendid tan, as if he'd been holidaying on some Indian Ocean beach.

It wasn't fair that he should look so carefree, Christa thought miserably. She began to feel even more paranoid, as if he'd turned up specifically to increase her wretchedness rather than to vote. For now she saw him, she realised still more how much she'd missed him.

Luckily Leda and Mallory were both at the far end of the table. Leda sent Christa a warm smile as she sat down, but Mallory's gaze passed over her in a way which made her want to hurl an inkstand at him.

The meeting began, and Governing Body started to drone through the initial items on the agenda. When she wasn't trying to ignore Mallory, or try yet again to come to a decision about Leda, Christa couldn't stop her mind from straying to Randall, and what she was going to do when he made her an offer. It was almost a relief when tea-time approached, and she had to think about her coming encounter with the Master instead.

'Are you all right?' Piers asked in an undertone, as two stewards staggered in with laden teatrays and the Master announced a twenty-minute break. 'If you hadn't told me otherwise, I'd say you were in a thoroughly bad way about our enigmatic colleague over there.'

'Don't be ridiculous,' she snapped. 'I'm going to talk to someone else if you can't think of anything better to discuss.'

People were already getting up and drifting towards the side table. Christa managed to insinuate her way through a knot of sycophants surrounding the Master. She was encouraged by a definite, though rapidly banished, look of apprehension as she arrived at his side.

'May I speak to you alone for a moment, Master? It's to do with a forthcoming item on the agenda.'

'Of course,' he said urbanely. 'Shall we retire to a corner?'

'It's extremely confidential. I'd prefer to go outside.'

'Indeed?' He raised faint grey eyebrows. 'In that case let us adjourn to the Queen's Parlour, though I'm afraid I can only allow you a limited amount of time.'

The Parlour, originally designed as a private closet for the Queen of Bohemia when she occasionally visited the college, was reached through a connecting door. It was a small intimate room with linen-fold panelling, a bay window whose upper panes contained the Queen's coat of arms in stained glass, and a ceiling heavily pargeted with the Stuart emblem.

The Master walked over to the fireplace and turned to face Christa. Outwardly no one could have been less threatening. He'd taken off his gown during the break, and with his grey hair, grey face and grey clothing, he appeared to merge into the fusty atmosphere, except where a coloured patch of sunlight gave him solidity as it fell through the stained glass on to his suit. It made him appear truly a master of deception, or the djinn to which Wes had once likened him.

'I am all attention, Miss Keith,' he said.

His voice was as soft as the ashes in the grate. It seemed odd to be taking part in such a quiet battle, unaccompanied by shellbursts or gunfire. Christa took a deep breath.

'Some information has come into my possession, Professor Slade, which concerns your academic reputation.'

His face showed no emotion, but he moved very slightly and the patches of light shifted like a camouflage net to a different part of his body.

'I assume you are about to impart some unpleasant rumour arising from professional jealousy. Let me tell you I've been dealing with that sort of thing ever since I discovered the Waylandsbury Hoard. You may as well save your breath.'

'This is no rumour. I assume you remember Violet Quinn at the Waylandsbury dig?'

The Master moved so suddenly that Christa was left bemusedly staring at a patch of colour on the floor, before she realised he'd gone to the window and was standing with his back to her.

'How could I forget her?' he said, in his usual dry, even voice. 'I was her supervisor. Poor creature. A most pathetic case of a fine mind lacking the strength to sustain itself.'

'Poor creature indeed. You know very well that she was the real discoverer of the Hoard.'

Christa longed to see his expression, but still he didn't turn round.

'I think you should be extremely careful what you say, Miss Keith. Violet Quinn was a hysteric depressive.'

'And you made her so. Don't bother to argue with me. I've seen her, and been told the full story. She's even shown me her research notes with your comments.'

The Master turned to face her. Lines of astonishment had cracked apart his bland expression at last.

'You've seen her? But she's in Australia! She hasn't been heard of for years.'

'I went there especially to find her.'

'Violet,' he repeated softly, looking almost approachable. 'I can hardly believe this is true.'

'It is true. Look, here's her writing on this envelope.'

Christa held out the letter addressed to the Vice-Chancellor. A flicker of real emotion passed over the Master's face.

'I was genuinely fond of her, Miss Keith, though you may find it hard to believe. In other circumstances I might have married her. How is she?'

'Well and happy, I'm glad to say. But extremely disturbed to hear about your proposals for the Gabriel's Mill site. She wants you to drop them immediately.'

'Ah!' said the Master. 'So that's why the envelope is addressed to the Vice-Chancellor. We've at last arrived at the real purpose of this discussion.'

'Exactly. She's offering you a trade-off. Your reputation in exchange for keeping Professor Saltash's promise to the Gabriel's Grounds Estate. Personally I think you're incredibly lucky. She could have simply decided to expose you to the media. So how about it?'

He sat down on the window seat, and locked his hands together round his knee. The speed with which he'd regained his composure was beginning to worry her. She could sense he was assessing potential moves as coldly as a computer playing chess.

'Knowing Violet as I do, it's hard to believe she'd want to stir up so much unpleasantness after so many years,' he said. 'She was never vindictive. She'd hate the publicity if I didn't agree to her terms. She couldn't stand the strain.'

'She's more than willing to go through with it, for the sake of the students and the people of Gabriel's Grounds,' said Christa, praying that the ability to bluff, learned during many games of poker in foreign bars, would again come to her aid. 'If you don't agree, I have her full permission to deliver this letter from her to the Vice-Chancellor, together with a copy of her research notes. So how about it, Professor Slade?'

He still seemed less disturbed than she'd hoped and expected. He'd unclasped his hands, and was leaning back with one arm along the window ledge, tapping his fingers against the wood in a secret, jaunty tune.

'Miss Keith, I must tell you that I also am in possession of some adverse information regarding a member of college. A member whom I believe you hold in high regard.'

Christa stared at him suspiciously.

'Who?' she demanded, immediately thinking he meant Mallory.

'Dr Lennox. I am sorry to say it has recently come to my knowledge that she is breaking the law on the university's premises.'

Christa tried to appear calm, but inwardly she froze. She could only hope that he was bluffing too, exaggerating some very minor transgression for his own end.

'So what's she done?' she demanded. 'Walked on the college grass?'

'How I wish that were all,' he said in a sanctimonious voice. 'Unfortunately it's something much more difficult to overlook. She is conducting unauthorised experiments on an endangered species, imported, I suspect, from the wild.'

Christa was too stupefied by the accuracy of his information to pretend ignorance any more.

'How can you possibly know? No one does.'

'Ah, so you've found out as well? I should have guessed you might. And you should have known that everything reaches me in the end.'

'But who told you?' Christa persisted.

'Luckily someone who is the soul of discretion: Miss Harker. She made the discovery a couple of days ago. She was trying to find Dr Lennox to give her an urgent message, and stumbled on the secret by mistake. I gather there was a faulty lock on an outer door. Dr Lennox wasn't there, and Miss Harker did the sensible thing and consulted me. I persuaded her to leave the matter in my hands. She knew how harmful to the college a public disclosure would be.'

Christa was silent, imagining Miss Harker's distress. She would have been cast into even greater agonies of indecision than Christa herself.

'Your astonishment is gratifying, Miss Keith,' said the Master with a faint smile. 'I was beginning to wonder if anything could deter you in your pursuit of the truth. And you'll no doubt be even more astonished to learn that my original intention on learning this news was not to prevent Dr Lennox from becoming Master, but merely to warn her that her activities must henceforth cease.'

'I'm not astonished at all,' said Christa slowly, at last beginning to collect her wits. 'Because that way you could blackmail her into doing whatever you want when she is Master. You'd still be in charge, though you'd retired.'

'Exactly,' said the Master. 'Well done. However, because of Violet Quinn's threat, that happy outcome is not to be. I'm sure you realise that we have reached a rather different kind of trade-off, as you call it. Dame Leda's reputation in exchange for mine.'

Christa was again reduced to silence as she realised the implications for Gabriel's Mill.

'Yes, you'll have to take a chance on the vote on the Mill, and so shall I,' said the Master. 'It'll be an interesting contest, but I must warn you that I think I shall win.'

'You're revelling in this, aren't you?' said Christa angrily.

'The college is my life. As long as my academic reputation remains intact I can still exert some influence, even when I'm merely an Emeritus professor.'

'But don't you care about the students? You act as though it's some kind of chess game. You forget the pieces are living people.'

'Life is a game of sorts, and academic advancement particularly so. Sometimes we have to compromise. Indeed, civilisation is the art of compromise.'

'Not your sort of compromise,' said Christa, loathing the way she'd again been forced into a typical Oxford quandary. Constantly throughout the past few months she'd been made to see life less in terms of absolutes.

If she exposed him, Leda and her research would be ruined, and she'd never become Head of House. If she kept quiet, Leda's research and the future of the college would be saved, and there was still a slender chance over the Gabriel's Mill vote. Christa would have to go along with the Master, though she despised herself utterly for it.

'All right, I agree,' she said, feeling sick as she spoke. 'But never forget the evidence still exists against you, in case you're tempted to change your mind.'

'You've made a good decision. I shan't change my mind,' said the Master, getting up from the window seat and already beginning to glide towards the door. 'We've kept the fellows waiting long enough, so now that little matter's disposed of, I suggest we finish our tea and resume the meeting without delay.'

Back in the Bohemia Room Christa went over to Leda and manoeuvred her discreetly to one side.

'You look as bad as I feel,' Leda said. Her face was haggard. 'I take it you've decided?'

She shut her eyes for a moment, clearly gathering her strength for the anticipated blow.

'Yes, I have. And I'm sorry it's taken me so long. I want you to know I'm going to keep quiet about Yatima. But you must give me your assurance that you'll never attempt anything like it again. And you must get her out of the country at once.'

'Thank God,' said Leda, closing her eyes again and letting out a long sigh. 'You have my promise. I could hardly believe you'd do so without warning me first, but I thought you might have been telling the Master about her when you both disappeared just now. I got the results I wanted this morning, and Yatima will be going to Ireland tomorrow.'

Christa felt as if she'd been thrown gasping from the grip of a tidal wave. Miss Harker was still pouring out tea, but even the thought of it made her feel queasy.

'I'd have given a lot for you not to be caught up in this, but it was for the greater good,' Leda went on. 'I'm deeply in your debt, and so are a great many children, which I hope is some recompense.'

'It's always for the greater good in Oxford.' Christa couldn't stop the bitterness from creeping into her voice, or prevent her gaze from straying towards Mallory. 'That's the problem with this place. And a huge problem when people like the Master, and even you to a certain extent, manipulate the higher good for their own ends.'

'I'm sorry,' said Leda again. 'This must have been tremendously stressful for you. If there's any way I can help you, either now or in the future, you have only to ask.'

'You've already helped me,' said Christa, trying to appear

unconcerned as Mallory passed by her to speak to Miss Harker without a sign of recognition. 'But the sooner I leave Oxford now, the better. I just hope the Gabriel's Mill vote goes our way, otherwise I shall think all my time here has been in vain.'

'Of course it hasn't been in vain,' said Leda. She at least was looking considerably better. She gave Christa one of her professional looks. 'I think you need to have that talk we missed yesterday. Let me take you out to dinner as soon as I return from Ireland. I insist. I need to thank you properly, anyway.'

Reluctantly Christa agreed, just as the Master called them back to the committee table.

'Ladies and gentlemen, your attention, please. Shall we reconvene?'

Christa still felt dazed as she sat through the ratification of Leda's appointment and the committee's congratulations. She'd discovered she didn't have the steely determination it took to purvey the absolute truth, and another foundation stone of her life had been removed.

When the Master announced the final item, the future of the Gabriel's Mill site, she felt so pessimistic about the outcome that she had to force herself to concentrate. She was astonished by the impassioned debate which ensued, and the number of dons who had gravitated to the cause of the Gabriel's Grounds Estate. Leda and Mallory's speeches were outstanding, but Christa knew there was a hard core of fellows who wouldn't dare desert the Master, because they owed him too much.

The Master was clearly counting on them too. He was as unruffled as ever as he brought the discussion to an end, though everyone else was clearly longing for the traditional schooners of Jubilee sherry laid on in the common room after meetings of Governing Body.

'And now, fellows of Gabriel, I must call you to account,' he said, briskly rapping the table. 'We shall proceed to a decision by a show of hands.'

Christa was wondering numbly if she could bear to stay for the vote, when it dawned on her that there was a tremendous commotion going on outside the committee room. Someone was arguing violently with the porter guarding the door.

A moment later it flew open and Gervaise hobbled into the

room, leaning heavily on an ebony walking stick. He looked round with a sardonic smile.

'I see nothing's changed. And I gather I'm not too late to vote on the matter of Gabriel's Mill. Fred tells me you've only just finished discussing it. Damned car broke down on the way, or I'd have been here from the start.'

Christa felt like kissing the old man. Mallory, with a huge grin, leaped up and solicitously escorted him to the table, lowering him into the empty seat next to his own.

'Well, well, let's get on with it,' Gervaise said testily.

The Master looked like a landed fish.

'We're delighted to have you with us after such a long absence, of course, Professor Burford, but . . .'

'Balderdash. Of course you're not delighted,' Gervaise interrupted. 'Just stop prevaricating, and let the meeting continue.'

'I was simply about to question whether it's wise for you to vote, when you can't possibly be apprised of the full background to the affair.'

'I'm very well apprised, Vernon. Dr Farrar has kept me more than adequately informed, and I believe I knew the late Master's mind better than anyone else here. In case you'd forgotten, I am the Senior Fellow.'

'Then we'll proceed to a vote. As I was about to say, I shall call first for a show of hands from those in favour of the motion, and then from those against.'

Christa's heart was hammering so loudly that the sound seemed to fill her ears as the voting took place, and it became apparent that the numbers were exactly even.

'Twenty-two on either side,' said the Master with a triumphant smile. 'So in that case I have the casting vote.'

Leda's face was almost as anxious as when Christa had discovered her secret. Mallory's grim expression was back again. But Gervaise looked like Rumpelstiltskin bent on mischief, and not in the slightest dismayed.

'I think not, Vernon,' he said. 'How lucky that I am present to give you the benefit of my advice, though I fear you may not welcome it. On matters affecting the leases of the Bohemia Bequest, the Senior Fellow has the deciding vote. I can remember a similar occasion, well before your time, when I was the most junior member of college present, and opinion was equally divided on the lease of land to be used as the site for a cinema. The Senior Fellow cast the deciding vote then.'

'Is this so?' said the Master, rounding on the Dean in a voice which made him search for his inhaler.

'I'm not sure Master,' he wheezed. 'During my term of office there's never been an equally divided vote in connection with the Bohemia Bequest. And unfortunately my copy of the bequest document is with the college lawyers just now.'

'No matter,' said Giles. 'The original is here in the room. Let us unlock the case and see for ourselves.'

'Impossible! The parchment is much too frail to handle,' said the Master. 'I cannot sanction anything which might damage our most valuable treasure.'

To Christa's delight, Piers, who'd been scribbling an extremely crude limerick on his blotter about the Master of Gabriel Hall, suddenly spoke up.

'I distinctly remember a conversation with an expert from the BM who came to inspect it only last term,' he observed in a throwaway tone. 'He said it was good for another five hundred years at least.'

Defeated, the Master nodded at Miss Harker. The document was extracted and laid reverently on the table in front of Gervaise. He was enjoying himself enormously, heightening the suspense by searching all his numerous pockets for his reading spectacles, and settling them with great deliberation on his nose.

'Here we are,' he said at last. ' "In the matter of the disposition of leases, if opinion be equally divided, the fellow most senior by virtue of his years as a member of Gabriel Hall shall take precedence over the Master and be allowed an additional deciding vote." '

'For God's sake, why didn't you tell me this?' the Master hissed at the Dean.

Mallory's voice struck across the table as the Dean tried to speak through his wheezes.

'Intimidation isn't going to work, Master. Not now, or ever again. I call upon the fellows to join me in asking Dr Burford to cast his deciding vote.'

There was a roar of assent. Gervaise smiled gleefully round the table.

'I vote for the carrying out of Professor Saltash's promise, for the Mill site to be developed for the benefit of Gabriel's Grounds, of course,' he declared. 'And now give me your arm, Dr Farrar, and let's go and celebrate! I gather from Fred that there's still some 1980 Bollinger left. I told him to instruct the cellar steward to put a dozen magnums on ice.'

Christa arrived back in Jericho with her head aching from more than champagne. For her the revelry in the common room had been more slow torture than a celebration. It was agonisingly difficult to pretend to herself and everyone else that Mallory's return meant nothing. Fortunately he'd left with Gervaise after about an hour, and she was able to escape without losing face.

The phone was ringing as she entered the sitting room, echoed by Poppaea who had recently learned its warble to maddening effect. When she answered, the voice she'd been dreading to hear made her hurriedly sit down.

'It's Randall, Christa. I've been trying to get you all afternoon. Did you see the midday news?'

'No. I was in college. What's happened?' she asked. Her stomach felt as if it had hit the floor.

'A massive outbreak of fighting in Chechnya, in spite of the truce. Looks as if it's going to escalate too. The assignment's made for you. I've hijacked Jim Albury from Channel Six to replace Matt. I know you've always admired his work. It's all set up and ready to go. You're both booked for the first flight out of Heathrow tomorrow.'

'For God's sake, Randall, hold on a moment,' she said weakly. 'Chechnya – it's one hell of a place – I'm not sure – I've got to have a little time to think about this.'

'Not sure?' he bellowed down the line. 'Are you crazy? What is it? Money? I'm offering you another 10K on your old salary, plus the usual bonus. It's a life-time's opportunity. Believe me, there are very few other women to whom I'd offer Chechnya.'

'It's not money. I just feel – I've changed somehow since I came here.'

She knew how feeble she must sound, and didn't blame Randall for thinking so too.

'Rubbish!' he roared. 'It's simply stage-fright – perfectly understandable when you've been away so long. You'll snap out of it the moment you're back in the thick of things. You'll forget you've ever been away.'

'That's what I'm afraid of,' she said slowly.

'Last September you would have jumped at this. I don't have time to fart about listening to your hang-ups now. I'm too busy. You know what it's like when a big story starts to break, and this one could be huge. You're a professional war-correspondent, Christa. You know the score.'

'Yes, I know the score,' she repeated dully.

'Right. So I'll give you half an hour to decide. I expect an answer from you by seven.'

Christa put down the phone in an advanced state of shock. Randall was right. To be offered Chechnya was an enormous compliment, and nine months ago she would already have been running to pack her bag. Now all she could think of was that she was bound to be sent to Grozny first, at the height of the earlier fighting one of the grimmest places on earth. She'd be plunged straight into every kind of human misery and degradation again.

She paced up and down the sitting room for five minutes, then wandered restlessly through the kitchen and scullery to the garden at the back of the house. The scent of the white lilac overhanging the path was heavy in the air. Its flowers sprinkled her face and hair with water droplets from a recent shower as she passed.

The leaves of her half-grown lettuce plants were a vivid green against the moist black soil. Christa remembered digging the plot with Mallory, and the care with which he'd set the fragile seedlings in the earth. She wouldn't gather them, for the house would have to be sold in order to buy a flat in London near Apollo and Heathrow. Pansy would begin to forget her again. She'd grow away from her family, and she'd grow away from her new self.

She walked on down to the canal's edge, and stood gazing into the water, watching an eddy silently bear away a handful of dead wildflowers. The distant thud of the ironworks seemed to stamp her decision into her brain.

She wouldn't go to Chechnya. She'd have to try another sort of reporting as Mallory had suggested, something which didn't cut her off so drastically from normal life. Randall would be furious, but when he'd calmed down he'd give her the professional contacts to help her set out on a different path. Yet even though her mind was calm and clear at last, she was trying not to cry as she walked back to the house. For without Mallory to share this new venture, half its meaning would be lost.

21

Ten days later Christa was again at Heathrow, this time in the departure hall. Randall, after bawling her out for a good five minutes when he heard her decision, had nobly come to her aid and pulled more strings.

As a result John Nisbet, the head of features at Apollo, offered her a contract to produce and present a six-part documentary on the lives of women in China. This was a preliminary research trip before preparing a shooting script.

'You're bloody fortunate to get it, considering you haven't done any producing before,' Randall had grumbled. 'It's only because of your high public profile that Johnny Nisbet was willing to take a chance.'

At least there was no risk of encountering Mallory in China, Christa thought. As it was, they hadn't met since the day of the vote. Leda at their dinner together said he'd intended to stay with Gervaise for some time while he worked on a proposal for his new book.

Christa tried to stifle the pang of longing still induced by the thought of him, and looked again at the departures board. She'd arrived early and there was almost an hour until she need board her flight. The huge hall was crowded. Queues of travellers stretched back across the floor from the check-in desks. All around her people were saying goodbye, mothers hugging daughters, grandparents smothering babies with kisses, lovers locked in embraces from which it seemed they'd never tear themselves apart.

Normally she would have gone through immigration to the departure lounge, but today she felt unaccustomedly forlorn, as if she wanted to hold on to familiar things as long as possible.

It was such a childish thought that she went in search of coffee to brace herself, and retired with it to the quietest corner she could find, hoping she wouldn't be spotted by the resident Heathrow photographer or any passing member of the press. After an Apollo publicity release about her new assignment, the media's interest in her had renewed. China should put a stop to that, she thought, drinking the coffee and reviewing the events of the past hectic ten days.

Leda, aided by a consortium of Oxford businessmen, had started raising funds for a community centre and small business park on the Mill site.

Rebekah was caretaking the Jericho house, and would do so again when Christa went on her longer filming trip. Christa had pulled some strings of her own. She'd shown the students' video to the head of personnel at Apollo, and as a result Justin and Steve were offered traineeships with the company when they graduated. Her father was again on the short list for the librarianship at Gabriel, and Leda had assured her that this time he would almost certainly be appointed.

Equally satisying but much more surprising was Philip's behaviour at a family lunch given by Emma, now fully recovered, on the day before Christa's departure. He'd solemnly taken her on one side in the hall, with such a hang-dog expression that she began to worry in case something else was wrong with Emma.

'I feel I should apologise to you before you go,' he said, looking anywhere but straight at her. 'Emma told me the true content of your conversation before her accident. I misjudged you. I'm sorry.'

Though it was a strangulated and almost inaudible apology, Christa was touched. Coming from Phil it was on a par with an international political détente.

'It's OK,' she said casually. 'I guess I did come on a bit strong sometimes too.'

For once he didn't carp at her slangy expression. He swallowed hard, Adam's apple bobbing up and down in the neck of the sports shirt which looked entirely wrong on him, and held out his hand.

'Good,' he said. 'Then shall we both try to aim for a period of positive readjustment?'

He really was impossible, Christa thought. Anyone else would have hugged her, or at least tried to sound less like a Brussels diplomat. But again she was touched, and solemnly shook his hand.

'All right,' she said, trying not to laugh, 'though perhaps it'd be safer to call it a trial truce.'

Her mother had been in an even more positive mood, brimming with enthusiasm about a job offer from a neighbour with a small business which planned children's parties.

'She wants me to help with the catering. Some of her ideas for birthday cakes are a little odd – I'm not convinced a toddler would really appreciate a sponge shaped like a vampire bat – but I'm sure I shall be able to cope.'

The occasion continued to be astonishingly full of sweetness and light until the very end, when Pansy descended into a massive sulk after Emma refused to take her to Heathrow to see Christa off.

'No, I will not,' Emma said briskly. 'I'm teaching all day tomorrow and you must go to school as well. You have to learn, Pansy, that the world doesn't revolve round you.'

'Chel saw her auntie off to Torremolinos last year,' Pansy wailed, retreating in high dudgeon to the cupboard under the stairs, where she gave Christa a very damp embrace on her departure.

'I won't have any fun while you're away,' she muttered. 'It's not fair. And I wanted to be your bridesmaid, too, but you went and spoiled it all.'

Christa was glad Pansy couldn't see her face in the darkness.

'I can think of lots more exciting things to do than that,' she said, recalling her own single appearance as a bridesmaid, to Emma, which had been an endurance test from beginning to end. 'If you come out of here and say goodbye properly, I'll take you to Paris Disneyland when I get back.'

*　　*　　*

Christa smiled as she remembered Pansy's instant recovery, and almost wished she hadn't discouraged her family from seeing her off. She finished her coffee and looked at her watch again. Still half an hour to go before her final call, but it made no sense to keep hanging around.

She picked up her rucsac, checked for photographers again, and headed towards the barrier. As she did so she heard an excited, high-pitched screech, exactly like Pansy's. She decided she'd imagined it because she'd been thinking of her, and carried on.

The screech came again. She turned, and saw Pansy skimming towards her across the highly polished floor in a dress of pink ruffled taffeta. Emma was hurrying to catch up, wearing a resigned expression.

'Surprise, surprise!' Pansy shrieked, skidding full-tilt into Christa and clutching her round the waist.

'I thought we wouldn't get here in time,' Emma puffed. 'We were stuck for ages in a traffic jam. I'm so sorry, Christa, but I had to bring her. She wore me down in the end.'

'It's wonderful to see you both! What's the dress in aid of, Pansy?'

'We've just bought it for Chel's birthday party next week,' said Emma. 'She insisted on showing you.'

'It's much, much frillier than Chel's,' said Pansy, twirling around.

'So you've got something better than hers at last,' said Christa with a grin. 'I think we should go up to the bar and celebrate with a drink.'

'Yes, yes!' Pansy was dancing with excitement. 'Can I have a cocktail? Please let me, Mummy, please!'

Emma, carried away by the pervading spirit of bonhomie, found herself sitting five minutes later at a table situated discreetly at the very edge of the bar area, while Pansy contemplated with awe a large daquiri minus the rum and topped by a cherry speared with a parasol cocktail stick.

She sipped her own drink sparingly, remembering she had to drive home, and realised how much she'd miss Christa.

'I'm glad you'll be back soon. It's been good to have you around.'

'Funnily enough, I'm glad too,' Christa replied. 'And I never expected to hear myself say that.'

She was wearing the frayed white jeans and shabby blue cotton cardigan she'd had on when she first arrived at Ethelred Road, and looked as relaxed as someone going for a country walk. In her place Emma would have been in a turmoil over vaccinations and currency and the huge, seething continent ahead. Yet in spite of her sister's apparent contentment, Emma sensed there was something wrong still. She longed to ask Christa about it, but couldn't quite make herself, in case she spoiled their last minutes together.

Pansy had been mercifully quiet, alternately dunking the cherry and blowing bubbles through the straw, while she surveyed the comings and goings of the other travellers. Emma glanced at her to make sure she wasn't spoiling her dress, and saw her suddenly tense with excitement.

'Mummmee!' Pansy shrieked, leaping from her chair. 'See over there! It's Mallory!'

Emma stood up and turned in the direction of Pansy's pointing arm. Mallory stood at the far side of the refreshment area, impatiently scanning the crowd. Even from a distance the absolute determination in his manner singled him out.

'I'm going to fetch him!' Pansy announced, and skipped away before anyone could stop her.

Emma glanced at Christa. She'd got up and was staring at Mallory as well. She looked as if someone had punched her in the ribs. Emma's astonishment increased as Christa flung her rucsac over her shoulder.

'I can't take any more of this,' she announced wildly. 'I have to get out of here. Sorry, Em, but I'm going through immigration now. Explain to Pansy for me, please.'

Emma could feel Christa trembling as she pulled away from a snatched hug. All at once she comprehended everything. It was no different from their childhood, when Christa had to be stopped on the brink of some enormously rash but cherished scheme and made to think about the consequences for herself.

She grabbed the rucsac from Christa's shoulder, dumped it in a chair, and sat on it. Not even Christa would dare fight her in public to get it back.

'You're not going anywhere,' she said. 'You'll stay here and speak to Mallory. And I don't care if you miss your flight.'

Christa was glowering at her. Her eyes had become an intense, brilliant blue as they always did when she wasn't getting her own way. Her expression heralded a major onslaught, but Emma had no intention of dealing with it herself.

Pansy rushed up to them like a very small, very determined tug piloting a battleship. Mallory, striding along behind her, looked quite unlike his usual laidback self. He glared at Christa. He had a good line in basilisk stares as well, Emma thought, and felt an awful urge to laugh.

'I've been looking for you all over the whole damn airport! Why didn't you tell me what you were up to?' he shouted at Christa. 'Apollo wouldn't give me your flight number – some rubbish about security. We've got to talk.'

'I didn't want to be looked for! I don't want to talk to you!' Christa bawled back. Heads turned at the bar to look at them.

'Yes, she does!' Emma said to Mallory, feeling as if she were in charge of three children, not one. 'Come along, Pansy. We're going to look at the shops.'

'But I don't want to look at the shops.' Pansy's voice was outraged.

'Just for once, you'll do as your mother tells you,' Emma snapped, slinging Christa's rucsac over her shoulder. She took Pansy firmly by the arm and propelled her towards the down escalator and the entrance hall.

'And the same applies to you,' said Mallory, grabbing Christa and steering her just as forcefully into a relatively quiet spot behind an escalator.

'Why the hell didn't you tell me what you'd decided?' he demanded. 'You might at least have given me another chance.'

He was gripping her as if he expected her to disappear in a puff of smoke. Her legs had turned to marshmallow. She couldn't have gone anywhere if she'd wanted to.

'I knew nothing about what's really been going on until I got back to Oxford this morning, and met Leda in the common room,' he went on furiously. 'She told me everything. About what you'd done for her, what you told her when you had dinner together ... She more or less ordered me to come after you. God knows how many speed traps I've been in on the way.'

'She told you everything?'

Christa felt dizzy as she remembered all the stupid, gutless things she'd said to Leda about missing him.

'Everything,' said Mallory, 'and don't even think of trying to get out of it.'

He'd loosened his grip and put his arms round her instead.

'Jesus, I was so scared I wasn't going to catch up with you.'

His hands were under her cardigan. Her own were round his waist.

'I'm going to miss my flight,' she said.

He smiled. 'There'll be another one. I was hoping you might like me to come with you, anyway.'

'In what capacity? Personal trainer?' she asked, beginning to laugh.

'Anything. We could even get married,' he answered, as they surfaced from a long, invigorating kiss. 'Leda was very hot on the benefits of commitment for us both.'

'But you don't know my mother,' she said weakly. Things she'd thought important seemed to be sliding away from her enormously fast, and she didn't mind at all. 'She'd go crazy if we didn't have a formal wedding. When Emma married she organised everyone to death.'

'You don't know my sisters. We'd just have to support each other through the ordeal.'

'Even with Pansy as a bridesmaid?' said Christa.

'No problem. Poppaea as well, if you want.'

As they came up from another kiss they were greeted by an explosion of flashbulbs. The official Heathrow photographer was beaming at them, and half of Wapping too.

'Gotcha, Christa!' one of them yelled.

'I couldn't have put it better myself,' Mallory said.